Dragonsworn

Impervious Book 2

Brady Hunsaker

Lightfire Publishing

Contents

To all those who wanted more dragon

COLANDIA
LUEDAN
COLMINAN
OKWAN
MAVENDA
MIGAZAT
XHI
ANKAMIR
PESKAN
CASTIA MONT
SHIANSAN
SOUTH FORK
NANSHA
SAL
TIAMJIN
THE FACILITY
RED BRIDGE
BAIGRA
FORT SAL
KOMBIDA
HITAR
ABAS
ENDEL
SUWAIN
ISHKAJEN
GOGOBA

Chapter One

Dragons

Zein Huan

Gray walls surrounded a single chair in an otherwise empty square room. A glowing light, powered by dragonblood, hung suspended directly above the chair where Zein Huan sat with his arms and legs crossed in front of him. He wasn't sure how long they'd kept him down here. Days, perhaps weeks. He'd expected torture, which, to his great relief, they had not yet used on him. They hadn't even threatened him with it.

Instead, they'd isolated him. Sure, they brought food and water. They tried to get him to speak by being casual with conversation. They'd questioned him. Zein had not said a single word. Clearly, they wanted answers, and if they wanted them, they would need to provide him with answers in return.

He still did not know exactly who it was that had taken him captive, but that was his primary interest. Perhaps it was a competing research organization or even one of the lords or ladies who had invested in his own facility. On a more sinister level, perhaps it was the same organization that had enlisted Dami. There were even... worse options than those.

He'd known he was treading dangerous water when he'd gotten into this whole research. If it hadn't been for the exorbitant cost of the blood of dragons, the dragonsbane to control the subjects if needed, and then the wages for the doctors themselves, he would have tried running the operation on a smaller scale. They hadn't expected the results to be so effective. Similar tests had failed many times on other subjects prior to the final batch. All those previous subjects had died, but the wave with Dami and Mia was nothing short of miraculous.

If he was asked to give an honest answer for what had made their group successful, Zein would only be able to guess. There were supposed to be controlled factors involved with these kinds of things, but in truth, he'd been so astounded by their success that when they went back to check some of the controlled variables of the test, the data was already diluted. He had to come to terms with the idea that there was no *easy* answer even though there was an *implied* one.

A distant click indicated that somebody was approaching. It had only been about an hour since they'd come to take his emptied dish away, so this was an unanticipated visit. That meant it was time for questioning once again. The footfalls were heavy, a tell of the large but amiable man who usually led the interrogations.

Zein released a sigh, weary of these pitiful attempts. The isolation was not something he enjoyed, especially where he was accustomed to working with a skilled team. He wondered how everyone was getting along. Ven and Mia may very well have been killed, as well as

Dami. His research would be ruined. A couple of the bodies of students from the facility had already gone missing before they'd been able to burn them, which didn't seem to be an issue once the subject died and their individual cells died as well. Though he was pleased that their bodies decomposed normally, he was uncomfortable with the idea that some of the bodies had been taken, no doubt to be studied. With access to such data, he was certain that it was possible for others to discover what had given the subjects the impervious adaptation. That frightened him more than anything.

The door opened, the hinges sliding smoothly. This was no dungeon. Spots and scratches on the floor indicated that objects had been moved out of the room at some point, probably to make room for him.

In came a large man with a thick, bushy beard and broad shoulders. He had light skin and a forehead riddled with wrinkles, though he was likely in his low forties. He wore a plain white shirt with shorter sleeves showing his muscled arms and a neatly-laced neckline that was just low enough to reveal a tuft of chest hair.

"Good evening, Zein," the man said, his tone and expression neutral.

"Is it now, Hufad?" Zein said, keeping his own expression as bland as he could, something with which he had great experience. This was the first time Hufad had offered such a greeting, and Zein could only suspect that today would be different than the previous encounters. Or perhaps that was merely his hope speaking.

Hufad shrugged and put his hands on his hips. "You're to come with me." He gave the slightest of nods, eyes flicking to Zein's chair.

Taking the hint, Zein rose to his feet, keeping his expression stolid, though he allowed a bit of excitement to spark within him. Perhaps now he would finally have an opportunity to get answers. He'd been patient. All this waiting would need to be for something. Zein had no restraints. They hadn't bothered, knowing Zein well enough that they would never suspect the doctor of trying to attack his captors. He'd certainly made a reputation of his own peaceful nature despite being surrounded by violence.

"After you," Hufad said, gesturing to the door.

Zein approached the door, noting a figure in the hallway just beyond, leaning up against the gray wall. She was a lean woman wearing simple armor, a long dagger at her belt and a small buckler braced against her forearm. She pushed off the wall, jerked her head toward the hallway, and led the way. Zein followed, Hufad coming from behind. It felt good to stretch his legs. Pacing in his small room had only done so much. He'd been concerned enough about muscular atrophy that he'd been spending much of his time walking, stretching, and holding meditative poses, all activities that had helped sustain his sanity during the isolation.

There was a stillness to this building that hinted at infrequent use or abandonment. He'd been blindfolded when they brought him here as though they worried that he would recognize the location. In truth, he hadn't the slightest idea where they may have taken him. They had waylaid him on his way to Castia Mont where he'd been hoping to confront both Dami and Lady Sitena Rosars. A group of six people had emerged from the woods, crossbows aimed at him.

Two of those bolts had taken his powerful Zebadon horse right in the chest.

Ruthless. He was still furious. Such majestic beasts were not so low as to deserve treatment like that.

Though Zein had done worse. Not just to beasts, but to humans. He'd done *much* worse. The early days of his treatment studies with dragonblood still haunted him. It was best not to think of it at all.

They passed several other rooms on either side of the long hall before reaching a staircase that led to the ground floor of the building. Late afternoon sunlight filtered in through a two-story window to the left. Zein took a deep breath. He hadn't seen sunlight since they captured him, and seeing it now was reinvigorating. Zein was a doctor and a scientist. The pursuit of good truth was something he'd committed himself to. He *would* have answers.

Their footsteps echoed as they crossed a large room, decorated with lavish furniture, though most of the items were covered by white drapes. Zein grunted to himself in satisfaction, realizing his assumption that the building was in disuse was correct. The building itself was anything but simple. Walls were inlaid with wooden decorations and columns, painted with hues of dark green and brown to emulate a deep forest. It was quite possible he was dealing with one of his former investors here. If that was the case, then his time here had likely been a waste.

After crossing the large room, they went to a stairway that led to a second floor exterior balcony, white railings surrounding a circular patio. The patio overlooked an elaborate garden that, at first glance, appeared as though it was in great need of attention, but Zein thought it had a more natural beauty even as most of the plants had lost their leaves. The remnants of snow still clustered in the shadows. Snow was not common in the valleys and usually only occurred two or three times each winter.

Winter. That meant he'd been in that basement for months.

A cast iron table and two padded chairs were the only adornments on the otherwise empty space. In one of the chairs sat a woman wearing a brimmed hat and trousers. She looked extremely healthy, somewhere in her mid-thirties, but her eyes had a strange tinge of violet color to them, just around the irises. There were very few people who might understand such significance. It wasn't merely a unique trait, it was actually a sign of something ancient, like the old magics that had belonged to ages past. If what he knew of it was true, then it was likely she even had some ability to control how much of the color in her eyes was visible.

Yet here she was, hiding none of it.

Zein was instantly able to conclude one important thing. His time alone in that room was worth it. He'd already received an answer here, but there was more to learn.

The woman gestured to the chair opposite her.

Zein obliged, bones creaking as he sat in the chair, lacing his hands in front of him. "To whom do I owe the pleasure?" He ventured to ask. From what he could tell, the woman was not nobility. Her clothing was fine, yes, and she had questionable origins, but there was a certain lack of ladylike grace he'd grown far too accustomed to seeing in the nobility. She was leaning back in her chair, one leg crossed over the other. It was too nonchalant.

The woman smirked as the two guards took position. Hufad went and stood at the edge of the railing while the younger woman remained at the door, arms at her sides.

"Why is that always the first question people ask?" the woman asked, then sighed as if bored.

"It is customary," Zein said.

"I will be straight with you, Doctor Huan," the woman said. "Your operation with the impervious subjects has not been replicable. Do you know how many people we've killed trying to make it work again?"

Zein's mouth dropped. This was what he'd feared. He knew others were trying to recreate the Impervious Project, but... this? "What have you done?"

The woman shrugged. "Nothing too dramatic. We pilfered enough papers from your facility to understand how the operation was to be performed. We repeated it on others, not only those who are terminally ill, but many others. Mostly children, hoping to recreate all the same factors. We had over a thousand subjects and all of them died. Not good odds."

A sinking feeling of dread squirmed down Zein's throat. He would have thought this woman a monster, but his own testing had been equally dramatic. Certainly he hadn't killed as many children, but at least she knew that it had a chance of saving them. He'd been doing it for the sake of science, studying the various reactions. Oftentimes the children would immediately see improved health only to suddenly die, their blood literally boiling inside of them. He'd spent years viciously trying to discover how to remediate such an issue. They were always so close to a solution, but it evaded him for years.

Until one simple group of subjects simply didn't die. Their bodies had adopted the dragonblood as their own, reproducing it from their own marrow.

What had made them so different?

"Do you want to know what I think it is?" the woman asked.

Zein frowned at her, unsure of how to respond. "I..." his voice trailed off. Of course he wanted to know, but at the same time, this was his research. He did not know who she was nor what her intentions were.

She smirked at him, perfectly white teeth flashing. "I think it's the dragonblood you used. You see, I have connections. I traced your sources. Technically, the blood you had was pooled from a facility that had traces of dragonblood from many years ago, mingled with a bit of fresh blood from that dragon in Peskan."

Zein couldn't restrain his gasp.

"You didn't know we'd confirmed that?" She laughed. "It was more than a suspicion, Zein. Your family was into some nasty business there. Bleeding a dragon for generations all while preaching against the use of dragonsblood? Quite nasty, indeed. I'm glad you'd been estranged. Perhaps that's why you didn't follow their creeds."

"I had never confirmed," Zein said, detecting the shakiness in his own voice. This revelation crashed into him harder than he might have thought. Sure, it was always rumored that the Huan family kept a dragon in the dungeon, but to hear this confirmed by... He narrowed his eyes at her once again, wary of what she was trying to do. He had to remind himself that they were keeping him here for some reason. They wanted something from him, and this was all a part of the scheme to try and persuade him.

The woman tugged at the finger of one of her gloves before continuing to speak. "I always wondered if you'd known. You had to consider the idea that fresh blood was getting into the market. That facility you were purchasing from, well, they were using old dragonblood to do manual DNA replication that was sometimes replenished by fresh dragonblood from a couple sources. It turns out, one of their shipments they sent you must have had some kind of mutation involved. I'm assuming it had something else stuck in the mixture that allowed it to successfully be taken on by the human host. I suspected this for a long time, but I needed one of your subjects in order to confirm." Her smirk returned, and Zein's stomach dropped even further.

Seeing his reaction only caused the woman's smirk to broaden. "No, Doctor Huan, I am afraid that even with their blood, we were not able to replicate what occurred. You see, we needed the original blood sample in order to recreate the operation correctly. Even the blood of the subjects is now a separate mutation that must have occurred after they survived the initial transfusion. This is why you still had so many subjects die from that test group." She shrugged. "So it appears the one in a billion chance has already passed."

"What has been your interest in all this research?" Zein asked, desperate for answers.

She considered him for a moment. "As you may have ascertained, dragons are not dead. We've been disguised as humans for generations."

Zein licked his dry lips. "We?"

"Myself and the other dragons, of course."

Zein let out a quick breath and glanced at the guards. She had said too much, clearly not expecting him to be any sort of threat if she was sharing this.

"Don't act so surprised," the woman said. "We've had an interest in dragonblood research for quite some time. It was amusing at first to see what qualities our blood had. We'd never experimented with such things, but it was very... inspiring. Some of us even started some of our own experiments, including human transfusions well before you started doing it. Our results were different. It turned the humans into empty vessels which we can control with a mere thought. It did not turn them into the adaptive beings you created."

Zein's heartbeat pounded in his ears. This was not at all what he'd been expecting. If dragons had been pulling the strings all along, then what could she hope to gain by speaking with him? "Why have you detained me here?"

She shrugged. "I didn't have all the details initially. We thought we might glean more from you through interrogation, but other methods proved more fruitful. In truth, I almost forgot you were even here."

"Why come now? Just to let me know that all my research was in vain?"

"I'm not one to gloat, Doctor Huan," the woman said. "I wanted to personally inform you that Dami is dead, but Mia somehow eluded everyone, including the Yashke boy I planted at your facility."

"Ah. So you're the one responsible for the facility's destruction."

"I cannot claim that, unfortunately. If it had happened the way I wanted, none of the subjects would have escaped. Here I was hoping you knew who was assisting Dami. Since the list of surviving investors is a lot shorter, I'm sure we could discover the culprit without too much effort."

Zein nodded. Mia was out there, alive. That must have meant that she too had managed to get the killswitch removed from her neck. She was completely unfettered, though he wasn't worried about her ravaging the world. Her psychological analysis had been quite favorable with Ven's help. Earth doctors like him and his parents certainly had a way of helping in areas where he had failed.

Mia on the loose was the least of Zein's concerns however, especially if dragons were still secretly in power. This was something the world needed to know about. How far away was the ultimate demise of humanity? How long would it take before they were enslaved by dragons once again? Or perhaps the dragons had learned their folly and would simply coexist. They'd been doing so for years it sounded like, biding their time for something.

"You're hoping I might know Mia's location," Zein stated.

The woman shrugged.

"I unfortunately do not. I will be of no use to you." Though he wished otherwise, he'd spoken the truth. He was surprised Mia was even able to stay hidden from these people for very long.

"That's a shame," the woman said. "But all is not lost. These new experiments of yours did teach us something useful." She reached for a thin chain tucked beneath her shirt and withdrew a necklace. It bore the image of a silver dragon coiled around a red vial. "I'm here to offer you a blessing, to be one of the first."

Zein tilted his head. "The first of what?"

"Of my dragonsworn. You see, if I inject some of my own blood into your bones, it will fuse you to me. You will not be impervious like your subjects were, but it does offer some benefits, though at the cost of most of your free will. Your mind will still be intact, so I don't lose that intellect of yours." She gestured with her head to the two guards and they approached.

A sinking in Zein's gut told him this was what the dragons were really after. Forced obedience. This was a side effect of his research that was far worse than anything else. A metal clasp pinched over one of Zein's wrists, pinning him to his chair.

Hufad picked up the woman's necklace and tapped it with a fingernail.

"Don't worry, Doctor Huan," Hufad said. "Dayelle is a benevolent dragon. She will take good care of you."

No. In fact, Zein had heard enough. His final secret would be revealed. Zein yanked his arm free of the clasp, metal breaking beneath his strength. Everyone gasped, but Zein wouldn't give them a moment to work through the shock. He burst forward, knocking Hufad aside. The woman guard was quick, her blade slashing across Zein's side, but it hardly left a mark. Zein hadn't worked much on his own imperviousness, but he was still considerably resilient to physical damage. Yes, he had performed the operation on himself immediately after seeing the success on his subjects, a secret he'd kept hidden for years.

Zein jumped over the railing, falling to the ground below. He took off at a run without looking back, hoping the dragon, Dayelle, wouldn't be able to catch him.

Chapter Two

Cellular Learning

Ven Yashke

Ven Yashke took his time to pack things into his bag as the other students all filed out of class. They had a lecture to get to, but there was a question that had been burning in the back of Ven's mind for the last few months. Nine months and thirteen days to be exact. Ever since the day he'd packed that dirt over—

He bit his tongue, drawing his attention back to the present. The room was arranged with a few mock operating tables. Today's discussion on gastrointestinal surgery was not of particular interest to Ven. After attending the university for eight months now, he was finding himself increasingly disinterested. Thankfully, they did a lot of tandem work at the nearby hospitals, but it was difficult to focus. His therapist said he still needed to work through his trauma and that something was still holding him back from being able to move that weight off his shoulders. He told her that he didn't know what it was, but the truth was, he still wasn't ready to let it go. How would he explain to a therapist that he'd been to another world, watched people die, and even killed a couple people, including someone he'd cared about?

The last of the other students filed out, and Professor Lee stood by the door, waiting for Ven to exit before her. Ven gulped. Words usually came easy to him, but he struggled finding the right way to ask his question.

Professor Lee jerked her head to the open door as if to tell him to hurry up but seemed to notice Ven's hesitation as he shuffled his feet. "Ven, are you well?"

Ven pursed his lips and shook his head. "Professor, I..." He paused a few steps away from the professor.

She folded her arms and looked up at him. He was tall, and she was so short that the top of her head wouldn't even reach his shoulders, so he'd stopped farther away from her on purpose so she wouldn't have to strain herself to regard him. "You can tell me," she said, glancing toward the door again as if to indicate that she had some time, but not much.

Ven gripped the straps of his backpack and took in a big breath. "You worked as a surgeon before coming to the university. Did you ever lose some of your patients?"

"Ah." Professor Lee's posture relaxed as she leaned back against the open door. "It was an unfortunate result, but yes, I lost a few patients. Are you worried about the prospect of losing patients if you go into the surgical field?"

Ven rubbed the back of his neck. "No, I... I lost one already."

"I see," Professor Lee said, her eyes looking off at nothing before returning to meet his gaze. "From working with your parents?"

"Sort of." Ven shrugged. "I was curious how you cope with it. Sometimes I feel like it's my fault. Though I know it's not, there's just that lingering sense of guilt. It's like I failed."

Professor Lee's thin eyebrows rose as she shook her head. "You really wanted to come at me with a difficult question. We need to recognize our own limitations. Not everything is within our control. We simply do the best we can. As long as you aren't the one who put the patient on the table, then you aren't to blame."

Ven gulped. He'd done more than put her on the table. He'd pulled the trigger. Literally. Her answer was not unexpected. Even his mother had always talked about keeping thoughts focused on things they could control. Did Ven have a choice? Certainly. He could have *not* pulled the trigger, but he knew that Mia would have died either way. His method had been *necessary*. If only that knowledge were enough to keep his shame at bay. More than that, he was still in mourning. He wasn't just ashamed of what happened, but he'd cared about Mia. When he spoke with his therapist, she thought his feelings of loss were related to his parents, which was true, of course, but he also missed Mia. Her death had been so much more personal. He *watched* her die. He *hauled* her dead body away. He *buried* her.

It was not the same as simply losing a patient. He'd been on the front lines of diseases and calamities all over the world. Death was not unfamiliar to him.

Professor Lee glanced back at the open door. The message was clear.

Ven nodded to her. "Thank you." He shouldered his bag and hurried out ahead of her.

"Ven?" she said from behind him, but he didn't turn back.

She wouldn't be able to help him. The best thing he could do now was move on. No use dwelling on the past. If only it was as easy as a thought. Something was off. Trying to move on like life was normal seemed like the best path forward, but it conflicted with what he knew to be true. He'd been to another world. Dragons were real. His parents had been involved with something there, and he still didn't have all the answers. Months had passed, and instead of feeling peace, his unease only grew, like a giant, anchor-sized fish hook was jabbed into his abdomen, tugging harder and harder with each passing day.

He placed his hand in his pocket. The familiar round shape was still there, smooth and cool to his touch. He took it with him everywhere, a constant reminder that there was more to life than what was before him. It was the key. It was what would allow him to return to Orund, though the very idea of doing so brought with it a whirl of conflicting emotions.

A long, deep breath filled his lungs. Chatter from other students echoed down the hallway as he headed for the Carl W. Walter Amphitheater. Today they were supposed to have a guest lecture from a renowned doctor from Germany who worked in some form of privatized research. To Ven, it seemed like some kind of strange way to hide a company that was creating biological weapons or something, but apparently the speaker came with high commendation. Microbiology wasn't something Ven had ever taken particular interest in, and most of his experience was more along the lines of emergency care, though his parents had also done plenty of work with infectious diseases.

Before his escapade in Orund, he would have thought his parents had nothing to do with research and had focused more on clinical treatment, but perhaps those had been meshed together. Maybe there was more research going on behind the scenes than he'd thought. If he'd been in the right state of mind, he might not have left Orund so abruptly after burying Mia. He would have questioned Dayelle more about his parents' involvement in dragonblood research. What he wouldn't give to interrogate Zein Huan on their business relationship.

When Dayelle had originally recruited him to help take down Zein's research facility, she'd wanted him to get in on the research side of it. Instead, he'd been assigned a patient. Working with patients was more in his nature. A fond smile snuck its way onto his lips.

He checked his phone and there was less than two minutes before the lecture was supposed to begin. He quickened his pace, squeezing into the doorway of the amphitheater. Most of the students were already seated, but the front row was mostly open, so he headed straight for it and sat down.

Voices died down as a staff member entered. She was younger, probably a graduate student working as an aide. A few lights dimmed at the back and the woman smiled. "Everyone please be seated. We're going to jump right into this week's guest lecture because I know she'll want the full time to go over this exciting new development in the realm of cellular research that could lead to what they coin as 'the cure to everything.' Without further ado, here's Doctor Dayelle Georgiou." She gestured her arms to the side and stepped down to sit somewhere to Ven's left.

Light clapping filled the hall, but the sound was distant to Ven, like it was behind a wall. That name. Could it be? He squinted at the doctor who walked up before them as she smiled at the students and professors who filled the amphitheater. She was instantly recognizable. He'd know that face anywhere. Her hair was dark, her skin a light brown, her smile dazzlingly bright. Her eyes rested pointedly on Ven. The touch of violet that had hinted around her irises was gone, but it was her.

Ven's emotions flared, though he wasn't sure which emotion it was, only that his hands felt cold, his face was hot, and his heart thundered in his chest. What could Dayelle possibly want? Surely she wasn't here by coincidence.

Dayelle's eyes flicked away from his and she smiled at the crowd. She spoke to them all generally, her gaze never returning to Ven as the lecture began. "Medical science is on the precipice of revolution. Cell research shouldn't just be an area of study in the medical field, but it should be the primary method of solving any issue. You may think my opinion extreme, but we often underestimate the power of a single cell, let alone an entire organism made of trillions of cells." The projector on the wall behind her lit up to show a single-cell organism of some kind.

"Consider viruses for a moment. Why does getting sick give the body a stronger immune system once you've recovered? That's right, the body *learns*. Without you having to give the order, the white blood cells know what to do. When observing single-celled organisms, these lifeforms do not have brains, but they adapt." A few charts popped up on the screen indicating data points. He could already see where her study was leading. This was the same vein of thought that led doctors on Orund to perform the dragonblood transfusions on people like Mia. They'd done more than cure diseases, they'd made the subjects completely impervious to everything except dragonsbane.

"Our research team has run several basic studies on single-celled organisms, finding that they would adjust to differing controlled settings presented to them. This also led to a clear understanding of habituation, in which the cells learned to behave in certain ways after repeated exposure to both sound and vibrations of various frequencies. We continued to repeat such studies using different cells as the controlled variables and started to find some very interesting results." She paused and a smirk curved her lips.

Ven's heart continued pounding in his chest, his ears burning as questions hammered against his skull. Why was she here? Why was she talking about this subject in particular? Did this have something to do with the research his parents had been involved in? Was she here to try to convince him to come back?

He rubbed his fingers across his lips, a nervous habit he thought he'd kicked, but it was all he could do to keep from jolting upright and sprinting out of the room. Perhaps that would be the right move. He already knew, however, that if Dayelle wanted to confront him, she would. There would be little he could do to avoid her.

Instead, he remained in his seat, even though it felt like he was simmering over the coals of a fire.

Dayelle's lecture continued, but it didn't go into things that were too farfetched. He'd thought the intricacies of the dragonblood transfusions to be almost magical, and perhaps it still was to some degree, but at the core of it, he knew it was laced with what modern science and medicine could confirm as valid. Perhaps it wasn't simply a transfusion that had changed people like Mia; there had to be something else to it. Their bodies had changed. That was more indicative of a mutation or restructuring of some kind, maybe not on the cellular level as Dayelle addressed, but perhaps deeper than that, like an adaptation of their very DNA. Hadn't Mia told him that imperviousness could be passed on if she ever had children?

Vaccines or immunities didn't work like that.

Now that Ven had some more practical experience with real hospital devices, he wished he'd gotten a chance to see what type of equipment they'd actually had at that facility Zein Huan had been running. He doubted they had the right kind of machine to modify an individual's very DNA. If they were unequipped with such technology, then that couldn't reasonably be what they'd done.

No.

He narrowed his eyes at Dayelle, who was still going into detail about some study.

Ven wasn't really sure what had made the subjects of the Impervious Project impervious, but perhaps it *was* something to do with the cells. That would explain Dayelle's fascination. Now he wondered if anybody else here knew if she was some kind of off-world secret agent. Her connections on Earth were good enough for her to be giving a lecture at Harvard. That couldn't have been an easy thing to arrange.

She continued blathering—well, *he* considered it blathering—for what seemed like ages, and the heat that seemed to burn at him only intensified. Each painful memory was crashing down on him. He'd thought of Mia and Orund every day. Every single moment since stepping back through the portal had carried with it the weight of what he'd left behind. Even his dreams had left him without respite.

Despite his best efforts to make that hooked feeling in his gut go away, it remained. It wasn't just because he was unable to let something go. His therapist hadn't been able to help him, and now, with Dayelle before him, he realized why.

The feeling wasn't wrong.

Perhaps his place wasn't here at Harvard at all. Maybe he wasn't meant to be on Earth. Orund called to him. It needed him.

But why?

The burning became unbearable enough that he shot up from his seat and hurried from the room, ignoring the others who stared at him in surprise as he ran by. He was a few paces down the hall outside by the time he stopped, sucking in deep breaths. With each inhalation, he envisioned the swelling of mist beside a waterfall, filling his lungs. As he exhaled, the mist rolled out, streaming across a forest with birds chirping and bugs humming about.

When his nerves were calmed, he opened his eyes. He'd gotten good at meditative breathing, quickly being able to harness his emotions. The heat that had been burning at him was gone, though the hook in his gut remained. It would never leave him. Perhaps his parents had felt the same way. He gasped at the sudden thought. Was that why they couldn't stop visiting Orund?

The door to the amphitheater swung open and people poured out. The lecture was concluded, which meant it was time. He strode through the crowd, pushing through the other students as he went the opposite way. Ven would not wait for Dayelle to approach him. He would have answers from her.

He got into the room, and most of the seats were empty, but Dayelle remained at the front, speaking with those who passed as they, for the most part, thanked her. She spared a glance for him as he approached, her eyes glistening with a knowing look, but her attention remained on acknowledging those who thanked her as they went by.

Ignoring propriety, Ven stopped directly in front of her. "Why are you here?" he demanded, distinctly aware at this moment how aggressive he might appear. He was, after all, taller than everyone else in the room, and he'd filled out a bit more in the last few months. Therapy and exercise had both done him a lot of good since leaving Orund, and taking a martial arts class had just seemed *right*.

One of the other professors spoke up first, a man Ven vaguely knew had the last name of Krivorsikov or some other difficult pronunciation. "Uh, apologies. Might I introduce one of our students—"

"No need," Dayelle said, eyes now fully rested upon Ven. "I once worked with Ven's parents, and even if I hadn't, how could I not know about the student with a perfect score."

Ven did *not* have a perfect score. He'd been docked on an essay, a fact that the professor seemed to gloat about for reasons Ven still had yet to comprehend.

Professor K pushed back his glasses and nodded at that. Indeed, Ven had made a bit of a name for himself. The idea that he'd practically already been working as a doctor in other countries seemed preposterous to many, but it was hard to question his practical knowledge and his *near* perfect scores on every assignment.

"Come along, Ven, perhaps we can talk outside," Dayelle said with a jerk of her head towards the door. "Thank you everyone." She offered a quick wave to everyone else.

Ven hurried after her as she made for the door without another word. Her pace was quick, but with Ven's long strides, he was able to catch up.

Dayelle gave him a sideways glance, looking him up and down in that measuring way of hers. "You look like you've been busy, Ven. You're not quite as lanky as before." Her accent was still so unique that he had difficulty putting a finger on it. She'd apparently been involved with some research facility in Germany, but her accent seemed more obscure. When he'd first met her, he assumed it originated from South America, but now he had to wonder if it was something Mediterranean. Even that was probably an incorrect assumption. She was from Orund after all, but then again, he hadn't noticed anybody else with an accent like hers on Orund. She remained a mystery.

"What are you doing here, Dayelle?" Ven asked. "I don't buy the whole lecture thing."

"Pity. I do fancy myself a bit of a connoisseur of scientific advancement."

"And yet you bullied me into helping take down a facility that was dedicated to the advancement of human health."

Dayelle clicked her tongue and frowned at him. "It was a mutual agreement."

"Coercion."

"An exchange. A very successful one at that, in which we both benefited. Besides, you saw it for yourself. What they were doing was not acceptable. You made all of your own choices. I wouldn't call that coercion."

Ven grunted. There was some truth there of course, but he was wary of Dayelle. He didn't believe that she'd lie to him, but she would certainly convey information in a way that was borderline manipulation, withholding just the right parts. Based on the lecture she'd given, she was clearly highly intelligent, not only regarding the way things worked on Orund, but also showing a profound understanding of Earth science. The message was clear to Ven.

Dayelle knew *exactly* what she was doing.

"Did you come here to make demands of me again?" Ven asked. "Or to arrange another one of your mutual agreements?"

"I did not come to make any requests," Dayelle said.

They passed through the door outside where a cold wind greeted them. Ven tucked his hands into the pocket of his sweatshirt. He hated the cold of Massachusetts, and with it being late February, these were the worst days of all. This was certainly nothing like living in Florida. Spring couldn't come soon enough.

Dayelle was unperturbed by the cold. She strode over to the base of a tree bordering the plaza and folded her arms.

Ven stopped in front of her, knowing that there were arguably a hundred better places to have this conversation. "Alright, you've been dodging my questions, Dayelle."

Dayelle smirked, her perfectly white teeth flashing. Out here under the mostly blue sky, that hint of violet in her eyes returned, hinting at her otherworldly origins. "You are aware of my connections with communications networks." She nodded to herself before continuing. "I came across some information that I thought you would like to know."

Ven restrained himself from breathing a laugh. What information could possibly be worth traveling here for?

"Mia is alive," Dayelle said. The smirk was gone from her expression, her eyes penetrating.

The hooked feeling in Ven's gut tugged a little tighter as his eyes narrowed at her. "I killed her, Dayelle. I buried her corpse!" He looked over his shoulder after realizing how loud his voice had gotten. Fortunately, the wind and cold had swallowed his voice and kept most people indoors.

Dayelle shrugged. "Well, I hate to break it to you, but she deceived you."

"How do you know?"

Dayelle pursed her lips for a moment before responding. "She was spotted in a village a couple days' travel southeast of Castia Mont."

"Impossible." Ven shook his head. Why was Dayelle doing this? "It could have been somebody else."

"Come now, Ven. You know I would have vetted this already before coming to you."

Ven still couldn't believe what he was hearing. He'd pulled the trigger that activated the kill switch in Mia's neck. He'd *buried* her. Unless... perhaps she faked it. Was it possible that she'd removed the kill switch from her own neck the night before? He *had* fallen asleep after all. That would have given her an opportunity. He pressed a hand to his chest, hoping it would suppress the growing pain as his heart hammered.

"I couldn't be certain of the facts unless I saw it for myself," Dayelle said. "It took a few months, but we scoured the area until we found where you'd buried her." She raised her eyebrows at him. "It is a shame you don't have better training at hiding your trail, but when we found the location, we saw traces of her there. She has a powerful aura that my trackers could sense. I can confirm the details. Her burial spot was empty. Traces of her aura trickled into the forest beyond but were untraceable after too long. She's alive, Ven."

Ven rubbed his lower lip and turned away from Dayelle as his thoughts raced. Mia had deceived him. This whole time, he'd been thinking of himself as her killer. He was far too relieved to be angry, but if she had tricked him in order to fool everyone else into thinking she was dead, then that meant she didn't want to be found. Her plan had failed. If they knew Mia was alive, they'd go after her. *Dayelle* would go after her. She'd already expressed her stance on the matter; the subjects of the Impervious Project were too dangerous and needed to be exterminated.

All these details made Ven more suspicious about Dayelle's present motivation. Why was she here telling this to him? He rounded on her. "You want me to find her. You want me to finish the job. Is that what this is about?"

Dayelle shook her head, eyebrows furrowing with concern. "No, dear boy. You are a doctor, not a tracker. We have many skilled agents that will be able to locate her in time. Her existence also isn't the concern that I thought it would be. We've determined that the operation that made her what she is cannot be repeated using the blood of another subject. Others have been trying unsuccessfully." She reached up and patted his shoulder. "But I know that she was dear to you. I did not want you going about with the weight of her death on your shoulders. I may have been callous about the suppression of Zein's research, but that does not mean I am past feeling."

Ven only blinked at her, unwilling to dismiss his suspicion that she harbored some ulterior motive. This revelation was so jarring that he felt like his chest would burst. He needed to think on this—gosh—he needed to *breathe*. There had to be more to this. Dayelle wouldn't come here just to let him know unless she wanted something. "What else do you have to tell me?" he said, practically gasping the words.

Dayelle tilted her head, that subtle violet hue in her eyes appearing even brighter than before. "Zein Huan escaped."

Ven frowned. "Doctor Huan? Didn't you apprehend him?"

"Yes, but he proved to be... keeping secrets of his own. He is involved in greater schemes than I originally anticipated."

"What's that supposed to mean?"

"He was not so innocently trying to cure diseases."

Ven shrugged. "Alright, and why do I care?"

"He will pursue her, Ven. He considers his work to be… unfinished."

Ven narrowed his eyes at Dayelle. "You'd hunt her down as well. She's as good as dead no matter who gets to her, right?"

"Not necessarily. I'm no longer convinced that her death is required. Eventually, yes, but she is still young, and she has proven her character to be free of malicious intent."

Ven took a step back from her. Dayelle needed to work on her delivery, as she was not instilling any confidence. Perhaps that was the point. He felt like he was *too* smart for catching on that easily. Dayelle was manipulative, yes, but even she knew that he was not the same gullible boy that he was a few months ago. Her methods here would be different. His blunt questions had probably revealed his sentiments all too easily, thus allowing her to respond in the best ways to prey on his weaknesses.

Or he was reading into it too much. He'd certainly become wary since their first encounter.

"How is Harvard treating you?" Dayelle said, suddenly changing the subject. Her eyes drifted lazily across the cold campus.

"Sufficiently," Ven said, hoping that fewer words would make him less readable. He had no desire to speak of trivial things and felt that their conversation was over. Dayelle had planted her little seeds this time. He'd probably fall right into doing whatever she wanted from him.

"So guarded suddenly." She offered him an amused smile. "I can assure you, I have no requests to make, Ven. I can't help but feel somewhat responsible for the heartache you have experienced with all this... loss. I do hope you have the brightest future with whatever you plan to do." She nodded at him and lifted her bag as though to leave.

Ven did not stop her. He did not say goodbye as she turned to go and walked away along the path, cold wind whipping at her hair as she completely ignored it. There were no words he had to offer. Dayelle did not make a request of him, because she already succeeded in her design. He knew exactly what it was that she wanted of him, and he would, unfortunately, fall straight into it.

Ven placed his hand in his pocket, feeling at the marble. The key. He had to hope that he could find Mia before Dayelle or Zein did, a seemingly impossible task, but he did at least have a single hint. A hunch. Hopefully that would be enough.

Ven gave one last look up at the university buildings and took a deep breath as the hook in his stomach loosened just slightly. His destiny held a different path, one that apparently did not involve a degree from Harvard.

Mind resolved, he turned away, the hook loosening even further as it too acknowledged that he'd stopped denying himself. He had a plane to catch.

Chapter Three

Fireweed

Mia

Snow crunched beneath her boots as Mia strode across the valley floor, dragging a sled full of firewood behind her. She took deep breaths through her nose, not because she needed to, but because she savored every moment of being in the fresh mountain air. It was a warmer winter day, and the evening sun made the snow glitter. She'd been warned about avalanches under such conditions before she came out here, but she didn't believe she'd have much to worry about.

She couldn't stop smiling at the idea that she would actually be caught in one, something that would have terrified any normal person. She was merrily climbing her way up to the thicket of trees she would cut for firewood when her foot slipped and it looked like the whole mountain was sliding toward her. Snow billowed into a cloud as it charged down from the side of the mountain, roaring gradually louder. Instead of fear, she watched with wide-eyed fascination. If she was anybody else, she would jump on the sled to try and get ahead of it, but what was the point of being impervious if she didn't experience things that would kill somebody else?

When the avalanche caught up to her, she laughed at first, keeping one hand firmly gripped on the sled, but her laugh cut off as the snow packed all around her. She wouldn't be able to breathe under the snow if it covered her head. Suffocation was something that could *actually* kill her. Probably. Realizing how much of a fool she was, she tried swimming through the snow, pumping her muscles to try and stay on top, all while keeping that one hand on the sled.

The force was surprisingly powerful, and it was only with great difficulty that she was able to keep her head up. She tried bracing the sled against her chest, hoping it was possible to keep it on top of the snow to help her along. The snow did eventually slip over her head completely, but the avalanche stopped moving only a couple seconds later. She pushed her hand up, forcing snow away from her face, but found the pressure to be incredibly heavy. This was not what she'd expected.

It took all her strength to push the snow up and slowly maneuver her body. If not for her immense strength, she probably would have died under the snow. After a solid six or seven minutes of digging, she was finally able to get her feet pulled up high enough to stand and get out.

Of course she would say nothing of this to the others when she got back to the village. The last thing she needed was for people to be aware of her unique qualities. They already commented on how different she was. Her very appearance was different. The way she moved was different. She even sat still differently than others, and they noticed.

Thankfully, Maisie-Jane never questioned her about any of it. She seemed to catch on to the idea that Mia was running or hiding from something, and rather than press her on it, she merely supported her, giving her a place to live and work, not even asking about Mia's past. It was refreshing to learn that there were other people in the world who were genuinely kind. Maisie-Jane wasn't using Mia for anything. She didn't know about Mia's procedure or history. She just saw a girl in need and wanted to help, offering her a bowl of soup almost as soon as Mia entered the village when she'd first arrived.

It was no wonder Mia had been drawn to this place. The woods she'd traveled to were a good hike away from the village, but the low buildings were already in view across the valley's expanse. The valley was small but sported its own little lake that then filtered out through a large stream on its eastern side. Boulders dotted the landscape, but in the late summer when Mia had arrived, the entire valley floor had been covered in flowers. She'd never smiled so big in her life. Even thinking of it now made her heart flutter with warmth.

Her pace quickened as she followed her foot trail back to the village. It was difficult to repress her own ability at times, particularly her speed. She couldn't very well be caught sprinting across the valley floor at the speed of a horse as she hauled a sled full of wood. Keeping her identity a mystery was paramount. She'd worked too hard to earn her freedom.

Smoke billowed up from the chimneys of the buildings, built of a combination of stone bricks and thatched wooden roofs. She wasn't sure exactly what she'd expected before coming here, but the village was larger than she thought it would be. There were nearly two hundred residents, most of whom had lived here their entire lives. A few of the homes were down on the west edge of the valley where the main road led down out of the valley, and there were two ranches on the south end where a couple families maintained herds of sheep and big hairy cows. Those were coincidentally the biggest families, and their ranches generated a lot of the mountain village's economy.

What people did to survive was always somehow one of the first questions that came to her mind whenever she'd crossed a different settlement. How did they get food? How did they find time to build shelters? Maybe she was just nosy.

Maisie-Jane had been scraping along all by herself. She owned a cow and two goats, which seemed like a staple of every home in the village, but she also spent much of her time either working at a kiln when it was cold or harvesting various herbs and berries from the wild in the warmer weather.

When Mia had first been taken in by Maisie-Jane, she'd enjoyed exploring the valley, hunting for specific plants. Maisie-Jane explained every little thing from where the plant would grow to what it would be used for. Learning about the plants was like a dream. They had plans to grow a few things around Maisie-Jane's home once winter was over, and Mia couldn't wait to watch the process from the very beginning.

She was close enough to the village that she slowed down. The village was far from quiet in the winter like she'd expected. Snow and cold did not do much to slow down the people, and they'd taken measures long ago to make stone paths and keep trails clear with shovels.

Everyone greeted her with a smile. Peton, with his ridiculously thick mustache, nodded to her, his grin hidden behind the wiry hairs. He had two fish hooked on a rope slung over his shoulder as he passed her going the other way.

Maisie-Jane's home was right on the edge of the village, its wooden gate wide open as Mia pulled the sled through and off to the side where the wood was stocked under a rough shed. She grabbed the timber and put it away bit by bit, occasionally grunting for added effect.

"There you are!" Maisie-Jane said as she emerged from inside, a massive smile beaming on her face. She had dark hair already streaked with the occasional gray, though she was only in her mid-thirties. She wore heavy woolen clothes, as did practically everyone in the village. Her home was a modest size, as she was the only one living there. Her husband had died seven years ago, and they'd never had any children. This hadn't diminished her cheerful demeanor.

Mia smiled back. Maisie-Jane hadn't questioned how long it took Mia to return. Normally a trip to collect firewood wouldn't have taken so long, but getting trapped in the avalanche had certainly impacted Mia's typical trip time.

"I've got soup ready inside," Maisie-Jane said. "We have a little less salt this time, so hopefully it's not bad."

"I've never disliked any of your soups, Maisie-Jane," Mia said, putting the last of the wood away before following Maisie-Jane into the home. She shook off her coat and placed it near the fireplace to dry while Maisie-Jane ladled out a bowl of soup for her.

Mia hadn't known her own mother, but she imagined it would have been something like her relationship with Maisie-Jane. It was simply... warm. There was still a layer of deception, of course. Mia wasn't sure if she'd ever truly be able to be her pure natural self with anybody like she'd been with Ven, but that was a consequence of an operation that she'd had no control over. It wasn't her fault she was immortal.

"I saw that avalanche," Maisie-Jane said, handing a bowl over to Mia. "Were you nearby?"

Mia tried to restrain her smirk, but no amount of biting her lip prevented her lips from curling. "I may have been right next to it. You were right. I should have been more careful."

A frown creased Maisie-Jane's brow. "I'm glad you're alright." There wasn't a critical note in her voice at all, merely relief that Mia was well.

"Me too. I was lucky. I've never seen one before, and you were right. They're a lot more powerful than I expected."

"I do know a few things about the mountains." Maisie-Jane tapped the side of her head before taking a slurp of her own soup.

Mia nodded. "I will be sure to make better use of your counsel in the future." Mia pointed with her elbow to a dried flower hanging from the side of the mantel. "When are those back in season?" she asked, remembering how gorgeous the mountainside was with all the fireweed flowers when she'd first arrived.

"Ah, that won't be until summer. They're among the later blooming flowers in the valley. Are they your favorite?"

"Yes," Mia said, remembering the bright red color. It made it look like the whole side of the mountain was on fire. It was beautiful. She sat down and leaned back, enjoying her soup, contemplating how simple life was here in the valley. She could just live. There was no murderous friend to stop. No experiments. There weren't even any expectations. She could simply do as she pleased. Was this what life was like for normal people? The only thing she was missing here were books. Nobody in the village appeared to have any, but Maisie-Jane said that peddlers would come in the summer, and it wasn't uncommon for them to have books.

"You're not alone there," Maisie-Jane said. "We get most of our visitors in the summer. Many people come from distant cities to see the flowers. Kind of like you did, though most of them don't stay." She offered Mia a smirk.

Mia laughed. "Well where else is better than here?"

"In the winter? Many places, I'm sure. I hear there are places on the shores of the ocean where almost every plant grows some kind of fruit and nobody goes hungry. Here we stash the plainest food just to get through."

"That does sound good, but it's hard to leave the mountains," Mia said, taking a closer look at Maisie-Jane's bowl of soup. It looked watery. Had the woman been sacrificing some of her own necessary food stores in order to provide for Mia? How had she not considered such a thing before now? Sure, Mia was often hungry, but she didn't experience pain and need the same way Maisie-Jane's body would. She needed to find out where Peton got those fish.

Other than the constant need to acquire food, life here was so simple. Mia had wondered if she would feel odd without any major obstacles or requirements in life, but in truth it was more of a relief. Her brain was finally able to relax. Everything was fine. There was no impending doom. She could simply live today and leave tomorrow to tomorrow. All she really had to worry about was if something changed.

Summer in the valley was beautiful, yes, but it introduced the one true threat to her peace. It brought visitors. She was certain her plan had worked. She'd even deceived Ven, and he was the cleverest person she knew. But he was also naive. Was it possible that things had been foiled? Would people be out there hunting for her? She shook her head and took another slurp of soup, pushing the thought aside. She had to hope that things here would be safe, but only time would tell. When summer came, she would just need to expose herself to as few people as possible to minimize risk.

That was it. Things would be fine.

Chapter Four

Orund

Ven Yashke

Two things were distinctly certain to Ven. First, Dayelle was baiting him into returning to Orund, the land of exterminated dragons. Second, he had no shot at resisting the urge. The problem with this scenario was that Ven was also going to be serving somebody else's interest. One way or another, he feared that he wouldn't be able to avoid whatever it was that Dayelle was trying to get him to do.

If people had successfully tracked him to find out where he'd buried Mia, then Dayelle, with all her resources, would easily be able to follow him into Orund. Unfortunately, Ven did in fact have a very good idea of where to find Mia. He knew exactly what she'd wanted out of life, unless she'd somehow deceived him on that as well. Also possible. She could very well have been playing on his weaknesses. But was it a weakness to care about her? Was it a weakness to want her to pursue her own happiness and freedom?

Probably not. Unless it was at the expense of other people maybe, but he didn't see that happening at all. Not from Mia.

The main thing Ven needed to do was find a way to get to Mia without being tracked. He'd considered his options. Dayelle clearly had connections in both worlds. He wasn't sure how techy things worked, but everything felt traceable. Phone calls or text messages, plane tickets, credit cards—all of those left a trail. It seemed a little crazy to think that Dayelle would have access to that level of information. She would need FBI or CIA tier data, but he didn't want to underestimate her. Instead, he bought some Visa gift cards. Borrowing a friend's phone, he made some calls to pay for most of his arrangements ahead of time.

What he hadn't anticipated was the layover in Denver due to bad weather. It only set him back a few hours, but every minute felt precious. After all, the man who'd ruined his family was out seeking to harm somebody else again. He wouldn't let that happen. Not that he could physically do very much, but he could at least warn her.

At least that's what he told himself he was doing. Maybe there was a more selfish reason. Deep down, there was the urge to just see her. He'd said that he loved her. Even in his own immature, adolescent sort of way. All this time, he'd thought her dead. He knew what it felt like to lose loved ones. The absence of his parents was absolutely more glaring than what losing her felt like. His parents had been a part of his everyday life, whereas Mia had only been a smaller portion. That of itself left a deeper hole, but it in no way diminished the pain of losing her too. Losing her had been harder to move on from, not because he loved her more than his parents, but because he bore the burden of responsibility for her death.

An unnecessary burden.

He sighed and shouldered his bag as he exited the door to the Bozeman Yellowstone International Airport. The clear mountain air was exactly what he needed, despite the considerable chill. Montana was surprisingly warmer than Massachusetts. He saw something that said it would be in the mid-forties today.

It had taken him three days to get here since Dayelle's initial warning. If Dayelle was expecting Ven to head into Orund, he had to hope that she didn't know which portal he'd use or where he'd end up once he crossed over. Perhaps she already knew exactly what he was doing. It was quite possible that all the portals between Earth and Orund were known to her and that she'd be monitoring each of them. Whatever resources her organization had seemed to be expansive, but everything was complete speculation unless he simply tried something.

He headed straight to the area where cabs were waiting. The number of vehicles was sparse. It seemed like they didn't expect many people to be getting off of a Thursday flight in the middle of the day.

"Where ya headed?" the cab driver said, offering to take Ven's bag. The man appeared to be in his late fifties, but he had a firm stride and carried himself like a much younger man. He wore a beanie on his head.

Ven kept his bag on his shoulder. "Livingston. A little east of that, actually."

The man nodded. "No worries. I can get you there." He opened the back door and ushered Ven inside.

Ven got inside and sat down, the smell of car air freshener hitting his senses like a wave. He set the bag down beside him and buckled in as the cab driver started up. He hadn't brought a phone with him. He would have loved to leave his wallet behind too, but that would be unavoidable. There was nowhere here in Montana he'd be able to stash anything realistically. It would all go with him.

"Where ya from?" the man asked after a few minutes of silence as they drove down the road.

"Nowhere," Ven said, voice quiet.

The man looked at Ven through the rear view mirror but redirected his eyes as Ven stared back. A little nod was all the man did after that, and the rest of the car ride was blissful silence. It didn't take long before they reached the mountains that stood between the two cities. They were still packed with a decent amount of snow, but there was a surprising amount of exposed ground where the sun had been melting it away already. Tomorrow was the first day of March. Even though February had the fewest number of days, it always felt like the longest month of the year, and he couldn't wait to see it pass. It did make him wonder if seasons were all the same in Orund based on where he teleported from. If it was still a frigid winter there, maybe he wouldn't find Mia at all. She'd be chasing some other pretty scene perhaps.

When they reached Livingston, Ven provided instructions for where to go next. He'd been down this road often enough that the route was second nature. When they pulled off the main road and went down a trail leading up to the compound of buildings, a sense of nostalgia trickled down Ven's spine. Even though he was alone this time, the warmth of memories of coming here with his parents left a smile on his face. It would be best to savor good memories with them rather than to make it sour with the idea that there wouldn't be any new ones. He wouldn't diminish the beauty of what had been.

"You can stop right out here, thank you," Ven said as they pulled up to the compound. There was a ranch-style house, a couple barns, a stable, a shed, and even a secondary home that was occasionally rented out to visitors. They'd stayed here once when their plane arrived super late one time before they were able to set out the next day.

Ven paid the driver and got out, eager to be on his way.

"Have a good day," the driver said.

Ven only nodded as he closed the door and heaved a breath. The car drove off, and Ven faced the compound. He took a few steps toward the front door of the primary home, but it opened up before he ever got there. He wondered if the family would recognize him even though he was over a foot taller than the last time he'd been here. It had been almost four years since he'd actually come directly up to the building.

In this case, he hadn't even tried to rent but had said he needed to outright purchase a horse, offering a lot of extra money to ensure the horse would also be fully equipped by the time he arrived. The Thompson family didn't even seem to blink at the offer. They'd simply said it was okay and he'd put down a deposit right then over the phone.

"Mr. Smith?" a woman said as she pushed open the screen door and took a look at Ven. She was a middle-aged white woman who looked vaguely familiar, but he doubted she'd recognize him with how much he'd changed.

"That's me," Ven said. He'd even used the name of the friend whose phone he borrowed as a means of hopefully throwing off Dayelle in case she was somehow tapped into all the communication. He really was paranoid about what she could do.

"Alright, I'll let everyone know you're here. You come sit down inside while we get things ready." The woman, Mrs. Thompson, held the door open and Ven nodded to her as he stepped inside. She kept her eyes toward the road as if expecting something else, then asked, "You didn't bring a trailer?"

"No, no." Ven rubbed his hand on the back of his neck. "I don't actually have my own vehicle. I'll be riding the horse home from here."

Mrs. Thompson raised her eyebrows at him but only shrugged and closed the door behind them. "Do you want some coffee or anything?" She gestured to a chair in the parlor.

"I should be alright, thank you."

"Okay, let's make sure that horse is ready. You sure you don't want something to eat while you wait?"

"I'm fine, really. I ate before I came." He flashed her a reassuring smile.

"Alright then." She tapped the wall before disappearing down the hall.

He was just glad they were trusting him enough to sell one of their horses out of the blue like this. Granted, he was pretty sure they had like twenty of them at least, and he'd told them they could pick which horse he'd get.

It felt strange not to have his phone with him. He had the impulse to pull it out and check the time or flip through to see how many missed calls he had for suddenly not showing up to classes. It probably wasn't common for one of the top students at Harvard to simply disappear, though he'd made arrangements for his room and also his general estate, if it could be called that. He still had way more money than any eighteen-year-old should, and the more he understood about how much money doctors made, the more he realized that his parents were even more wealthy than they should have been. At least on paper.

At the close of his job for Dayelle, she'd probably paid him a lot. He'd had a coin and a gem appraised and estimated that everything he'd received would possibly equate to half a million dollars in US currency. It was almost absurdly excessive like she was daring him to stay on Orund. The gems were apparently extremely high quality, and he had to wonder if they were more common Orund than on Earth. The gems were not as liquid as the coins, but he'd brought the entire stash anyway, stashing it in a plastic bag before wrapping it in a cloth sack and tucking it in his pack.

Mrs. Thompson popped her head around the corner. "Let's go around and I'll introduce you to Butch."

"Butch?" Ven asked, rising to his feet to follow Mrs. Thompson back out the front door.

"The horse. We named him Butch after Butch Cassidy. Well, my son named him. He was crazy about cowboys back then, but that was seven years ago."

Ven smirked, remembering his own experience naming his first horse, the Zebadon that seemed like it was built for charging into battle. The best name he'd come up with was Horsey. "That's a great name."

Mrs. Thompson only chuckled as they went through the compound toward the stable. Most of the ground was covered in gravel or crumbled paving that had worn away, and he avoided the occasional muddy spot as they crossed the distance. The building was connected to a large fenced area where a few horses roamed. Mrs. Thompson opened the front door and led Ven inside where a single large LED light hung in the middle of the building.

A boy stood there next to a brown horse with a white diamond on its head. The horse was saddled, eating from a trough of grain as the boy, probably a year younger than Ven, brushed at its shoulder. He stopped brushing the horse and turned to face them, scratching it with his fingers instead. "He's good to go."

"Thank you," Ven said. "I'm guessing you're the one who named him Butch?"

The boy snickered. "Yeah, that was me."

Ven smiled back and approached the horse, pulling an apple from one of his large side pockets for this exact occasion.

The boy stepped back as the horse lifted his head from the trough and regarded Ven with its dark black eyes. He held out the apple and it gave out a tiny snort before accepting the treat. Ven carefully allowed it to take a couple bites before it grabbed the whole thing up with its lips and chomped away. He then moved a step closer and began scratching the horse's neck.

"Butch is eleven years old," Mrs. Thompson said, "so he still has a good life ahead of him. He's generally pretty healthy, and we've had him trained for giving rides to people for several years now."

"He seems great," Ven said. "You made a good selection." Butch adapted well to Ven. He could already tell the beast was comfortable with him, which would likely translate well to when it was just the two of them. He paid the remaining balance and checked the bags on the saddle. He'd asked that they equip it with a few extra things and all was in order. This time around, he even thought to bring a water filter with him so he hopefully didn't catch any offworld parasites or something when drinking water from streams. Orund admittedly seemed a lot cleaner than Earth, but it was best not to take any unnecessary risks. He didn't need some Oregon Trail dysentery experience.

Ven mounted up and steered Butch out of the compound. The boy followed him all the way to the front of the property, waving goodbye, though clearly not for Ven. He felt bad, but then again, they'd been the ones to pick the horse.

The day had grown warmer as the afternoon rolled in. He could practically feel the snow melting as he led Butch across the street and toward the familiar trail. It led up into the mountains alongside a stream. Before leaving his apartment in Cambridge, Ven had looked up the trail and searched all around on maps to see if there was any valley or town in the area. There was not. It was pure wilderness that led straight on down into Yellowstone eventually. He wasn't sure how his parents planned on hiding it from him long term when any map could reveal that there was no town in the mountains. Perhaps they didn't expect to keep it a secret forever.

The temperature dropped as Ven started up the trail. Mountains rose up on either side. The forest was dense with leafless trees and several evergreens. Surprisingly, the trail actually had seen enough use even in the winter that Butch's footsteps weren't paving the way through the snow. Squinting through the reflected sunlight, he saw tracks from deer, people, and dogs. He just hoped there wouldn't be people around when he got higher up on the trail where the portal was. But did he care if people saw him disappear? It would be amusing to see a reaction, but he wouldn't be able to enjoy it.

Instead, he focused on the task that lay before him. If he knew Mia, she'd be where the beauty was. There were lots of beautiful settings, but he knew her particular draw to mountains and flowers. He'd told her specifically about the town he used to visit as a child with his parents and that she needed to see it someday. He had to hope that she would be there. If she wasn't, well, he could see himself spend months or even years scouring every mountain village in Orund. It was winter, however. It was still very possible that she'd gone to see the flowers then simply moved onto the next thing.

That didn't seem unrealistic, and it would be the wise approach. Unless she didn't expect anybody to be looking for her. She believed everyone thought her dead. She wouldn't anticipate anyone hunting her down. Or perhaps she would and he was assuming too much. Mia was a smart woman. Probably smarter than him. He could only imagine the effect the impervious trait had on the physical function of her brain.

Butch made steady progress up the trail, but it was clear that Ven would have to spend at least one night camping in the snow. He'd prepared for this, but wasn't feeling very enthusiastic. If things had worked how they were supposed to, he would have arrived yesterday evening, spent the night, then started first thing in the morning. That would have allowed him to get to Orund today. Perhaps this was better though. He'd arrive in Orund before noon tomorrow, giving him more time to scope out Mavenda.

Another realistic concern about staying the night here was bears. He had mace of course, but the idea of a bear stealing his food in the night did not seem too pleasant, especially when he was alone. "Well, not completely alone," Ven muttered to himself as he bent forward to scratch Butch's neck.

Despite the other tracks in the snow, Ven didn't cross a single soul during his trek. He kept Butch going until it got too dark to see ahead, then they pulled off to the side of the trail in a generally flatter area. The trail had been steep for the last little while, which was a good sign.

He slid off the saddle and quickly started caring for Butch. The horse would need water and food before Ven settled down for sleep. Urgency pressed against Ven's chest, so he took deep breaths as he went through the motions. There was nothing he could do to make time go faster. He had to accept what was before him and what he could reasonably control.

***

Ven was up early, and he got Butch on the trail within a few minutes. He did a poor job tying his tarp back up, so it slung over Butch's back. He'd at least put in enough time to get his thermal sleeping bag stuffed into its tiny bag. Butch was eager to be on the move. The horse had good energy, and even though Ven was a little out of practice, getting back into riding felt completely natural.

They proceeded up the mountain at a good pace, and Ven was grateful the trail was gravelly or they'd be tromping through straight mud. The temperature rose quickly as they got a little higher up and the sun finally reached them. Water gushed down the mountain, melting off as though eager to bring spring. Ven hadn't ever been here in the winter, but seeing the familiar mountains was comforting. He could almost hear Mom and Dad talking as a conversation of theirs came to mind. They'd been right here on this trail.

"Daniel says I'm rich and pompous and that's why I don't go to school with the rest of them," Ven had said. How old was he then? Fourteen? They had just bought their home in Southwest Ranches, Florida and moved in two months before that trip. Ven hadn't had much time to make friends. A lot of the other kids his age all attended school together, but he at least connected with them through tennis and swimming.

"Daniel called us rich?" Dad asked incredulously.

Mom actually laughed.

Ven didn't know it then, but Daniel's family was easily one of the wealthiest in the whole neighborhood. His dad had sold a software company for nine figures.

At their reaction, Ven smiled as well.

"You know, he's probably right," Mom said, "because there's a lot more to being wealthy than having money. We're wealthy because we get to spend all our time together. Not everyone gets to bring their kid with them around the whole world."

"We're wealthy because we love each other," Dad said, looking back at Mom with a smirk and that softness to his eyes. He shifted his gaze to Ven and the smile broadened as Ven rolled his eyes and shook his head.

"Yeah, but what if I did want to go to school with the other kids?" Ven asked.

"Oh," Mom said, looking back at Ven with her brows furrowed. "Do you?"

Ven thought about it. Honestly, it kind of sucked not being as close to other people his age. He didn't really have friends because his family spent ten out of twelve months every year on the road somewhere or in another country. They hadn't had an actual home until just a few months ago. It would be nice to have someone he could talk to that wasn't just his mom or dad or a random patient.

On the other hand, kids were often mean and dumb. The immaturity around them bothered him, and he found their humor to often be rude, judgemental, or inappropriate rather than intellectual. He didn't have to worry about that with his parents, and he genuinely believed that they had his best interest in mind.

Maybe they weren't as fun or relatable all the time, but they were reliable.

Ven sighed and said, "No, I guess not. It's just hard to not have friends."

"You're good at making friends though, Ven," Dad said.

"Yeah, I guess," Ven said, though what he truly meant was that his friends always seemed temporary. He had a phone with a few numbers in it, but nobody he ever stayed in touch with. As soon as his family moved on to the next place, that was it. No more contact.

Perhaps it was for the best and Ven was really just meant to have this sort of doctor-patient relationship with everyone. He would help them, and when the time was up, they'd each move on. Ven's job would be done. As long as he helped improve their quality of life somehow, that was all that was needed of him. He *should* be able to just move onto the next location and help more people. That's how his parents did it, and they never seemed to worry about having friends.

That was it then. He wasn't a doctor yet, but he was like his parents. He might not be able to perform surgery, but he could still help in his own way. When people were sick or injured, they still needed somebody to talk to. They needed a friend. He could be that person, even if it was temporary. He could give of himself. That's the kind of thing doctors did.

Resolved, Ven looked to his parents to find that they were pulling back so that they would be riding on either side of him.

"Time to close your eyes," Mom said, reaching her hand out to his. Dad grabbed Ven's hand from the other side, giving him a gentle squeeze.

Ven knew the procedure, closing his eyes as requested, though this time, he kept an eye open just a sliver, peeking through his eyelashes as he watched his dad withdraw a marble from his pocket and pop it into his mouth. That seemed a strange thing to do, yet Dad was a very smart man. He'd know what he was doing.

"Close your eyes," Mom said again, squeezing his hand from the other side as if sensing his spying.

Ven jolted, body shivering. He looked around, finding that he was not in a lush green forest in the middle of summer, but he was back on Butch, riding through the snow. Despite his excitement, he must have dozed, but looking ahead, he found himself at that exact spot, a thrill of realization shocking him to full attention. Immediately to the right of the trail was a large, pillar-like stone jutting out from the snow with another smaller one on the left. The stones didn't look particularly unique from any other stone or cliff face exposed on the mountain, but this portal was much more evident than the one Ven had gone through back in Florida.

Now Ven was suddenly faced with the question of how in the world his parents had found *any* portals. It wasn't like they could just randomly stumble upon them. Or perhaps there was a means of identifying where portals were located. He was still a few steps away, but he quickly withdrew the marble key and popped it into his mouth. He squinted at the stones, wondering if something would reveal itself, but they appeared the same as before. Of course. That would have been too easy.

Being totally honest, he'd expected that a world with dragons would have also had a little more magic involved. He'd heard the phrase that magic was just misunderstood technology, but the marbles acting as a portal seemed nothing short of magical. He couldn't fathom a logical explanation for how the little ball could send him to another world. How did his body survive the transfer? Was it like a wormhole? If he ever saw Dayelle again, which he was sure he would somehow, he'd have to ask her.

He was almost between the stones. In his mind, he pictured the scene, imagining the mountains around Mavenda on Orund, as he now understood that they were completely different from the Rockies. His breath caught in his lungs as anticipation tingled across his skin. Right as his body went between the two stones, that sucking feeling caused him to lurch forward in his saddle as though a wave of water crashed into his back. He forgot to close his eyes and quickly clamped them shut as his vision swirled.

Beneath him, Butch whinnied and shook his head before increasing to a trot.

In the same instant, everything settled. Ven's vision returned to normal and the weight on his back vanished. The trail ahead was noticeably different. He was still on a path on the side of the mountain, but there was a larger peak in the distance, and it was most certainly not the same place he'd been a minute ago. A trail extended ahead of him, but it was wider than what he'd been on, with ruts driven into the ground that looked like they'd been made by wheels.

Butch slowed back to a walk after the feeling passed, but he grunted his disapproval at whatever had happened.

Ven scratched the horse's neck as they came around a bend. The trail ahead led between a couple low ridges on either side. Once he passed through there, the trail would wind up into the valley where Mavenda rested. He filled his lungs. Yes, there was still the mountainous, earthy smell, mingled with pine and mud, but it was somehow different than it had been before. He sat up straighter in the saddle, eyes locked on the trail ahead as he drew ever closer, resisting the urge to lead Butch into a trot.

The temperature on Orund was even warmer. There were even patches of ground where the snow had already melted away, revealing soggy grasslands beneath. In spring and through the summer, these grasses would be exploding with flowers.

"Good boy, Butch," Ven muttered before rising up on his feet in the stirrups as if the added height would allow him to see the village sooner. He was preparing himself to be devastatingly wrong about finding Mia here, but energy pulsed in his chest, a hope that made their speed achingly slow.

Ven withdrew the marble and sealed it in a plastic baggie before tucking it into his pocket. It was the most valuable thing he had with him, even counting all the Orund money he'd brought. Everything else he had was all new. He was familiar enough now with the crazy spy tech that existed here and was keenly aware that Dayelle or one of her agents could have planted something in his room or on his clothes, so he'd acted in due measure. The only thing he had with him that he'd owned prior to her showing up at Harvard was the money she'd given him. He realized of course that something could be hidden within the coins or gems potentially, but each item looked as innocent as the next. Without cutting everything in half, there was no way of knowing if they'd been tampered with.

When Mavenda came into view, the warmth in Ven's chest intensified despite the cold. The beautiful little valley had a massive mountain rising up on one side. The ridges that rose up and formed the oval-shaped valley on the other sides were less than half as tall. A stream gurgled out of the mouth of the valley through which Ven entered, trickling away from the thawing lake. The village was nestled not far from the lake, many of the buildings stretching down toward the south end of the valley.

A smile spread across Ven's face. This was one of the few places he'd regularly visited. There would be people here who'd probably recognize him, as he and his parents would often stay here for several days at a time, and though the village often had visitors in the warmer seasons, in a small place like this, they remembered who they saw.

The cold weather didn't stop the villagers of Mavenda from getting out and about. There was a constant bustle of activity, and even from this distance, Ven caught a lot of attention. Children blatantly ran out and started shouting to each other about him, shamelessly pointing and asking who he was.

Ven bit his lip to avoid smiling. He wondered how strange he must seem. He'd come here wearing jeans before, but today he had on a pair of dark olive hiking pants with some kind of built in stretch fabric and a zip-up coat. The villagers would be accustomed to seeing visitors in strange clothing, but certainly not in winter.

Word spread quickly of Ven's arrival, and people spilled out from their homes or stopped their tasks to get a look at him. Ven proceeded toward the middle of the village, centered around a stone well. A couple stood in front of it. The woman had her arms folded, and the man had an axe in one hand, though he was holding it by the head, indicating it wasn't being held in a threatening way, but more like he'd been in the middle of something when Ven arrived.

They both had dark brown hair, graying on the sides more than the last time he'd seen them. When their eyes widened with recognition, Ven could no longer restrain his smile.

"Is that little Yashke?" asked the man, Drin.

"It is indeed," Ven said, drawing Butch to a halt. Then he addressed both of them. "Drin, Elena, it's so good to see you." He climbed down from Butch to greet them, surprised to find that he was taller than Drin, a man who had once seemed so big with his broad shoulders and thick build.

They both came and shook his hand in turn, patting his shoulder at the same time.

"My, you have grown," Elena said, squeezing his shoulder. Ven and his parents had stayed with their family whenever they came to visit. In truth, Ven had spent more time with these people than he had with anybody besides his own parents, with the exception of Oliver of course, who was still house-sitting for Ven while doing online classes. The house was probably a wreck without Ven there to keep him in line.

Elena looked at the road behind Ven expectantly.

Ven sighed and gulped hard. "I came alone. My parents..." He bit his lip, preventing it from trembling. He hadn't expected to be overcome with such grief. "They, um, they passed away last year."

"Oh, Ven." Elena gave Ven a hug while Drin placed a hand on his arm in a strong grip.

Ven couldn't explain the relief he felt to have somebody he could properly grieve with. That tightness in his gut that had been wrenching at him loosened just enough for a single shudder to rock his shoulders. He tried not to think the thoughts, but they came at him regardless. He would never hug his parents again. He would never hear any more of their nuggets of wisdom, either the blunt way his mom expressed things or the verbose way in which his dad spoke. They hadn't just been his parents, they'd been his teachers, his confidants, and ultimately, his best friends. It was a loss he could never replace.

The hug lasted a few seconds until Ven sniffed and withdrew, letting out a huff. He nodded to them both and wiped his eyes before another tear could fall.

The other people who'd gathered around to see who it was started to disperse. There were several other vaguely familiar faces, but they clearly didn't want to be intruding on the moment, much to Ven's relief. If he'd been a little smarter, he would have scanned each face, trying to see if he could spot the one he was looking for among them, but he'd been caught up in the sight of Drin and Elena.

"Could we get you some tea?" Drin asked, hand still gripping Ven's shoulder. "How long have you been on the road?"

Ven nodded. Oddly enough, he felt better than he had for months. It was good to be somewhere familiar. This was a kind of healing his therapist hadn't been able to offer. "Yes. In fact, there's a lot we have to discuss."

Chapter Five

Reunion

Mia

Mia pulled her hood over her head and stood behind one of the homes, a hunting knife gripped tightly in her right hand. Her heart did not pound rapidly. Her hands were not sweaty. Her breathing was steady and calm. Despite her body's inability to react, Mia was nervous. Her hearing was exceptionally sharp, and she could tell the people were excited about something. A visitor had come to the village. As far as she knew, this was not the time for visitors. That wouldn't happen until the snow on the valley floor was practically gone.

If she was trying to be inconspicuous, she was failing. Shayna, one of the other villagers, walked right by Mia with her eyebrows raised at Mia's posture. "I don't think he'll bite," she muttered.

He? Mia peeked around the side of the building. She needed to get over to Maisie-Jane's house. This could very well be somebody who would be looking for her and she needed to ensure that Maisie-Jane was safe. She slammed her knife back into its leather sheath. No.

Nobody was looking for her. Everyone thought she was dead. She was being paranoid.

Her first stomp back onto the trodden path into the village was forced. She wished she'd been here when the newcomer arrived. It would have been a lot easier to get a look at him, and now she had to be worried that it was someone who would recognize her. The safest thing for her to do would be to hide outside the village until night rolled around, then sneak inside and see what Maisie-Jane had learned about the visitor, but she didn't want the woman to worry about her, so she'd at least let her know that she was going out to try hunting and wouldn't be back for a while.

Mia reached the home and pushed her way into the small building, stopping dead in her tracks as soon as she entered. She was about to turn around and bolt back outside, but Maisie-Jane addressed her immediately.

"Mia, we have a visitor," Maisie-Jane said, gesturing to a man who had his back to the door. He was seated in front of their fire, but he turned upon hearing Mia's name.

A trickle went up Mia's back as goosebumps spread across her skin, putting to shame all the winter days that had failed to do so. She'd be lying if she said she hadn't imagined this moment coming, especially after she first arrived in Mavenda. For some reason, she'd expected Ven would see through her deception. He was always so perceptive, but perhaps she'd overestimated him. As the year had waned, so too did her expectations. It was a strange idea to begin with. Hadn't she deceived him with the very intent of being on her own for a while? Why then would she secretly want him to show up?

But she'd found a place here. Sure, it was temporary, but it provided Mia the opportunity to see what a normal life may have looked like. It was good that he hadn't shown up. But now that he was here... she was stumped.

"Hello, Mia," Ven said, rising to his feet. His voice was slightly deeper than it had been even a few months ago, and he was not quite as gangly as she remembered. His blond hair was longer, as though he hadn't cut it since she last got a good look at him, which, she realized, was when he'd been throwing clods of dirt onto her face. She'd opened her eyes only enough to peer up at him through her eyelashes so he wouldn't notice.

Ven's eyes were as wide as a full moon, and he looked like he was seeing a ghost. If Mia honed in her hearing enough, she'd swear that she could pick out his heartbeat thumping rapidly. He must have truly thought she was dead. It probably *did* feel like seeing a ghost.

Mia took a step toward him, a smile twitching at her lips. But then the reality of his presence sent her mind spinning. He wouldn't just turn up here out of the blue. Something had spurred this meeting. If he'd truly believed her to be dead, then there was no other reason for him to come. "You came looking for me?" It was more of a statement than a question.

Ven finally blinked and nodded. "I did." He glanced at Maisie-Jane, sending Mia the unspoken message that he couldn't say everything he needed to. A smile revealed his teeth. "I'm glad you happened upon MJ here. Her soup is probably one of the best things to bless this village."

MJ?

Mia had to remind herself that Ven had been coming to the place a long time before she'd arrived.

Maisie-Jane laughed. "Please, I already ran out of salt. You can hardly taste it. Mia, I'm surprised you didn't tell me you knew the Yashke family."

Ven forced a laugh as well while Mia watched him closely. "Ah, well, she never met my parents." His smile wavered, but then he gestured to the door. "Mia, perhaps we could go for a walk."

Mia nodded and rushed outside. If Ven had known she was alive, did that mean somebody else knew? Maybe he'd returned to visit her burial site to find that the space was empty. She knew she should have moved the soil back over the hole a little more neatly.

When Ven got outside, the first question that she blurted out was "So where did I mess up? How did you know I was alive?"

Ven shook his head to himself and took a while to respond as they made their way to the edge of the village. It was only then that Mia realized he was wearing unique clothing, particularly his boots, which had a strange looking material on the very bottom. He didn't say anything until they'd gotten a few steps away from the nearest building. "It was my fault."

"What do you mean?"

"Somebody followed my trail when I took you out of Castia Mont. I didn't know you were still alive. They found where I buried you, but you were gone. They're going to keep looking for you. I should have done a better job concealing things somehow, Mia. I'm so sorry."

"Wait, who?" She should have known her little scheme wouldn't work. Outsmarting geniuses and powerful organizations was not something she really should have hoped to do so easily.

"Doctor Huan. Also, Dayelle. She's that secret employer I had. I don't know what her organization really is, but she's the one who initially wanted me to kill you."

"Oh, lovely." Mia turned her head toward the tall mountain to the east. She should have known that a life here was too good to be true.

"I'm so sorry, Mia." Ven had turned away from her and was rubbing a hand across the back of his neck.

Mia pulled his arm down and turned him to face her, surprised at how easy it was for her to interact with him on such a physical level. He looked down at her, frowning as though he was pained. "It's alright, Ven. It's not your fault. It was the best we could do given the circumstances. Please don't blame yourself." Then she hugged him. It was hard not to squeeze tightly, but she'd gotten better at moderating her strength. Instead, it was just tight enough to press her face right into his chest.

At first, Ven didn't hug her back, and she worried she'd done the wrong thing or read him incorrectly, but a second later, he wrapped his long arms around her, nuzzling his face down into her hair. His body was so rigid. She hadn't realized how incredibly tight he'd been until she felt him start to loosen up. His back and chest became softer the longer she held him. While she'd been living in paradise these last few months, it had been another story entirely for Ven. Perhaps she hadn't fully considered what he'd been going through.

"I'm so glad to see you, Ven," she said. "I'm sorry for tricking you."

Ven took a long while to respond, but he didn't let go of her. She knew he did this at times when he was trying to collect his thoughts. She'd hurt him. That much was clear.

"It's alright," he said, though his voice was a little strained. "I understand why you did it. I needed to be convincing so they wouldn't try to confirm your death." Then he sighed and withdrew from the hug. "I'm glad to see you too, Mia." He smiled at her, probably hoping it would be reassuring, but the smile didn't reach his eyes. Something in him was still pained. She didn't blame him for it. In fact, she completely understood. Perhaps he would never fully forgive her and their relationship would never be as it was before.

Mia brushed her hair back. "If I'm being honest, I always thought we'd cross paths again. I don't know why, I just suspected you would find me."

"You weren't wrong."

"Yes, and I even thought it would only be a few weeks, like you'd somehow know exactly where I was going."

Ven laughed. "Well, I suppose I did guess correctly once I heard you were alive." His smile vanished suddenly as if he'd just realized something.

"What is it?" Mia asked.

Ven shook his head and ran his fingers across his lips in thought. "I just—it's a little strange to think that it took people so long to find where you were buried. I don't know how tracking really works, but Dayelle only came to me a few days ago. The timing doesn't really line up to me."

Mia grunted. "Right, like if they were tracking you, they would have been right behind your trail. They would have known for quite a while that I wasn't actually dead, so she would have known well before then." Mia narrowed her eyes. "Why did she come to you at all? Who is she really?"

Ven took a couple steps away, arms folded, boots crunching on the trodden snow. "She claimed that she wanted me to have a clear conscience, so I wouldn't feel guilty for your death since you were actually alive."

"Did you?"

"Yes, I did feel that, but I know the reasoning was justified—"

"I'm sorry, Ven. I didn't mean to lay that on you."

"It's alright—"

"No, it's not. I can tell it hurt you."

"Mia." Ven turned to face her and grabbed both her shoulders, his brow furrowed with sincerity as he said, "It's alright. You did what you thought was best. That's all we can ever ask of anyone. I admit, I was a little lost, and yes, I was hurting, but you aren't responsible for my feelings. That lies with me." He stepped back once again and looked down at himself.

Mia bit her lip as emotion welled within her. Not enough to cry. She felt like she was beyond that as the truth of his words rang to her core, but she still felt sorry for the suffering he'd experienced.

"And you might be right," he said. "I knew I was supposed to come back to Orund. I don't know why, but I always had this feeling in my gut, like I was caught on the end of a fishing line, and it was tugging me back here. If I'd only listened I could have gotten here that much sooner. Maybe you would have seen me a few weeks after getting here, but I ignored it. I wanted to move on." He ran a hand through his hair.

Mia didn't know how to react, so she only nodded. She hadn't known he'd been so conflicted.

"Sorry," he said after glancing at her expression. "I think I felt like coming back here would make this all too real. If I stayed on Earth I could maybe distance myself from all of this, but it only made it worse."

"Earth?"

Ven's jaw hung open for a moment as he stared at her. He took a long breath before letting it out and pressing his fist to his lip. "Um, right. Well, I'm not sure how to explain this, and we probably need to talk about it more later, but I'm from a different world."

Mia pursed her lips then looked up at the sky before tilting her head at him. "Like... another planet?"

Ven turned his hands up before dropping them. "Look, I know it sounds crazy. That's because it is. I don't know how any of this actually works, but I'm able to go through a magical portal or something that lets me go between this world, Orund, and my world, Earth. I went back to my world after... after everything happened here. I went back to studying to become a doctor—a real one—and I'd been there this whole time until Dayelle came to my world and told me about you."

Mia smiled and nodded. "Okay."

"Okay? I just shared like the craziest thing and you just say 'okay'?"

"Yes, I mean, it makes sense. I always thought you were a little weird. I didn't know you were a complete alien. That adds up though."

Ven's jaw dropped again before he clamped it shut and smiled, folding his arms and leaning back as he glared down at her. "Good one."

"Thank you. But honestly, I'd believe anything at this point. I mean, I've got the blood of dragons running through my whole being. Tell me how that makes more sense than you coming through a magical portal."

Ven shrugged. "Touché."

"What does that mean?"

"Good point. But anyway, before we get too distracted, you'd asked me who Dayelle is and, embarrassingly, I don't really know. She knew my parents. She knew about Zein Huan's facility. She knew about the dragon imprisoned in the Huan's castle in Peskan. She even apprehended Zein himself. Well, her organization did all that at least. I'm not sure where she stands in that whole situation."

Mia blinked at Ven. Box it all, this whole thing went far deeper than she thought. She suddenly felt so small. This circumstances seemed so insurmountable to her. She was eighteen. Even as an immortal test subject, she was nothing but a child to all the strange things going on. "The... dragon?"

Ven nodded vigorously. "Yeah, that girl you saw in the Huan's castle dungeon—Dayelle said she was a dragon. She said they took care of her." He used two fingers to make some strange gesture she was unfamiliar with, but she got the point. Dayelle's organization's actions were morally ambiguous at best.

"And she came to tell you that I was alive?"

"Yeah. So that I didn't feel guilty, but I suspect she had an ulterior motive. She wouldn't go to a whole different world, orchestrate some crazy scheme to get into my university, and give a lecture exactly where I would be just to get an opportunity to tell me something like that. She could have delivered the message in a much simpler way."

Mia let out a breath that she hoped didn't come off as too seething, but she looked around, suddenly anxious about the idea that someone was after her. "And why did you come?" She hadn't meant her words to be so sharp, but there was fire to them.

Ven shrugged. "I don't know. Maybe I shouldn't have, but I felt convinced that they were coming after you. Dayelle seemed certain that at least Zein Huan was looking for you, and she didn't hide the idea that her organization is after you as well. I didn't want you to get caught up in their schemes again so I figured I could at least warn you."

"Dayelle didn't ask or request that you come here?"

"No. She didn't ask me for anything."

"So she wanted you to feel like it was your own decision and not some machination of hers?"

"Yeah, I think that's what it boils down to."

Mia closed her eyes. So much for paradise. "Alright, we have to go." She strode back toward Maisie-Jane's home.

"Go? Where?" Ven hurried after her.

"Ven, think about it. An organization that wants to find me went out of its way to tell you I was alive so that you could track me down. Why would they do that? Did they hide some device in your clothes like they did to Doctor Huan?"

"No, I went full undercover spy mode to—I mean, I took very specific measures to make sure that I couldn't be tracked here."

"Just like you did when you buried my body?"

"Well, no, I did better than that. I know how to do sneaky things on Earth better than I do here on Orund. Hopefully."

"Even when it means hiding from some organization like Dayelle's with seemingly ridiculous resources when they were clearly planning on tracking you here as a last-ditch effort to locate me?"

"Would you rather I didn't come and warn you?" Ven asked.

Mia stopped right in front of Maisie-Jane's door and turned to look at Ven. She realized her hands and chest felt hot. She'd been practically stomping the whole way. "Sorry, Ven. I'm not angry with you, I just... I wanted my freedom. I always thought if I saw you again it wouldn't be so..."She waved her hands in the air, unsure how to word what she was feeling.

"Stressful?" he suggested.

"Yes. I didn't want to leave here."

Ven nodded, face solemn as he looked down at the ground.

A smile grew along Mia's lips. "You were right though, Ven. About Mavenda." She gestured around her. "It really is as beautiful as you said it was. I couldn't believe how many flowers there were. I was just biding my time until spring." Her smile wavered. "It will be a shame to leave it behind."

"I'm glad you got to see it," Ven said. "And I don't know how Dayelle will track me, but you're probably right. She'll find out I came here."

"I just wish we knew how much time we had."

"We could probably... experiment with that," Ven said.

When Mia narrowed her eyes at him, he continued.

"I mean, the people here are amazing. We could let them know that somebody might come here looking for us. They'd keep us hidden, or at least let us know so we could find our own way to get out of here."

Mia tapped her chin. "That's actually not a bad idea. As long as whoever is after me doesn't come in full force."

Ven grunted. "Knowing Dayelle? It'll be a lot more subtle. Even Zein. They'd both slip in and try to manipulate us somehow."

"Or worse yet, sneak in while I'm sleeping and cut my throat with a dragonsbane blade or something." Despite being impervious, Mia still needed to sleep. Her body didn't view sleep as an impediment, otherwise she would have started forming some peculiar adaptation. She did need less sleep than the average person, but she didn't like it. It was the moment she was most vulnerable. No level of sharp senses and imperviousness could save her from somebody sneaking right up while she was sleeping.

"I bet we could come up with a way to prevent that, but if you're fine with it, I can start talking to the villagers and let them know that somebody could be coming after us. They'd be all in on helping us out."

"I believe it," Mia said.

"Ultimately, I would hate to have you living every night in fear. There has to be some way to create an assurance of safety."

There was such sincerity to Ven's words. The concern in his eyes reminded her of when they'd first met. He always wanted to help and solve everything, and not in a naive way, but by taking it head on. She reached out and squeezed his arm, grateful for how natural it felt to do so. No awkward heat came to her cheeks, but a familiar comfort washed over her. Despite what she'd done to him, he was still Ven. He still cared about her. Hopefully he was a little less naive, as was she, but she'd only been on her own now for a few months. They were still just youths who had been forced to grow up in a harsh world. Or, in Ven's case, two harsh worlds, apparently.

Mia released his arm. "So you're recommending we stick it out here until we know? Would that put the villagers at risk?"

"I hope not. I can't see either Zein or Dayelle wanting to do anything to bystanders. I like to think I can read people a little bit, and neither of them seem like Dami in that sense."

"Alright. Let's do it. How do we set up?"

Ven smirked. "I have a few ideas."

Chapter Six

The Royal

Ven Yashke

Ven finished setting up the last bell inside MJ's house and tested opening the door. The motion loosed the string and the bell fell to the floor, creating a distinctly loud, metal sound as it clattered on the stone.

Mia grunted her approval, arms folded across her chest. Each of the windows had also been set up with a similar rigging. This way, nobody would be able to catch Mia asleep. If she was awake when somebody tried sneaking in, then *they'd* be the ones who'd have to worry. Ven doubted anybody in the entire world would be able to stand up to a fully conscious Mia.

"I'm hoping that's a satisfied grunt," Ven said as he bent down to pick up the bell.

Mia rolled her eyes. "Yes. I'm satisfied."

"MJ," Ven said, "I hope you're okay with this."

"Pff," MJ said with a wave of her hand. "This is good. This has my full support. I tried not to ask about her past on purpose, but I knew she was seeking safety."

"Maisie-Jane, I really appreciate you doing this and taking me in," Mia said. Her eyes sparkled as she spoke. It was all Ven could do to keep from staring at Mia. She was still as stunning as ever. No, more so. It was like her moment of freedom had released so much unseen tension that her true self had been able to flourish. It made him regret coming with such unfortunate news.

"You are always welcome, Mia," MJ said. "This is what we do here in Mavenda. We care for people."

Ven smiled. It was such a beautiful notion to think that this place was where he and his parents would come for vacation. A place that cared for people. A place where they stood by the same principles his family had lived for.

"Are you staying here as well, Ven?" Mia asked.

Ven felt heat rise to his cheeks as he looked around MJ's meager home. "Uh, I'm," he stammered. "I'll be staying at the Andersens. It's where my family has always stayed when we've come here."

"Wouldn't it make more sense for us to stay in the same place?" Mia asked, brows pressed together in confusion. "What if somebody tries to get *you*?"

"We'll do a similar setup over at the Andersens."

"Yes, but you don't have the same... training that I do." There was a fierceness to Mia's voice. "It would be safer for you if you remained here."

MJ watched their interaction with folded arms, glancing between them with obvious interest. Ven could tell that Mia wouldn't let up on this either, and she made a good point. It would leave him feeling admittedly more confident in their security. He could work past the strange feeling of being in Mavenda and not staying with Drin and Elena's family.

Ven huffed. "Alright, true enough. I'll have you know though, I've been training a bit."

Mia gave him a skeptical smile. "Training what?"

"Fighting—not with a sword or weapon—but hand-to-hand combat."

Mia's smile grew, but MJ was aghast.

"You? Learning to fight?" MJ's jaw was unhinged.

Ven shrugged. "My parents were murdered, MJ. I had to adapt." He hoped they wouldn't have to resort to fighting, but if there was no alternative, he'd do what had to be done. That was a bridge he'd already crossed.

"Tomorrow you'll have to show me what you can do," Mia said, and Ven thought her smile came off a little mischievous.

"Mia, I have tried not to ask questions, but the two of you are now making me a little too curious." MJ shifted from one foot to the other.

Even though Ven had known MJ for years, he didn't feel comfortable sharing anything at all. Quite frankly, he felt like his ability to fully trust people was extremely limited. Was it possible that Dayelle had agents embedded in Mavenda? Yes, but MJ didn't seem likely to be one.

Mia, on the other hand, didn't hesitate to start talking about her upbringing. She didn't share about the dragonblood transfusion and her imperviousness, but she did talk about her combat training and that she was generally more physically capable than the average person. It was a clever way to tell the truth while leaving out the most significant details.

"So that's why people are after you?" MJ asked. "Because you escaped their testing facility?"

"Sort of," Mia said with a shrug. "It gets a lot more complicated really, but we can just leave it at that."

MJ raised a hand in acceptance. "That's quite alright. I know you didn't have to tell me any of that, but I appreciate that you could trust me enough to tell me what you did."

Ven was grateful that MJ was so unintrusive, even though she'd been exceedingly generous to house Mia all this time on her own dime. He could only imagine the financial strain that had placed on the woman. He didn't know what she did for income, but he hadn't failed to notice the thinness of the soup he had earlier. The bones of her cheeks and hands were more prominent than he remembered. She'd no doubt been providing for Mia without complaint. She was too modest.

Mia and MJ talked a bit more as Ven fished through his bag and located a couple coins. His memory was sharp enough to remember the respective value of Orundian currency, so he knew it would be way more than enough when he handed the coins to MJ.

MJ frowned at him in confusion.

"MJ, I hate to ask this of you," Ven said, "and I know we're already imposing on your home, but I had to travel a lot to get here and was a little low on supplies. Could you see about getting us enough food for a while? Enough for all three of us."

"Oh." MJ beamed. Her smile was so genuine that he knew she'd been stressed. "Well, of course."

"Thank you," Ven said as MJ hurried out the door.

Mia pressed her hands together and smiled at Ven, mouthing her own wordless thanks.

The rest of the evening went by quickly. Ven relocated Butch, and the Andersens came over with their two daughters, now twelve and eleven, bringing some more food so they could all eat together.

Mia was so full of smiles and laughter that it warmed Ven's heart like nothing else. It was only then that he realized that pain in his gut was completely gone. No more hook. This was what his soul had needed. It had yearned to see the truth, that Mia was alive and that she could know joy. This was true healing. Every time Mia's eyes lighted on him, a warmth spread over his whole chest and neck. His own smile was so pure that he wished the moment would last forever.

Maybe Zein or Dayelle would never come. Maybe this could be every night, smiling, laughing, and bathing in the ecstasy that was Mia's radiant smile. But he knew it couldn't be so. Something would change, as it always did. At least he could cherish this moment and hold onto it for times when life got harder.

When the Andersens went back to their house and the only light left came from a single candle at the center of the home, Ven threw down some spare padding on the floor. This would be his sleeping place for the foreseeable future.

"You know, I could try the floor," Mia suggested as Ven knelt beside his makeshift bed.

Ven breathed a laugh. "No, you deserve all the comfort you can get."

"Don't you deserve comfort as well?"

Ven thought to protest, but when he looked up at her, she stood so close to him. Her flawless skin glittered in the candlelight, black hair glistening like stars in the night sky. He could stare at her eyes forever. Unbidden warmth spread throughout his body and he suddenly found that it took all his willpower to prevent himself from standing just to reach out and touch her chin. His fingers ached to feel the smoothness of her skin, to run across her neck. He was hanging on a precipice, but he couldn't bring himself to move. All the pent up emotion was surging within him. With most of his anxiety, grief, and heartache pushed to the side, what remained was his passion. What he felt for Mia wasn't simply the infatuation of youth or the obligation of caring for someone in need, it was love.

"Sorry I don't have any more blankets," MJ said from across the room, her eyes flicking between the two of them. "You're sure the floor will be fine, Ven?"

Ven gulped and blinked rapidly as he twisted to regard MJ. "This-this will be just fine. Thank you, MJ. I have slept on the floor a lot over the years actually. Especially with all the traveling my family did." With all the pillows they had provided him, this would be a lot better than other places he'd slept, especially those dirt floors with nothing more than his clothes and a single blanket. He lay down to make his point, shifting around on the collection of pillows and blankets. It actually was rather cozy, and what the blankets lacked in softness, they made up for with warmth.

"Perfect," he stated, placing his hands behind his neck with a smile.

"Alright, well, goodnight, Ven." Mia's voice was just more than a whisper, and the corner of her lips curled just slightly, providing Ven more comfort than any blanket or pillow ever could.

MJ blew out the candle, and the home fell into stillness as the others settled into their beds.

Ven couldn't sleep. Despite how wonderful the day had been, he couldn't even bring himself to close his eyes. Minutes passed until MJ's breathing became a steady rhythm. He knew Mia didn't sleep as much as a normal person, so she would probably be awake as well. She shifted at one point, but Ven remained still. Perhaps if he didn't move at all, he'd be able to fall asleep, but it never came. Minutes turned to hours until even Mia seemed to be asleep.

In his restlessness, Ven sat up. What was wrong with him? It wasn't like he was jet-lagged. The time zone difference would have only been two hours off, if time even went the same way on this planet. Moonlight spilled through the uncovered window, illuminating the home in a dim, pale glow. Despite the blankets, he was cold. He should have just brought out his sleeping bag. MJ wouldn't have batted an eye over Ven having strange things.

A shadow passed by the window just beside where Mia was sleeping. Ven shot up, suddenly wishing he had some kind of weapon, but he'd brought nothing of the sort with him from Earth and hadn't had a chance to try to get anything now that he was here. He didn't want to wake the others in case he was being paranoid, but he slipped on his coat and boots and carefully retrieved a knife from the shelf.

He stood alert, waiting. It could have been a fluke. Somebody could have been up late. Surely there were things people needed to do in the middle of the night in a small village, right? *Probably not.* Ven remained there near the center of the room, waiting to see if there was any other indication of movement. He wouldn't do anything rash, but he'd at least be prepared in case something happened. Unless people came charging in with dragonsbane weapons, Mia would be able to react so quickly that there was ultimately very little chance for an opponent to succeed.

But Ven and MJ were not impervious.

After considering if he was just seeing things, the shadow appeared again in another window over the wash basin. This time, it lingered. It was shaped like a cloaked head as they peered inside. Ven's blood went cold, wondering if they could see him there, shivering in the dark.

Ven would not act first. He was safest inside, but perhaps it would be wise to rouse Mia.

A new shadow appeared beside the head. It was a hand that waved back and forth before beckoning Ven toward the window. He frowned but wondered if this was perhaps a villager who knew about the alarms on the door and windows but had an urgent message for them.

Ven approached the window tentatively. When he got there, he brushed back the thin curtain that barely veiled half of the window as the person outside pulled back their hood, exposing their face to the bright moonlight. Ven's eyes widened with recognition.

Huan.

Chapter Seven

Conspiracy

Mia

Without any weapons of her own, Mia stood across from the newcomer with a readied stance. She was close enough to the table that she could easily fling the entire heavy wooden furniture directly into his body if necessary. It was difficult to keep her eyes off of the familiar dragonsbane sword sheathed at his waist.

Even in the dark with little more than a bit of moonlight, Mia was able to pick out his features clearly. Her vision was well adapted to the dark, a subtle change that she hadn't known to be so significantly different from normal humans, but with the blood of dragons running in her veins, everything about her had been altered.

This was one of the few people in the world who knew Mia's true nature, and he was the only person Mia had ever willingly told about her adaptive condition.

Siwen Huan, Zein's cousin, and heir to the throne of Peskan.

"How did you find me?" Mia asked, her voice barely more than a whisper.

Maisie-Jane still slept like a rock. She hadn't even stirred after Ven woke Mia up and they opened the door for Siwen to enter.

Siwen's slim eyes closed for a moment before answering. One might not assume that Siwen was a noble unless they got a good look at that sword on his hip. He was otherwise adorned in simple traveling clothes and smelled strongly of smoked meat with an undertone of moistened dirt.

"Only a few days after the events at Castia Mont, I was contacted by the Drekis Alliance to provide my tracking services," Siwen said. "You are familiar with my particular skill there."

"The Drekis Alliance?" Ven asked, still holding the knife casually in one hand though his arms were folded as he leaned back against the wall.

"Yes. The same organization that pulled you into all this." Siwen's expression was stoic, but Ven's soured. "They said they needed to locate someone. This led me to the scene where Ven buried you. I instantly realized what I was looking at as there were still the recognizable hoofprints of Ven's Zebadon there. Such tracks are not easy to hide. On seeing the empty grave, I knew what you had done. I was tasked with locating you. It was difficult and it took a full day to finally pick out your path, but I was able to trace it, eventually leading me here. I had to report back to the Alliance, but I told them it was untraceable."

Mia blinked at him and Ven remained silent. "Why?"

Siwen let out a long breath. "I do not share the same level of confidence in them I once had. Their choices around you and Dami felt questionable to me. I could not in good conscience say that I align with their same moral decisions. I thought it better that if Mia had escaped alive, it should remain that way. As you know, I'm a man who seeks to pursue the best moral path, and Mia's potential execution does not seem justified."

"So they *did* know that Mia was alive for quite some time now," Ven said.

"Oh, yes indeed," Siwen said. "I would surmise that they were right behind you for the entirety of your venture, Ven. They would have scoured the gravesite perhaps only an hour or two after you left. It is within that timeframe that I assume Mia was able to uncover herself and run away, right before the agents would have arrived."

Mia shared a look with Ven. This meant his assumption was correct. They'd only told him about her just recently, even though they'd known she was alive for several months.

"And why did you come back now?" Mia asked. "Conveniently on the same day as Ven."

"I was given some disconcerting information regarding my cousin." Siwen's expression hardened.

"Zein escaped custody somehow. Dayelle told me about that," Ven said.

"Yes," Siwen said. "This appears to be the catalyst that has brought us both here, but it's even worse than that." He shifted his weight between legs, hand hovering over the pommel of his sword, but one glance at Mia caused him to stop and fold his arms. "It would seem that my cousin shares similar... characteristics as Mia."

Ven's jaw dropped, but a flare of anger simmered in Mia's chest. Zein. The man who had tortured and used not only her, but dozens of people like her, was also a subject to his own test. Perhaps he'd been after power all along. It wasn't about helping people.

"Why would that lead you here? To me?" Mia asked, trying to keep her voice steady. Maisie-Jane stirred in her bed.

"He knows you're alive. He will look for you," Siwen said. "I came here because I thought I was the only one who would be able to warn you." He glanced at Ven. "I was wrong."

"Can you tell us more about the Drekis Alliance?" Ven asked. "Who are they? What do they really want?"

"Yes," Siwen said. "They are an old group. I believe the organization has existed for centuries, but they're motivated to root out the use of dragonblood for research and technological advancement. I ascribe to the same creed, as has long been the tradition of my family since we killed our overlords. My role under my family's fiefdom has been dedicated to enforcing the law, and it was extremely evident that illegal dragonblood research and technology production was rampant. My vigor in addressing the situation caught the attention of the Drekis Alliance, and I have been associated with them for some time, as they would often provide useful information regarding movements within Peskan. That is about the extent of my knowledge regarding them."

"But what is your sentiment toward me being alive?" Mia asked. "Clearly, you did not pursue after me when you located me originally, but what's your stake in the matter?"

Siwen clasped both his hands in front of him. "Just as I do not destroy existing dragonblood technology and merely work to prevent future developments, I have the same feeling toward you." He shrugged. "So long as you do not attempt to murder or enslave my people, or until my commanding lord orders me to come after you. On a personal level, I have viewed you as an ally. We have fought together against a common foe."

Mia nodded, content with his answer, but Ven was tapping a foot.

"How are things back at Peskan with your father?" Ven asked.

"We do not speak much," Siwen said, his face returning to an impassive facade. "He has been unlike himself in the last few months since that prisoner was smuggled out of the dungeon."

"The dragon," Mia said, her voice a whisper.

"I was under the impression she was dead," Ven said. "Dayelle said she'd been taken care of."

Siwen's lips became a thin line. "I wondered if it was her doing."

"She didn't tell you?" Ven asked.

Siwen shook his head just slightly before snapping his attention to Maisie-Jane. She sat up in her bed, eyes as wide as the full moon as she stared at them. Mia hadn't even noticed her movement.

"MJ," Ven said, smiling at her. "Uh, we may need to ask you to keep a secret. Or two."

Chapter Eight

Spring

Ven Yashke

Ven shook his arms out, attempting to stave off the weariness. Siwen had elected to remain with them as they anticipated some kind of assault, but none came. Two months passed, and a few people had already visited the village.

In the meantime, Ven had taken to practicing with Mia and Siwen. His martial arts classes weren't incredibly relevant to the art of killing, but the structure of moving through combat strokes and maneuvers was at least tangentially applicable. Siwen provided Ven with an additional sidearm to practice with, but they didn't really get into sparring. The warrior lord seemed hesitant to even draw the dragonsbane weapon from its sheath and instead demonstrated all of his techniques by using a stick. There was a sort of reverence Siwen held for the weapon.

Mia struggled to provide instruction. She was obviously an unmatched combatant, but she lacked the ability to teach the skills she used. This was understandable, as her techniques were all implemented with her full strength and agility behind them, things that Siwen and Ven would never be able to match or fully comprehend. She was even quicker than she'd been a few months ago. It seemed she still hadn't reached her maximum potential if there truly was a cap. Her body simply continued adapting.

"Again," Siwen said, lifting his stick.

Ven raised the shortsword and swung through the motions, shuffling his legs and trying to maintain the same posture that Siwen demonstrated. They'd been through this at least a hundred times today, but there was little else to do as the days passed, so Ven practiced.

And Siwen was not a casual instructor. He pushed Ven to the extreme. It had only been two months, but they'd been absolutely grueling. As they practiced, Siwen himself looked like he was pulled straight from some Chinese warrior movie, excluding all the gravity-defying stunts. Those were left to Mia.

The village found the demonstrations amusing in two parts: first, that Ven, the doctors' son, was training as a warrior, and second, that they were training in combat forms at all. This was a village that had never known war. Human aggression was simply unheard of. The only weapons any of them had used were bows, and those were strictly for hunting. Thankfully, none of the people minded it at all.

MJ was still the only one among them who knew that Mia was something different. She didn't know the exact details that made her different, but Ven knew MJ was no fool. From what she'd overheard, she could surmise that Mia had some kind of connection as a subject of dragonblood technology research. He still didn't know if anybody in Mavenda even knew about dragonblood tech. He'd certainly never seen any of it here before.

"Are you sure your father isn't going to mind that you've been gone for a couple months?" Ven asked, finishing up the sequence Siwen was running him through.

Siwen shrugged. "He'll mind a little bit, certainly, but I have no specific duties."

"Weren't you supposed to get married?" Mia asked. She was crouched down by a budding plant. There were loads of little green shoots that had started appearing the last few days, and Ven had no doubt they'd turn into some kind of flowering specimen.

"Ah." Siwen actually stuttered, freezing in place. "Yes, not yet. I do have a formal engagement. We were going to be married in the summer, but there was a delay due to some of the recent complications back at Peskan. The disappearance of the woman—the dragon—has been quite the disruption. The disturbance at the castle between your escape and hers has created a bit of gossip in the city. It caused the proposing family to have second thoughts about my family's security. They want assurances about their daughter's safety. I completely support their decision." His arms were flat against his sides and his face had resumed that flat expression.

Ven smiled and looked at Mia, but she only shrugged. "Siwen, are you second-guessing your engagement?"

"No," Siwen said. "She is an excellent pick. Healthy. Articulate. Quite intelligent. She is a very skilled dancer and comes from a strong family with four younger sisters. Her mother is the baroness of Luedan. It's not as close as I would like, but they are a well-connected family that would actually place our children within the line of ascendancy to the throne, though very distantly."

"So, why the hesitation?" Ven asked. "Not from her family, but I mean from you."

"I don't know what you mean." Siwen was as rigid as ever. "I consider myself lucky to be able to make this connection between our two families. She and I could have a strong relationship."

Ven smirked. If there was one thing Ven had gotten good at, it was reading people. Siwen often did a good job at hiding how he felt about something, but he only reached complete rigidity when he was trying to turn or suppress something. Denial. His noble honor would prevent him from voicing something negative on this subject.

"Of course," Ven said, not willing to press. He was still breathing heavily from the exertion of the drills. "This upcoming wedding means you will need to depart soon."

"It does," Siwen said. "In fact, I will need to depart tomorrow. There are preparations to make. I anticipated something would have happened here already."

Ven looked toward the village. The first visitors of spring had already started showing up, though they were still few in number. The snow on the valley floor had melted quickly once things were consistently warmer. The lake filled up, and the stream leading out of the valley was now a gushing river. Visitors meant potential exposure.

Now was one such occasion. A bit of excitement echoed up from the village center as a cart arrived, pulled by two horses.

"Should we check it out?" Ven asked.

Siwen put his stick down and nodded as Mia joined them, pulling her hood over her head just in case. Nearly every eligible bachelor in the village had at one point or another fought to get Mia's attention. Understandably so. Beauty like hers was almost unnatural. Other people appeared to completely avoid her, though they'd still stare. If Ven didn't already know her personally, he could imagine that she'd seem unreal or untouchable.

Villagers crowded the cart. This was the first trader to arrive, and they were already getting set up to start selling or trading supplies. Ven, Mia, and Siwen watched from the fringes. Five people had come in aboard the cart, and two of them immediately brought out a barrel full of salt and started selling it off. Sometimes the villagers traded with goods like wool and cheese, but there weren't many trade commodities produced in the village. A lot of the actual money the villagers made was from tourism, which seemed like a strange concept for a society where things mostly ran on horsepower. There was a lot that Ven didn't understand about Orund. He felt like he needed history and geography classes.

In the flurry of trading, Ven hadn't noticed another rider coming up at the back of the procession. It was only when Siwen nudged him and pointed with his chin that Ven squinted over. The new-comer was a middle-aged man with a thick beard and broad shoulders. A covered axe was strapped to the side of his saddle but he didn't appear to have any other tool. Ven wasn't sure how he knew, but the axe looked like it wasn't the kind that was used exclusively for chopping wood. The man looked directly at them before veering his horse toward the far end of the village, avoiding the center, then disappearing behind a building on the other side.

Siwen tied a band over his head and said quietly, "I'll do some reconnaissance. Watch for any other newcomers." Then he stepped forward, mixing into the crowd.

Mia stepped closer to Ven and folded her arms across her chest. Ven ran a finger across his lower lip. It was difficult for him to focus on all the activity ahead of them while in such proximity to Mia. There was this sort of invisible aura around her that made everything feel... warmer. Was he the only person who she affected like that? He didn't remember it from before. Maybe it was psychological and something he felt because of past experiences with her.

Ven cast a sideways glance at her, but her eyes were concealed behind the hood. A thought had been simmering at the back of his mind for weeks now, one he was still afraid to confront. If she needed him to believe she was dead, why hadn't she told him she was alive once they got out of Castia Mont? He knew he needed to bring it up to Mia eventually, but part of him hoped he could simply suppress it. History had shown that was not effective for him. It would only fester until things got even worse.

What he didn't want to admit was that he was afraid to learn the truth. He still remembered that night when he'd confessed his love for her. She'd never returned the sentiment. She'd merely used his proclamation for her own purposes.

Mia tapped Ven's arm. He'd been rubbing his lip hard enough that she'd picked up on it, casting him a curious look, perfect brown eyes glinting at him.

"Just nervous," Ven said, electing to stuff his hands in his pockets to prevent himself from resuming his nervous habit.

The traders only stayed for another hour or two before they ran out of supplies. Being the first trader to arrive after winter certainly had its perks, especially since the supplies would be greatly needed for all the small industries in preparation for summer. Mia learned that they'd come from a big city down southwest called South Fork. They were regular visitors that came two or three times a year. From their position, she could overhear all the conversations in the whole circle. Siwen had tracked the other visitor, but he'd gone to the ranches on the south end of the village and was apparently a business associate who was merely there to arrange exports.

Everything was clear.

"Perhaps there is no threat after all," Mia said as they walked back towards MJ's home.

Ven nodded. He'd had so much confidence that no matter what he did, Dayelle would be able to track him. Maybe she couldn't, and all the precautions he'd taken to get here were actually effective.

"Dayelle is clever," Siwen said. "I'm worried we're looking in the wrong place altogether. If what you said regarding the dragon in Peskan suggests that Dayelle loosed the monster or merely transferred its slavery, then I have deeper concerns regarding the motivations of the Drekis Alliance."

"So like… they want us here?" Ven asked, trying to wrap his head around the politics of it. Individuals he could understand, but organizations were a completely different beast.

"Something along those lines, yes," Siwen said. He'd grown more stern these last few months. It seemed life had hardened him. They'd all been dealing with some semblance of that. Save for Mia. She seemed... better.

"That's not so bad," Mia said. "I can imagine much worse places to be."

Ven smiled. "She has a point, but I don't understand why they'd want us to be here."

"Neither do I," Siwen said. "That's what worries me." He paused before they reached MJ's home. "I'm actually going to scope out the road around the lower valley. I'll return before nightfall. Then I will need to depart tomorrow to reach Peskan. I have a suspicion they know you are here and are content if you stay. That, or it's taking them a considerably long time to get here. Either way, I would recommend you leave."

With that, Siwen clapped them both on the shoulder before jogging off to fetch his horse. He had a Zebadon, the largest and most powerful type of horse. He'd be able to scout a large area if necessary.

Now that Ven was alone with Mia, the question tugged at his mind, begging him to ask. He took a deep breath and aimed toward the back of the home rather than going inside. "So, Mia."

"Hmm?" She looked up at him, eyebrows raised.

"I was just curious about something." Ven wiped his hands on his pants. They'd inevitably started sweating. "After Castia Mont, when I'd successfully gotten you out of the castle grounds. I lugged you around for a few days straight. Was it absolutely necessary to keep up the ruse? Like, couldn't you have told me that you were alive? I mean…" Ven shook his head, remembering his months of suffering, fully believing that he'd killed her. "Why?"

Mia sighed and looked down, folding her arms. He already knew he wasn't going to like her answer. "Ven, I'm—look—I'm sorry. I thought it would be necessary in order for you to get back to whatever life you had before."

Ven shook his head. "Mia, I couldn't go back to normal." He squeezed the back of his neck as the memory of his pain rose in his chest like a filling balloon. "I thought about you every day. I felt like I'd done something terrible. I went to see doctors and they couldn't help me. Mia, it was… it was torture."

Mia frowned at the ground, refusing to look up and meet his eyes.

He wished he could just forgive her, but she wasn't telling him the whole truth. "Mia, I pretended to be a doctor. I pretended to be three years older than I actually was, and people believed me. I think I could have pretended you were dead."

"Okay." Mia threw her arms up. "What do you want me to say? Maybe I *did* want to hurt you, Ven. I don't know. I just needed time to myself." She returned to a firm stance, arms folding once again. She was resolute.

"I see," Ven said. He set his jaw. She didn't feel the same at all. He shook his head, thinking himself silly. The pain, the guilt, the shame—it had all been meaningless. He'd suffered those months for no reason at all, except that she might live in peace without him. The realization hit him like a kick to the gut.

Still, he'd been drawn back to Orund for a reason. If it wasn't to be with Mia, then what was it? Clearly he was not meant to go back to Earth and get his degree from Harvard. He'd burned that bridge two months ago. It was also clear that Mia didn't need him. He had nothing to offer her. She was an immortal, and he was just some kid who hardly knew anything about this place. There was no point for him to be here.

Siwen was right. Dayelle wanted them here for some kind of distraction. He'd fallen for it. Dayelle knew of his infatuation.

"I should help MJ prepare supper," Ven said. He walked past Mia, ignoring that her mouth worked in silence as she couldn't come up with a response. Ven already knew there was no adequate response. If she wanted time to herself, then who was he to deny her?

Chapter Nine

Wings

Mia

Mia didn't sleep all night. She lay awake staring at the ceiling and fuming. Ven hadn't spoken to her the rest of the night except for a polite good night. Maisie-Jane had been oblivious to their discord, chatting about all the things she traded, but Siwen was quiet and broody. After Siwen left to go sleep wherever it was he hid, they all went straight to bed.

Mia's mood darkened as the hours passed. Ven had a right to be angry. She'd manipulated him. She could have told him once they'd gotten away safely, yet instead she chose to keep pretending she was dead. She'd wanted to get away without anybody knowing she was alive, including Ven. Was that selfish of her to want complete freedom? She'd known it would hurt him, but she wasn't responsible for his emotions. The thought felt hollow. If she'd punched him, and he got angry about it, would she be innocent?

Somehow, the worst part about it was that Ven wasn't angry at all. He was indifferent. Instead, Mia was the angry one. She didn't want to feel like she'd done something so insensitive, especially to a man who'd basically do anything for her. She'd thought caring about other people was what had separated her from the other subjects like Dami and Ambrose. To them, it didn't matter who they hurt so long as they got what they wanted. Was she a little like them?

She continued to brood, sometimes clenching her fists and rolling around in bed, but no comfort came. When the first light of a new day started filtering through the window, she was relieved. It would likely be another hour or two before everyone woke up, but she slipped out of bed and removed the alarm bell from the door before going outside. The village was asleep, but Mia had an overwhelming urge to move. She pulled off her stockings, bare feet absorbing the cool touch of stone. She ran to the edge of the village at a normal pace.

Once at a good distance, she burst into full speed, arms pumping at her sides. The crisp smell of damp foliage calmed her senses, and she enjoyed the feeling of the soft ground squishing beneath her pounding feet. Her hair, still tied in a braid from yesterday, flapped behind her.

Mia was faster than any horse, but she suspected her body had limitations due to size. If her legs were longer, perhaps she could run even faster. At full speed, it still didn't trigger her adaptation response. Few things did that anymore. It would take hours of hard work to trigger it in most cases. She needed her run to go quickly, so she went all the way to the edge of the valley, then turned back around. It only took a few minutes, but it was effective at clearing her mind. She was still able to get back before any of the others were awake, offering her plenty of time to clean off her feet where mud had gotten properly caked between each of her toes.

Siwen was the first to arrive. She heard him coming from several paces away. It was interesting how, if she really harnessed her attention, she could tell exactly who approached based on their gait. Siwen was steady with a stride that was not overly confident, but had a semblance of lightness to it, suggesting he was ready to change course at any moment.

When he arrived, he took one glance at her mostly clean feet and smirked. "Took an adventure this morning, no?"

Mia smiled back, grateful to have somebody treating her normally. "Had to clear my head."

He only nodded back. "I hope you aren't too distressed that I'm leaving. You could come with me, of course, though I can't say your face will be altogether welcome in Peskan around the castle. Normally I'd say enough time has passed that you could probably lie low in the city without being recognized, but yours isn't a face to go without recognition."

"That's alright," Mia said. "Thank you." She didn't want to leave Mavenda. The flowers were just about to start blooming again and she felt like she'd waited her whole life for this. And if Dayelle or Zein didn't feel like coming after her, then good riddance.

He remained outside with her, inspecting some of his gear while she finished cleaning up. Maisie-Jane and Ven woke up and the door swung open a second later, Ven's wide-eyed face appearing in the doorframe. When he saw her sitting there just outside, his expression vanished. "Ah. Good morning."

"Good morning," Siwen and Mia said at the same time.

Ven pushed the door all the way open and let them in, but he continued out the building, heading further into the village.

Mia and Siwen went inside and helped Maisie-Jane prepare a meal. Ven made it back a few minutes later with Drin and Elena who brought some additional food. Mia remained quiet for most of the meal, choosing instead to see how the others interacted. The Andersens were pure joy, laughing and smiling constantly.

"One of my favorite memories," Elena said, "was when Ven was absolutely convinced that he could ride one of our goats."

Ven covered his face with a hand, failing to hide a smile as his cheeks blushed.

"He tried climbing on its back but it jumped away then head-butted him right in the chest, knocking him over. He tried getting back up, and then it hit him in the back again." She could barely get the words out as she laughed. "Drin had to rush in and grab the goat so Ven could get inside."

Drin smiled, and his face was red with silent laughter.

Their joy was infectious and pierced through Mia's moodiness. She still didn't engage much in the conversation, but at least she was enjoying the moment.

Ven was her friend. He would be able to move on from the pain. He was the same person who preached about everyone needing healing. She'd gotten used to life in Mavenda and it was great to have him around. The relief of having somebody she could be completely real with was the one thing she'd been lacking, and yet, she'd know-ingly pushed him away by not letting him in on her plan.

After the meal, Ven stood and cleared his throat. "I wanted us all to come together today because I'll be leaving with Siwen."

Mia's head jerked back like she'd been slapped. She gulped down the shock and looked at each person to see if they heard the same thing she did. Ven was leaving? But what about the threat from Dayelle and Zein? He couldn't really leave her here. The idea had never crossed her mind.

"Well, it was good to have you for as long as we did," Drin said, clapping Ven's shoulder.

Elena placed a hand to her forehead. "Don't tell me you're running off to be a soldier. Is that what this man has gotten you into?"

Ven laughed. "Hopefully not, but you never know what can happen out there. Things have always seemed safe here in Mavenda, but people fight, and I need to be able to watch out for myself."

"Well, yes, as long as you don't go looking for trouble," Elena said.

Ven looked straight into Elena's eyes. "I promise I'll only do what I must, but Siwen and I are going to look into some things that could be dangerous. And he's to be married soon, so I'll want to be there for that."

Siwen stood with his arms to his side, observing the exchange with a quizzical expression. Mia had a feeling that Ven had just sprung this on him from out of nowhere. She would have expected him to at least discuss this decision first. He was acting rashly. Heat rose in her chest. He was just doing this to make a point. She clenched her jaw and glared at him, but he barely gave her a passing glance.

"When do you leave?" Maisie-Jane asked.

"My intention was to leave right now," Siwen said, crossing his arms. "Especially with Ven's horse. We'll need all the time we can get."

"Then we must send you off with whatever provisions you need," Elena said, immediately bending over the table to start wrapping the half-eaten loaf of bread into a cloth. Everyone started fussing about getting Ven prepped to go while Siwen stood by the door with his arms folded.

Mia imagined this was how a family would function if their own son was leaving. Still baffled by the announcement, she slunk over to Siwen. "Did you know about this?" she whispered to him.

Siwen's unenthusiastic frown accompanied his response. "No, but perhaps it will be necessary."

"Necessary for what?"

"Ven's a sharp lad. Hopefully his insight can help me figure out what's been going on in Peskan, though I suspect this is bigger than that."

Mia leaned back against the wall. Doubtful. Ven just wanted an excuse to leave.

"Ven, fetch your horse, then I can lead you over to my camp and we'll head out from there," Siwen said before opening the door.

Ven hugged Elena, Drin, and Maisie-Jane before slinging his pack over his shoulder. He paused in front of Mia before offering his hand to shake hers. "Mia. It was good to see you again."

Mia took Ven's hand, trying not to sneer. How had things deteriorated so quickly? Just yesterday, Ven had seemed like her best friend in the world, and now he was leaving her with nothing more than a handshake?

He gave her hand a squeeze, then pulled away. The warm touch of his skin slipped away like oil from water. When he turned and went out the door, something clenched at her chest as she fought against the idea that this was the last time she would see him. Everyone followed them outside and said their goodbyes, but the words disappeared in the air as though Mia couldn't hear what anyone was saying. It was like time moved through water.

Mia took a step in their direction, feeling as though she should say something. A tightness grew in her stomach, but she couldn't think of any words. All she could do was stare at the back of Ven's head as he disappeared.

Fine. It didn't matter. He didn't care if somebody came to assassinate her. He wouldn't make a difference in such a situation anyway, so what reason did she have to be bothered? There was none. And yet, tears watered her vision. She blinked them away rapidly and turned towards the big mountain to the east. She needed some time to herself.

With that, she marched out of the village. She ran, not at full speed, but headed straight to the mountain. A lot of it was still covered in snow and ice, but she didn't care. She started scaling up the steep incline, aiming for the exposed stone whenever possible. This was something she excelled at. Even if she hadn't been a subject of the Impervious Project, she wanted to believe that climbing would have just come naturally to her. This had always been her greatest escape at the facility. The exercise and the coolness of the mountain helped clear her mind.

She decided to stop atop a large rockface, feet dangling over the edge as she turned and looked out across the village. It had probably been a full hour or two since Ven and Siwen left, and now that she was alone and her frustration had simmered down, she was surprised to feel gradual tears welling in her eyes. Part of her believed that this was simply the end and she would never see Ven again. They were going off to find something good to do in the world, and yet here was Mia, quite possibly the most capable person on the planet, and all she wanted to do was look at flowers. But just because she could do something didn't mean she had to.

Mia remained in place, breathing the mountain air, bouncing her heels on the stone, watching the valley as the sun slowly shifted overhead. She knew Maisie-Jane would be worried about her being gone for so long, but Mia couldn't muster the will to head back. It would feel too quiet.

Evening was already approaching when Mia saw smoke start to rise from one of the homes. That wasn't too unusual, but it seemed like a lot more smoke than would be necessary for a simple fireplace. She leaned forward over the edge, squinting even though her vision was already as sharp as possible. A building was on fire.

She clucked her tongue and scrambled down the cliff as panic bubbled in her gut. It could very well be a coincidence that this fire was happening after Ven and Siwen left, but Mia did not suspect it was coincidence.

When the screams reached her, Mia abandoned caution. She bit her lip and started jumping down the ledges, which she was more adept at than she would have thought. She reached the bottom of the mountain in seconds before taking off at a sprint down the sloped foothill. The screams continued, and she cursed herself for going so far away. Flames erupted from another building with the sound of a roaring bear.

No, no, no. This couldn't be an accident.

And then she saw them. A column of soldiers marched through the center of the village two abreast, each armed with a spear and shield. They wore intricate metal helmets with strange ears that looked like the wings of dragons, their eyes hidden behind a toothy maw, the rest of their body covered in scaled armor.

They were killing the villagers.

Mia snarled and came in at full speed, holding out her arms as she rammed into the soldiers. She barely even thought of the risk of them wielding dragonsbane weapons. They would not hurt these people. Bodies went flying as she crashed. The soldiers didn't even scream. Their eyes didn't widen with surprise. Those left standing merely took up position to face her.

Several spears jabbed at her, but she was far too quick and impervious for any of it to matter. She yanked a spear away, kicking the wielder off the other end. He went soaring, clattering into some of his fellow soldiers, body crumpling with the force. She moved like a blur, using the spear more like a battering ram as she hammered it into people. Stabbing was too slow. It only lasted for five strikes before it split in half across a soldier's face. Again, no screams. No cries of pain. It was like they weren't even human.

Villagers still scrambled away from the village. The soldiers were spreading out, and Mia couldn't reach all of them. There were hundreds.

A few spears streaked across Mia's body here and there, but nothing caused so much as a scratch, though her clothing started to tear along her arms and back. Mia grabbed a soldier who stabbed at her, ripping the woman's helmet off as she lifted her in the air by the breastplate of her armor. "Why?" Mia roared.

The soldier did not answer. Her face was a pure mask of neutrality as she simply kicked and clawed at Mia, her efforts completely harmless.

Mia screamed and slammed the body down. This was senseless. Who could benefit from killing these villagers? Even for her to kill these soldiers, it was meaningless violence. She hated this. She hated *them* for attacking. But they didn't stop. Her ferocity didn't scare them. They merely pressed on. More buildings burned. More villagers died.

She managed to wrench a soldier's sidesword away and used this to attack the others. She was a wolf among ants. They came at her, heedless of the danger. She could see how Dami, Ambrose, and Baze had reveled in the pure destruction. She wasn't technically made for killing, but her expertise would certainly make one wonder if this was her purpose. Pure unstoppable, destructive power.

Warm blood poured across her skin as she severed a man in half. Her sword had been blunted down to a dented piece of iron, but her raw power allowed her to break through bodies with ease. It was disgusting, and her lips were pulled back in a sneer as she tore through their ranks. Her body burned with anger.

Where was Maisie-Jane? Where were Elena and Drin? What about their children—would she be able to protect them all? She simply couldn't cover all this ground, and with the strange, unnatural reactions of the soldiers, the only screams came from dying villagers. When she saw the first bodies, her heart wrenched. An entire family lay dead on the ground, skewered as though their lives had been meaningless.

Flames surrounded her on all sides as the buildings burned. Mia rushed to some other soldiers, but a new opponent froze her in place.

Soaring on giant, batlike wings, a woman dropped down in front of Mia before the wings practically sucked into the woman's back and disappeared. Black hair, eyes tinged with violet. Mia had seen her before—this was the woman Siwen and Ven had talked about. Those wings—those eyes. Dread clawed at Mia's throat as the pieces came together. This was Dayelle, and she was no ordinary woman. She was a dragon.

And she'd come for her.

Mia's grip tightened around the battered weapon in her hand. It was not dragonsbane, but she would see how much force a dragon could take before it broke. She moved to lunge but her body suddenly spasmed. She screamed, barely able to take a step. Every muscle in her body trembled, refusing to obey. Something was terribly wrong with her.

Another woman dropped down sharply on draconic wings just beside Dayelle. This was the woman Mia recognized from the dungeons of Peskan's castle. Her dark skin was lined with so many scars, and her expression was that of barely suppressed rage. A muscle in her neck twitched feverishly as she glared at Mia.

Not one but *two* dragons. Box it all, Mia had been right.

A groan escaped Mia's throat as she took another step forward, fighting for control over her body.

Dayelle took confident stride towards Mia until she stood directly before her. She clicked her tongue and easily pulled the sword from Mia's trembling grip. She stroked Mia's jaw with the blunted tip of the sword. "You are strong. I'm glad I decided not to kill you."

Dayelle nodded to the other dragon and the woman forcibly flexed her muscles, a vein on her forehead popping with the strain.

Mia was overcome with an intense pressure, as though she'd been dunked underwater. The pressure built inside of her as well, like something was trying to force her eyes out of their sockets. She would have screamed again, but no sound came. Instead, her vision went black.

Chapter Ten

Peskan

Ven Yashke

"**I** would have appreciated a bit more communication before you announced that you'd be coming with me," Siwen said as they descended the mountainside.

The warrior lord rode atop his massive horse just in front of Ven. He'd almost forgotten how big Zebadons were. Butch kept pace, but Ven had a feeling that Siwen was holding his beast back from going faster. It often snorted as though impatient. Butch had more energy than before, probably excited to be on the trail with someone besides Ven.

"Yes, sorry about that," Ven said. "I figured it would be the easiest way for me to leave. Mia doesn't want to go, but I agree, we only seemed to be there as a means of distraction."

"She is disappointed you left her," Siwen said, looking over his shoulder at him.

"It's complicated, Siwen. She lied to me. I needlessly suffered." And in truth, if Mia needed time to herself, then Ven needed to have that same liberty. He needed to be somewhere he could process this all on his own. He wasn't going to just brush it off. That would feel disingenuous.

"True, but she is young. Both of you are. And given her background, I can only imagine how much she would have wanted to experience freedom, unfettered by any obligation."

"I wouldn't have tried to hold her back."

"She may not have trusted you. Again, can you blame her? With all that she's been through, I can understand why she would have difficulty."

"Yes, but I didn't—" Ven couldn't finish the sentence. He was going to say that he hadn't lied to her or kept secrets, but he had. It had taken him a long time to confess that he'd been working with a separate organization and had been tasked to help eliminate her. No wonder she didn't trust him. *Maybe I overreacted.* Leaving without notice wasn't really like him, but now he was too committed to turn back and look like a fool. The fact of the matter was that he'd gotten offended because Mia didn't feel the same way about him as he did for her.

Thankfully, Siwen didn't press him.

They rode mostly in silence, pausing when Butch needed a moment. Siwen's horse always got impatient when they stopped, but the farther they dropped in elevation, the greener everything was. Spring was in full swing below the mountains, and both horses foraged ravenously.

Ven watched carefully as they passed the portal location and proceeded farther down. This was uncharted territory for him, and he figured now was as good a time as any to further educate himself on Orund. Siwen was a nobleman and probably had a better understanding of this world than the average person, but he still didn't know that Ven was from a completely different world.

"Siwen," Ven said, "I must admit that I am not well traveled, and I was hoping you could explain where everything is. In fact, I'm not familiar with politics to any degree. All I've really learned about is from my medical studies."

"Where are you from again?" Siwen asked.

"Um." Ven scanned his mind. He'd read over these details from the paperwork Dayelle had forged for him before sending him to work at Zein's facility. He recited the location from distant memory. "Red Bridge."

"Why the hesitation?" Siwen said with a smirk.

Ven shrugged. "It's really a small estate outside the city, but my family traveled a lot before we settled at the university there."

"You traveled a lot and yet you are unfamiliar with the geography and political structures?" Siwen's raised eyebrow hinted at his skepticism.

Ven sighed. He wouldn't last under any real interrogation for a story he hadn't fabricated himself, but he wasn't about to throw in the towel just because of a few questions. "Yes, this is why I'm asking for help. We had other people that carted us around. We provided medical assistance all over, but this was mostly in my youth, and with so much going on, remembering the names of all the places we visited was the last thing on my mind. You'd be surprised to know that I have not personally even looked at a map."

Siwen chuckled. "I must admit I expected you'd be a man with broader education, but I suppose when your life work has been dedicated to healing, other details become less significant."

"Exactly," Ven said. "I would appreciate any opportunity to expand my horizons."

Siwen grunted. "I see. Well, I suppose you are speaking to the right person for this conversation. Having been raised as a nobleman for one of the greatest houses in Shiansan, I was taught about this from infancy. Borders and lineage are quite important to those who collect taxes." He looked forward, eyes going blank as though sifting through his memory. "We can start with our current location. Technically, we are in the nation of Okwan. They're a relatively large nation, but they're not quite structured in a cohesive way. They operate with a noble council instead of a king, and their fealty is more like a military and domestic alliance rather than a single cohesive government."

"Uh." Ven scratched his head. "Maybe we can just focus on the geography for now."

Siwen smirked. "Apologies. I will avoid political discourse wherever I can restrain myself." He waved a hand at their surroundings. "We will head south when we get down from the mountains, then start moving west. We'll actually pass Castia Mont eventually, but once we cross a river over there, we'll be in Luedan. That's where my betrothed is from. It's another country. After a few days, we'll reach Peskan, which is part of the nation of Shiansan."

"Hold on, so there's an entire nation between here and Peskan?"

"Yes, though it isn't a particularly large nation. Luedan and Shi-ansan combined are smaller than Okwan. In fact, we'd probably have to combine all of Kombida to equal the size of Okwan."

"Kombida?" If Ven was hoping to hide his ignorance, this conversation was not an effective means of doing so. He was still trying to visualize the layout, but without a map, he struggled.

Siwen cleared his throat and dug around in one of his saddlebags. "I keep a map with me here," he said, finally pulling a folded sheet of parchment from a bag. He handed it to Ven. "It's a crude drawing, meant for quick reference only, but it should at least give you a general idea of locations."

Ven unfolded the paper and scanned over it. From the way things were labeled, he was able to ascertain that there were eleven countries listed. He even saw Endel, which was oddly the only country he remembered. That was the place Mia's fake identity had been from when she'd posed as Lady Demora. It was all the way on the west end at the edge of the paper. With so many countries displayed, it had him wishing he understood the scale. How far apart were all these places? There were rough sketches of mountains, rivers, forests, and even some kind of sea down in the southeast corner.

As somewhat of a geography geek, Ven had to compare it to the relative scale of countries in eastern Europe, like Montenegro or Albania, but he could be completely off. "So how long does it take to get to Peskan?"

"With your horse? Hopefully just eight or nine days."

Ven did the math in his head. If they traveled at about twenty to thirty miles a day, that would mean it was roughly two hundred miles to Peskan. "Alright, this helps, thank you." Ven went to hand the map back, but Siwen held his hand up.

"You need that more than I do."

Ven laughed and tucked the map away. "True. Now, about all those political things, maybe you can tell me about how things work in Shiansan. You're a nobleman, and the Huan family rules over Peskan, but how does that work?"

"Ah, yes, we are from a great house. We've ruled in Peskan for generations, but Shiansan was part of a greater nation that was the first to liberate ourselves from the dragon overlords. Together, we helped liberate other peoples, but they formed their own coalitions. Shiansan used to encapsulate Luedan as well, but there was a faction split between two sons. Thankfully, they didn't go to war, and it was a peaceful arrangement. We still have strong ties with them, which is why I'm marrying a woman from Luedan. Both nations have a ruling monarchy. You may have seen it on the map there, but my king and queen rule from Xhi. It's a powerful fortress city, even more defensible than Peskan, much to our family's dismay." He paused to smirk.

They spent the next few hours talking about feudalism, geography, and eventually politics. The political side to it seemed like an unavoidable component as it influenced how things were run and how they'd changed over time. Ven kept pulling the map back out for reference, though Siwen really did seem to have the entire thing memorized. Shiansan was relatively small compared to its neighboring countries, but Siwen asserted that it maintained good relations and significant trade agreements.

"Every nation has a road that leads to Peskan," Siwen said. "So while Xhi might be the center of prime military prowess in our part of the world, Peskan remains a larger commercial hub. Not to say that our military isn't very capable as well."

Ven kept his mouth shut. He had no military training at all, and even with Mia's help, he'd still battered his way past two or three guards. "What about people like Sitena Rosars? Where does she fit into things like this?" She was the wealthiest investor in Zein's research, and her castle was where Ven had killed Dami. Again, with Mia's help.

Siwen grunted. "She is an odd one. She functions outside of the normal structure of nobility. Her castle lies within Luedan, as you may have noted, but she is significantly wealthier than the Masterson royal family—Garion and Jada Masterson are the ruling king and queen of Luedan. If she wanted to assert herself, she could easily usurp the throne, but if she'd really wanted that, she would have done so years ago."

Ven had so much to wrap his head around, but true to his word, Siwen was a good instructor. Sometimes, when they stopped for Butch to take a break, they would continue sparring. They were three days into their journey back to Peskan when they stopped to spar outside a trading settlement that was apparently about a day's ride from Castia Mont.

"Should we get a weapon for me?" Ven asked. He'd still been uncomfortable with the idea that the only thing he had close to a weapon was a Swiss Army knife.

"Don't worry about that," Siwen said. "These roads are quite safe, and the best weapons you could find would be at Peskan."

Ven swung the sword around a couple times before handing it back to Siwen. The horses started stamping. It was time to be on the move again. "I've been thinking about using a mace and shield."

Siwen looked Ven up and down before nodding. "Not a bad choice, though a spear and shield with a shortsword on hand would work wonders as well. Your height could give you excellent advantages as long as you keep your swings tight and arms in."

"Are there different techniques I would learn with certain weapons?" Ven settled back into the saddle, ignoring the soreness in his body. He hadn't done this much riding in years.

"Oh, absolutely, and don't you fret, I can get you connected with our instructors at the castle. There may be some soldiers who find you familiar, but you have changed a bit since last you were there, and I recommend you let that stubble of yours keep growing out."

Ven scratched at his jaw. He hadn't ever let his facial hair grow very long, but he didn't want a guard trying to throw him in prison. Their pace was quicker now that Butch had broken in a bit more. He was already a healthy horse, but perhaps he was encouraged by Siwen's Zebadon. It took half the day for them to pass by Castia Mont. There was still some scaffolding in place where people were hard at work repairing the damage of Dami's assault. He'd completely shattered the lower gate, but the repairs seemed to be nearing completion.

"Imagine that kind of power bridled under the right hands," Siwen muttered so quietly that Ven barely heard the words.

"What do you mean?" Ven asked, looking over the castle.

"Dami was a wildfire," Siwen said. "He was sent out on his own to do terrible things, but if he'd been supported by the right army or a specialized team with good leadership, even Mia wouldn't have stood a chance. It frightens me to think of how close we came to such utter domination."

Ven had no response. He couldn't fathom what that would be like here. He'd never seen war in action, only the aftereffects of its devastation. If things were bad on Earth, he couldn't even fathom how terrible war would be here. Did they have anything like penicillin here? He would honestly be surprised if they didn't, especially given his parents' interest in this world's medical practices.

Siwen didn't let up on the discussion regarding politics. Once they were back on the road, he spoke freely, and Ven could fully appreciate how Siwen's father, Yubo, had been able to call their bluff when they'd tried to pose Mia as a distant noblewoman. They knew a lot more about each individual family than Ven would have thought.

He was grateful for the distraction and fully immersed himself in the conversation. It allowed him to push off the nagging feeling that he'd simply abandoned Mia. However, he too needed to find his own purpose.

To Siwen's credit, they arrived in Peskan in the late morning of the eighth day. Butch had done a wonderful job getting them here, and Ven was fully committed to finding a new batch of apples to give him.

The city looked just like Ven remembered, with so much bustling activity. The high walls were formidable enough that he had a hard time picturing how Xhi could be more of a fortress than Peskan. Ven had done a lot of traveling on Earth and he'd certainly seen a few castles, but he realized that this and Castia Mont were the only castles he'd seen that were in active, legitimate use, and specifically for actual defensive measures and not for aesthetic appeal.

Ven rubbed his finger across his jaw. He'd never let his facial hair go so long without at least a trim, but it was no longer as itchy as it had been a couple days ago.

"I'll have to show you how to get a proper trim," Siwen said as he eyed Ven's beard. Siwen himself had maintained a completely clean-shaven appearance as part of his morning routine.

When they reached the gate to Peskan, Ven fell in behind Siwen. The traffic in and out was stifling. Now that Ven had a better understanding of the various countries, it made him wonder where everyone was from and what they did for work. He kept an eye out for any dragonblood technology, but didn't see anything.

A couple guards saluted to Siwen and gave Ven little more than a passing glance. Regardless of Siwen's reassurance, Ven's palms still sweat with anticipation. Some of these guards had imprisoned him at one time. They'd beaten him.

He kept his eyes down until they were significantly farther up the street. The sights filled him with memories, but it was accompanied with regret since he was here without Mia. He wondered how she was getting along. Hopefully she was still safe.

Instead of heading straight to the castle, Siwen led them down another street to the markets. "I have something to pick up here," Siwen said as he dismounted. "I'll just be a minute."

Ven got off Butch as Siwen entered a two-story building that smelled of oil. Siwen didn't need to tie down his Zebadon. The horses were highly intelligent, and nobody would dare try to steal one. Ven stretched his limbs as he held onto Butch's reins.

A hand clamped over Ven's face from behind, smothering his mouth and nose. The grip was incredibly strong as he was jerked back, hands ripping away from the reins. His shout was muffled, legs kicking around as someone much stronger than Ven dragged him into an alley.

Chapter Eleven

Sworn

Mia

Mia started with a gasp. A persistent pain throbbed inside of her head, but nothing so trivial would keep her down. It was like she'd been asleep for days, her dreams haunted by fire, blood, death, and the frightening image of dragons' wings flapping overhead. The dark memory of sticky, warm blood covering her arms and spattering across her face brought a grimace to her lips. Screams echoed in her ears.

She jerked up, launching to her feet before instantly falling back to her knees as her body shook with tremors.

"Ah, ah," a voice said. Dayelle.

Mia whipped her head towards the voice, her voice growling in her throat but unable to form words.

They were inside one of the buildings that apparently hadn't been burned down. Dim light filtered in through the open door and an uncovered window, hinting that it was either early morning or evening. The building was empty save for Mia and the two dragons.

"Go easier on her this time, Rowan," Dayelle said.

Rowan. The dragon was concentrating on Mia, her brow furrowed. She looked as human as ever except for the red glint in her eyes. The power she held over Mia was supernatural.

"She is strong," Rowan said, baring her teeth. Her voice carried a hint of a growl and was surprisingly deep.

"And you are stronger," Dayelle said without regarding her companion. Her eyes remained on Mia. "We have something to show you." Without being given any verbal command, two of those senseless soldiers entered the room, dragging a couple people in with them.

Mia's breath caught. It was Elena and Drin. Neither of them struggled against their captors since sharp metal pressed against their necks, keeping them in line. Both of them looked haggard, faces sunken, shoulders drooping, skin spotted in soot and blood. Mia tried to speak to them, but her body was still seized.

Dayelle crouched in front of Mia, meeting her at eye level. "As you may have ascertained, Rowan and I are dragons. Our magic affords us the ability to disguise ourselves as humans, which has allowed our species to survive, but we have not been idle." She tapped her fingernails on the stone floor in thought. "It's amazing the things you can learn while in hiding, but we have had some very interesting insights from Zein's research."

She rose to her feet and strode over to the soldier holding a speartip to Drin's neck, placing her hand on the soldier's shoulder. "We've always known our blood could do marvelous things, and we've been running some experiments of our own."

Mia suddenly found herself wondering who these soldiers were. From what little Mia actually knew about dragons, these people had to be insane to knowingly follow them. In reality, they probably *were* insane. She still remembered their complete lack of expression even as she dashed them to pieces. Perhaps they weren't really human at all.

"No doubt you found fighting against my dragonsworn to be... interesting," Dayelle said as if reading Mia's mind, "but I want you to fully understand what is about to happen." She pulled a necklace up from inside her shirt. The symbol fit within Dayelle's palm, a depiction of a silver dragon curled protectively over a vial.

With her other hand, Dayelle grabbed Drin by the ear and shoved him to the ground before pouncing on his back. The big man roared and struggled, clearly aware that something terrible was afoot.

"Get off me you witch!" he yelled.

Elena screamed and tried to run to him, but both soldiers restrained her.

Mia's entire body trembled, shaking as her muscles refused to obey. She had to watch as Dayelle drew a precise cut across the back of Drin's neck with her own fingernail. Drin roared and fought to break free, but Dayelle was inhumanly strong and kept him in place. He couldn't even budge. Dayelle pressed his face into the floor and dangled the necklace over his neck when a single drop of thick, red liquid dripped down from it directly into the fresh cut. Then she pushed her hand up against the wound and closed her eyes.

Drin's roars turned into frantic whimpers. "Elena," he said, his voice small and broken. "Elena."

"Drin!" Elena repeated his name over and over, but there was nothing she could do.

Drin's voice cut off completely. His body shivered and twitched before going completely still. Elena stopped uttering his name and broke down into sobs, her body sagging against her captors.

Dayelle stood and returned her attention to Mia. She gestured to Drin's limp form. "You see, we started some of our own experiments. When I applied my blood directly to the nervous system of a human, I discovered that I was able to form a connection." The thin smile that curled at the edges of Dayelle's lips caused a shiver to go down Mia's spine.

Drin heaved himself up off the floor.

"Drin?" Elena's voice broke out through her sobs. "Oh, Drin, my heart."

Mia saw that look on Drin's face, however. It was the same blank expression she'd seen on the soldiers. The room heaved as Mia's vision spun. She was witnessing a horror far beyond anything she could have imagined.

Dayelle's wicked smile never left her face as she observed Mia's reactions to what played out in front of her.

Drin dropped to a knee in front of Elena. Tears streaked down Elena's cheeks as Drin lifted her chin with a finger. "My love," Drin said, his voice a dark monotone. Elena dared to smile just before Drin slapped her across the face. She gasped and dropped her head, hair covering her face as her shoulders rocked with sobs.

Mia's heart broke. A physical pain stretched across her chest like it would tear her in half. No amount of imperviousness could protect her from that.

Dayelle bent down in front of Mia. "I wanted you to understand, Mia. It gives me complete control over them. They lose their autonomy. I wondered if our blood had similar effects on the subjects of the Impervious Project. It took a lot of digging, but I was finally able to locate the source of the dragonblood that was used on you." Dayelle looked over her shoulder at Rowan, whose eyes were ablaze as she glared at Mia.

No. Please, no. Tears burst across Mia's vision as terror squeezed the air from her lungs. This was why she couldn't move. Ven should have killed her. She should have left that poison in her neck. Anything was better than this.

Dayelle bent closer, looking deep into Mia's eyes. "You understand." She nodded to herself. "Rowan will take you now. You'll help us turn the rest of the village into dragonsworn, then I'll have a very special task for you." She tapped Mia on the nose. "We'll need you to go kill your friends Ven and Siwen. I was hoping they'd be here for the show. This demonstration with Elena and Dris would have been much more fulfilling." She stood and nodded to Rowan. "Take her, Rowan."

Rowan's response was to bare her teeth. The convulsions in Mia's body increased in rapidity as Mia put all her effort into maintaining that frail autonomy, but it felt like tendrils of cold water were slithering across her skin, then inside of her, stretching across her entire being. The last of her to plunge under the cold embrace was her head. At that very instant, the pain was gone and Mia rose to her feet, her vision clouded as though through a blue haze. Unbidden, her body strode to Elena, ignoring the woman's sobs as she threw her to the ground and held back her hair to reveal the back of her neck.

Even though she wanted to, she couldn't turn her eyes away from what happened next. She was a monster, and there was nothing she could do about it.

Chapter Twelve

The Doctor

Ven Yashke

Ven grasped for anything, hoping beyond hope that he wasn't about to get knifed right there in the alley. He was dragged behind the building and thrown up against the stone wall, pinned there by the hand clamped over his mouth and nose. A hooded figure held him in place with a strength that defied reason.

With their free hand, the figure placed a finger to their lips before drawing back their hood, revealing none other than Zein Huan.

Ven's desperate struggle to free himself did not cease, but his feet and hands could only clap at the stone wall, and no amount of clawing managed to loosen Zein's grip.

"I know you need to breathe soon," Zein said in his steady voice, "and I do not wish to harm you, but I need you to be silent. It is no longer safe here. Or anywhere. Any undue attention would be ill advised. Understood?"

Ven's lungs screamed for air, but he knew better than to trust Zein. This was the man who had killed his parents. Anger burned in Ven's chest, but he tempered himself. If what Dayelle had told him was true, then Zein was impervious. All signs indicated that this was indeed true. Ven would stand no chance without a dragonsbane weapon anyway. He could play his part. Ven stopped struggling and tried to nod his head.

Zein nodded back, a small, simple motion, then released Ven.

Ven dropped about two inches to the ground and quickly caught his breath. He tried to feign more surprise than he felt. "Zein, I don't fail to notice that you just held me up against the wall with a single hand." He recalled how Zein's age had always been in question. He couldn't tell if the man was thirty or fifty. Now the reason was much more obvious. The only hair the man seemed to grow was on his eyebrows, and they knit together as he scrutinized Ven.

"We all have our secrets," Zein said. "Mine is now out."

"How long have you had it?"

"I performed the operation on myself shortly after I realized the effectiveness on Mia's test group."

Ven nodded. He could only imagine the level of pain he would have had to endure to perform such an operation on himself while fully conscious. There was only so much a local anesthetic could help with something like that.

"Alright," Ven said, glancing back toward the entrance of the alley. "Siwen probably won't take long in there."

"I understand, though I'm not sure my cousin can be trusted."

"Quite frankly, I'm not sure *you* can be trusted, Zein."

Zein's eyes narrowed just slightly. "I understand your skepticism, Ven, but I've had to keep my own secrets. I would already be dead if knowledge of my own operation hadn't been hidden. I haven't undergone enough tests to adapt like the subjects have."

Ven only grunted, trying not to seem excited to learn that Zein was hopefully more susceptible. He was still inhumanly strong though, so Ven likely wouldn't want to trust in anything besides a dragonsbane weapon if it came to that. "Everyone always has their reasons to lie."

Zein shook his head at Ven. "Move on, Ven. I know you'd been planted at the facility. I took you on because I knew of your parents, but I did not know that you were somehow manipulated by the dragons. Did you at least know that much?"

"Oh, yes, I've heard of your connection to my parents," Ven said, his voice going dark. He rolled his right wrist as he subconsciously prepared to punch. He'd never been so instinctively violent.

Zein took a step back and folded his arms. "And yet you still decided to work for them? You are not what I expected, Ven. Perhaps this conversation is over."

Zein threw on his hood and turned as if to leave, but Ven grabbed the clothing of Zein's shoulder. "Hey, I'm not done talking to you. What do you think happened to my parents?"

There was fire in Zein's eyes as he regarded Ven, a dark fury that he'd never seen in the otherwise impassive man's face. "They were murdered." His voice came as an unexpected growl. "By none other than the dragons themselves. You didn't know, then?"

Ven shook his head. "I have no idea what you're talking about. You're the one who killed them. Don't lie to me."

"Me?" Zein let out a huff. "They were my dearest friends, Ven. It appears we have much to discuss, but now is not the time. I need you to meet me at Juns Hall. Can you do that?"

Ven bit his lip. He still held Zein's shoulder in a tight grip, but his emotions rattled through his brain. He wanted to understand, but he was missing all the pieces. Everybody was lying to him, but the hook in his gut flared, yearning for truth. The need to know drilled at him. He clenched his jaw before sighing and releasing Zein's shoulder, not that he would truly be able to hold the man back anyway. "I'll find a way."

Zein nodded before grabbing the wall and jumping to the other side in one swift motion.

Ven shook his head and ran out of the alley to find Siwen looking around frantically.

The young lord threw up his hands. "You left the horses. Where did you go?"

"I, uh... had to pee," Ven said.

"In an alley?"

"Couldn't wait."

"Never again," Siwen said, shaking his head as he mounted up.

After watching Ven get dragged off, Butch had apparently just gone to stand beside Siwen's Zebadon as if he didn't have a care in the world. Ven mounted and followed after Siwen. "Actually, I was thinking of going through the markets today."

"Don't want to assist with wedding preparations, then?" Siwen said, looking back at him.

Ven smiled. "I would actually be quite interested. I haven't seen a wedding in Peskan yet." Ven had barely caught himself. He was about to say he'd never seen a wedding on Orund. "I might find the preparations intriguing."

Siwen barked a laugh. "Well, we still have three days before the wedding, so there will be plenty of time for that. I recommend we get you settled into a room at the castle before you head off to the markets though."

"And you're sure nobody will recognize me?"

"Frankly, no, and my father is quite keen. As long as you avoid him though, you should be fine."

Ven's unease did not alleviate. When they reached the castle, Siwen got them through without any issue. They rode to the stables and dismounted as a couple servants came out to greet them.

"See to it that my companion's things are taken to the secure guest room in the verdant quarters."

"Yes, lord," the servant said. She had similar features to the Huans, with black hair, brown, narrow eyes, though her skin was much paler. There was also a blue and red ribbon tied across her forehead. The most notable feature of the clothing was the sewn-in patch of a coiled dragon being skewered through the mouth by a sword. He vaguely recognized the insignia from when he'd been here the first time, but the details hadn't seemed so important back then. The other servant was dressed the exact same but without the headband.

"That room is currently vacant, correct?" Siwen asked.

"Yes, lord. I have kept it available, as you've requested."

"Very good." Siwen handed the reins to the other servant. "Ven, I want you to meet Carina. If you need anything, she's as reliable as they come. I'll need to run and find my father, but you go ahead and get settled."

Siwen hurried off, leaving Ven with Carina, who immediately started leading Butch into the stable.

Ven made sure to grab his big bag off of Butch's back before anybody else could try to lay their hands on it. The items in the saddlebags weren't incredibly vital, but he didn't want to lose all that money. After getting Butch squared away and handed off to a stableboy, Carina guided Ven up a very narrow wooden stairway that led up the stone side of the castle wall. She took him through a door one floor up.

Down here, it was a lot different than the hallways on the upper floor. The hallways were narrow and dark, much more like a fortress. There was none of the elegance Ven had been expecting. But then again, he'd toured old castles a couple times before, and this seemed consistent with those ones.

Carina led Ven to a room that ended up being a little bigger than he'd thought, with enough room for a large bed, a dresser, and a table and two chairs. He quickly put his bag down and switched it out for a satchel he'd brought that would be much more lightweight. He waited for Carina to leave before transferring over his bag of money, then hurried back out.

It was probably a bad idea to go rushing over to meet Zein without telling Siwen what he was actually doing. Though Zein couldn't trust his cousin, Ven was certain Siwen was the only person in this world he actually could trust, except Mia of course. A twinge of guilt tugged at him as he all but ran out of the castle grounds. He hoped Mia was doing well, but he also wished it wasn't so hard for him to just stop feeling bad about other people's experiences. Mia was strong and smart. She would be able to handle herself. Besides, when he was done here and had some time to himself, he could return to find her.

Though he hadn't been here for months and had only stayed briefly, the streets of Peskan felt so familiar. Perhaps the uniqueness of it all had simply burned itself into his memory. It was like he'd only been away for a week. The two-story buildings with their wide eaves belonged in fairytales. His footsteps easily brought him to the entrance of Juns Hall.

The building was large and very active. All sorts of people came and went freely, though a burly man stood at the door. Ven had just enough sense to check over his shoulder before stepping up to the door as naturally as if he'd done this a hundred times. He had the feeling that something was off, but he couldn't quite place it. Regardless, he entered the building, quickly drowning in the chorus of voices that greeted him as a large crowd of people milled about inside. Many sat at the tables near the dining area, but most people bustled about between the gaming tables. The air inside was warm and humid from all the bodies.

Ven followed the familiar route to the more exclusive section of the building, shouldering his way through the ever-shifting host of people. As the tallest person inside, it was easy to navigate and people generally tried to stay out of his way, but when he reached the open entry that led to the back area, a man stopped him.

"You don't have access back here," the man said, holding a hand up as he took a small stick from between his teeth.

"Actually," a voice said from around the corner. A familiar man came into view. "I'll lead him back." It was Tem. Ven had almost forgotten about the assistant. He'd been working with Ven while at the facility. He'd assumed that Tem had been killed by Dami when he'd gone back to the facility, massacred the place, and burned it to the ground.

The man standing between him and the exclusive area of the building stepped aside, and Tem gestured to the hallway behind.

"Tem," was all Ven could think to say.

"Yes, I did not get mutilated thankfully," Tem said. He had a kind smile and an eager jump to his step.

"I can see that. Where have you been?"

"Here and there," Tem said. "Without my job, I went back to see my family for a while before coming here. I knew Doctor Huan had disappeared and would eventually end up at Juns Hall, so here I am." He gestured to a table at the back of the room where Zein, still with his hood on, sat in the unabated darkness.

"I'll leave you to it," Tem said, then gave Ven a wink and patted his arm as he went back the way he'd come.

There was nobody else in the room.

"Time is valuable," Zein said.

Ven approached the table. Even if he hadn't already known it was Zein, he could have identified the man merely by his posture. He sat with perfect form, hands clasped before him on the edge of the table, back straight, forming a ninety-degree angle with his legs. Ven stopped short, unwilling to sit with this man.

Zein peered up at Ven, still keeping his head covered by the hood. "Who do you work for, Ven?"

"I'm unemployed."

Zein sighed in annoyance. "Why did you work with Dayelle?"

Ven rubbed his thumb across his lower lip. He'd been too trusting of everyone. Mia loathed this man for overseeing her torture for years, all of his actions cloaked behind the false ideal of working to cure diseases. Instead, he'd gone and used the operation on himself. He hadn't been selfless or noble at all. There probably wasn't much of anything to gain from a conversation with this man, but he'd bite and see what lies Zein wanted to weave.

"She offered me information about my parents if I helped take down your facility."

Zein nodded. "Are you the one who removed the kill switch from Dami's neck?"

"No. They had other agents planted there."

"What do you know of Dayelle and her organization?"

Ven sighed. "Practically nothing except that they are incredibly wealthy, detest dragonblood research, and that Dayelle is able to travel—" he stopped short. Keeping track of who knew what secrets was always difficult. He'd almost mentioned the portals.

An uncommon frown creased Zein's brow. "I know of Earth, Ven. Your parents traveled there at times. I did not know Dayelle possessed such ability as well." His jaw clenched repeatedly. It was the starkest emotional reaction Ven had ever seen from the man.

Ven leaned forward, placing his knuckles on the surface of the table. "What do you know of my parents?"

"The Yashkes were my business partners, even well before the Impervious Project. I spent a lot of time with them. You may need to be more specific with your question."

Zein's delivery was completely empty of emotion. His parents were nothing like him at all—how could they have partnered with such a person? "How did my parents die, then?"

"That I do not know. I'd tried keeping in touch with them, but they disappeared." Zein looked down. "I believe it was my letters that got intercepted which led to their exposure. I have no proof, but this Dayelle and her organization are likely responsible."

Classic. More finger pointing. "Why?"

"Ven, there's no easy way to put this, but Dayelle is a dragon."

Unbidden, Ven shivered. She didn't look anything like a dragon. "What do you mean?"

"She kept me prisoner because she wanted to figure out how I was able to perform the operation. She failed. Instead, she discovered something else that might actually be worse."

Ven shook his head. "But why are you telling me this? Why bother meeting me here—if this is true, then shouldn't you be trying to convince the nobility of the danger?"

"My duty is not to them, Ven. In pursuit of greater knowledge, I have denied the law of the land. Your parents were complicit in my ideas, which is why they ultimately fled to Earth and remained there for a few years. I understand I'm not fully responsible, but I do carry some of the weight regarding their death, which is why I accepted you at the facility."

"You knew I was their son?"

"It seemed extremely likely."

Ven threw up his hands in disbelief. "Then why did you not say anything?"

"Several reasons. In all honesty, I thought you had been aware of my relationship with them. I do not pry into people's personal matters. I also suspected you might be a spy using the guise of the Yashke name, which is why I placed Tem with you. When I saw how you worked with Mia, it appeared even more likely that you were from Earth. I understand doctors have more training in psychological treatment there than we do here."

"But still you said nothing."

"Yes." Zein laced his fingers together. "I did learn that you stole a pair of keys and handed them off to Dami, so my suspicions about you being a spy also seemed likely. I considered the possibility that you were both a spy and their son, which, apparently, was correct."

Ven flopped into the chair, trying to consider all the details. The weight on his shoulders was heavy. There was so much to try and make sense of. "My parents are from Orund?"

"Just your mother," Zein said. "She is from Colandia, and would have become the queen there if she hadn't stolen the ancient key and gotten involved in dragonblood research. That had gotten her disowned by her mother, the very woman she'd been working to try and find a cure for."

Ven shook his head. "No." This was too much. It had to be made up. "That's insanity."

"It's true. She was only sixteen when she'd been disowned. She fled to Earth and met your father. I don't know all the details after that, but it's quite the tale. You could ask any of the nobility. They will still remember it. Well, everything but the portal. That's supposed to be a family secret of House Sokanof. Her disappearance was quite a scandal."

"There's literally no way this is real." Wasn't his mom from New York?

"I only say this to provide context to my answer," Zein said. "I came to you and wanted to share the information regarding the dragons with you because I am partially responsible for what happened to your parents. The dragons have persisted. I believed that perhaps they only existed in captivity for harvesting purposes, but they are free, somehow. I wasn't able to save your parents, but I might be able to save you." He reached into his cloak and pulled out a very small metal tube and placed it on the table in front of him.

Ven's jaw dropped and he slowly shook his head. He knew exactly what Zein was proposing. That vial contained dragonblood.

Chapter Thirteen

Bringer of Peace

Mia

Mia would have sobbed if she had any control over herself. Instead, she merely observed as she brought each villager over to Dayelle, split their neck open from the back, and applied some of Dayelle's blood to each of them. For reasons she didn't know, they only used Dayelle's blood and none of Rowan's. Perhaps the dragon was already wounded enough that they didn't want to spare any more of hers, but Rowan watched every single time. They proceeded until every single adult had been "harvested," as Dayelle put it.

There were no children. She didn't even want to think about what had happened to them.

Despite having no control over her body, the tearing pain in her chest did not subside. but clawed at her with the turmoil of the damned. She had already done unspeakable things, and it would only get worse. She knew how powerful she was, and now that power was in control of one of the monsters that had dominated humanity for thousands of years.

When the last of the villager's had been taken, Mia knelt with Rowan standing behind her, stroking her hair the way a human would pet a dog. She would have shivered. She would have screamed and fought, but she possessed no ability to defy. They rested until night came. Dayelle and Rowan discussed things with sharp tones.

"I want to burn it all," Rowan hissed.

"I understand your pain, sister," Dayelle said. "Peskan will burn."

"673 years!" Rowan slammed her hand into the table, snapping the stone in half. Her other hand yanked on Mia's hair. "Bled by these vermin."

"Yes, Rowan, but these are strong vermin. If we act too hastily then we could end up back in the same predicament."

"What are we waiting for?"

"We are not waiting at all," Dayelle said, her voice a little harsher. "We are growing. With forces of our own, we can fight back, but politics among the humans is more volatile. They have known peace for so long, but I have laid a foundation that will put us back in our rightful place. Do you not trust me?"

Rowan growled, a guttural, inhuman sound. "I have no choice. You saved my life. That is enough."

Dayelle smiled, and a soft purring emanated from her throat. This didn't seem like a conversation a human should have been hearing, but she was completely under Rowan's control. The information would be useless. Nonetheless, Dayelle's eyes shifted to Mia. Mia didn't even have control over her eyes. She stared straight ahead.

The conversation between the dragons resumed, but they no longer spoke in a language she could understand.

She expected their language to be something harsh and terrible but was surprised to find the words and pronunciation to be smooth and simple, like they belonged in a song. The light outside continued to darken until Dayelle rose, stroked Rowan's hair, and then bent down beside Mia.

"It's time, Mia," Dayelle said. "Ven served his purpose by leading us to you. Admittedly, it took me longer to track him than I would have thought. He was more clever this time around, booking things in his friend's name and using a temporary card to pay for everything. It took some extra digging, and I had to rally the troops, but here I am, and Ven is already gone. I need you to go kill him. Doctor Huan will be drawn to him, no doubt. There are plenty of experiments I'd like to test with him, but it would be wisest just to kill him. I'm not one to let curiosity get the best of me. You don't live a few thousand years without learning to exercise caution and precision, so I'll have you kill the doctor if you see him as well."

Dayelle put her hand on Mia's shoulder, and she yearned to punch it away and throw the woman across the room. Her body trembled, the tell-tale sign that some portion of her refused to be a pawn, but it was no use. Mia rose to her feet.

"This will be good for you," Dayelle said. "With both of them gone, all remnants of the facility will be eradicated, leaving only you, the pinnacle of human creation. You will be a god among them, and they will flock to you as you usher in the renewal of Orund's true leaders." She nodded to Rowan.

"He's been spotted in Peskan," Rowan said.

Mia strode toward the shattered door wishing she could scream. She was going to kill Ven. She was going to have to watch it. The pain of her heart tearing only expanded, but it did not impede her body from moving unbidden.

"You'll be much more subtle than Dami was," Dayelle said, following Mia outside. "You'll be the perfect assassin."

The village was in ruins. Only one other building had not been burned to the ground. The livestock had been herded, most of them slaughtered to feed the army that had recently swelled in numbers thanks to Mia's help. She'd led the dragons here. She'd brought this destruction. She should have known that they could flee, but she hadn't wanted to leave the village. Spring was coming, and she'd wanted to see those flowers. Didn't she deserve to see the spring flowers?

The smell of fire hung so heavy that she was sure it would never disperse. Mia burst into a sprint, running at unthinkable speed. The last bit of sunshine dipped behind the mountains. Outside the bounds of the village, after passing the crumbled buildings, there were flowers, but without sunlight, the petals were folding in on themselves as they closed. She would not see the spring flowers in bloom. No, she would only see their end.

All of this was just because she'd wanted freedom, and now she was more a prisoner than ever before. The pain to her soul was crushing. If only she'd actually let Ven kill her that day at Castia Mont. Perhaps death was the only peace she could have hoped for. If death was peace, then she would be the bringer of it.

Chapter Fourteen

Fire in the Veins

Ven Yashke

Ven's heart pounded as he stared down at the metal vial on the table. "What are you proposing?"

"A chance to live," Zein said. "In the coming days, things will only get worse. Dragons have supposedly been exterminated for so long, but all this while, they have been in hiding. Can you imagine what such ancient creatures could have been doing behind the curtain all this time? They are not foolish. Their intelligence far surpasses our own. Their cellular regeneration never corrodes with time. I can guarantee you, they have not been idle."

Ven shook his head. "Zein, I don't think I can do this." Nausea squirmed in Ven's stomach.

"Of course you can. And quite frankly, you would make much better use of the qualities than any of my subjects. Mia, though she has a wonderful heart, is too afraid. Too timid. You have kindness in you, and a desire to help others. You fought even when you lacked training. You have the heart of not only a warrior, but of a good man.

You have the same heart as your parents. They gave everything to help others. I can think of no better purpose for this bit of blood than to preserve that kind of heart."

Ven couldn't take his eyes off the vial. He wanted to say that this shouldn't even be an option. An operation like this shouldn't exist. Mia was immortal. *Zein* was immortal. But also, dragons were real. That hooked feeling in his gut quivered as though on the precipice of shrinking or growing. His decision here would be of tremendous impact. He pressed a hand to his head. If he was being totally honest, he wanted to be immortal. He wanted purpose. With this kind of resilience, he could make a difference here on Orund. And Mia... perhaps she would see him differently. Perhaps he wouldn't simply be an afterthought.

He had his answer, but before he could voice it, Zein snatched the vial away with lightning speed. A swordpoint lowered toward the doctor. Ven jerked back with a gasp, but that was a dragonsbane sword, and the wielder was Siwen Huan. He'd snuck up on them.

"Cousin. I should have known you were up to something," Siwen said. "You should go, Ven." He didn't even spare a glance at Ven. "I will handle this rabble."

Zein shot to his feet and rounded the far side of the table, opposite Siwen. "You don't even know what you're dealing with here, cousin. Lower your sword. Go back to your lord and your wedding preparations."

"I will lower your head when I separate it from your shoulders," Siwen said. "Ven, I recommend returning to the castle."

Ven gulped and glanced between them. It was likely Zein could simply flee, but Siwen was at an advantageous enough location that he could also possibly get a strike in against him before he'd be able to get away. Zein probably had other options, such as throwing the entire table at his cousin, but Ven had the impression that Zein did not wish to harm him. He was conflicted. Only moments ago, he'd wanted Zein to die, believing he was responsible for killing his parents. Now, he wasn't sure what he believed, but he felt like Zein's story was more believable than Dayelle's.

"I am not your enemy," Zein said. "Ven. You have a choice here. How will you proceed?"

"Just because he's an enemy to the Drekis Alliance, it does not mean he's an ally, Ven."

"I'll do it," Ven said, ignoring Siwen.

"Do what?" Siwen said.

"Siwen, put that sword away. Zein is not a threat," Ven said.

"Didn't he have your parents murdered?"

"That was likely a lie fabricated by the dragons," Ven said.

Siwen frowned. "Dragons?"

Zein sighed. "There is much to discuss, but we should go to a more secure location. One where, apparently, Ven cannot be tracked so easily."

Ven swallowed. He was still worried about that. If he was so easy to track, then Mia might still be in danger, and if Dayelle was a dragon, did she possess the means to kill Mia? She wasn't as safe as he'd thought.

Siwen's sword lowered just slightly. "If you are wanting to remain hidden from Dayelle, then I fear she may already be aware of your presence here, Zein. She has a particular interest in both you and Peskan."

"Reasonably so," Zein said. "This is the city where the banner of resisting the dragons was first raised, and it shall be the same place where it is raised once again." He rounded the table slowly, and Siwen made no move to stop him. "Is she not tracking you as well, Siwen? I know of your association with her, though I hope you too were not aware of what the Drekis Alliance truly is."

"I am not entirely convinced of your own opinion regarding that, but I can confirm that I was not followed, though I would be surprised if they did not have an agent planted here." Siwen looked over toward the back area through which he'd come.

"Are you that agent?" Zein asked, his voice surprisingly dark.

Siwen's brows creased. "Dayelle and the Drekis Alliance no longer have my confidence, and they have never had my allegiance if that's what you're asking."

"Then save your sword for the dragons and follow me." Zein strode past Siwen and went to the hallway beyond.

Ven shrugged at Zein and followed. Siwen only sighed before sheathing his sword and coming behind. Zein steered through the hallway as they dodged around a server holding a tray laden with dishes. Ven's tastebuds exploded at the smell, and he became distinctly aware of the fact that he hadn't had a freshly-cooked meal for a few days.

Zein entered a small room, and Ven had to duck under the doorway to get inside. It was dark, but Zein shuffled around with something until there was a grinding of metal on stone followed by a heavy thud. Next, there was a click, and a light flickered on from down below.

"This way," Zein said, proceeding down a few steep steps. "Watch your heads."

Ven had to walk with his head bent down. The path ahead was short, narrow, and long, lit by a few bulbs of dragonlight that shone from one of the sides. They provided only minimal light, perhaps a sign that they used only the smallest fraction of dragonblood to operate.

Siwen grumbled about this being an absolutely ridiculous trap and how they were fools for following his cousin down here, but he still came along.

"Information regarding this tunnel should not be shared," Zein said. "As you know, I own several of the properties in this district. This leads directly to a safehouse. I have certain equipment set up there. Siwen, how much do you know of my research?"

"Too much," Siwen said. "Mia and Dami were some of your subjects."

"That knowledge will be sufficient."

"I'm wondering though, Zein," Ven said, changing topisc to something he still wasn't sure on. "If you were a prisoner of Dayelle, how did you get away? Did she not know you were impervious?"

"She did not. The only reason I remained captive for so long is because I was determined to discover who my captor was. When she finally came to me, it was merely to gloat, revealing that she can use her blood to create thralls out of humans. Once I learned who she was and what she was doing, I simply ran away."

"She couldn't catch you?" Ven asked.

"I didn't even see them pursue," Zein said. "It is possible Dayelle has limitations for changing into her dragon form, but I assume she is electing to keep that hidden. The sight of a dragon would certainly create significant alarm. Part of their plan, whatever it is, must rely on subtlety."

Zein reached the other end of the tunnel and paused there, regarding Ven with his blank expression, skin glowing blue under the strange light. "Ven, do you feel that Siwen can be trusted?"

"More than I can trust you," Ven said, which, depressingly, was not a lot of trust. Every action Ven took here seemed like a mere calculated risk. Dayelle was likely the person he could trust the least. Zein was only a marginal step up from there, but Siwen had been more reliable. He'd assisted Ven and Mia more than once, and if dragons were going to be a real issue, then Siwen would be one of the few assets capable of withstanding such a force.

Zein grunted. "That will have to do." He worked on the mechanism of the slanted doorway at the top of the stairs before swinging it up. They emerged inside of a room packed full of crates and barrels with enough dust on them to suggest the place had not been in much use for months. The entire building was otherwise empty. Nobody else was here.

"I saw that Tem survived," Ven said to Zein.

"Yes, for that I am glad. He is a tenacious one. Dutiful. Helpful. Not overly self-seeking or ambitious. He was the first person to assist your parents and I as we embarked on the Impervious Project." Zein closed up the trap door and led them through the building. It was not a large place, but it appeared almost like an older home on Earth. The floors were tiled and there were built-in cabinets with a wood-burning stove and a stone fireplace. The next room looked like it was pulled straight from a science lab, similar to those he'd seen at Zein's facility. There was a stainless steel countertop and several glass jars,empty for the most part, though one contained cotton balls and another had oily fluid. A few cabinets on the wall were closed. A beam of dragonlight stretched across the whole ceiling, filling the room with white light. Lastly, a padded bench sat at the center of the room, distinctly reminiscent of an operating table.

The room was cold, and goosebumps went up Ven's arm in a wave.

"What exactly are we doing here?" Siwen asked.

Zein didn't answer the question immediately. He moved about the room, grabbing this and that, placing them on a metal tray. "In a sense, I failed Ven's parents. The best I can do to remediate this is to offer Ven immortality. If the dragons do in fact return, as I predict, then we can hope that he will persist where others will burn in the fire of vengeance."

Siwen stammered before saying, "Is that truly possible? You can make more?"

"Only one," Zein said, placing the metal vial on the tray he was assembling. "I still have a fraction of the blood that was used for the original transfusions performed on Mia's group. It's from the same batch I used on myself. I will now use it on Ven."

"I'm not sure such an operation should be performed," Siwen said.

"I have made my mistakes, Siwen, but Ven will do this voluntarily." Zein offered Siwen a blank stare. "Are you going to stop me?"

Siwen made no response. He just remained there, frozen in place.

"Ven, remove your shirt and lie on the table," Zein said. "Brace yourself. I will give your body a simple infection as well. It will help to create a hyperactivity in the transfused blood to assist in increasing the chance of a successful adoption of the new cells. They are dominant, but there is a ninety-two percent chance of failure if it is not able to identify an immediate threat and begin the adaptation phase. In such a case, it will identify your very body as the threat and slowly deteriorate your healthy cells until you are withered and dead. The disease I'll infuse you with is dormant, but it should still create the trigger within the infused blood. This will be painful."

Ven clenched his teeth, worried that they would start chattering if he let his jaw loose. "Disease?" he asked through his teeth as he put his bag down and started to remove his shirt.

"Yes," Zein said. "It is necessary for optimal chances of effective adaptation. This was a hard-learned lesson from some of our test subjects and is why our terminally ill patients were the ones who saw the highest chance of success, but don't worry. The disease is minor, far less significant than what the dragonblood will do."

"Zein, that is not reassuring," Ven said. "How did you ever get into medical practice making statements like that?"

"I did the research, mostly. Your parents were more the experts on interacting with patients."

"I can see that." It was increasingly apparent why the facility's operations had gone so downhill. Zein truly lacked skills in some of the areas where his own parents had excelled. Ven lay down on the table, trying to relax against the cold leather cover.

Zein flicked a needle before pressing it into Ven's arm. "That's the disease," Zein said. Ven watched as Zein injected him. To think that Zein had somehow performed this operation on himself was wild.

"I'm afraid I have no anesthetics," Zein said. "You will need to go into the operation fully conscious. Fortunately, the pain will also increase the effectiveness of the adaptation, decreasing the failure rate to eighty-nine percent."

"So, lots of pain for a two percent increase. Excellent," Ven said, noting how his voice went a little higher.

"Perhaps you should have him bite down on his belt," Zein said to Siwen.

Siwen frowned at the whole scenario, but after Ven removed his belt, Siwen placed it in Ven's mouth. Zein held up a tool that looked like a massive screw with a crank.

"Ready?" Zein asked.

Ven managed a quick nod but his body shivered against the cold. This was a stupid idea. What was he thinking? This was absolutely unnecessary.

Zein pulled the bottom of Ven's pants up to his knee.

Ven needed to tell him to stop. Imperviousness wasn't what he'd come back to Orund for. There was some other purpose.

But he said nothing. Instead, he only bit down as Zein pressed cold metal against Ven's shin.

"Brace," Zein said, and then there was pain.

Ven wanted to seem strong, but he roared as he clenched down on his belt. Pain stabbed into his leg, sharp and deep. The pressure made it feel like his leg would snap in two, but it was gone a second later, only to be repeated on his other leg. He shivered, screaming. Tears ran down his cheeks.

"You're being dramatic, Ven," Siwen said. "Zein hasn't even started drilling yet."

"What?" Ven yelled incredulously through the belt clenched in his teeth. He picked his head up to look down at his legs only to see a bloody hole on his right shin while Zein still worked on his left.

"I was... joking, of course," Siwen said, putting a hand on Ven's shoulder as if to encourage him to look away.

But Ven couldn't. Steam issued from the wound, which was no longer bleeding.

Zein's movements were a blur as he quickly moved things around Ven's other leg. He spared a glance at Ven. "Stitches come last," Zein said. "I must perform this same exercise at three other locations. If things work properly, you may not even need the stitches, but we'll keep an eye on that."

Ven's body shivered fiercely. The pain did not subside, but watching the operation gave the pain purpose. He could survive this. He didn't come to Orund just to die in some silly operation, and he still had questions for Zein. Curse it all, he still had questions for Dayelle, but he would never get to her if he was some weakling. If she was truly a dragon, it would take power like Mia's for her to take him seriously.

Zein moved to Ven's right side and urged Ven to take a deep breath just before he twisted a tool into his sternum. He let out his breath with a long groan. This seemed so wrong. He was not even ill. Perhaps they should have saved this operation for somebody who needed their life saved. But that was how Zein saw it. Ven was on some path to destruction. In truth, he had to wonder why Dayelle had kept him alive for so long already.

The pain Ven felt started to change, and he became distinctly aware of a sizzling sound coming from his chest. He still had the memory of how his bones had ached during his growth spurts. This was similar, but it was every bone. He went rigid as pressure built. He no longer shivered. Instead, he burned.

"Just two more, Ven," Zein said right before drilling into his hip.

Ven's arms clenched tight. Every muscle in his body flexed like he was receiving shock therapy. A few more minutes passed and Ven wondered how he still maintained consciousness.

"Last one," Zein said. "You are strong, Ven. This is good."

The words meant nothing to him as Siwen helped him sit up. The last spot was at the back of his neck in the craniocervical junction, right where the first vertebra met with the skull. It was the same location where Mia's kill switch had been installed. By this point, it was the least painful part of the procedure. Perhaps he'd become numb to the pain. The hole in his chest left a small portion of his sternum exposed to the air. He had seen plenty of bones before, but seeing his own like this made him consider his own sanity. This operation was happening of his own volition.

Finally, Siwen set Ven back against the table. The shivers returned.

"I can't believe I just participated in this," Siwen said, leaning over to look into Ven's eyes. "How long does the process take?"

"If it works, about thirty minutes," Zein said, washing his hands in a basin of water that filled and drained from a pump beside the steel counter.

"So we just stand here and see if he dies or not?"

"Essentially," Zein said. "Though there will be signs if it is working or failing." Zein gave a disapproving grunt. "Well... he shouldn't be shivering any more, and there's some seepage from the penetration points on the leg which should also have passed already. Not good signs."

"What do you mean, Zein? Fix it! You can't kill him!"

That was the last thing Ven heard before the pain overcame him and everything shifted into blackness.

Chapter Fifteen

Immortal

Zein Huan

Zein stared in disbelief at Ven's still body.

"Zein!" Siwen yelled, shoving his shoulder. Zein stumbled away from his cousin, still looking down at Ven in confusion.

"I don't understand," Zein said. "I did everything right."

Siwen ignored him and started shaking Ven's arm. "Ven, this is a really stupid way to die. You can't let this happen. I need you to get up and punch my cousin in the face, do you understand? I would do it myself, but I'm afraid I'd just end up stabbing him with the dragonsbane sword."

Zein looked at each of the exposed wounds. They had stopped bleeding. He stepped up beside Ven and placed a hand on his neck, feeling for a pulse. Nothing. His stomach sank. He stepped away, mortified. He'd killed him.

"Zein! Curse it, you're a doctor!" Siwen pointed at him. "Don't just back away. His heart has stopped beating, what do we do?"

Zein swallowed hard, pushing past the darkness that threatened to overtake him. Why did he always somehow do the wrong thing? He'd wanted to save the boy, not kill him. He'd done this same thing to so many others. What was the point of all his research if it meant he couldn't save those he wanted to?

"Zein!"

Snapping back to attention, Zein hurried to the counter and pulled open a drawer, withdrawing a tool that Ven's parents had helped him design. He'd seen them use it a couple times, but that had been many years ago inside this very room. He pushed a button, and the device came alive with a tiny hum of energy as the dragonblood technology whirred. He placed the device on Ven's chest, just above the wound, and pushed another button. Ven's body jolted in response and a grunt forced out of his throat.

Zein withdrew the tool, and Ven's body continued to twitch around his shoulders. Steam resumed rising from his wounds and Ven snapped his eyes open, gasping for air as he screamed.

So he was... not dead? But his wounds should have healed already. If the imperviousness had taken hold, Ven would be describing the warm flush as his body adapted to the damage. Instead he remained wild-eyed, gasping for air. He shot to his feet and dashed across the room, bracing himself against the counter as he stumbled.

"Ven, calm yourself," Siwen said, shoving at Zein again as he went to help the boy.

"It hurts!" Ven said, spittle flying from his mouth as he spat the belt out. He pounded his fist against the counter as he groaned.

Something was wrong. Zein had never seen this kind of reaction from anyone, and he'd performed this operation nearly two-hundred times.

"What are you feeling, Ven?" Zein asked. He needed to treat this like a normal assessment. The best he could do was determine if there were similar factors at all so that he could perhaps provide treatment. The fact that Ven wasn't dead was a good sign, even if everything else was still not responding as expected.

"It burns," Ven said, voice haggard. "My bones."

Burning in the bones. Zein tapped his finger on the counter. "Is it hot and feeling like your bones will snap from intense pressure?"

"Yes," Ven said, bending over as though he might vomit.

"Does that mean something?" Siwen asked, eyes narrowed at Zein.

"The pressure is a good sign," Zein said, speaking faster than usual. "His body's response is unusual, possibly because he's not from our planet. That could mean various things about him operate differently, all the way from bone density to the microbial communities in his systems that could impact the way he absorbs or responds to invasive cells. So he could potentially still be adapting to the dragonblood correctly, it may just take longer to be effective."

"Whoa!" Ven said, jerking upright while keeping his eyes on his chest. The wound had closed. He looked between Zein and Siwen, eyes wide.

"Does that mean it's working?" Siwen asked.

Zein heaved a sigh and nodded. "It's working. You are now looking at the newest immortal."

Chapter Sixteen

Murder

Mia

Resigned to her fate, Mia tried not to be astounded at her own ability. She'd managed to keep running for three days straight without even pausing to sleep. She reached Peskan in the dead of night. She had no idea how her body knew where it was going. Perhaps Rowan flew along somewhere nearby, guiding her with her thoughts.

No, I am not resigned. She would fight. She had to. If she didn't find a way to resist Rowan, then she would kill Ven. Nothing would be able to stop her but herself.

When she reached the tall city walls, she ran and jumped up the surface, flinging herself to the other side with a slap of her hands on the parapet. There was no guard nearby. She would have heard their breathing or their heartbeat. People were so easy to detect when she listened for it. She hit the ground with a roll, not to prevent damage to herself, but to reduce the sound. Her feet padded on the cobbled streets. She'd lost her boots and stockings while running. It was no loss. She didn't need them at all, anyway, unless she wanted to walk more quietly. Stockings would have been ideal.

Windows were all dark. Only an occasional lantern provided light down a main street. She approached the castle from the side, heading straight to a sheer portion of the wall that stretched up twice as high as the wall around the city. Instead of attempting to jump, she crawled up the surface. Her fingers and toes clenched easily against any groove with a grip so strong it would surpass that of a metal clamp. She even snapped the edge of a brick away by pulling on it too hard. She glided up the wall with ease. At the top, there was a slim parapeted wall just in front of a slanted roof.

The breathing of a person reached her ears, the presence several strides down the length of the wall. She went the other direction. Did Rowan know where Ven was? She had to wonder how the dragons were so well informed. The only possibility she could think of was that they had spies all over the city. She reached a staircase and pattered down the steep, narrow steps. The large open courtyard was familiar, even in the dark, but she didn't head to the large doors leading into the castle keep. Instead, she sidled over to another staircase on the other end of the open space. This was somehow even smaller than the other staircase she'd just descended, and the wooden door she went through squealed with age.

Inside, all was black, but she felt her way along the walls until she came across a single door. A flickering light shone under the crack of the door. Without hesitation, she pushed her way inside. Something fell with a jingling, the same kind of alarm trap Ven had used in Mavenda to warn them of danger. It wouldn't do Ven any good.

And there he was. He sat up in his bed, blond hair disheveled. His eyes sparkled with recognition, smiling past his initial shock.

He wasn't alone. A woman stood beside Ven's bed, holding a tray of empty dishes as though Ven had just finished eating. Mia could still smell the fresh scents of onion and garlic. This seemed a strange time to be eating. Had Ven been unwell? Who was this woman?

Mia's body cared for none of this. She was driven by her objective.

"Can I help you?" The woman asked.

Mia shoved the woman to the side, sending her crashing into the wall where she crumbled in a heap.

Ven's eyes widened in horror. "Mia! You might have just killed her!"

Mia grabbed Ven's foot and yanked him down so that he flopped back against the bed.

"Mia!"

Mia's muscles trembled as she fought to regain control. If there was ever a time to try to free herself it was now. She could *not* kill Ven. She couldn't. This was all a lesson from Rowan and Dayelle to teach her how powerless she was. Inside, she screamed, and her body perspired, something she hadn't experienced in years.

"Please," Ven said, eyes pleading.

Mia raised her hand. She would have struck already, but her will struggled against the command to strike. After only a moment of hesitation, her arm pounded down, straight into Ven's throat. The flesh collapsed beneath her blow, leaving Ven's neck a ruined mess. He choked and spat blood from his mouth. He was going to die. Box it all, he was going to die. She had done this.

No, not her. Rowan had done this.

Ven, of all people, was the last who deserved something like this. He was one of the few people she genuinely cared about. If he died, she felt as though her own humanity would die with him. She could sense her sanity cracking as she stared down at his blue eyes. They blinked up at her pleadingly, but she'd already dealt the blow.

Mia wanted to embrace him—to beg for his forgiveness. The tearing pain in her chest grew wider as if her whole soul were about to explode. She gripped his hand, squeezing tightly, but not tight enough to break his bones. That was not the action of a killer. She couldn't stand to watch Ven die. She withdrew her hand and stumbled to the door. Her body shook with the effort. Walking had become so incredibly difficult, like a weight was crushing down on her.

The fading sound of Ven's choked sputters wrenched at Mia's heart. She couldn't get away fast enough. She hated Rowan and Dayelle for doing this to her. This was not what she was meant for. She reached the door to the outside and fumbled into the railing, crying out. The pleading look in Ven's eyes haunted her. She should have been able to stop herself. The tearing pain in her chest continued to flare until she couldn't bear it. Her ragged scream echoed across the courtyard as the pain tore her in half, encompassing her mind with the blissful peace of unconsciousness as she fell down the stairs.

Chapter Seventeen

Impervious

Ven Yashke

Ven's vision swirled with stars as he watched Mia leave. He couldn't breathe, and when he tried to sit up, his neck wouldn't hold his head and flared with pain. He remained lying there, waiting to die. He had seconds at best. The lack of oxygen made his lungs burn. From Zein's assessment, imperviousness adaptations took longer for Ven's body to grasp than a native of Orund. He'd have to survive longer than an Orundian in order for the adaptation to take effect.

Though the pain of the blow was nothing short of excruciating, it didn't compare to what he'd experienced earlier in the day after undergoing the initial procedure. Even with all of that, Mia being the one to come in and throw down the deadly blow was the most painful thing of all.

Why?

She could have killed him at any moment back in Mavenda if that was something she'd truly wanted, but that look in Mia's eyes when she'd struck at him was terrifying. Her eyes and face were completely emotionless. The only sign she'd shown of any remorse was a slight twitch in her eyebrow right before she'd chopped at his neck, crushing his trachea and esophagus into oblivion.

Stars swam in his vision. Something in his neck popped and more blood flooded his mouth. He tried spitting it out, but from his position on his back, and with no strength to force it out, it remained at the back of his throat. It wouldn't make a difference. He was dead anyway, drowning in his own blood. He'd helped his dad pump the stomach of a woman who'd had way too much to drink, collapsed on the floor, and choked on her own vomit. She'd been out long enough that even with her lungs clear, she'd suffered so much brain damage from the lack of oxygen that she'd been stuck in a coma. That was maybe his best case scenario. He touched his neck gingerly, feeling the mushy flesh beneath his fingers

His eyes grew so heavy, all he could do was close them. Images of Mia flashed through his mind as he recalled her chopping down at him, but he also remembered the moment they met. That look in her eyes, pleading for help. He'd given it. He'd saved her life, dragging her out of the river and resuscitating her. He recognized that as the moment he'd fallen in love with her, hoping that she would live because he couldn't see how life was supposed to go on without her.

But then she'd asked him to kill her anyway. And perhaps he should have. Maybe she'd come back to kill him because he'd undergone the operation.

Ven snapped his eyes open, a ragged breath filling his lungs. Looking down at him was Siwen. Carina stood just behind him, cradling a broken arm.

"You can go now, Carina," Siwen said. "Get that arm taken care of."

Carina dipped into a quick bow then hurried out of the room. Ven vaguely remembered Carina getting batted out of the way as Mia had charged up to him.

"My word," Siwen said, eyes on Ven's neck. "You really are committed to surviving, aren't you?"

Ven's blurry mind was getting clearer by the second, and a warmth spread across his body. Zein had said that was the common sensation of an adaptation taking place. He certainly wouldn't mind expediting the adaptation process. The structure of his trachea snapped into place as the flesh reformed properly, allowing him to take in a full breath. At the same time, his presence of mind restored, memory returning in sharp clarity. He touched his neck gingerly, but the flesh had knit itself back together as though nothing had happened.

"Carina described what happened," Siwen said. "I told her to keep confidence regarding the attack, but Ven, is it what I think?"

"Mia," Ven said. He shook his head, still unsure if he could believe what happened. "She did this to me. Did anyone else see her? How long was I out?"

"I am not certain. Carina said she came straight to me after it happened, so not too long."

A loud knock came at the door. "Lord Huan," a voice called.

Siwen unsheathed the dragonsbane sword in a quick motion. "What is it?"

Ven hurried off the bed, ready to run out and find Mia himself, even if she was going to try to kill him again. Her actions didn't make any sense. A ravenous hunger gurgled in his stomach, and he suddenly remembered how much food Mia ate. It seemed necessary in order to continue adapting effectively, which was why Carina had brought him a bunch of food.

"Lord, we found a woman in the courtyard just outside. She is out cold. Doesn't look like one of the servants."

Siwen muttered a curse under his breath and hurried out the door. Ven barely had time to stuff his feet in his boots, laces left loose, before running after Siwen. The servant who'd alerted them ran at the head as they rushed through the hall.

"The guard, Albert, is watching her currently, lord. We haven't moved her since we discovered her. It looks like she fell down the stairs," the servant explained.

Had Mia hurt somebody else? Ven was extremely grateful that he'd decided to go forward with the operation. It couldn't have been more timely, and though it had been the most physically painful experience of his life, it had allowed him to survive an attack that would have otherwise killed him. Other people wouldn't have been as lucky.

They got outside and bounded down the steps. It was still dark, and the air was freezing, making Ven wonder what he'd have to subject himself to in order to adapt more to both the cold and the dark. Probably nothing pleasant.

Sure enough, there was a woman lying on the ground at the bottom of the steps. Ven's emergency training kicked in. He snatched the torch from the soldier and got down to her side, ready to check vitals, when he realized it was Mia. He looked up at Siwen, eyes wide, but the lord merely lowered his sword to Mia's chest.

"Don't kill her!" Ven putting his hand out and pushing away the blade in his own foolishness. Even touching the metal scalded his flesh. Right. It was poisonous to him now.

"I'm not killing her," Siwen said. "Just keeping myself ready in case it is necessary."

Ven shook his head. "Something is off—"

Siwen shushed Ven and gestured at the soldier. "You are dismissed, Albert. We have it from here."

"Aye, sir," Albert said, saluting before walking off.

Ven took the opportunity to check Mia's condition. "Her heartbeat is steady. She's breathing." Something was clearly amiss with her. She was unconscious. It would take something quite drastic to have such an effect on her.

"So she tried to kill you then passed out as she fled?"

Ven rubbed his lower lip in thought. "That appears to be the case."

"From what I understand, though, she's been through quite a few... studies. Isn't her body virtually impervious to everything? What could cause this kind of reaction?"

"I have absolutely no idea," Ven said. "We may need to involve the other doct—"

He didn't finish his thought as Mia blinked, staring up at him with bleary eyes. By impulse, he shot to his feet and took a step away. Siwen held the sword a hair above Mia's chest, ready to stab in case she tried anything.

Mia's face twisted in pain as she blinked up at Ven. She tried to rise, but her chest poked into the tip of Siwen's blade and she flinched back down as it stung her. Her eyes didn't look away from Ven, but there was life to her expression now, something that hadn't been there earlier when she'd tried to kill him.

"Ven," she said, her voice shaking. Tears welled in her eyes. She gasped when she regarded his neck. Her lip trembled as she said, "How did you... How?"

"The real question," Siwen said, tone laced with anger, "is why you tried to kill him."

Ven still wanted to respond to Mia's question, but he knew that getting the truth from her was much more important.

Mia shook her head. Tears flowed freely down her cheeks. "I can move." She paused as a sob wracked her shoulders. "I cannot be trusted." She continued to cry.

"Stay clear of her reach, Ven," Siwen said.

Ven looked at his feet. If she wanted to, she could reach out and grab him, but she made no move.

"Mia, what's going on?" Ven asked, ignoring Siwen's warning. A horrible feeling crawled across Ven's skin. Mia wasn't just afraid, she was downright terrified. He fought back his own panic as he tried to consider what could possibly do this to her.

"The dragons sent me to kill you, Ven." She raised a hand to wipe the tears from her face. "They can control me."

"What dragons?" Siwen's voice was darker than Ven had ever heard.

"Dayelle and Rowan." Mia squeezed her eyes shut and pinched the bridge of her nose. "Rowan can control me because the dragonblood used on me came from her."

"What do you mean she can control you?" Ven asked, the blood draining from his face, horror washing over him. Had Zein known about this? Had he given Ven the same operation so the dragons could control him?

"It's horrible," Mia said. "She can take complete control over my body. I lose all autonomy. It's how she was able to send me here to kill you. They wanted me to see how powerless I was to overcome them."

"What about now?" Siwen asked. "Can you control yourself now?"

"Yes," Mia said. "I don't know why. I felt Rowan's control fading as I tried not to kill Ven. After I struck him, something... broke in me. She no longer has control."

Ven nodded. He had to remember that Mia had an incredible ability to self-evaluate. "Do you think she could reassert herself and take over again?"

"It's possible," Mia said. She'd stopped crying, and her beautiful dark eyes settled on him. He had a flashback of her chopping down at his neck and the intense, mind-numbing pain the blow had dealt him, and he looked away with a shiver.

"They made me do terrible things," Mia continued. "All of Mavenda, Ven... It's... The dragons can enslave people, like they did to me, but worse."

"No," Ven said, shaking his head. The idea of a dragon actively trying to kill people was an absolute nightmare, but taking over people?

"You should kill me," Mia said, pressing herself up against the tip of the sword. "Please. I can't do that again. I couldn't even stop myself from hurting Ven. Killing me is the only guarantee that I won't do it again."

Ven shook his head slowly, despite the doubt that wriggled across his brain. If Mia could be possessed in such a way, then Ven was also susceptible. "You threw her off once, you must be able to do it again."

"Yes, but not until after I'd already thought I killed you."

"But I'm impervious now. I can survive if she makes you try again. You must be able to get better at resisting."

Mia's eyes widened. "I worried about that. How did you... What happened?"

"Long story short, Zein found me. He gave me the same operation."

Mia laid her head back on the stone, closed her eyes, and heaved a long breath. "That means she can control you as well."

"And Zein. He performed the operation on himself years ago." Ven rubbed his eye. "That's how he got away from Dayelle. Once he learned she was a dragon and that she wanted to turn him into some kind of thrall, he broke out and ran away."

"Then the answer is simple," Siwen said. "We must kill these dragons. And I mean not you two. You'll leave this to the dragonslayers."

"But there are none. Technically," Ven said.

Siwen raised an eyebrow at him. "Not yet, but there will be soon. Fortunately, a few of those I would consider for such a task will be coming to attend my wedding, so as long as we can keep you two out of the dragon's influence for a couple days, then I can probably start coordinating something."

"What do we do? Hide in a cell?" Ven asked.

"That might work for you," Mia said, "but I don't think there's a cell that could hold me."

"No, probably not," Siwen said. "So we might need to maintain good faith that if you are controlled again, you'd be able to withstand it. If thinking you'd killed Ven was able to break you free, you can perhaps focus on those same feelings again to try and hold back."

"I'm not sure," Mia said.

"Well there isn't much of another option because we aren't going to kill you," Ven said. "I would die before I let that happen again."

Siwen withdrew his weapon. "Mia, you will not have sanctuary here within the castle. You will be recognized."

"You should head over to Juns Hall," Ven said. "Zein is there. He'll have somewhere for you to stay."

Mia scowled and rose to her feet in a fluid motion. "I do not care to see him."

"I don't like him either, Mia, but he will help," Ven said. "If staying hidden prevents you from being manipulated by Rowan, then he'd be the best person to check with."

Mia folded her arms.

"I will get you out of the castle in the morning," Siwen said. "Sneaking a woman out of the castle grounds in the middle of the night would not be seemly. I will need to get some sleep, but we can discuss an agenda tomorrow. Are we all in agreement?"

They each looked at each other, and Ven nodded. He was in deep. Somewhere along the way, perhaps he'd made some terrible choice that led him here, and now there was no escape unless someone killed a dragon. What if they ran away? If they fled to Earth, maybe this wouldn't be a problem at all. That wouldn't be a real option though. If Dayelle could get to Earth, so could Rowan. They'd be in danger no matter where they went.

Mia nodded as well.

Siwen sighed. "Alright, in the meantime, try not to kill each other. Or me."

Chapter Eighteen

Wedding

Mia

Mia hid behind a head bangle and a thin veil that went down over her eyes and nose. It was just enough to hide her most distinct features. Zein had discouraged her from attending, but since she'd insisted, such ornamentation would be sufficient. Most other women weren't dressed in such a manner, but at least it allowed her to be here at all. Mia had been cooped up inside of some empty house by herself. The only upside was that it had a small yard. Ven had gone over yesterday to practice meditation with her.

"I don't know if it'll help," he'd said, "but meditation can be a good way to help mediate your emotions. Perhaps it can help us maintain some of our own control if Rowan tries imposing herself." They'd practiced visualization, relaxation, and breathing for over an hour.

Mia wasn't sure if it would help with resisting Rowan, but it at least helped to calm some of her anxieties. She would have to exert control wherever she could and recognize there were some things that were beyond her.

Flower petals started to flutter down from the sides of the castle courtyard as a horse-drawn carriage pulled in from the gate, signaling the arrival of Siwen's bride. The carriage had been painted white and was decorated with pink, red, and purple flowers. Even the two horses pulling the carriage had been dressed with flowery bridles. Cheers filled the air, echoing off the stone walls. Most people clapped, so Mia joined in. Ven stood beside her, wearing his own subtle disguise that consisted of a pair of spectacles and one of those broad-brimmed hats. He hadn't met her eyes all day, and she could tell he was conflicted about something. Even yesterday, when he'd come to help her with meditation, he'd seemed distant.

When she glanced at him, a broad smile split his face as he clapped along. Right. This was a joyous occasion. She snapped herself back to the present. The flowers *were* quite beautiful. A few of the petals fell around her, and she couldn't help it when her own smile broadened. She'd never seen a wedding and was still unfamiliar with the significance of such an event, but it was clearly no small matter.

The crowd was separated behind a removable balustrade that had been built into either side of the courtyard. The wedding itself was going to take place inside the actual castle where only particular guests would witness the event, but these sections had been prepared for the general public to attend. Once the wedding was done, the couple would come back out to greet them.

Several soldiers working as crowd control stood on the other side of the balustrades, their metal helmets looking particularly shiny for the event. Each of them were armed with poleaxes and tower shields.

The carriage stopped in front of the stairs, vaguely reminiscent of the time Mia had pulled up to the castle in a similar fashion. Beside her, Ven bit his lip, holding back a grin as he looked down at her. It was the first time he'd looked directly at her since the other night after they'd found her lying on the ground. Perhaps he was remembering the same memory of when they'd come to steal the dragonsbane dagger from the Huan family.

Cheers grew even louder as Siwen's bride exited the carriage. Mia and Ven had such a good vantage from their position that they were able to see her the instant she stepped out. Siwen had told them her name was Morgan Lauron and that her family ruled from another castle settlement similar to Peskan but all the way on the north end of Luedan. He and Ven had spent another hour discussing the different noble families of Luedan, much to Mia's boredom.

Morgan was beautiful. Her black hair was shorter than Mia typically saw, with straight-cut bangs and more flowers mingled into the rest of her hair. She wore a dress of dark, shiny green with pink flowers. It was significantly more beautiful than the dress Mia had worn when she'd feigned as a potential suitress, though its form was such that it would not have been very suitable for running, as it remained slim down Morgan's thighs.

A woman held out her arm to Morgan as she came down, presumably Morgan's mother, as their appearances were very similar. Morgan faced the crowd and waved to them before proceeding up

the stairs into the castle with a small entourage. Once they disappeared inside, the crowd changed from cheering to chatting.

"Ven," Mia said.

"Yeah." Ven kept his eyes on the castle.

"What's the significance of a wedding?"

Ven frowned and looked down at her briefly. He admittedly
looked so much more mature with that facial hair of his. It mostly
grew on his upper lip and down around his chin and was a lot sharp-
er now that one of Siwen's servants had helped him take care of it. "I
suppose it's different depending on the culture," Ven said. "I haven't
seen one here in Shiansan, but if it's similar to what I'm familiar
with, then marriage is important because it signifies a commitment
to each other and the formation of a new family."

"A commitment?" she leaned towards him to be heard over the
crowd.

"Yes, which again, might vary, but it's typically a promise that you
will take care of each other and be responsible for one another. It also
usually involves a promise of fidelity, like that you won't go out and
try to have romantic or," Ven paused and lowered his voice a little
more before adding, "sexual relations with anybody else."

Mia nodded. "So they are committing to spend their whole lives
together."

"That's my understanding, unless traditions here are different,
but that part at least seems to be a universal concept. For govern-
mental leaders, like the Huans and the Laurons, it might also act as
a means of tying their two families together."

"Why does that matter?"

"I don't know, really. It's probably a good thing I'm not a nobleman." Ven's expression hardened after he said that, and he turned
his head away.

Mia found his reaction strange but didn't comment on it. Her
thoughts drifted back to the terrible feeling of chopping down on
his neck. Why did the image keep recurring? Her stomach clenched,
and she could at least in part understand why Ven wouldn't meet
her eyes. They still hadn't spoken about why he'd left Mavenda or
discussed her feelings towards him. She wanted to ask him what was
wrong with the way things were, but now didn't seem like the right
time.

Her discomfort remained, and she continued having flashbacks
to the things she'd done, not only while being controlled, but before then, when she'd been butchering the dragonsworn who'd attacked the village. She kept seeing the dead people in the streets. Her
breathing became heavy, eyes blinking rapidly as she stared at the
ground. Instinctively, she grasped Ven's hand and squeezed.

Ven squeezed back and bent down, whispering in her ear. "Eyes
up. Look at the flowers. Big breaths. What colors do you see?"

Mia let out a long breath and regarded the flowers on the carriage.
"Red, pink, and purple. One of the flowers has a white coloration
near the tips of the petals."

"Good," Ven said. "Can you smell them? Breathe it in. Let it fill
your lungs, then breathe all the way out. Breathe with your stomach.
Does it smell good?"

Mia inhaled deeply and a chill went up her spine. Ven squeezed
her hand again, and she nodded to him. They had the distinct scent

of nectar, so sharp she could almost taste it. "They smell wonderful."

"Good," Ven said. "Keep breathing. Think of the smell. Think of the sky. Notice the sounds of those around us. Notice the ground beneath your feet." He gave her another squeeze.

Mia continued to breathe as he instructed, and calmness washed over her. She smiled at him, those bright blue eyes of his looking back at her. Box, his ability to calm her was too magical. "Thank you," she said.

Ven gave her an accepting nod, then released her hand.

A moment later, the doors to the castle opened again and out strode Siwen and Morgan, hand-in-hand as the cheering intensified more than ever. Ven gave a loud whistle, and Mia couldn't help but laugh.

There was some exchange between Morgan's parents and Yubo. Mia realized only just then that perhaps Siwen's mother had passed away, which would explain why she'd never seen her.

The smiles that Siwen and Morgan shared with each other were so jubilant. Even their eyes sparkled with a joy she had never known. This wedding had been an act of love.

A horse rode into the courtyard at full gallop. By his uniform, it was one of their soldiers, but he was stopped by the guards and forced to dismount. There was alarm in the man's expression. Mia nudged Ven and they watched the soldier get escorted by one of the guards directly to Yubo Huan.

Mia wasn't entirely sure, but she suspected that interrupting the lord at his son's wedding was probably something that was only reserved for very serious situations. Indeed, Yubo's expression darkened as he received the news. Mia wished the crowd wasn't so loud or she might have been able to hear what they'd said.

Siwen was also far enough from his father that he likely couldn't hear the report, but he gave his father a questioning look. Yubo waved his son off with a smile but gave the guard and the soldier an order, and they both ran off at a full sprint. Despite the smile on Siwen's face, he looked pointedly at Ven and Mia. When they made eye contact, he pointed with his chin at the soldier running back toward the gate.

Mia sighed. "I guess we're going to be his spies now, aren't we?"

"That seems to be the case," Ven said. "I'll follow the guard. You go after the soldier."

"On it," Mia said, slipping off to weave through the crowd. She kept her head down, carving a path through the onlookers until she emerged at the edge of the balustrade where the soldier had just gotten back to his horse. With the crowd now behind her, and being only a few steps from the horse, she was able to tune in and hear the soldier.

A guard spoke to the soldier as he mounted the horse. "What did Lord Huan have to say?"

"I need to report back to Captain Wanli to mobilize," the soldier said.

"Mobilize for what?" the guard asked, releasing the horse's reins now that the soldier was ready to go.

"War," the soldier said before heeling his horse onward. "Gogoba invades."

Chapter Nineteen

Invasion

Elise Sherwood

Commander Elise Sherwood squinted south at the snaking line of the invading forces as they worked their way across the open plains. The plains were pockmarked by blackened stones that formed lumps on the uneven ground. Small bushes grew in the stones' shadows, but the immediate area was mostly devoid of plant life.

Fort Sal, upon which Elise stood, was the first outpost bordering the nations of Gogoba to the south and Kombida to the east. It had been in excess of a hundred years since they'd had any clashes with either nation, and the fort had been in operation for at least a few centuries. It was in place to protect much of Shiansan's southern farmland.

Elise had been sent here to command the fort after being informed that it was a quiet post where they'd mostly just inspect trade routes. Instead, here she was, three weeks after accepting the assignment, staring down a host of three or four thousand hostile soldiers. The fort was defensible, built up atop the highest hill in the area, one side a sharp cliff. It was stockpiled with plenty of resources to withstand a siege, and it housed a good sixty-three soldiers with an additional twenty-nine civilian personnel who served in other capacities, but holding out against thousands would be impossible. They would need the full might of the Shiansan army to defend against such a force.

If the Gogoban army moved straight into an assault, the fort would perhaps only be able to hold them off for two days at best. The more likely scenario was that they would be overrun within hours, depending on the kind of equipment the Gogobans brought with them.

"Renden," Elise said over her shoulder, "any word from Captain Termot about those reinforcements?" There was no response. She looked behind her to see that Renden was no more than a corpse beside the staircase that led back down to the fort, and the archer who'd been standing with them seconds ago was in a pile of his own blood. A single figure, a woman, stood a few steps down, staring at Elise with folded arms. She wore a robe over simple clothes, though she was spattered in blood. She held no weapon that Elise could see, but this was not somebody who worked under her employment. The indication was clear.

Elise whipped her sword out and stepped toward the intruder. "Who are you?" she demanded. Elise wasn't the greatest fighter, but she was adept. This assassin may have caught her fellow soldiers off-guard, but Elise would make her pay.

The woman tilted her head at Elise, ignoring the sword as she took the last two steps to the top of the tower.

Elise would not be taken for a fool. She stepped toward the intruder, shifting her hold on her sword to a striking position, elbow bent to provide extra arc to a swing if needed. "Answer the question or be struck down."

The woman bore no expression, but she dabbed at some of the blood that had spattered across her bare forearm with a finger before raising the finger to her mouth, licking the blood off.

Elise's lips curled back. "Who are you?" she demanded again.

There was no answer. Instead, the woman stepped toward Elise.

Without hesitation, Elise struck, swinging her sword straight for the woman's throat. She backed her head away, narrowly dodging the stroke. Elise swung again, though the woman dodged again. Then she stepped forward, stabbing at the woman's midsection. Instead of dodging, the woman slapped her hands onto either side of the sword, palms pressed against the flat of the blade, pinning it with her grip. The tip of the blade was a mere finger's width from its target.

Elise snarled and pulled her sword back before trying two quick swings from either side. The woman smirked, deftly avoiding the first swing then slapping the sword away with the back of her hand on the second. The woman was toying with her. Elise stepped back to reassess. How had the other two died? Renden's throat appeared to be completely missing, as though it had been torn away. The archer was face down in his own mess so that his wound was not visible. This assassin was skilled and had somehow managed to kill both of them without so much as a single sound to alert her.

A sick feeling rose in her stomach, and Elise's lips curled even more. "What are you?"

The woman nodded. "I am ancient. I am the one that reigns. I am the master of these lands."

Elise shook her head. No. "We're under attack!" she shouted, knowing that her voice could be heard from down below. They wouldn't be able to reach her in time if this lunatic was going to try killing her. At least she wouldn't go down without a fight. There was no way this woman would be able to get at her without injury.

"Why are you doing this?" Elise asked.

"To reclaim what's mine."

"And who are you to claim these lands?"

The woman shrugged. "That won't matter to you." She walked almost playfully over to the archer's corpse.

"How did you get in here?" Elise wanted to keep the woman talking. It would give her other soldiers enough time to get here and provide assistance. There was no way this strange woman would be able to resist all of them.

"We had an agent planted here among the staff for a few months now. This plan has been in the works for some time."

Elise's eye twitched. Gogoba had been planning an invasion for this much time? Why? There were only three people who'd been new to this location in the last few months, and she was one of them, as well as her younger brother who'd taken the assignment to come with her. She knew exactly who the plant was. It was no doubt that cook with the half grin. The previous cook had died of food poisoning. The new one, Tafyen, would work longer hours, and preferred to stay in the castle rather than the village below. He'd often be found wandering the grounds. "Tafyen. The cook."

"Very astute," the woman said. "He smuggled us in with some food supplies. You see, I'm not from Gogoba, but we enticed them to invade. As part of the arrangement, they wanted assistance taking your little fort here. From their level of hesitation, I was expecting something impressive. To be honest, I thought it would have much better fortifications, but I'm a little underwhelmed. Needless to say, we did our part. We killed a few officers and pilfered the food supply."

"That seemed necessary?"

The woman shrugged. "Not really, but we ultimately want the Gogoban army to feel that they have support. We also wanted them to have the satisfaction of taking the fort to encourage them farther into Shiansan. We want them hungry for more than just a little farmland. Your crushing defeat here will be tantalizingly invigorating for them. Humans really are such emotionally persuaded creatures."

Elise shook her head. Footsteps approached from below, and the woman smirked. Elise's tactic to stall the assassin was not a surprise to her. She didn't even seem to care. She lurched toward Elise, so she hacked at her, but the woman dodged with blurring speed, grabbed Elise's sword arm with one hand, then snatched her around the throat with the other. She lifted Elise off the floor with surprising strength. Was this woman even human?

With her free hand, Elise slipped out a knife and rammed it into the woman's armpit. The small blade went through the thin layer of clothing and pressed up against her target's flesh, but she felt no indication that it pierced the skin.

The woman's grip around Elise's wrist tightened. The pain was so sharp that she dropped her sword. She withdrew the knife and tried to stab again, but with the sword gone, her opponent grabbed her other hand, ripped the knife from her grip, and threw it over the parapet.

Elise's lungs were empty. The woman's hand squeezed tight enough around her neck that she couldn't breathe. They wouldn't have any time for reinforcements to arrive, and if their food stocks had been plundered, they wouldn't last long in a siege. The village to the north would be sacked in another day's time. Her hopes for a peaceful assignment for her and her brother were gone. She should have known that an outpost at the fringes of two other nations would be one of the riskier locations. Her vision started to blacken.

"You have a good spirit," the woman said. "I think I will let you die fighting the Gogobans. There is more honor for you there, if humans care for such a notion."

Elise worked her mouth, but no words emerged. She sputtered, and her vision swarmed with stars. Before she knew it, she was on the floor again.

"Commander Sherwood!" a voice cried. It was a man, dropping down at her side to help her rise. "What happened?"

Elise looked up at him, her vision clearing as she gulped down air. The woman was... gone. That left her alone with this gory mess atop the tower.

Lieutenant Baatarin had just reached her, along with two other soldiers, their weapons drawn. "Commander," he said, his voice a gruff rumble. He bent his head down to see her face better.

"Assassin," Elise managed to say. She flexed her arm, gauging the damage to her wrist. It hurt but was likely just bruised. No sprain. "Did you see her?"

Baatarin looked around the tower top. "We saw no one, sir."

"It's like a monster did this," muttered one of the other soldiers as he inspected Rendel's torn throat. Elise had forgotten the soldier's name. She was still getting used to the new assignment, and learning nearly a hundred names was not one of her strengths.

Elise reinspected the scene. The only evidence that the strange woman had even been here was a single, bloody footprint near the dead body of Rendel. She couldn't have imagined the strange woman, but the assassin also couldn't have simply disappeared. Then again, she was... otherworldly. Elise retrieved her sword and hurried to the edge of the tower, peering over the side. "Then she escaped," she said. "Put everyone on high alert. We must search the castle immediately. There may have been other assassinations. And we must check our food supply. It has supposedly been ransacked."

"Aye, sir," Baatarin said. "You heard her, lads. Nal, you head to the barracks and put everyone on alert. Fitner, head straight to the gatehouse." The three of them dashed back down the stairs, leaving Elise alone with the scene of a nightmare displayed before her.

She'd understood that this kind of career choice could result in seeing death. Shiansan was at peace, but there were still murders and accidents at times. Nothing like this, though. Nothing like what she would see on the morrow. That approaching army was already setting up camp not too far away. They'd probably launch an assault in the morning.

Elise rounded the whole tower, glancing down the sides. There were no ropes. No indication of how the woman had gotten away. What *was* that woman? The way she'd talked about people almost made her feel inhuman. Elise shivered, pushing back the pang of guilt for leaving these bodies here. They'd take care of them later, but for now, she needed to get everything prepared, and she needed to find her brother.

Without another thought, she hurried and flew down the winding stairs. There were already other shouts echoing through the fort's courtyard. Fort Sal was not significantly large, but it was formidable. At peak capacity, it had room to house and supply nearly three hundred people. That didn't seem like much when compared to an invading army of three thousand, but it was a very defensible position. Assailants would only be able to approach from the west and north sides of the fort since both the southern and eastern sides were elevated high enough that no ladder or grapple would realistically be tall enough for them to be able to scale the surface.

All of the walls were built with doubly thick layers of stone which would require considerable hammering from siege engines before they'd ever give way. She knew exactly why the Gogobans would want the fort taken down in order to feel confident enough to invade the rest of Shiansan. Otherwise, it would remain a thorn in the side of any army.

When she reached the bottom, Elise burst out across the courtyard, dodging between a couple other soldiers.

"Commander Sherwood," said one of the servants. "Half of our food supply has gone missing."

"Understood," Elise said, trying not to appear too frantic as she went straight for the keep. The door was wide open as she went inside.

"Leric!" Elise said, seeing her brother already on his way out, helmet in hand.

"Is it time?" Leric said, eyebrows furrowed, voice grave.

"Not yet, but we've had some kind of infiltration already."

Leric didn't pause, but made as if to exit.

Elise grabbed his arm. "Leric, we won't last long. Run to the village. The Gogobans will go for them next—they need to flee."

Leric frowned at her. "Then send the servants out. I am a warrior, Elise, not some messenger boy."

"It's an order, Leric!"

Leric puffed out his chest. "And what of the rest of the soldiers? Are they to remain here, defending the fort so we can buy the people enough time to evacuate?"

Elise tried to come up with some response other than the affirmative, but her hesitation to come up with anything else had Leric nodding.

"I thought so." Leric grunted. "You told me that I wouldn't have any special privileges by coming here with you. I guess I shouldn't be surprised that you'd go back on your word when it matters most."

"We will all die here, Leric." Tears stung Elise's eyes. Her grip on her brother's arm tightened. "One more soldier won't make much of a difference. Uncle is on his deathbed, and you will be the remaining descendant. Weren't you hoping to marry Hatya?"

The muscles of Leric's jaw twitched. "There will be no Hatya if we fail to do our duty."

Elise clenched her fists. He was right. The whole point of Fort Sal was to be a watchtower that alerted the nation to gather its defenses, then to hold out long enough for them to arrive.

"And what if there was a way for us to not simply die here, Elise?" Leric said, lowering his voice.

She shook her head. "No, Leric." She knew exactly what he was talking about. "Using *that* would be treasonous. There'd be no hiding it."

"Would you rather be dead or punished? Why would you have brought it with us to begin with if you weren't going to use it?"

"I said no, Leric. Now if you plan on staying here and dying with the rest of us, then you can at least help Denar's crew set up the anti-siege equipment on the west wing."

Leric's nostrils flared and he hesitated only a moment before saying, "Very well, sir. As you command."

As Leric walked away, Elise's heart thundered. Could she do it? Why was it even more terrifying than dying in battle? Perhaps because it would feel like a denial of her convictions, but if it truly came down to doing that or dying, she already knew what she would do.

***

Two hours passed before the Gogoban army began their assault. They had not hesitated to mobilize. All hope for Fort Sal rested in that single messenger they'd sent off after receiving the declaration of war. Elise had read the note herself before sending it off with the rider. Gogoba had accused Shiansan of abusing their control over the bordering river, but even more egregious than that was their free use of dragonblood technology.

Admittedly, Elise had been witness to many uses of dragonblood technology within the country, though it would never be blatantly displayed or used by any of the nobility. If such information ever reached the king and queen, the responsible party would be subject to losing their lands and titles.

However, enforcement of the law against dragonblood technology seemed to be limited to the creation of new devices rather than the use of existing ones. Thus, it was not altogether uncommon to see things like people driving those powered vehicles or lighting the inside of their homes with dragonlights. The saved expense for lighting alone had a tremendous impact, not only for residences, but for industrial facilities. That was part of what she was supposed to help moderate in her role here at the fort. Trading of dragonblood technology between nations was illegal, and if any of her troops ever came across a cart containing such devices, the items would be seized and moved to a different facility. It was a difficult law to enforce, and she knew that transactions for dragonblood-related products were virtually impossible to stop.

Even still, Elise refused to be guilty of the same laws she tried to enforce.

Elise braced herself as a rock crashed into the wall just beneath her. The wall trembled but held. It would take many shots like those to destroy the walls of Fort Sal. The engineers were already aiming the counter siege engines to fire back. The mangonels would hurl a smattering of burning debris at the assailants. It took longer to set them up than she preferred, and the enemy troops were already drawing near with a battering ram.

The first mangonel released its load, launching out toward the enemy catapults. The Gogobans had brought three catapults with them as well as this battering ram and several ladders. The ladders would be a last resort as the enemy hoped to soften up the fort's defenses. Fort Sal's mangonels had exceptional reach, as they were built in at the top of two of the fort's towers. She watched the launch, hoping it would land successfully. Ultimately, the debris shot over the catapults but landed amid some of their troops stationed around it. She wasn't sure what kind of damage they'd done, and the war cries of the Gogobans drowned out any kind of reaction.

The battering ram was getting dangerously close, and they needed that other mangonel to fire at it. Elise walked along the parepets, repeating some of her orders to the archers. "You will fire at will once they draw near enough. Do not bother aiming for the battering ram. That will be taken care of by the engineers. You must aim your efforts at their archers and ladder-bearers. They will be less protected."

The fort had been equipped with around two thousand arrows. At best, she could hope for twenty-five to thirty percent efficiency, seeing that the incoming forces were well armored. This would only scratch a dent in the Gogoban forces, and she knew those numbers were optimistic anyway. That wouldn't stop them from trying.

The second mangonel released its launch, scoring a direct hit on the battering ram. One of the stones broke through the top and crushed one or two of the soldiers pushing it forward. The screams of pain were poignant, marking the first guaranteed casualties for the enemy forces.

Another stone crashed into the wall to her left, grazing the top of the parapet. A soldier who'd ducked behind the wall was unable to avoid getting his leg crushed by the impact. He nearly fell off the wall as he tumbled and screamed. The bone at his shin protruded through his trousers. She looked away. They had a protocol. Two neighboring soldiers ran over to help pull the man into the cover of the tower.

This was war.

Hopefully the rest of the enemy's shots would not be so accurate. She retrieved the soldier's bow and grabbed three arrows. The battering ram's momentum had not slowed at all. They had less than a minute before it would reach the gate. They really needed two more good hits from that mangonel. Two more stones flew toward them. One went right over the wall but crashed into the far side while the other one hit the middle, a splintering of stone blasting out.

Their mangonels both launched again, but her eyes were fixed on the battering ram. They hit it again, but it was more of a glancing blow to the rear, though it did crush a few of the soldiers who were trying to sneak in behind and provide backup to the device. That was the last shot they'd have before it reached the wall. She rushed into the gatehouse, checking for the tenth time that they were adequately stocked. They weren't, but it would have to do.

Next, she went up a flight of stairs that brought her to the top of the gatehouse. This area was where she'd concentrated the largest portion of troops. There were sixteen of them here, all armed with bows. There was another large pile of rocks here. Primitive, of course, but a well-aimed rock dropped from thirty feet could still be deadly, even if the target was wearing heavier armor.

As she'd expected, the mangonel was not prepared in time to get another shot off. The battering ram was too close to reach. Instead, it launched a volley at the troops who snaked out behind it. Shields did them little good.

An arrow whizzed right by Elise's face, close enough to graze the edge of her helmet. She ducked down with a gasp. "It's almost here," she said to the others as they prepared to attack the battering ram. A chorus of shouts rose up from below just before the first blow from the battering ram smacked against the gate.

"Now!" Lieutenant Baatarin said from the center of the gate-house. More arrows flew by as they exposed themselves to throw down two entire pots filled with tar. A soldier leaned over the edge and dropped a torch. If successful, they'd light the whole battering ram. The soldier who'd thrown the torch yelled and spun away, an arrow embedded in her shoulder. Screams came up from below, but the pounding against the gate didn't cease.

Elise nocked an arrow and peeked over the edge. "Ladders!" she shouted as she spotted the groups of Gogoban soldiers now running at the walls. She popped up ever-so-briefly, took aim, and fired at one of the runners. The arrow slammed right into the base of the man's neck and he tumbled away. She ducked. Two archers fired at her. One arrow overshot, but another clanged against the wall.

"Got one!" shouted another of their soldiers.

One. Even with her quick glance, there'd been at least ten ladders. The gate below continued to tremble.

Another archer got hit as arrows kept flying over and threw the slits. She nocked another arrow and stood. The gatehouse extended slightly farther than the rest of the wall, allowing her to see anybody coming at the sides while protecting her from the archers firing at them from the front. Two ladders reached the wall on that side. She pulled back and fired, hitting one of the exposed soldiers in the side. Unsupported, the ladder fell, but the other one was getting settled into place. More soldiers came to pick up the one that had dropped. She'd only had three arrows, so she nocked the last one and shot another soldier.

"Post here," she ordered two of the other archers.

A shattering echoed up from below and the Gogobans cheered.

"Focus on those ladders," she said to Baatarin. He nodded and directed the soldiers as Elise ran down the stairs. The enemy soldiers flooded into the murder hall that stood between the front gate and the rear gate. Right here between the walls, their heads were exposed to a hole in the gatehouse. Her fellow soldiers were already hurling rocks through the gap, crushing the Gogobans below as they started hammering their weapons into the rear gate.

Elise ran over to help another soldier lift a heavy rock from the pile. They shimmied over to the large, open space and dropped the rock down. It clattered directly onto the shoulder of an enemy soldier who bent under its weight with a scream. The wall trembled.

She and the others continued throwing the rocks down to the final brick. A pile of bodies built up, but the soldiers kept coming. The sound of weapons clashing rang down from the walls. Elise cursed and sprinted back up to the walls to find a melee. The ladders were set, and Gogobans had reached the top of the walls. She drew her sword and dashed to the nearest ladder where one of her soldiers was engaged in battle. She slid over and shoved the assailant, pushing him back over the edge of the wall as her sword tore across his side. She picked up a hooked pole from the floor of the wall and placed it up against the top of the ladder. The other soldier helped her as they heaved, pushing the ladder away. A Gogoban who was already near the top of the ladder tried pushing the pole away, but to no avail. He screamed as the ladder fell back.

One of Elise's other soldiers had managed to pull a ladder up and over, preventing the enemy from using it at all. A different ladder was firmly in place, with seven enemy soldiers already atop the wall, purchasing more ground to keep the flood coming. Arrows from atop the guardhouse were aimed at that location, however, picking off some of the soldiers who were attempting to climb that ladder. Perhaps they could win the area back.

Elise hurried over, tugging another defender along with her. Three of her own soldiers were already dead, and a fourth got skewered through the gut just as she arrived to help. The terror of the scene threatened to overwhelm her, but she already knew that if she didn't fight, they would all fall faster. As soon as she arrived, a spear caught her near the hip. She grunted off the pain and spun, blade arcing. She nearly severed a man's arm in that first swing and she kept her momentum. The attackers withdrew slightly as she cut down two of them, but a blow from a mace rocked her forearm, one of the few places she wore plated armor for that exact purpose.

Breathing through the pain, she bent down and retrieved the spear from a fallen attacker, using it in a one-handed grip to jab at opponents as she hacked with her sword. Two more defenders came in from the other side, though one of them fell instantly. Elise's companion dispatched an attacker, leaving only two more of them on the wall. Elise and her comrades quickly overwhelmed the force and pushed off the ladder, thanks to the assistance of the archers on the gatehouse.

The inner gate cracked.

A force of sixteen soldiers waited just behind the gate, each equipped with spear and shield. They'd be able to hold that position against a larger host for a while, but even still, they'd be overwhelmed. Open combat was not something they could endure, and the outer gate had broken in much sooner than she'd hoped. Once the inner gate was forced open, it would be a matter of minutes.

Elise jumped down the ramparts to join them. She didn't have a shield, but she'd still be able to provide support.

When the gate finally did give way, the first enemy soldier to step through the opening hurled a spear at the line, which was deflected by their shields.

"Push in!" a voice bellowed from the other side.

Elise clicked her tongue and her defensive line moved in to stand right behind the crumbling gate. They needed to prevent a larger force from getting through. The murder hall only allowed enough room for three soldiers to fit side-by-side, so their best hope was to bottle them in as they maintained three rows of five with a relief option. They successfully kept the forces at bay for quite a while until three of the frontline soldiers got stabbed by enemy spears. Gogoban soldiers from behind were throwing rocks and javelins over.

The line rotated as another defender fell.

"Hold them back!" Elise ordered. One of the soldiers stumbled after taking a spear to the shin. She jumped down and stabbed the attacker with her spear, but they wouldn't hold out forever. Another of her defenders screamed as he fell from the battlements and crashed down behind her.

A spear lanced into the face of the soldier beside her, and she flinched away as his blood flicked across her face. She staggered back. The mass of bodies that had accumulated at the gate was disgustingly large. Elise became so starkly aware of the mortality of man even as her own sword had to jab forward, cutting through the muscle along a man's arm as he tried to stab her.

She stepped back further. The other soldiers filled in as the shouts and screams of battle became deafening to her. The soldiers of Fort

Sal were down to the last five, though one of them was barely able to stand as she bled profusely from a wound on the side of her head.

The Gogoban forces spilled in as they pushed the defenders back.

It was over.

They hadn't even held for more than an hour. It was utter defeat.

Elise flicked the blood from her sword as the enemies rushed toward her. She would try to take at least one more of them with her, but a blinding flash of yellow light stopped her in her tracks.

No.

Not this.

She shielded her eyes and looked over her shoulder. Leric came running toward the battle, the ancient weapon held in his hand. It was the very item she'd buried in the chest in her room. The device was simple with an open musket, but the handle encased a palm-sized crystal that had been formed by condensed, dehydrated dragon blood. The weapon had been passed down for generations, the design getting refined over years until her mother had been executed for egregious use of dragonblood research after one of her experiments exploded, killing five aides and burning their laboratory to the ground. Her mother had barely made it out alive. The execution was practically a mercy.

They'd sworn not to follow in the footsteps of their ancestors, enlisting in the army instead, but Elise had been a fool, bringing this device with them. Perhaps it was fear that had influenced her to do so.

But the weapon... It was both horrible and magnificent.

As Leric pulled the trigger, it unleashed a torrent of energy at those toward whom it was aimed. Their bodies appeared to be caught in a powerful gust. At first, it was unclear how it was working, but then the targets' hair vanished, burned away in an instant. Their clothing burst into flames, their skin shriveling and popping. It was supposedly built to mimic the effect of dragon fire.

In this case, the results were devastating. Within seconds, it had melted away the enemy forces, turning them into little more than charred husks. Elise had to run away just to avoid the heat, but it still left her feeling burned.

Leric roared, teeth bared with pain. His leather gloves had burned away and his fingers were blistering just from holding the device. An arrow struck Leric in the chest.

"Stop, Leric!" Elise cried. The weapon had the heart of a monster. It would only consume.

Leric redirected the weapon, scorching those atop the walls.

All other defenders were dead, Elise realized. It was just the two of them that remained to defend the fort, but the weapon consumed, the attackers disappearing one by one, never sating the fire.

Leric dropped to a knee as the weapon clicked off, clattering out of his charred hands. Tears streaked his face.

"Leric, you are a fool," Elise said as she stood beside him. Heat emanated from the weapon, and the handle glowed with the dim red light of embers.

"Go," he said, voice slightly gurgling. He coughed up blood. That arrow in the bottom of his neck had clearly struck the windpipe. His lungs were filling up with his own blood. She bit back thoughts of the inevitable.

"Do you realize you've justified their entire invasion?"

He only blinked up at her. His hands were trembling.

"They attacked Shiansan because they say we have embraced the use of dragonblood. We've been accused of harboring dragons all this time rather than executing them, so they've come to do the job we couldn't. Do you realize the implications of using that weapon?"

Leric merely coughed up more blood. His inhalation made a slurping sound, and he coughed even more. When the fit ceased, he glared up at her. It made her angry. She'd wanted him to live.

In the midst of all her roiling emotions, Elise couldn't help it when she slapped him, but then she immediately dropped down in front of him and hugged him. *My baby brother*. He didn't hug her back. His weight started to feel heavy in her arms as tears stung her eyes. "You weren't supposed to die like this."

"Go," he said again, growling the words out. "Live. Apologize to Hatya for me. She'll have to marry a better fool." He went completely limp.

Elise laid her brother down and sniffed. How was she supposed to live? Would they take prisoners? The fact that they'd bothered declaring war over the dragonblood technology gave her the impression that they'd be ruthless and unapologetic. Her brother had just used a devastating weapon. It would be difficult to hide what had happened.

Shouts alerted her. War provided little opportunity to grieve. She pressed her fingers to her lips then placed them on Leric's cheek before closing his eyes. There were four horses left in the stable, and they were all saddled in preparation for just such an event as this, but she needed to take the weapon with her and limit the evidence. She let out a seething breath and launched to her feet.

Fort Sal was lost.

Chapter Twenty

Call of War

Ven Yashke

Ven breathed heavily as he faced off against Mia. His own dried blood caked across his chest where she'd cut him. That was one of several cuts he'd received, but the wounds sealed a few minutes after they were delivered. Sweat glistened across his bare torso and arms. They had little room to maneuver in the small space of this property, owned by Zein.

Zein stood in the doorway to the home with a clipboard in hand, giving Ven a creeped out feeling as he made the automatic connection to the research facility.

Mia wore a frown, but she wasn't even tired. They'd been sparring for the last couple days, but Ven had also been sparring before coming over here as he trained under a grizzled drill instructor who worked with the soldiers at the Huans' castle. It had been three days since they'd learned that Gogoba, the nation to the south, had declared war on Shiansan. Ven was still learning about the customs on Orund, but Gogoban had apparently delivered a formal declaration stating that Shiansan was guilty of atrocities dealing with dragonblood and alleging that they kept dragons alive on purpose.

They hadn't been wrong. And the guilty party was quite literally Siwen's own father and Zein Huan himself.

Why dragonblood usage was outlawed still made little sense to Ven. It obviously had remarkable uses. The rejection of such technology just seemed foolish, though he could understand, at least to some degree, the moral issue with having to actually use the blood of a dragon, essentially torturing the beast and keeping it imprisoned in order to farm from its body. But if they all hated dragons so much, then why would that be a concern?

"Hmm," Zein hummed to himself as his lips disappeared into a thin line. "Pause for a moment."

Ven gratefully lowered his weapon. They'd been using actual swords, much to his chagrin. He'd really wanted to use a mace and shield because they seemed less technical, but the shield would just get destroyed in sparring with Mia. She was trying to go light on him, otherwise a single stroke from her would probably snap his sword and cleave him in two at the same time.

"Look at this data," Zein said, turning the clipboard to Ven. There were various neatly assorted notes all over the sheet of paper, but Zein tapped his fingers against a table he'd drawn up. "I've been recording the time it takes for your wounds to heal, and it appears to be fairly similar in each instance, regardless of depth and severity."

Ven noted the times recorded and nodded. "Yes, but then there would be an issue with tracking the exact instant the wound was inflicted and the exact time it closed. There's a difference regarding depth, severity, and location of the wound. We've been sparring, so we haven't been able to measure those specifically."

Zein nodded. "My thoughts exactly." He met Ven's eyes.

"Ah," Ven said. His shoulders slumped a second later. "Is this... necessary?"

"If we want to confirm effectiveness, yes. It's already clear that your body responds to the imperviousness differently than all the other subjects—myself included."

Ven sighed. "Alright. This will be fine. It's better to know what's going on."

"Excuse me, but what are you referring to?" Mia asked.

"Oh, well if we want to know how my body is responding to various traumas, we'd need to test against certain independent variables. While sparring, my injuries are randomized, so precise timing isn't possible, but if we deliberately give me a cut in a particular location and depth and start the timer at that exact moment, we'll have a better idea of how effective my adaptations are."

"I see." Mia folded her arms. "So you will undergo tests like I did."

"Not quite so extensive," Zein said. "It would be wise to understand how his adaptation functions."

The next couple hours were solely devoted to discovering how Ven's body recovered from cuts. Zein would make an incision on Ven's arm and record the time it took for the wound to seal. The first cut took three minutes and eight seconds to heal.

Zein cut a different spot, up on Ven's shoulder. Time to heal was another three minutes and eight seconds. He then sampled with Ven's leg and got the exact same time. He then experimented with different severities, sometimes cutting deeper and longer. Ven gritted his teeth through the whole process. With all his blood loss, he was sure to need some massive amounts of food.

Mia had already gone off to eat, leaving Ven to the experimentations.

"It's strange," Zein said, tapping the clipboard. "I would have expected some kind of adjustment by now."

"On the topic of controllable factors, perhaps you could try cutting the same location," Ven suggested. He sure appreciated the ability to heal quickly, but he'd been hoping to show signs of adaptation. His body was not growing more resilient.

Zein grunted and pulled out his blade again, placing it against one of Ven's sealed cuts. He sliced and tracked the time. Ven waited, surprised by how quickly it closed up. *I'm getting accustomed to the pain.* Strange. It still made him sweat, but he could even watch the cut happen without flinching.

When the flesh sealed shut he wrote down the time. Three minutes and six seconds.

"I recommend we try this same spot again, but also do another fresh spot to ensure it's not universal," Zein said.

They spent a few more minutes working on it until they found a couple consistencies. They explained it to Mia when she came back after eating.

"Wait," Mia said, holding up a hand, "so you adapt more slowly than I would, but it also only adapts in areas where you've received the damage?"

Ven folded his arms as the disappointment simmered. "Yes. So if I get stabbed in the gut, my entire body doesn't adapt to getting stabbed, only my gut adapts. We also tried this with a glass knife, and my body reacted as though it had never experienced any adaptation, so it's specific to the material that causes the damage as well."

"It appears only the specific cells that are affected are the ones that adapt," Zein explained. "And they only adapt to the specific type of thing that inflicted the damage. I'm not sure why it is having this effect. I suppose the blood's age could have been a factor since it was simply sealed up this whole time. Also, Ven being from a different world might have some impact on the effectiveness."

"Alright, so I'm not as impervious, but I still adapt, it just takes way longer. Neat. At least I heal, so if..." Ven trailed off, subconsciously running a finger along his throat, remembering the distinct texture it had taken on after being crushed. Trying to fill his lungs had only resulted in creating a painful tightness.

"Which is admittedly the most significant feature anyway," Zein said, pulling Ven back to the present.

He blinked at Zein. "True. I won't have to worry about cancer."

"It would be terrible to build up your resilience," Mia said. "Think about it. If you wanted to be resistant to someone slitting your throat or stabbing you in the back, you'd literally have to survive that exact experience first." She visibly shivered.

"I would prefer *not* to think about it, actually," Ven said. Nevertheless, he did. There was no way he was about to go through such extensive training. Also, his body's ability to adapt to things seemed like very gradual progress, whereas the previous subjects all appeared to adapt much faster. That didn't make it very appealing to build up his resilience intentionally. Not unless he was planning on running at the front of an army, but that was most definitely not on his agenda. And yet, he'd been spending most of his time training for combat. Perhaps fighting was inevitable.

"I must see to some reports," Zein said. "Tem has every resource out there trying to locate Dayelle and Rowan. They are the real threat. I'm sure my brother has some of his own contacts out there trying to locate them, but he is not known for his information network. I hesitate to say it, but this might be the kind of thing we'd want to use private resources for investigating."

"What do you mean by private resources?" Ven asked.

Zein folded his arms. "You let me worry about that. I need you to see if we can get Siwen involved once Rowan is located. If she can control Mia, she can control all three of us, which means that she controls the most powerful weapons on Orund, second only to the dragons themselves. Is Siwen joining the march tomorrow?"

Ven shook his head. "I don't know. Would that not be expected?"

"Typically, he would," Zein said. "It is likely that he will march with the army, but it's your job to remind him that it will be more important for him to aid in the hunt of the dragons. He would need to find a good reason to remain in Peskan. There are several excuses he could propose, but that will need to be up to him."

Ah. That made sense. "Understood. Do we have any other means of killing a dragon? None of us would be able to fight them so long as Rowan is alive."

"As I said before, I will look into other resources."

Mia gave Ven a shrug.

"Alright," Ven said. "I guess I'll go have a chat with Siwen."

As Ven jogged back to the castle, he wondered how the adaptive trait would start to affect things like his endurance and strength. Perhaps it would be like working out but more effective? The more he pondered about his new characteristics, the more he worried he'd end up fighting. That was not his inclination. If it came down to a war, he'd rather leave Shiansan than fight. He couldn't imagine that Mia would want to go join them in battle either, but... then again, she'd fought to defend the people of Mavenda. Would he have done the same?

He was glad he hadn't been there to see the horrors, but he still hated to think of all those who had died. Or worse, those who had been turned into Dayelle's thralls. He wanted to be angry with her, but instead he was just sad.

His friends. Were all. Dead.

And he wasn't even sure what to consider Siwen, Mia, and Zein. Comrades perhaps? His feelings toward Mia were muted. She'd been a star amidst darkness. He'd thought it was his *cause* to save her, but she didn't need saving. She just needed space.

And me? What do I need?

For once in his life, he didn't know, and that was more frustrating than anything. At least they could be unified on one thing. As much as he hated to admit it, Rowan needed to die. Dayelle probably did as well. Killing a practically extinct species wasn't something he was very keen on, but he couldn't deny that they both seemed sadistic and manipulative. Were they evil? Perhaps. They'd committed atrocities, but he also knew that their trauma was a significant factor. He could only imagine the crazy lives they must have lived after their entire society had nearly been eradicated. If Mia had psychological damage from being raised in the facility, what kind of mental health issues would Rowan be suffering from after hundreds of years of imprisonment and torture?

His natural inclination told him that freedom was the right thing, but not if Rowan was going to enslave humans and force them to kill each other in turn.

When he reached the castle, he slowed back to a walk and nodded to the two guards posted at the gate. They were familiar with him by now. All the soldiers stood straighter than they had a few days ago. War had them all on edge.

Yubo Huan was in the courtyard addressing a group of officers. Ven navigated along the edge of the wall, keeping as much distance from Siwen's father as he could. He'd managed to avoid any interaction with the man since he'd arrived and would hopefully keep it that way. Siwen had explicitly said that if anybody were to recognize Ven from the whole scuffle the last time they came, it would be Yubo.

Siwen was also in the courtyard, though he stood at the entrance to the castle keep, his new wife at his side with her hand on his arm. He had a sword belted on either side of his waist. Defeating the dragons rested on that man's shoulders.

Ven climbed partway up the wooden staircase that led to the second floor where his room was, but he leaned out over the railing, hoping to catch Siwen's eye. Siwen nodded up at him but remained in place as he listened to Yubo's instructions. He was mostly briefing them on logistics. They'd already assembled most of their resources for the march south, but a contingent of riders was supposed to leave within the next few minutes.

The thought that the war declaration was a consequence of Yubo's own actions made Ven shake his head. How the Gogobans knew about Yubo harboring the dragon was another mystery entirely.

Yubo finished his address, and the officers hurried off. Siwen and his father shared a few words before Yubo entered the castle. A few servants rushed out and started loading things into a wagon, and there were a few other horses that were brought out from the stable, Siwen's Zebadon among them. Siwen and Morgan approached Ven's position together.

Ven went back to the bottom of the stairs to meet them.

Siwen cleared his throat before speaking. "Ven, you could probably come with us to the south. I've watched you spar with some of the other soldiers here. I think you could be a useful asset against the invasion force."

"I can't go, Siwen—and neither can you."

"What do you mean?"

"You will be needed for" —Ven paused to glance at Morgan— "a different threat."

Siwen lowered his voice. "You may speak freely. I trust Lady Lauron with my life."

That caught Ven by surprise. He eyed Morgan again. He knew virtually nothing about her on a personal level, but he knew Siwen would want complete confidence in her. He'd married her after all.

"Very well," Ven said. "We are trying to locate the dragons. If we find them, we'll need to make it a top priority to kill them. Otherwise, there are three impervious people who could be controlled to essentially take over the world against their wills. Somebody armed with a dragonsbane sword would be paramount."

Siwen's lips thinned before he replied. "I understand the gravity there, Ven, but I am an officer. I cannot sit idly by awaiting news of the dragons' discovery while my comrades get slaughtered on the front lines. My place is with them."

Ven's mouth dropped open. "What? Then what are we supposed to do if we find them?"

Siwen's jaw hardened. "I don't know. That relative of mine probably has some scheme in mind, but it can't be me. Not while we are at war."

"Siwen!" Yubo shouted from across the courtyard. He nodded to Siwen before mounting his horse.

"It's time," Siwen said. "If the chance arises, I will assist. Do not think that me fulfilling my duty means that I do not understand the gravity of the dragons' return. I understand their threat, but right now, my nation is under attack, and even if the other lords and ladies don't know it, I know that my own family is at least partially responsible for this invasion. I would be a fool not to try and make things right."

Morgan squeezed Siwen's hand, and he nodded back to her.

"Ven, Carina knows how to get in touch with me if you must send communication, but I am going. The campaign could potentially take a full year, but hopefully we can push the Gogobans back with a firm strike and I can return much sooner." Siwen hugged Morgan before rushing off to his horse as the procession started on its way out.

Ven remained in his place, dumbfounded. Morgan stood where Siwen had left her. Her hands were clenched into fists for a brief moment before relaxing. They watched as the thanes of Peskan departed the castle. An ominous sensation of dread sank into Ven's stomach once Siwen was out of view.

As the courtyard fell into silence, Morgan looked over her shoulder at Ven, her voice calm and steady as she said, "Tell me what you know of these dragons."

Chapter Twenty-One

Will

Mia

Mia watched from a hill outside the city walls as troops marched out the western gate. There were hundreds of soldiers. They'd left later in the day than they probably planned. Wagons of inventory were hauled behind them. She could only imagine the complexity of keeping so many people supplied.

A group of heavily armed horsemen had departed much earlier in the day, many wielding lances. She wondered what the battle would look like. The tactics used in war had to be complex. The different weapons everyone wielded had to play some kind of role in gaining various advantages. Perhaps the structure wasn't so easy to coordinate and the battlefield would just be pure chaos.

Mia rose to her feet as the last of the soldiers disappeared from view. The sun was already getting low, and she guessed they'd only get to march for another hour or two before stopping, but at least they'd be that much closer to reaching the southern border.

She took her time in the stillness of evening to practice some of the breathing Ven had taught her. There was a light breeze that carried so many earthy scents. A couple trees on the side of the hill were bursting with blossoms, bees buzzing between them. Her eyes closed as she filled her lungs, letting calmness wash over her like a warm blanket. She remained like that for a long moment, breathing, smelling, feeling, listening. It was beautiful.

But the calm worried her. There was a war going on. People were in turmoil. The citizens of Mavenda were all either dead or forced into mindless conscription for the dragons. It was because she'd wanted to hide. She'd wanted peace. But after delivering so much destruction, maybe peace wasn't a real option.

The calm sensation cracked as a *presence* pressed down on her.

No. No, no, no.

Her muscles went taut. She'd been so calm. So in *control*. But that control was gone in an instant. Her eyes snapped open. The evening light was fading, leaving the sky with a light purple hue as night approached. It was the return of darkness.

Somewhere nearby, hiding in shadows, was Rowan. The dragons had found her. Mia tried to do as Ven instructed her, clawing for the peace in desperation, but her breathing came in pants. Deep down, she'd known his instructions wouldn't work. Pain had been her only way out before. If she was forced to attack Ven again, this time she would probably be forced to ensure that it was more thorough to guarantee he died.

Mia's will to fight dissipated as the dragon's control clenched over her like a constricting blanket. She was a shell of a human, caught within the confines of her own flesh, forced to witness but not command. This was her penance. Perhaps she never should have survived as a child. Whatever disease had afflicted her was supposed to kill her. She was a product of humanity's folly and could very well prove their ultimate demise. At least there was some semblance of peace in knowing that whatever happened now was beyond her. If she was forced to destroy, then so be it.

She was pulled away, quickening to a sprint that drew her farther away from the city. The direction brought her hope that she wouldn't be forced to try and kill Ven again. Perhaps the disguise they'd had him wearing since the assassination attempt had been effective enough to make Rowan believe that Mia had been successful.

Mia reached a thicket and slowed to a halt, frozen in place as Rowan emerged in human form, though her eyes lingered on the city of Peskan. The red in Rowan's eyes sparked as though alive with flames as her brows knitted together. They remained like this in silence for a moment before Rowan finally shifted her gaze to Mia.

"I must apologize for my delay in coming to reclaim you. I felt your pain after you killed your friend. This is good. The pain is binding. It is resolute. Life lost can no longer be reclaimed and thus cannot bind you." Rowan tilted her head at Mia. "The pain has broken you, as it should have. If I hadn't been needed elsewhere, I would have remained close so that our bond wouldn't have shaken, but I want you to understand that from now on, you are mine. It is my blood that flows inside of you and keeps you alive. It is *my* blood and my will that commands you." She seemed a lot calmer than the last time Mia had seen her. Before, she'd been like an animal trapped in the body of a human, but now she was more in control, despite the fury that simmered within her eyes.

Mia could not speak. She could not move. She was nothing more than a vessel. Her one consolation was that she could at least believe that Rowan thought Ven was dead. There wasn't any reason for Rowan to converse with Mia like this since she had no ability to respond. Perhaps the dragon just enjoyed talking.

It was like she just wanted to convince Mia that her efforts to resist were meaningless, which was an unnecessary means of persuasion, as Mia was very aware of the fact. And yet, Rowan still tried.

"Dayelle's vision for you is yet to be fulfilled," Rowan said. "There is much work yet to do and the hour is at hand. I hope you didn't think you were done." When Rowan smiled, her sharp teeth glinted in the fading light. She always seemed like she was on the verge of tearing out of her human flesh into the monster that hid beneath.

Mia was not very different.

Without saying more, Mia took off at a sprint, knowing full well that she was about to commit more atrocities. At least she could settle with the knowledge that it was beyond her own choice.

Chapter Twenty-Two

Purpose

Ven Yashke

The trembling in Ven's body finally went away. Breath came in a heaving gasp, his muscles unclenching as the pressure released. He wiped the sweat beading on his face and collected his thoughts. That strain on his brain felt akin to compulsion—the absolute need to do something beyond his control. Instinctively, he knew what was happening. He'd felt his own bodily commands fighting against him, but he'd made it halfway down the hall away from his room even while the sensation persisted. He could resist. Potentially this was because Rowan wasn't trying to pull at him. She likely didn't know he'd received the operation. Perhaps she was pulling on somebody else.

Mia.

He burst into a full sprint out of the building and down the stairs. The last light of day flickered on the horizon as he ran out of the castle grounds, ignoring the question from the guard about what was wrong. How would he even be able to explain? Buildings and people passed in a blur. As he hurried through the streets, he forced back the worry building in his chest. He knew he should have been more discreet to keep his identity and destination better concealed, but none of that would matter much anyway if things were as bad as he suspected.

The final street he turned down was mostly empty save for a few other people. He reached the safehouse Mia had been bunked up in and knocked on the door. No answer came after a few seconds, so he tried the handle. It was unlocked. He pushed his way inside.

"Mia," he called. Fear pounded through him as his breathing intensified. Despite his run here, his skin felt cold. There was the very real possibility that she *was* here and that she would kill him. He pushed through the chilling thoughts and checked each room without finding her. Even the enclosed portion outside was empty.

The front door opened and Ven quietly hid behind a wall and froze, listening.

"Mia, Ven? Is that you?"

Recognizing the voice, Ven released his breath and emerged. Zein stood in the doorway, features barely visible.

Ven swallowed. "You felt it, too?"

"I did," Zein said. "It was a very strong compulsion."

"Yes. I remember how Mia described it, like my own muscles refused to obey. I caught onto it quickly though and was able to take a few steps without following through until it finally went away." Ven glanced around him. "I take it you haven't seen Mia, though?"

"I have not. And it appears we both had the same idea about Mia."

Ven could only nod. They both knew what had happened. "I don't understand. Why would she react differently?"

"That is the right question to ask, though we do not know the factors at play here. The dragons may not know we are here, and they likely don't even know you have undergone the operation."

Ven didn't even want to bother considering the implications at present. His real urge was to search the whole city. Perhaps Mia didn't get pulled along and was simply hiding somewhere, trying to resist the dragon's command.

"Is there anywhere else Mia might have gone?" Zein asked.

"I don't think so, no." Ven cursed himself. He should have been here with her. He'd taken to sharing dinner with her here in the drab home. Despite whatever conflicted feelings he had, it wasn't right to have her cooped up on her own.

"The dragon must have seized her again," Zein said. "When you see her next, it may not be under peaceful terms, Ven. We need to exercise caution and continue our search for the dragons."

Ven's hands clenched into fists. "We need to find them immediately." Perhaps the only way Mia would be free was if Rowan was dead. "You said you have resources that are searching."

"I do. We will find them in time."

"What about Sitena Rosars? Doesn't she have quite the stockpile of dragonsbane equipment? We could reach out to her about assisting us in the hunt."

"Absolutely not," Zein said. "She'd be just as likely to turn on us or attempt to utilize us for our own gain."

"But wouldn't she be willing to help locate and destroy them? We could use the resources."

"Ven, if my own family kept a dragon enslaved in the castle for generations, then someone like Sitena would do much worse. I do have other resources though."

Ven nodded. He too wasn't entirely keen on having to work with Sitena again, but he hoped Zein's other resources were reliable. He also had no desire to sit around. Though he had no loyalty to one nation or another, he felt the need to be involved somehow. Shiansan had broken some moral code shared by these other nations, but was that ground for declaring war? And Siwen had taken Ven in. He was probably the closest thing Ven had to a friend right now.

"I should try to locate the dragons," Ven said. "I can't be stuck here just waiting. If I find the dragons, then we can move against them."

"There is no quick resolution when it comes to war," Zein said. "Do as you wish, but I would at least like to supply you with a communication device so we can talk in case I have updates. I have identified the manor in which I was held prisoner and who the owner is. This might lead to finding some holdings maintained by the dragons in case there is some kind of headquarters. If they are amassing an army as Mia suggested, then they shouldn't be too difficult to locate, especially if that army is actively conquering cities."

"Any estimate on the number of days it would take to find them?"

"With any luck, maybe four or five days. Without any luck, upwards of a couple months, possibly longer. The dragons have been experts at hiding for a very long time."

Ven tried blinking away the weariness from his eyes. He couldn't wait until he was not as susceptible to fatigue. "And how far away is the southern border of Shiansan?"

"Eight to ten days on horseback."

Ven rubbed his lower lip. "And what if I were to investigate things to the east? I know the town the dragons raided. Perhaps I could find their trail."

Zein raised his eyebrow just slightly at that. "I suppose you could."

"Do you have anybody else planted in the army in case you need to deliver a message to Siwen?"

"I am not without connections there."

Man. Ven was still staggered by the idea that everyone seemed to have such networks established. "Alright, so if we need him to join us, then I can get a message relayed through you."

"Indeed." Zein folded his arms.

"Then it's decided," Ven said. "I will head east to find the dragons." If killing the dragons was the only way to free Mia from their control, then that's what Ven would do. Though in order to make that happen, he'd need a dragonsbane weapon and a pair of very sturdy metal gauntlets.

"If that's what you desire."

"It is. And I will leave tomorrow morning."

"Very well," Zein said, pulling something out from within his cloak. "Then take this. It will stick to the inside of your ear. It has a button that allows you to turn it off and on." He handed Ven a small, pale, fleshy looking device that appeared to have been shaded to Ven's exact skin tone already. "We can communicate through there."

"You've prepared for this," Ven muttered as he affixed the device to the inside of his ear.

"You train while I spend my time deliberating options," Zein said. Even in the darkened light, Ven could see Zein's eyes soften. "Take care of yourself. I recommend at least doing little things to build up that imperviousness whenever you have time."

Ven nodded. "I will do that. Thank you, Zein."

Zein said nothing else, but they departed out into the night. With any luck, Ven would find a way to get his hands on another dragonsbane weapon. His *gauntleted* hands, anyway.

Chapter Twenty-Three

Subterfuge

Mia

Mia slunk through the night. It had been two days since Rowan had taken control over her again, and she'd been sprinting for most of it. Her speed was unfathomably fast. Whatever she'd thought about her limitations, she was wrong. The adaptations continued beyond comprehension. That, or Rowan somehow knew how to make her even more effective than she believed herself to be.

Either way, here she was in some new city. She'd caught sight of a banner labeling this place as Red Bridge. She could have sworn she'd heard Ven mention this city before, perhaps as the place he'd studied to become a doctor, but none of his actual studies even took place on Orund. It took conscious effort not to be so invested in whatever scheme the dragons had her involved in. She yearned for disassociation.

If this was the destination, then things were not going to be getting better any time soon. The horrors were just about to start.

The dragons were certainly plotting something interesting with this move. Mia had stopped somewhere late yesterday to find a cache of gear stowed away near a roadside inn. She changed into new clothes, donned a sword, and even brushed her hair, which had gotten absolutely wild with all the running. The clothing bore some kind of emblem she'd seen in Peskan, but she was unsure what it meant. It was a uniform, like those she'd seen some of the soldiers wear.

Red Bridge was a bright city even though it was night. Every corner of the main road was lit with a lantern, though the flames inside always flickered with peculiar regularity. If she had to guess, they were fueled by dragonblood technology and the flames were intended to appear natural, but it would take close observation to confirm.

The streets were not as bare as she would have expected. Instead, many young people milled about and several shops and eateries bustled with activity. Perhaps tonight was some kind of celebration, but even in the snippets of conversation she overheard, it was unclear if this was a unique event.

Mia's face was uncovered. Usually, that alone would be enough to catch everyone's attention, but the uniform she wore made her stand out even more. Rowan was doing this on purpose. To her surprise, nobody tried stopping her or speaking to her at all. For the most part, they steered clear. She would normally expect someone to attempt speaking to her, particularly the men, but all she got were stares. It made her wonder if there was something about her that was particularly frightening.

After making it down a couple streets, she found the rest of the city to have the kind of night life she was more accustomed to. There were fewer lights and practically nobody outside. Her pace quickened as she headed toward a tall building ringed by a high wall. It didn't seem like a castle, but more of a large house. She rounded the perimeter for a moment until she paused at one location and started climbing straight up the wall.

Mia had to wonder what level of control Rowan had to invest in order to get Mia's body to perform such particular tasks. Did she need to focus on every detail? Did she simply give a command and Mia's body did its best to perform the task? Whatever the case, the meticulousness was remarkable.

Mia's strength made gripping the stones seem easy, even though her boots didn't help much. She lost hold with one hand as the stone broke away beneath her fingers, but her other hand held firm. She just had to find a new spot to grab and resume climbing.

Normally, this level of activity would have been exciting, but nothing good would come of this, and Mia wasn't in charge. The grounds were so small that the wall was immediately adjacent to the house, and even better was that she was close to an alcove with a door that led straight inside. Easy. Mia snuck to the door and hurried to a set of stairs where a guard gasped in surprise to see her approaching.

"Who are—" The guard never finished his sentence.

Mia slipped her sword out and straight through the man's neck in a single motion. She took the torch from the wall and snuffed it out. She was at the bottom of the stairs a second later. The inner courtyard was miniscule, without even enough room to accommodate a carriage. Rowan didn't bother having Mia scour the space for others. Instead she went right up to the front double doors and pushed one open where the interior was mostly dark. A single lamp burned beside the entryway while another one burned farther in the distance.

Mia eased the door shut and continued onward, steps light. By the way Rowan had Mia proceed, this part of the mission was a stealth operation. She went up a flight of stairs to the second floor and snuck down a long hallway. More lamplight flickered in the distance, some coming from the hallway and some outlining a door. A man stood outside the room, arms behind his back, while voices from inside the room rose and fell as though the occupants were in heated debate.

The person standing outside didn't even see Mia coming before she clapped a hand over his mouth. Her hearing was sharply attuned well enough that she knew the exact location of his heart before she stabbed him through it. She twisted the sword and pulled it out as the man dropped. The arguments inside the room continued, and Mia waited outside, ear close to the crack.

"I cannot endorse a declaration of war," a woman's voice said. "Not over a single letter."

"It's not just a letter, Zatla," a man said. "Even the Gogobans have declared war."

"What, for creating dragonblood technology?" Zatla said. "Yector, *we* use dragonblood technology every day! We could very well assist the Gogobans only to have them turn on us when the war is over."

"It's not just dragonblood technology, they were harboring a dragon. If this is true, then it is unacceptable."

"It is a heavy accusation that would require firm evidence. Do you really believe Shiansan could hide a dragon for so many years?"

"It's a stretch of course, but not impossible. You and I both know that the stream of dragonblood, though expensive, was oddly unending. Dragonblood only comes from one source, Zatla. There's no denying that."

"Even still, we would need proof."

The man scoffed. "Zatla, did you even read the letter? They will kill you! They will kill us all while we twiddle our thumbs. We are on the border. If things escalate, where do you think they will strike first? Here!"

"She's not saying we sit idle," said another man's voice. "She's saying we shouldn't encourage an outright declaration of war. I will still deliver a message to Queen Sophie requesting military aid, but merely as a precautionary measure."

Mia shoved right through the door, not even bothering to open it. Perhaps hearing that third man's voice was the confirmation Rowan was waiting for. Inside was a lounge room with five occupants. Nobody was lounging as Mia charged in. The person nearest the door only got a dagger halfway raised before Mia completely severed his arm and stabbed him through the chest.

Everyone screamed. Rowan's subtlety was discarded. One other person, a large woman with thick shoulders wielding a long, curved blade, moved to intercept Mia.

"Let us discuss this!" said one man as he positioned himself behind a couch. He was the one who'd mentioned delivering a message to the queen. The woman, Zatla, was unarmed, though she picked up a metal candlestick and watched with widened eyes.

The large woman swung at Mia, but she shot forward so fast that the woman couldn't react quickly enough. Mia grabbed her hand and squeezed, crushing the bones, then stabbed her in the heart. The three remaining people all had their mouths gaping.

"Please, whatever you want," Yector said. He had a thick mustache and equally thick eyebrows. His eyes caught sight of the uniform on Mia's body. "Ah, we—we have not declared war!"

Mia did not answer. She had no doubt that with the precision Rowan had over her body, she could force Mia to talk, but she didn't. Instead, Mia prowled toward Yector, head tilted slightly. She had no idea who these people were, but the terror in their eyes made her want to retreat. She could not unsee. She could not unhear. And when she lunged for Yector, sword slashing, she could not unfeel the blood that sprayed across her arm.

Zatla threw the candlestick, which bounced harmlessly off Mia's shoulder. The unnamed man tried shoving the couch at her as she spun toward Zatla. Mia rolled across the couch, shoving a foot into the man's chest that sent him tumbling across the room. She jabbed her sword at Zatla, piercing the woman in the shoulder. Zatla screamed and staggered back but was unable to avoid the next stab that took her through the heart.

That seemed to be a favorite stroke from Rowan, always aiming for the hearts. The ease with which Rowan controlled Mia was remarkable, and the way she was able to move Mia's body with clean precision suggested that the dragon had unquestionable expertise.

Mia turned and faced the man she'd sent sprawling. He sat on the floor. She'd kicked him hard, and he cradled an arm.

"I am a messenger," the man said. "Tell me what you want, and I will deliver it."

His clothing suggested the man was more than just a messenger, but Rowan did not have her question him. She raised her sword and pressed it down against the man's chest. His face twitched with pain, but he lay down flat on the floor, eyes bouncing between her and the tip of the sword.

When words came from Mia's throat, they were surprisingly calm. "Tell your queen that she can send her soldiers, but even when worms fight against birds, all they do is fuel the beast." Mia withdrew her sword. A small dot of blood colored the man's shirt.

The man scowled up at her, but Mia turned and ran back out into the night.

Chapter Twenty-Four

Blessed

Ven Yashke

Ven was halfway into the second day on the road when he started suspecting he was being followed. The roads at this time were a lot busier than the first time he'd headed east out of Peskan. There were several wagons going either direction. From what he could gather, wartime was encouraging a lot of hasty trade between Luedan and Shiansan. He was certain that Siwen's recent marriage had only strengthened the ties between the two nations.

Butch handled the traffic exceptionally and enjoyed being back on the trail, so they'd kept a good pace. Being on his own, Ven found that he was more observant than usual. He watched the people he passed, and he looked behind a lot more frequently, which is how he identified the same two horses on the trail behind him for an extended amount of time.

Today, he would confront them.

Ven spurred Butch into a light gallop as they went around a bend in the path with several trees on either side of the road. Once certain he was out of view, he steered Butch into the trees, weaving carefully through them and going far enough in to keep Butch hidden from the road before stopping. He dismounted and tied Butch to a tree. The horse happily started munching on the nearby vegetation while Ven ran back toward the road.

When he got back to the road, he crouched down behind a couple bushes near the edge, and waited. He only had to wait a couple minutes before a pair of horses rode by.

The voices of the riders were hushed as they spoke to each other, quiet enough that he couldn't pick out the words. He peeked out from behind his cover just as they rode past. They were two women, and, much to his surprise, he recognized one of them. He came out of his cover, startling the nearest woman, though her reaction was to draw her sword. She expertly maneuvered her horse to face him.

"Lady Morgan," Ven said. He folded his arms. "You've been following me."

Morgan resheathed her sword with a sigh. The other woman also had her weapon drawn but kept hers out.

"Indeed, I have," Morgan said.

They stared at each other for a moment as Ven considered what could have possibly persuaded the newly married lady to leave the city and follow *him*, of all people. "I'm slightly confused."

Morgan's lips drew to a thin line before she spoke. "My husband said to keep an eye on you."

Ven looked at their surroundings. "And that somehow included following me far outside the city?"

Morgan tilted her chin up. "My husband has fellow nobility and trusted officers to associate with, and yet the one person he told me to watch after you. All he said about you was that you are a doctor. Yet, when I see you, I see a man built like a giant with no association or allegiance to anyone, and I believe you are doing something important. Perhaps you might enlighten me as to why I'm inclined to believe you are no mere doctor and that you perhaps have some special assignment, even though you are not one of my lord's subjects."

Ven looked her up and down then glanced at her attendant who wore a very short dress with padded trousers underneath and a leather vest. She had a shield strapped to her back and a sword hanging at her waist, and he had no doubt she was probably more expert with the blade than he was.

"We're friends who share similar objectives," Ven said.

Siwen had said that he trusted Morgan, and she was admittedly sharp. "Which is why I'm coming to assist you."

"But you don't even know what I'm doing."

"Are you so sure about that?" Morgan's eyebrow rose as her lips curved into a smile. "You're after the dragons. From what I gather, you have a very short list of allies. Valerie and I can be useful assets in this endeavor. We will accompany you."

Ven glanced between them, contemplating the concept of traveling with the two of them. They were far from inconspicuous. Morgan had all the looks of a prim lady while Valerie struck quite an imposing figure. With that thought, he looked down at himself, realizing that he too was quite a difficult person to miss. Morgan had called him a giant. He'd always been tall, but had he really gotten much thicker in the last few days? "I'm still not sure this is a good idea. When Siwen said to keep an eye on me, I doubt that meant running around trying to find the most dangerous creatures on the planet."

Morgan shrugged. "He did leave much up to interpretation."

"Indeed."

"Besides, I don't believe you'd be able to keep us from accompanying you anyway. You may as well accept your fate and share what you know so that we can be of further use."

"I could just sneak away at night," Ven said.

Morgan smirked. "We'd find you. Valerie and I are excellent hunters, and your expertise clearly lies in helping people and not so much in hiding your tracks."

Ven sighed and looked at the ground. "Let me get my horse," he said after a moment. There really would be no getting out of it.

A few minutes later, they were back on the road, making a good pace. If the dragons had truly started amassing an army of people that they could control, how difficult would it be for them to relocate and keep such a force hidden? Though Zein was hesitant to reach out to certain people, Ven had no such hesitation, and now, having Lady Morgan Lauron with him would possibly open up a couple doors. He didn't need to be an excellent scout, he just needed to get information from those who *did* have excellent scouts.

"Is it true then, regarding my new father-in-law?" Morgan asked.

Ven rode at the front and looked over his shoulder to answer. "What do you mean?"

"About the dragons and the accusations."

Ven breathed a laugh. "Yes, unfortunately. I wouldn't be surprised if the war declaration is completely due to his involvement. The dragon he held captive is the one we're hunting."

"Ah," Morgan said. Ven looked back again to see that the two women were regarding each other and making hand gestures to keep information from him. The movements were subtle, but clear. "Siwen told me as much, but I wanted to know the extent of your own knowledge on the subject. I take it that killing this dragon will help free your friend."

"That's exactly right," Ven said, glad that he didn't have to explain that part. "In my opinion, it's even more important than the war going on. If the dragons attempt what we believe they will, then we are in for some very dire times." He didn't want to voice it, but in truth, if things became irreparable on Orund, he knew he at least had the backup of being able to flee back to Earth. Everyone else did not have that luxury. It made him wonder if it was possible for him to simply find Mia and take her back with him, but he had no idea if that would free her from Rowan's influence. In fact, since the dragons were able to get to Earth too, it would possibly set up another planet for domination as well. And from what he knew, dragonsbane was not a substance that existed on Earth, which meant it was practically defenseless against the beasts.

"In the event that you locate the dragons, what is your plan?"

Ven shook his head. "I don't think I'm equipped to handle them. It will simply give me an opportunity to notify the rest of the team that I have found them. The dragon slaying will be left to the professionals—your husband, ideally."

"But he is on the other side of the country," Morgan said.

"Yes," Ven said. "We'd still have to rally together of course, but at least we'd know where to strike. He would need some hard evidence to justify slipping away from the front lines of a war."

"And then you expect my husband to single-handedly kill a dragon?"

"I assume he'd have some assistance, of course, but that's the hope."

"Millions of people died overthrowing the dragons originally. You are aware of that, no?"

A chill went along Ven's entire back. "I... no, I did not know." There was a lot he still didn't know about dragons. Were they impervious like Mia? Better yet, after living for a thousand years, did that mean the dragons were considerably more impervious? Everything he knew about dragons came from some perceived mythological perspective he'd gained on Earth. It was entirely possible that they were not similar at all.

"They can't be underestimated," Morgan said.

"If they are so powerful, then what keeps them from revealing themselves?" Ven asked.

Valerie barked a laugh at that.

"If they did that, it would be a very simple means of uniting all of humanity against them," Morgan said. "My guess is that they are very few in number. You mentioned two, correct?"

"Yes, that's all we know of."

"And both are female?"

"Yes," Ven said, nodding to himself with understanding. "And one of them was a prisoner this whole time while the other one has been pulling strings behind the scenes."

"So we can safely assume that they will try to assert dominance while in human form. That can be advantageous for both us and them since dragons are supposed to be more susceptible when not in the form of a dragon, but there's unfortunately not a lot of information about their human forms."

"Could a normal weapon hurt them?" Ven asked.

"Possibly," Morgan said. "I'm not entirely sure."

Ven remembered the device stuck to the inside of his ear and reached in to touch the tiny button. "Zein," he said quietly, "can a normal weapon hurt a dragon in human form?"

A long moment passed in silence, leaving Ven to wonder if the device worked how he'd expected it. Perhaps it was like an audio message rather than a live feed. When Zein's voice finally came through, it startled him enough to cause him to jolt in his saddle.

"Possibly. It hasn't really been done, but in dragon form, other weapons can still harm them slightly, though it's similar to digging at a mountain with spears. Their skin is hard and thick enough in most places that it would be a struggle to cause any real harm. The primary advantage of dragonsbane is that it functions as a poison that kills the flesh and nerves so a blow to the back of the head, the neck, and upper back actually prove to be pretty effective at killing it. This is why we had a similar setup with the subjects to have poison injected there with the trigger release."

Ven's mouth hung open. He wondered why he'd never thought to ask this before. Did this mean he, Zein, and Mia were like dragons in human form? "Holy smokes…" He ran a hand through his hair as he tried to process his thoughts.

The road had been silent for the last few miles. A lot of the traffic had veered north once they'd reached the other side of the mountain. Ven checked his map just to get his brain focused on something else. To the north were most of the major cities of Luedan, as he'd surmised.

Distantly, the patter of horse hooves drew closer, though they pounded, suggesting that whoever approached was coming in fast.

Ven glanced over his shoulder at Morgan and Valerie, but they were looking around as well. The sound wasn't coming from the road. A second after Ven realized, several people emerged from the woods around them, including two people on horseback, one of whom went out in front, the other going directly behind Valerie and Morgan. They all had weapons drawn.

"Wait, wait, hold on," Ven said, lifting a hand up. "What is this—Are we getting robbed?"

"Right you are!" said the man on a horse in front of Ven. The man's smile revealed at least three missing teeth, and he wore one of those brimmed hats and a leather vest that made him look like he was some kind of ripoff cowboy, albeit a cowboy armed with a long, curved sword. "Make this simple. Dismount and throw down your weapons."

Ven looked around, estimating that there were at least a dozen people who'd surrounded them, and two of them had bows with arrows nocked. They could potentially attempt to ride away, but he already knew they wouldn't get out of something like that without getting skewered. He held back a curse and looked at Morgan. Her jaw was set and nostrils flared. When she met Ven's eyes, she shook her head.

"You should know better than to travel looking like that without proper guards," the man said, pointing the tip of his sword at Morgan. "My boys here can sniff out nobles like it's their job."

"It is our job, Alandir," said one of the soldiers on foot.

Alandir rolled his eyes. "Yes, that was part of the quip." He turned his attention back to Ven. "Anyway, go ahead and get down."

"Ven," Morgan hissed.

Ven looked back at her.

She held a weapon slightly away from her chest as though she were about to toss it down but said, "Dragonsbane."

Ven groaned. It was a long dagger, not too dissimilar from the one he'd used to kill Dami, though it was another few inches longer. The dragon-shaped crossguard was unmistakable.

That item alone was more valuable than everything else they had combined, and it was not something they could afford to part with. The fact that Morgan hadn't shared that she possessed such an item until now was vexing enough, but Ven forced the anger aside and focused it instead on their enemies.

He knew exactly why she'd told him now.

"Alright," Ven said, getting down from Butch's saddle. He had quickly grown accustomed to the feel of the mace at his waist. He'd opted for a longer one, which made it a little more difficult to maneuver with the extra weight, but he figured with a well-aimed, heavy blow, there'd be little that could stop him. He'd also felt quite a bit stronger over the last few days as he'd been trying to push himself to his limits. That warm feeling of an adaptation applying was becoming a familiar sensation.

And he was about to get a lot more of that.

A heavy sigh slipped between his lips as he pulled the mace off of his belt. A bow was aimed directly at him. The other thugs all stood at the ready, though one of them had his arms on his hips, a shortsword in one hand. He'd be the obvious target.

He couldn't believe what he was about to do, but he couldn't let them take the dragonsbane weapon. He held the weapon up as though he would drop it. Alandir gave him an expectant nod, but instead, Ven leapt toward the man with his hand on his hip. He swung a blow deftly aimed at the man's solar plexus. The man was too slow to dodge. Ribs crunched and the man fell without a scream.

An arrow slammed into Ven's back with enough force to push the air from his lungs. He moved into his next swing, smashing a man's arm even though the jagged dagger he thrust at Ven grazed the side of Ven's chest.

The pain was sharp and raw, but Ven was already pumped full of adrenaline as he spun and swung, putting force into every move-ment. He knew this was not the most elegant way to fight, but at the end of the day, Ven would be healed of whatever damage they dealt. His enemies would not be so fortunate.

Everyone sprang into action.

"Ah, kill them!" Alandir screamed in a voice that made Ven think of an overdramatic goblin, high pitched and garbled.

Another blade slashed across Ven's thigh right before he smashed the man's skull in. He focused on his objective, reminding himself that it was only pain. He still struggled to breathe, but he moved with ferocity.

Alandir spurred his horse forward, charging at Ven. He jumped away on his good leg and rolled into another bandit, dragging the man down with him. They grappled as another thug tried stabbing down at Ven with his dagger. Ven pushed with all his might, throwing the man he was grappling with into the path of the dagger just before it struck home. He rolled out and got back to his feet as another arrow narrowly dodged his neck.

Both Morgan and Valerie were still on their horses, weapons flashing. Perhaps he should have remained mounted as well, but he didn't want Butch to get hurt. A glint of metal had him flinching away as a thug jabbed at him with a short spear. Ven grabbed the haft and yanked, causing the wielder to stumble forward as Ven kicked up into the man's face. He spun to dodge another attack, but cold steel ripped across his back, right next to where the arrow still protruded from him.

The pain *invigorated* him. He leaned into it, taking whatever energy he could get. With one blow, he crushed a man's elbow, then swung at another target, bashing a robber's jaw out of its place, blood and spittle spraying from the man's mouth. He hurled the spear, skewering the archer who had just nocked another arrow. That arrow never flew.

As Alandir charged back toward him, Ven welcomed the man headon, sidestepping just enough to get to the side of the horse. Then he smacked the slashing sword away and grabbed Alandir's leather vest, yanking the man right off the top of the horse. Alandir smashed into the ground with a grunt, eyes wide as he stared up at Ven.

Another thug rushed to Alandir's aid before Ven could pummel him. A blade slid across Ven's forehead and over his eyebrow, spilling blood across his vision. Ven roared and punched the new attacker directly in the throat before bashing his thigh with the mace. The man crumpled.

Alandir was on his feet, sword slashing at Ven in quick, desperate strokes.

Ven stepped back, assessing the situation. Alandir's sword was long, and his strokes were practiced. He was possibly a former soldier with proper training. Ven could heal from most things, but he had no desire to get carved. Also, if he lost a limb or got stabbed in the eye, he wasn't sure the imperviousness would allow him to regrow a limb or organ.

Another arrow took Ven in the gut, embedding itself in his intestines.

He grunted and tried not to scream. This one hurt. He needed this to end. There was no way he'd die like this, killed by highway bandits. The dragons would ruin this entire planet if Ven didn't stop them. His limbs trembled as he stepped toward Alandir and batted at the man's sword. Alandir shifted his stroke and swung again, using quick motions. The blade slid by, not reaching its mark as Ven deftly shimmied forward at an angle. He brought his mace up, the end making contact with the bottom of Alandir's hand. The sword flew from Alandir's grip and the man screamed. He looked at Ven, eyes wide as he panted.

"What are you?" Alandir said in the same croaky voice.

One of the other bandits ran off into the woods, apparently not considering the wealth to be worth losing his life.

"Get out of here," Ven told the man. Truly, he deserved a jail cell, but Ven was not some kind of law enforcement officer, and the only justice he'd be able to serve was death. Wasn't that the same sentence Alandir had just declared upon the three of them?

But no, Ven was not the same kind of animal.

Morgan and Valerie didn't seem to have any problems from their end. They'd killed three other bandits and scared off another. Butch just stood there, eyeing Alandir as if he'd not just witnessed his rider get practically butchered. Ven would have made some kind of pun about that if he wasn't so focused on remaining alert without letting the pain of his injuries overwhelm him.

He could have sworn the whole fight had lasted less than two minutes. That energy that had surged through him was already dwindling, though.

Alandir held up his hands and ran away as Valerie steered toward him with her own roar. The bandit got back on his horse and spurred away, leaving his injured party members behind.

"What do we do with the rabble, my lady?" Valerie said.

Morgan didn't respond immediately. "Leave them," she said, eyes on Ven.

Ven looked down at his gut and gritted his teeth, arms trembling as he eased the arrow out, knowing that he should try to keep everything in its proper order. Even if his body healed, that didn't mean it would always heal in the right way. Unless the dragonblood imperviousness simply didn't work like that. Perhaps it healed to perfection and he was being needlessly careful.

Once the arrow was free, he tried to focus on his breathing, letting each exhale out slowly. Blood seeped from a dozen wounds, and he couldn't even see out of his right eye.

"Ven," Morgan said, her tone questioning.

"I'll be alright," Ven said, body still trembling from the pain. He'd hoped that what he'd endured on the operating table when undergoing the procedure would help build his pain tolerance. Perhaps it had, but certainly not enough. The chemicals in his body were dispersing.

One of the men he'd brutalized was trying to crawl away, but his left leg was an angled mess. He kept groaning about the pain.

A few other men were still. Unmoving.

He had done this.

Some of the blood on his arms was his. Most of it was not.

He'd been raised to be a doctor, and he'd sought to help people his whole life. This was something different entirely. Perhaps he should have felt some level of remorse. He knew all about the effects of trauma. Though he felt pity as he looked at the dead and broken, a different sensation filled him.

Pride. *He* had done this. He'd fought off at least six men all on his own. Morgan and Valerie were safe because he'd been able to fight. He smiled and let out a chuckle, shaking his head.

Morgan's worried expression deepened.

Ven cleared his throat and turned his shoulder to her. "Do you mind pulling that out?"

Instead of Morgan pulling out the arrow in Ven's back, Valerie rode over and tugged it out with a sharp jerk that tore off some of his skin anew. Ven took in a sharp, hissing breath and climbed back on Butch, who stood there still as a rock.

"It's alright, Butch," Ven said, patting Butch's side. The horse stamped and whinnied, but Ven was just glad Butch hadn't been injured.

"Ven, I—I don't know if you should be riding in that condition," Morgan said.

"I'll be fine," Ven said, and already there was a warm sensation washing over his body. He wasn't sure which wound was triggering the adaptive reaction, but he was grateful the process was starting. Ideally, he wouldn't receive many wounds at all in a fight. There was always the off chance that a blade could sever his spine or chop off a limb, but if he at least became slightly more impervious, then hopefully it would be worth it. He hadn't really been much of a video game player, but he imagined this was probably what it was like to level up.

"Let's just get to the next settlement," Ven said, urging Butch forward. He knew he'd need plenty of food and water to recover properly. Mia had a voracious appetite for a reason, and he could only imagine the ridiculous amount of calories his body consumed to heal wounds so rapidly.

Though the bouncing of Butch's trots did little to help the pain as Ven slowly healed, it at least provided some reassurance that he'd not only survived, but also that he was still progressing on their journey.

He didn't look back, but eventually the sounds of additional hooves following behind suggested that Morgan and Valerie had decided to go with him. One hand held his reins while the other remained pressed against his stomach. The warmth of the adaptation remained for several minutes, and he kept an eye on the gash along his arm as it proceeded to knit together, skin tingling as the cells moved to correct themselves.

Valerie pulled up beside him and brushed some of her dark hair back that had escaped her once-perfect bun, but a strand remained coiled by her eye. "That was brave, but we are concerned for your health."

"My wounds weren't that bad," Ven said. He rubbed a hand over his eyebrow, clearing some of the blood away so he could see better. That wound was already healing up as well. "Most of it is their blood, I assure you."

"We have eyes, Ven," Morgan said from behind. "You are blessed somehow, aren't you? Is this different from the condition that your friend has?"

"What do you know about that?" Ven asked, wondering how much Morgan knew about everything, and then how much Valerie was supposed to know. Siwen said he trusted his wife, but that didn't mean Valerie was included by default.

"Everything my husband knows," Morgan said.

"And Valerie?"

"She has my full confidence."

Ven glanced at the two of them before sighing. "It's similar. It was supposed to be the same, but it affects me a little differently."

"I see," Morgan said. "Do you share the same... concerns as she does?"

Ven assumed she was referring to the dragon's ability to control her. "I feel some of the effects, but it doesn't seem to impact me as much."

"And what of dragonsbane?" Morgan asked.

Ven took even longer to answer this question. "I assume it is the same. We have not tested that theory." He had a pair of metal gauntlets packed into the saddlebags in case he ever got his hands on a dragonsbane weapon. If it came down to it, he would not hesitate to strike at the dragons. To think that he had been so close to Dayelle on so many occasions, not knowing that she was using him for something. He was still unsure of her entire use for him. It was strange that she'd given him so much money, and he now had an even greater desire to get rid of it all just so he wasn't somehow indirectly under her influence. Maybe there really was some kind of tracking device hidden among the jewels and that was how Dayelle had known that Ven went to Mavenda.

Perhaps she was tracking him right this moment.

But he had to be paranoid. It was just like what he'd thought after deciding to return to Orund. It was only money—coins and gems.

"Alright then, blessed one," Valerie said. "Perhaps you might enlighten us as to the destination."

"Right," Ven said, pulling his thoughts back. "We're going to see an old... acquaintance of mine."

Chapter Twenty-Five

Flames of War

Siwen Huan

"Push the line!" Siwen bellowed. He shoved his shield forward, weapons and body parts bouncing off of it as he stepped into the movement. He slipped his sword through the gap in the side and felt his weapon rip across a man's arm. Roars and grunts vanished in the din of battle. They pushed forward again and Siwen had to step over a dead body to proceed. It was one of his own comrades—a man he'd known personally by the name of Yesper. He had three children—all boys. The youngest one had just turned three. Siwen would have to report back to Yesper's wife and mother to inform them that their husband, son, and father had fallen honorably in battle.

"They're retreating!" somebody shouted, the voice barely reaching Siwen's ears.

The Shiansan soldiers cheered and pushed harder, cutting down those who didn't run away fast enough. A wall of enemy archers stood not too far away, so Siwen called off the pursuit. They would get butchered if they took so much as another step forward. "Shields up! Fall back!"

Nobody questioned Siwen's order, and the other officers began repeating the command. They'd learned quickly. Those who didn't follow orders made the whole team suffer. This was hammered into them repeatedly at drills. Not only that, but not following orders also tended to lead to getting killed.

Their entire unit backed away. Siwen didn't turn until they were a safe distance, then their whole group fell back behind their ramshackle fortifications. They were at the edges of the region of Sal. The fort had been overrun in a single day, and the nearby town fell not too long after. Thankfully, most of the people had fled ahead of the invasion, but that left the entire region to fall under the foot of the Gogoban army.

The Shiansan camp had been thrown up in hasty preparations. The terrain here was choice farmland and of significant value to the entire nation. Many crops were already prime for harvest, and the Gogoban army had not held back in pillaging whatever they could. In truth, Shiansan leaders simply hadn't expected a war declaration, and thus the military presence had been minimal, focused entirely on policing rather than any actual combat.

Estimates placed the Gogoban army at a little shy of three thousand. There was only a single person who'd escaped Fort Sal during the initial invasion, Commander Elise Sherwood. She'd said they probably killed a little over a hundred of the invaders but that the fort itself had fallen within minutes. He'd hardly had any time to speak with her on that since they'd been thrown into battle within minutes of their arrival.

Siwen headed straight for the command tent, which had only been erected during the short battle. He looked down at the blood that now decorated his clothing. None of it was his. He'd been one of the lucky ones. He needed to stay lucky. They were outnumbered and unprepared for such an assault, and Siwen had only just been married. Morgan deserved more than this, and if he died here in battle, it would be his greatest failure. He needed more time with her.

The entire situation with Gogoba was entirely uncalled for. War was far too extreme a measure for something that should have started with diplomatic negotiations. Either the evidence posed against Shiansan had been undeniably convincing, indicating a direct threat against the safety of Gogoba so that war would have been the only reasonable conclusion, or the Gogoban nobility were seeking more lands for themselves.

Shouts from inside the tent indicated that he was about to step into a heated argument. The guard outside kept a stoic face as he nodded to him before Siwen entered.

"We can't flank them on the side with the cavalry—they have enough bowmen to pin each of us ten times over," Lord Tennisen was saying as Siwen joined the circle. Only one other nobleman in the tent was as battered as he was, and that was his father, Yubo, though this was visible merely as a bit of filth spattered across his lower body and speckled blood on his leather vambraces.

The Huan family didn't issue orders from the back line, they joined their forces in the fray.

Conversation stopped as eyes settled on Siwen.

"Siwen, you look like you bathed in the blood of our oppressors. How fares the front line?" It was spoken by Hesh Halimah, baroness of Nansha, one of the other larger provinces like Peskan. Siwen didn't fail to notice that she'd skipped using formalities.

Realizing his bloodied sword was still in hand, he sheathed it and folded his hands behind his back. "They have fallen back, thankfully. I believe they hoped to overtake us quickly, but in their haste, they were not set up to provide their front line with proper support, and they suffered heavy losses too quickly. They will likely rest for a moment before rallying and setting in on our camp. With their superior numbers, I believe they will attempt an assault this very evening, hoping that we do not receive additional reinforcements before then."

"Do we fall back?" Hesh said.

"And go where? Nobody is here to buy us any time," said Fennu Kye in his booming voice. He'd been the one doing most of the shouting, enough so that Siwen had to wonder if the man knew any other way to speak. His son and daughter stood to either side, both of them younger than Siwen.

"We wouldn't be in this predicament if you'd kept scouts ahead so we could establish a better-suited base of operation. Now we may very well die before the king even arrives," Yubo said, voice tempered in his calm anger.

"I was focused on getting my people to safety," Fennu said. "The fort was never supposed to fall so quickly." As lord of the Sal province, the safety of these lands was supposed to rest on his shoulders.

"We will have to make the best of this hill and hold out until the king arrives. We've brought enough supplies to last for a while," Yubo said.

Their location wasn't ideal. The hill they camped atop contained the remnants of an old tower, too decrepit for any official use. Though the walls provided meager cover on the northwest area of the hill, they provided little in the way of defensive operations. Regardless, there simply wouldn't be time to move and set up anywhere else. Not without heavy losses as the enemy army picked them off from behind, anyway.

Fennu rubbed a hand across his forehead, damp with sweat. He was a heavier set man, with already graying hairs streaking the sides of his otherwise black hair. "We should have positioned ourselves at my castle."

"That would have allowed the Gogobans to proceed through the rest of our lands, pillaging even more," Hesh said. "That would have meant handing over supplies that we will need in the next month. A successful invasion often depends on momentum. If we can halt them for long enough, then it will at least be a victory by attrition. The king's cavalry will open up a few new strategies as well."

"True," Yubo said. "I already have a scouting squad assessing the enemy supply and should have a report within a couple hours."

"Didn't that commander from Fort Sal say they have siege equipment?" asked Fennu's son, a young lad Siwen knew simply as Du.

"Yes," Siwen said, "but their army is trailing a bit. What we fought today was an advance force. To Lady Halimah's point, they've been riding on momentum for a while now. It would probably take the main force some time to catch up with them. We'll want to wait on my father's scouting squad to return to have a better estimate on timelines."

"So a flanking cavalry strike might not be advantageous then?" Hesh asked. Everyone in this tent knew that the Huans were the most dedicated military family present, so an opinion from one of them was not to be discounted lightly.

"It's not unreasonable," Siwen said. "It would be highly risky, but if it meant being able to disable some siege equipment at the rear of their formation, then it could prove significantly advantageous. We would need a highly accurate report before running any such mission though. I would not want to risk our forces getting caught back there."

Yubo nodded his agreement. "Let's get people fortifying our position in the meantime so we can survive until reinforcements arrive."

"I also have a militia force with another two hundred and fifty people who could be arriving within a day or two," Hesh said. "Fennu, you have some as well, don't you?"

"Another hundred or so," Fennu mumbled.

"That would put our numbers at what, thirteen hundred?" Hesh said.

"About fourteen hundred actually," Siwen said, not to mention the other non-military people who'd come along with them.

"Then we'll need to hold out through tonight," Yubo said. "I want that cavalry unit to pose a threat so they know we're holding onto another play. That means no raid today. It's more important that we keep our position until tomorrow. If they see reinforcements arrive, they may shift their tactic."

"Or they could press even harder," Siwen said. This situation was not good, but the Gogobans had to know that it would all be over once the king's forces arrived. They'd already received a forward notice that he was marching with somewhere around twenty-five hundred soldiers. Siwen didn't want to admit it, but his stomach twisted in knots just thinking about what the next two days would look like.

"Did we request a meeting with them?" Yubo asked.

"I did that already," Fennu said, lips pulling back in a sneer. "*Zula* Rakachi spit in my face and said he'd use our blood to cleanse this land of the dragon loyalist infestation. Based on that, I'm not sure they are open to negotiation."

"Is that all he said?" Yubo pressed.

"He used much more colorful language if you'd like me to use direct quotes," Fennu said.

A soldier popped his head through the tent flap. "A messenger has arrived with an urgent report," he said.

"Let them in," Yubo said.

The soldier disappeared behind the flap before another person entered, a small woman in light leather armor. She dipped into a bow, bending at the waist. "I regret to inform the assembled that Queen Sophie of Kombida has declared war against Shiansan."

Siwen's jaw dropped despite himself.

Fennu cursed and punched his fists together.

This changed everything. If both nations moved against Shiansan, they wouldn't stand a chance in open combat.

"On what grounds?" Hesh demanded.

Siwen refused to make eye contact with his father. This ruination rested on Yubo. Heat rose to Siwen's cheeks, but he snapped his jaw shut and assumed his confident posturing.

"Violent actions against the nobility and citizenry of Red Bridge," the messenger said.

"Absurd!" Fennu shouted.

Siwen had heard enough. The more they talked here the less they got done. He nodded in the general direction of his father before he dismissed himself and exited the tent, taking in deep breaths of the warm air outside to try and calm his nerves.

The soldiers outside were a mixture of units from the three provinces. Most were idling, some were nursing wounds, and a few were going about various tasks setting up the camp. He would address their activity soon enough, but it would require meeting with the various squad leaders.

In the immediacy, he had questions that needed answered. He made his way to the ruins of the tower, at the base of which was a woman in tattered armor brushing down her horse.

"Commander Sherwood," Siwen said, announcing himself.

The woman gasped and jumped at the sound before dropping the brush, hand flicking to the hilt of her sword. "Sorry, sir," she said, letting out a breath. "What can I do to help, Lord Huan?"

"We only had time for introductions earlier, but I hadn't yet had the chance to speak with you regarding the battle at Fort Sal," Siwen said, looking the woman over. She was a mess. Her hair was in disarray, her clothing and armor cut in a few places, and she even bore the markings of soot stains, suggesting there had been a fire. "I was hoping you could detail the battle for me. Hopefully I could learn a bit more regarding their tactics. They remain a superior force, and we need a couple days."

"Yes, of course," Elise said, brushing a stray strand of hair behind her ear. Her eyes darted about, settling on a sack loaded upon her horse before she returned her full attention to Siwen.

"It's alright," Siwen said, taking a step closer. "You don't have to be too detailed. You can just share the parts that might be important, particularly tactical details. Were you there for the whole battle?"

Elise nodded. "Yes, lord. I was." She cleared her throat and straightened her back. "We... estimated their numbers at around three thousand, though I now think their actual force was around three thousand two hundred and fifty. Their initial march was rather quick, though we did see them approaching for some time, which allowed us to get word out. The assault itself went about as we expected, though we'd remained hopeful. Ideally, we would have broken down their battering ram, but we weren't able to damage it enough before it got in range. They used ladders to scale the walls as well, and they used a lot of ranged coverage to keep our archers from being able to fire back effectively. We were overwhelmed within an hour from the beginning of the assault."

Siwen pursed his lips and resisted shaking his head. Elise folded her arms, then unfolded them, shifting from one leg to the other. Clearly she had more to say. "What else?"

Elise frowned and rubbed her forehead before speaking. "The strangest part about the assault was actually before the battle." She heaved a breath and dropped her arms. "I'm sorry, sir, I don't know if I experienced some kind of delirium, so I hope you will excuse my hesitation."

"It's alright," Siwen said. "Any information you can offer me would be helpful."

Elise nodded. "We were infiltrated. Somebody stole a large portion of our supplies. They also murdered several of our soldiers—I'm not even aware of how many were killed because I didn't have time to assess the losses before the invasion began—but it seemed to be part of some kind of arrangement made with another party."

Siwen's fists clenched, and he had to hide them behind his back as he considered the implication. He didn't want to say anything to interrupt her.

"We had a traitor among the staff. It would seem the attack on the fort was at least a few months in the making." Elise's frown deepened. "I spoke with one of the assassins, or perhaps she was the only one. I'm not sure. She was extremely formidable and was a much better fighter than I am—faster than anyone I've ever seen.

She defeated me in combat but allowed me to live as if she wanted me to witness what was happening."

That tickled Siwen's memory. He could think of at least one woman capable of doing something like that. "This was before the battle?"

"Yes, sir."

"So it was a power play?"

"I believe so, sir. Her efforts would have made little difference in the fort's ability to hold out, but she made it sound as though it was part of some agreement she had made with Gogoba."

Siwen was four steps into pacing before he stopped himself. "And what about you, commander, how did you get out? Did they release you?"

"No, sir," Elise said. Her posture was stiff, as though it took all her effort to keep herself as rigid as possible. Beads of sweat glistened on her forehead. "I escaped."

Siwen stepped closer to her. "There is no need to be ashamed, commander. How did you escape?" He suspected that she'd managed to hide somewhere or that she knew a different exit to sneak out. Those seemed the most likely. If she'd actually abandoned her post before the battle, that would be an entirely different issue, but she didn't seem the sort to do that. Something else about it was troubling her.

"There was a soldier among my ranks, sir. He... used an object that killed several dozen of the Gogoban force, enough for them to fall back for a moment—long enough for me to escape. I was the only one left at that time."

The sweat on her brow made a lot more sense. "I'm sorry for the losses you've experienced, commander. There is not much worse to experience in life than defeat in battle, especially one as grievous as yours. Recognize that much of what happened was well beyond your control."

"Yes, sir," she said before curling her lower lip in, failing to hide its tremble.

"What object did this soldier use that was capable of such devastation?"

"Something forbidden, lord," Elise said, no longer hesitating with her response. She took a step back and gestured to the bag on the floor. "I strictly ordered him not to use it, but he went against my command."

"And you brought the object with you?"

"Yes, lord, of course. This kind of object in their hands would have been very incriminating evidence for their claims."

Siwen's pulse quickened as he considered all the possibilities, jumping to the most immediate conclusion. "Is it a weapon fueled by the blood of dragons?"

"Yes, lord."

"What does it do exactly?"

Elise swallowed. "It imitates the fire breath of a dragon, sir."

"By the blood of my mother," Siwen couldn't help but mutter. "Does anyone else know of this object?"

"I don't know, sir," Elise said. "Other than those who developed the weapon, it's possible that some of the Gogoban soldiers saw it before falling back."

Siwen shook his head. The repercussions should such information spread would be dire. They were already at war with two nations now, but if this got out, he could scarcely think of someone that wouldn't seek to destroy Shiansan. "I will need to confiscate it."

"No!" Elise shouted, though she didn't move.

Siwen stared at her in utter surprise.

"I mean, no, sir," Elise said. "It belongs to my family. I brought it here. We must accept the responsibility."

"Commander Sherwood..." Siwen started to say but then trailed off, suddenly making the connection with her family name. They'd been nobles at some point, losing their title after word got out regarding their blatant use of dragonblood research.

"Perhaps you could end this war right now," Elise said. "Turn me over to them and say that my family was responsible for this."

Siwen knew a little of that pressure she was experiencing. "Commander, that won't solve our issue here. Even if we turned you over, I can assure you that it would not appease them. There is much more to their agenda than simply enforcing international laws against the use of dragonblood research and technology."

Elise looked down for only a moment before frowning back up at him. "Farmland?"

"That seems like the obvious reason. We know how hard the last few years have been on Gogoba. That's one of the issues with living in a land that's mostly desert. The dragonblood accusation merely allows them to justify the invasion."

"So how do we end it, sir?"

"I wish I knew," Siwen said, though he suspected it would probably boil down to blood. If his forces could make Gogoba's losses heavy enough, they'd back off. Kombida joining in the war would not make it easy. The one hope Siwen had was that it would likely take them quite a while to muster the appropriate force. In that time, Shiansan might have a chance to push back Gogoba.

Only to be crushed by Kombida.

They needed to devise a real tactic. One that wouldn't incur an invasion from any other country.

"What can you tell me about this weapon?" Siwen asked, nudging the bag with his foot.

Elise's shoulders dropped as she started to explain one of the most terrible things Siwen had ever heard of.

Chapter Twenty-Six

King Nikato

Mia

The amount of control that Rowan imposed on Mia's body was a marvel. She slunk through the darkened camp like a shadow. Her black hair was braided and tucked back. They'd had her change clothes once again; this time she wore some kind of clothing that seemed otherworldly, with a mismatched pattern of dark grays and greens, but she blended into the darkness like she was born there.

She'd spent the last couple days running at full sprint again. Why have her do all this? Wasn't this something Rowan could do herself? Perhaps there were simply risks the dragons didn't want to take themselves. It was easier to use an expendable force. Then again, they didn't seem against doing their own dirty work either. There was likely something Mia was missing.

Mia crawled through the army camp undetected. There were very few people who weren't sleeping. Whatever this massive force of soldiers was up to, they seemed weary after a long day of marching.

Those keeping watch weren't doing a very good job, either. Any kind of attack was not anticipated. The camp was so large that they couldn't cover enough ground to secure their border regardless, and the speed and silence with which Mia was able to move made her impossible to spot.

At times, Mia had to pause to gauge her surroundings, indicating that Rowan didn't know exactly where to lead her. This only occurred three separate times, but Mia's destination seemed quite clear once she was close. A large tent was erected near the center of camp. Two guards actively walked around its perimeter, and they were not taking their job as lightly as those who'd been on the fringes of the camp.

The camp was eerily still. The only sounds were that of the insects, a couple people snoring, and the footsteps of the guards as their boots scuffed against the tall grass. There was no wind.

Mia snuck in, body low, until she was beside a tent immediately adjacent to the one she was targeting. Most of the grass had been stomped flat, but Mia had to remember that these guards could not see anywhere near as well as she could in the dark. She would be just another shadow. She pulled out the long dagger she'd been equipped with and tucked it against her chest as the guard passed so he wouldn't have any chance to catch light glinting off the metal.

Once he walked by, Mia immediately pounced behind him. He was much taller than her, but when she reached up, she was able to clamp a hand over his mouth just as her dagger pierced him from behind, shoving straight up from underneath his ribs. She didn't stab just once, but three times, each one aimed at a particular organ, including the heart, of course, as was Rowan's obvious preference.

Mia easily held the man up as he died. She grabbed hold of his chest armor with one hand and carried him behind another tent and laid his body down.

"Holt?" the other soldier whispered, noting the apparent silence.

Before he could do anything else, Mia was already behind him, stabbing the exact same way.

Both guards dispatched, Mia walked right through the front flap of the tent. Judging by the uniforms of the soldiers and the insignia outside the tent, this was some important nobleman of Shiansan.

There was a single, sleeping figure inside the tent, bundled up on a surprisingly extravagant bed. She could only imagine the amount of time it would take each day to disassemble the interior of the tent and set it up again every day, but most things were still in moving crates, indicating that they didn't intend to stay here for more than the night.

Rowan didn't let Mia hesitate for a moment. Her body prowled right up to the sleeping figure. She withdrew a small vial from her pocket and emptied the contents onto a darkened cloth, then held it up to the sleeping man's face, smothering his nose. She held it there for just a moment before hauling the person out and slinging him over her shoulders. He was still alive, but he did not wake. The contents of the vial clearly had some way of keeping the man asleep.

With the man on her shoulders, Mia walked out of the tent. He wore a plain linen nightgown that would be a lot easier to spot than her own attire, but apparently the need for full caution was gone.

Mia ran through the camp like a blur, sticking to the same path she'd used upon entering. There weren't any people keeping watch in the center, only on the fringes of camp, so she merely had to maneuver past a single sentry who paced back and forth with the gait of a man who would have preferred to be sleeping.

Mia burst out into the night as soon as the guard's back was turned.

She ran for a few minutes until she stopped at a copse of trees and dropped the man down, leaning him up against the base of a tree trunk. It took another moment before he finally roused from whatever chemical she'd used to knock him out.

As his eyes fluttered open, he blinked around in confusion. In her stillness, he could not see her, and he tried rising to his feet. Before he got all the way up, Mia shoved him up against the tree and jabbed her dagger through the cloth at the top of his shoulder, pinning it to the trunk. His eyes flickered with both fear and defiance, even though he wouldn't have been able to discern any of her features.

"Who are you?" he demanded.

The flesh of his chest was feeble beneath Mia's palm. The ease with which she'd be able to crush him was an oddly familiar sensation. She'd come to think of people differently, she'd realized. The sharpness of her senses and the expertise experienced through Rowan's control made it too easy to discern not only the emotions of most people, but also a profound clarity regarding their anatomy. The man was old. She could sense some developing disease or deformity building on one of his internal organs, though she hadn't ever learned what each organ was.

"King Hinam Nikato," Mia said, ignoring the man's question. A king. Rowan was really aiming higher with her targets. Mia couldn't help but be intrigued by whatever the dragons were plotting, despite the impending doom all of their actions were surely bringing. "Shiansan is about to be utterly ruined. I don't believe you are in a position to be questioning your captor."

Hinam scoffed, that sense of defiance growing stronger despite the stench of fear that wafted from him like an aura. "Bold words. Everyone knows Shiansan boasts the most capable warriors."

Mia's lips curled in an unnatural smile. Rowan took pleasure in this discourse. "That may have been true centuries ago, but we both know Shiansan has been untested for generations and your once-great military has declined."

"Our glory has not ended."

"Speaking of those glory days, I was hoping the great king of Shiansan would be privy to some helpful information."

"You'll get nothing from me, you no-named—"

Mia slammed Hinam back up against the trunk with such force that the air evicted from his lungs in a wheeze. "Be aware that you are completely within my power. I walked into your camp by myself, killed the guards outside your tent, and carried you here over my shoulder."

Hinam sucked in air and struggled to remain standing. She'd hit him hard. "What... who are you with? Are you Gogoban?"

"I'm with an organization that predates all of that, which is why I need to ask you something"

Hinam rubbed a hand across his chest and frowned at her through the darkness. "Older? What could you even mean by that? Are you dragonsworn?"

Mia ignored the question this time. "Long ago, your family arranged an exchange, giving up half of the land north of Xhi in order to receive a single prisoner. What family did you arrange that with?"

Hinam's head reeled back. "That is… How do you know of this? The only record of that is kept in my family's…" His eyes widened.

"We went through your archives weeks ago, but there were a few gaps I was hoping you could fill in for me. Namely, what family did you acquire the prisoner from?"

"I don't understand. What prisoner?"

Mia jabbed a finger into Hinam's shoulder, pressing hard enough that it would leave a sharp bruise. "The prisoner that was kept in Peskan by the Huan family. We're aware of the arrangement you had there."

Hinam dropped his head back against the trunk of the tree and closed his eyes, face sagging with newfound exhaustion. "You are dragonsworn, aren't you?"

"No, I am someone seeking justice."

Hinam ran a hand over his face. "Is my fate sealed then?"

"It is," Mia said. "But we need to fit a few pieces. The people of Shiansan could potentially be spared, but we'd need to punish every leader who was involved in capturing and imprisoning that dragon. It's the only way we'd be able to appease the masses at this point."

"But the dragon is free. Should that not be a higher priority?"

"That has been taken care of already. We just need you to share the missing piece." Mia tapped the king's nose. "Who delivered the dragon to Shiansan?"

Hinam shook his head with a deep sigh. The first light of dawn twinkled on the horizon. His shoulders sagged. "Nobody did. It was a ruse. The dragon was captured as a baby, hiding in human form right there in Xhi. It was later into the rebellion when she was discovered, after most dragons had been slain. Humans knew at least to some degree the uses of dragonblood by then. It seemed like the perfect scenario to be able to harvest the blood freely."

"Exploitation," Mia said.

"Yes. It was frowned on by others who knew. The exchange was made with Colandia for an oath of secrecy, not for acquiring the prisoner. They knew because they were involved in the takeover."

"Are you protecting somebody, Hinam?"

"No," he said fiercely. "They did not want to be involved in the dragonblood exploitation."

"That does not make them exempt."

"This was generations ago. Even I had nothing to do with this. How would targeting them satisfy justice?"

Mia clucked her tongue. "Anybody who knew about that dragon is not exempt. They allowed that arrangement to be maintained. You could have ended it at any time. Yubo Huan could have done the same. Is there anybody else who knew?"

"I see," Hinam said. "The answer is no. That responsibility lies solely on the shoulders of our two families."

"Including your two daughters back in Xhi, unfortunately."

"No, that's not what I meant."

"But it is the case. We've already conducted our research on that matter."

"Please, don't do this."

"As a king, would you grant anybody pardon for committing a grievous atrocity?"

"There is sometimes room for mercy, yes."

Mia stepped back slowly. Something fluttered down from the sky behind her. There was enough light now that Hinam was likely able to see much better, and his eyes widened in abject horror at whatever had just arrived. Mia could make a guess.

Footsteps trod on the ground behind her, but she could not turn her head to see.

"You—you lied to me. You are dragonsworn!" Hinam's light brown skin paled as he blanched at the approaching figure. He gripped the dagger impaling his clothes to the tree, but it was embedded so deep that he couldn't make it move. He jerked away frantically, tearing his clothing away before stumbling to the ground just as Rowan stepped up before him. She hadn't retracted her wings. They seemed smaller than the last time Mia had seen them, and it became more apparent that the dragons had some kind of control over the size of their appearance. She wondered if they could transform back and forth between the two forms with ease.

Mia no longer had to speak for Rowan now that the dragon was present. Her voice was gravelly as though her dragon form was on the verge of breaking through.

"Can you imagine an existence of slavery as your blood is drained from you every single day?" Rowan asked as she bent down and grabbed Hinam by the jaw, raising him up to his feet. He clawed at her arm, trying to wrest himself free even though he must have known it was hopeless.

"I never even saw the light of day for centuries." Her voice was tinged with a hint of emotion that Mia somehow found surprising. Not only that, but Mia could *sympathize* with the monster. Hadn't she been in a similar situation? Justice wasn't a bad thing, but wasn't that what had driven Dami to his extremes?

No, that had been vengeance. But where was the divide? Rowan was being deliberate in her actions. It was against the nature of a dragon to be imprisoned and used, just like it had been an injustice for Mia to be kept at the facility. But she realized these questions regarding freedom and justice were beyond her. She didn't know what was right. Perhaps it was best that Rowan remained in control of Mia's body. Then these actions were beyond her. She was not responsible for what was happening.

But even then, what Rowan was doing to Mia was completely against the same principles Rowan was trying to enforce. Where did her logic betray her?

"You've exceeded your usefulness," Rowan said. "And besides, I believe you humans have a saying. How does it go? 'Don't play with your food.'" A devious smile crossed Rowan's face as Hinam's went even paler.

Rowan released him, and he scrambled away, but before he could even make it a couple steps, Rowan's head transformed, becoming a massive, elongated neck, glistening with black and red scales. The head was crowned by jagged horns, and the dragon's jaws snapped shut around the king's entire body, completely engulfing him. The head retracted a second later as Rowan resumed her human form. The only trace of the king was a spattering of blood wetting the grass.

"Well done, Mia," Rowan said, body shivering with pleasure as she turned to pat Mia's head like she was a dog.

Mia didn't have control of her body, but that didn't mean she was immune to emotional responses, and that sly smile on Rowan's lips filled Mia with a crawling sensation.

"I've played nicely for a while, and now that I have what I need and the other pieces are falling into place, I think I've earned myself a bit of... indulgence." That smile of hers widened to a full grin, and Mia's heart sank.

Chapter Twenty-Seven

The Price of Information

Ven Yashke

"You want to visit *her*?" Morgan asked as they veered off the main road and steered toward the large castle resting on a rocky hill nearby. The traffic was considerable as though they were preparing for something.

"She has people and information," Ven said.

"And she will likely try to use you in some way to further her own gain," Morgan said. "Believe me, wealth like hers doesn't come by doing favors. She would make demands."

"Which I anticipate," Ven said. "But this will be a simple visit. I will not be making high demands from my end of things, so she cannot expect to ask too much of me."

"You underestimate the value of information," Morgan said.

Ven smirked. He'd been pondering that value himself, which was why he deemed this visit entirely necessary.

The path steepened sharply as they wound back and forth to get up the hill leading to Castia Mont. Admittedly, Lady Sitena Rosars was not one of the people Ven could reasonably trust. She would, as Morgan noted, undoubtedly try to forward her own agenda, but that seemed of little consequence regarding the circumstances. He didn't imagine there was much Sitena could do to impede Ven's own objectives. But then again, she was very clever and had a lot more resources, and even Zein had warned him about coming here.

The traffic to and from the castle was hurried. People went in groups, and a surprising number of them were armed, though upon further reflection, perhaps that should have been expected. For all Ven knew, this was a normal day for Castia Mont. He'd only visited it before under extreme conditions.

When they reached the gate, a pair of guards greeted them. Morgan and Valerie were completely disinterested in engaging with them as they were questioned. Ven was the only one who had an objective here. "I've come to see Lady Rosars."

The guards gave Ven a solid lookover before inspecting his companions as well. "Who are you?" the guard asked, lips barely visible beneath a thick mustache.

"The name is Ven Yashke. She'll know me."

The guards chuckled at each other with no small amusement.

"I have urgent news that she may find interesting," Ven added.

"Sure," the mustached guard said. "Wait over there while we confirm." He gestured to an outbuilding where at least two dozen other people were milling about. The building reminded Ven of some old-timey inn with a few tables and chairs. They appeared to serve some kind of drink at least.

"Very well," Ven said before the three of them steered over and hitched their horses. From experience, he knew Sitena was serious about her security. He wouldn't be surprised if they'd be out here half the day, but the time he might be able to save with a single conversation with her would be worth the wait.

"You do know of her reputation, don't you?" Morgan asked. They did not take seats, but they roamed about near their horses, trying to find shade under the wooden rafters to avoid the midday sun.

"I've had the opportunity to work very closely with her once," Ven said.

"And?"

"And it was not an ideal business transaction," Ven said, giving Morgan a level stare.

Morgan humphed. "Very detailed response."

"Let's just say that she helped take care of a dangerous threat but betrayed us at the same time."

"At least she's consistent," Morgan said.

"Is that her typical approach to things?"

"I would say so," Morgan said.

"How does she maintain her status with such a bad reputation?" Ven asked. It would be strange for her to be an unreasonable person to work with while still maintaining a large enterprise.

"Oh, probably for the same reason you are here. She tends to be unavoidable. People *must* work with her."

Ven nodded. He had no idea what kind of trade Sitena operated under, but he did know at least a portion of it had something to do with dragonblood technology. Now that there was no dragon to bleed, he wondered how that business was working out for her.

Realizing it would take much longer than originally anticipated, they eventually settled down, taking a seat at one of the small tables.

"How did you end up becoming Morgan's... uh... guard?" Ven asked Valerie.

"Attendant," Valerie said with a smile. "And it was very simple, really. I am the daughter of Lady Lauron's mother's attendant. We are the same age and I grew up on their estate."

Morgan smiled fondly at Valerie. "We're basically sisters, though we have our different jobs."

"So will you get married as well?" Ven asked.

"Is that a proposition?" Valerie asked, raising her eyebrows.

Ven stammered. "Uh..." That hadn't at all been what he was suggesting.

Morgan and Valerie laughed before Morgan spoke. "It would be ideal, of course, for her to be wed as well. It is common practice to have attendants marry other key figures from the noble's entourage."

"I see," Ven said. "And just so we're clear, I simply made the connection that both of you are the same age, but Valerie is in a new place and might not know many men in Peskan yet."

"Oh, she knows a few of them," Morgan said, giving Valerie a sideways look.

Valerie simply smiled and shook her head. "Trying to gauge your competition, Ven? That's understandable."

Ven couldn't help but sputter a laugh. These two were good company, and Ven had to admit that he was grateful not to be alone, a feeling he'd been getting too accustomed to. It took a good couple hours of waiting before they ever got word back from the guard.

The same mustached man jogged over to the waiting area and called out Ven's name. There was another person with the guard, a woman who bore a serious expression that demanded no nonsense.

"Follow me, please," the woman said, turning back toward the castle at a quick pace, not even glancing back to see if they were coming. The three of them rushed to join her.

Ven was glad to see that much of the damage caused by Dami's assault was repaired. There were only subtle signs left of the damage, probably only noticeable by those who had seen the place before, like one of the side buildings being reconstructed slightly smaller than it had previously been.

This was a dark place in Ven's memory, and the image of dead bodies flickered through his mind, revealing themselves in flashes of lightning. He might not remember their faces, but their injuries were too sharp to forget. When they reached the upper courtyard, the one where he and Mia had fought against Dami, he could see the blood on his hands as if it had been seconds ago. That had been his first confirmed kill. His hands were a lot bloodier now.

The memory was not as haunting as he might have expected. Instead, it was a cold reminder of the role he had to play. If things needed to be done, Ven could do it. He *would* do it. Rowan and Dayelle would receive no different treatment. Ven was trained to treat people, but sometimes the right treatment was death.

"Are you well?" Valerie asked, nudging Ven's arm from beside him.

This pulled Ven from his dark thoughts. "I am, yes." He looked up at the large inner keep of Castia Mont. It was an impressive structure that would rival any of the most elaborate castles on Earth, with room enough to house several hundred people. The design was simple in most places, but the more elaborate gates and towers reminded Ven of some kind of hybrid between Gothic and Mesopotamian designs, combining geometric shapes, long lines, and fine details.

The woman led them straight into the main doorway and up a flight of stairs. Sitena was skipping her intimidation approach this time, it seemed.

"You weren't kidding about your name getting you in," Morgan said. "What kind of work did you do with her again?"

"Probably not the kind we could discuss right now," Ven said, "but it did involve helping make sure that some people who were alive were no longer doing that."

"What, living?" Morgan asked.

"Yes, that."

"So you killed them?"

"Maybe."

"Didn't you just say you shouldn't be talking about it?" Valerie said.

Ven didn't answer, but they stopped in front of a door where the woman leading them nodded to a guard outside and gestured at Ven. With a quick acknowledgement from the guard, the woman led them inside to find a cozy waiting room furnished with a few couches and a couple coffee tables. It was probably one of the only fancily decorated rooms in the entire castle.

Sitena Rosars sat with crossed legs on one of the couches, hands clasped over her knees. She did not bother smiling or standing. "Ven Yashke. It has been a while," she said. The powerful woman was probably in her late fifties, and she wore a sharp suit, complete with a vest and a high collar, a white scarf wrapped around her neck. "You brought company."

"I did," Ven said.

Sitena ran her eyes over the two women before nodding. "Good company." She raised her fingers at the woman who had escorted them, and she promptly left the room, closing the door behind her.

"Many people come to me seeking some kind of business venture or appealing to my sense of charity. I don't mind either of those things, but most cases are really of very little consequence and hardly worth my time. I was informed that you brought news for me, and at a time like this, I can only wonder what kind of information might be so significant that it would draw you here to my door." Sitena's eyes flicked over to Morgan. "And with such company as the newlywed Lady Lauron, no less. Did the Huan family die in battle?"

Ven breathed a laugh. "No, and actually, I was hoping this could be an exchange of information."

"Ah, a bargain," Sitena said, leaning back in her seat. "Do please elaborate." She gestured at the couch opposite her.

Ven took a seat as the two women sat to either side of him. He leaned forward on the couch and said, "I need to ask if you have seen any military operation recently within the vicinity, particularly an army gathering."

"The two neighboring nations nearest this location have just declared war on each other, so your question may not be entirely useful."

"Even still, I'd like to know."

"And what information were you hoping to share in exchange?"

"I'm sure you've noticed a decrease in the supply of dragonblood."

"Of course, but I already know why if that's what you were hoping to tell me." Sitena seemed bent on wringing out every bit of information she could. She rubbed a finger across her eye as if signifying that the conversation was boring.

"So you know about the two dragons that are on the loose, then?"

Sitena froze, only her eyes moving as she regarded each of them in turn. She took a moment before responding. "Is that theory confirmed, then?"

"It is. I have seen both the dragons with my own eyes."

"How many people know about this?"

"Not many. Maybe just us and the Huans, maybe a few others who were involved in the trade network. I'm guessing Yubo harvested the blood himself in order to reduce the number of people who would be exposed to the information."

"How have there not been more witnesses? Dragons cannot be easily hidden." Sitena shook her head.

"Simple. The dragons have been in human form this whole time, except for when they want to utilize their wings, anyway."

"Well," Sitena said, lacing her fingers together. "I'd say you earned your information. How did you come to know of this?"

Ven shrugged. "They are the ones who got me roped into that whole thing with Zein Huan's facility. They've had an interest in human affairs for quite some time now."

"Understandably so. What else could you share about them?"

"Their names are Dayelle and Rowan," Ven said. He folded his arms and sat back in his seat, making sure not to touch Morgan or Valerie who sat on either side of him.

Sitena was silent for a moment, lips pursed before she responded with a smile. "And you hope that I have information of equal value when you've just dropped one of the dirtiest secrets in the world."

"I do."

"Very well, what would you like to know?"

"I'm looking for a specific military group," Ven said. "They are described as wearing fairly unique armor and have been raiding villages that wouldn't be far from here."

"Yes, I'm quite sure I know exactly what you are referring to. You are very informed, Doctor Yashke. Perhaps you missed your calling."

Ven tried not to feel too self-satisfied but merely nodded to Sitena to continue.

Sitena squared her shoulders and said, "I am aware of two villages that have been completely razed. All residents were completely gone and several of the buildings burned."

"Is one of them Mavenda up in the mountains?"

Sitena hummed an acknowledgement to herself. "I have not heard anything regarding that location."

"Add it to the list. Where are the other two villages, and do you know when they were attacked?"

Morgan shifted uncomfortably beside him and Ven suddenly remembered that he'd been completely skipping the normal formalities of this kind of conversation. As a random individual with no title, he was speaking to upper nobility.

"It was the villages of Granfield and Willow. Both of them were hit relatively soon after one another, no less than nine days ago. There were even a couple other farmhouses that were hit with similar results. Do you know who is responsible, then?"

"The dragons," Ven said without hesitation.

"Of course they are." Sitena shook her head as her lips became a thin line. Her finger tapped against her knee. "So they are in the region."

"It would appear so. How far away was the nearest village?"

"That would be Granfield. It's a day and a half away on horseback."

"Very close," Ven said, absently stroking the wispy hairs growing on his chin. "I suppose that explains the bustle of activity I've seen around your castle."

"In part. The official war declarations between neighboring nations are one thing, but entire villages completely disappearing are admittedly more concerning. Knowing that dragons are behind it, well... It's like Dami all over again, but considerably worse."

"Which is part of why I wanted to come here," Ven said. "If anything, it will help to have other people know the true nature of what is going on. From what we understand, the dragons have also been experimenting with their blood, which was how I got pulled into working at Doctor Huan's facility."

Sitena's eyes shot wide. "Don't tell me they have been developing their own subjects."

"They have," Ven said, "but it's very different. The subjects don't appear to be developing any imperviousness, but instead they lose all sense of self, and the dragons are able to control them. We believe they're making an army. This is why I was going to ask if you've seen any soldiers wearing unique armor so we could verify who's been raiding the villages."

"There is no official confirmation regarding the identity of the assailants. I've had two of my scouts disappear when trying to discover the answer to that very question. If you want to volunteer to be the third, then by all means, but we've come to the conclusion that we should hold our position rather than trying to track them down."

"That's encouraging." It was the first thing Morgan had said.

"Who else knows about the dragons?" Sitena asked. "I assume not many people seeing as I've only learned just now."

"Very few. I would venture to guess only those who were responsible for keeping the dragon prisoner. I think they want to keep the information under wraps for fear of retaliation from the other nations, though we can see Shiansan is already suffering from the ramifications there, but the dragons have also been acting in secret. I must assume it's because they are trying to position themselves in such a way that people don't unite against them."

"That seems probable. You're very keen, Ven."

Ven almost smiled, but something about how Sitena was behaving unnerved him. The worry she'd had earlier was gone, and now she appeared more contemplative as she tapped her fingers together. A second later, she pressed a button on the table beside her seat, and the door opened to admit three of the guards.

"Perhaps too keen," Sitena said.

"Sitena," Ven warned, hands gripping his knees tightly. Morgan and Valerie tensed up beside him as they too noticed the change in tone.

"Take them to the prison," Sitena said, gesturing at Ven, Valerie, and Morgan.

"You're a dragonsworn," Ven said, still shocked at the words even as they left his mouth.

"Don't be silly," Sitena said with a wink.

Ven had been a fool. He should have listened to Zein and not come here at all.

Chapter Twenty-Eight

The Cruel Trade

Siwen Huan

"Where's the king?" Siwen demanded as he stormed over to the other lords and ladies, flicking the blood off his sword.

The other nobles were bickering amongst themselves atop a small platform while their soldiers fought and died on the front line. The occasional arrow flew by overhead, so Siwen kept his shield raised in his off hand as he faced them. His father was nowhere to be seen among them.

"He's dead!" Fennu bellowed. His son and daughter flanked him, fully armed, but still immaculate, indicating their complete nonparticipation in the battle.

The Gogoban army was currently assaulting the camp, thankfully without the siege equipment, though their arrows had already caused enough damage. The higher elevation of the camp could only help so much.

Siwen stopped directly in front of the others as they regarded him. Each of them was flustered. They feared they would lose. He could read it in their expressions. If they retreated, then they'd be making that fate sure.

"The king vanished in the middle of the night. His guards were dead," Hesh explained. "The only trace of him they found was his nightgown and a spattering of blood a little ways away from their camp."

"But what about his forces?" Siwen said, pushing to the relevant information.

"They are almost here," Hesh said. "We need to hold out just a little longer."

A man came at them, screaming, a spiked mace raised in one hand. He wore only light leather armor, and his face was painted with black charcoal, meant to intimidate.

Siwen moved to intercept, ducking under a hasty swing by the Gogoban soldier. His knee connected with the soldier's gut, doubling him over before Siwen stabbed down through the man's back. With the man down on his stomach in the grass, Siwen hacked at his neck, bringing the conflict to a quick end.

The Gogoban should not have gotten through. "How much longer?" Siwen said. A glance back at the clashing forces revealed that an entire troop of Shiansan soldiers was falling back. They didn't know how close they were to salvation and were giving up the front line. This would cause hundreds of them to die.

"Less than an hour," Hesh said, her eyes scanning over the battle as well.

"Reinforce your soldiers," Siwen barked at them. "Those look like your men falling back, Lady Hesh. If they don't push back, there won't be anyone here for the king's men to reinforce."

Siwen clapped a hand down on his helmet and hurried back to the line, glancing back to at least ensure that Hesh was joining him. She jumped down from the platform and mounted up on her horse before heading straight toward her soldiers.

"Turn, you cowards!" she shouted at them, her voice carrying with strength. She held a spear aloft and charged straight at the Gogobans. Her personal guard, who had been mounted and ready, had to heel their horses into pace to keep up. Hopefully she wasn't about to get killed.

On seeing their commanding officer join the fray, her soldiers turned and roared, pushing back against the tide of Gogobans.

Fennu was nowhere to be seen, but his children were running up behind Siwen, ideally not as liabilities. Minutes were all they needed, but that was still enough time to be devastating during a battle.

"Shields!" Siwen shouted as he jumped in, bashing his own shield against a Gogoban who was trying to stab at the side of one of Siwen's soldiers. "Shields!" he said, repeating the word until his soldiers started to form a more solid wall. Siwen sheathed his sword and scooped a spear up off the ground, ducking behind his shield to avoid an axe that swung over the top. He jabbed the spear out, feeling it graze across the top of something before he pulled back and jabbed again.

The next few minutes remained much like that, the two forces pushing up against each other. Siwen's arms grew tired, and he wished he could safely transition his shield to his other arm to at least shift the strain to different muscles.

When the comrade beside him fell with a spear to the face, his opportunity to do something different was forced upon him. Pushing the comrade back to save him from getting finished off, Siwen jumped to fill the gap, but there was too much space. With a low jab, he sliced into a Gogoban's thigh, deflected two weapons with his shield, the blows jarring his arm, then stabbed high, hitting another opponent in the neck.

The Gogobans, eager to widen the gap, pushed forward at the urging of their officers. There were few men who had as much combat training as Siwen, however, and after jabbing his spear into the gut of another man, he whipped out his sword and went to work. They came in fast—too fast to maintain ideal control, and Siwen's practiced strokes had blood flying around him like rain. His feet danced across the mottled grass, now more brown and red than green, as his body shifted expertly to dodge and strike.

Noting how several of their comrades fell, the Gogobans hesitated until one of their officers forced his way to the front and squared off against Siwen. The soldiers holding the line on either side struggled to keep their formation now that the extra shield was missing.

The Gogoban officer was marked by an iron helmet plumed with two large black feathers He was a large man, and when he jumped in, swinging his axe at full force, it broke through the outer leather of Siwen's shield and cracked the wood beneath. Siwen quickly swiped his sword in an arc as though to wipe the weapon off his shield, but his blade glanced off the officer's hardened vambrace instead of cutting flesh.

When the officer yanked his weapon back, it pulled Siwen's shield with it. Siwen adjusted his style and attacked with swift strokes. The first two were deflected by the man's shield, but the third stroke slid below the bicep of his weapon-bearing arm. The same move cost Siwen, for it allowed the officer to use his shield to bash Siwen on the side of his chest, knocking the wind from his lungs.

Siwen stepped back, nearly tripping over a fallen soldier. On the misstep, the officer took a quick step forward and kicked at Siwen, but he lifted his own leg, catching the kick across his plated shin. This threw the officer off balance, and Siwen hacked down, scoring a blow across the man's thigh. The officer's leg gave out and Siwen nearly finished him off, but another Gogoban jabbed a spear at Siwen that stuck into his armor on the side of his ribs, metal piercing through just enough to break flesh.

Siwen grabbed the spear and jumped back, wresting it from the hands of its owner. He unhooked it from his side and threw it back, scoring a hit in the man's face.

The officer had withdrawn, but two others pressed in.

Siwen was fatigued, but he'd trained to exhaustion so many times. The whole purpose behind it was to develop the mindset that as long as he was alive, his body could always do more. As they charged in, he slipped into rhythm, careful to try using a method that implemented quick, careful strokes that both deflected and attacked with the same motion. His continuous movement threw them off, and one stumbled away with a severed arm while the other collapsed with a slice across his belly.

Another of Siwen's comrades fell, making the gap even larger. They would get surrounded. Ideally, they would have a relief force at the rear, allowing them to fill the gaps with ease, but the battlefield was too wide, and the enemy soldiers too numerous.

"Give!" he shouted, bending down to pick up a discarded shield, but as he glanced back he saw none other than Commander Sherwood holding that dragonblood-fueled contraption. His heart dropped with horror. He repeated the order to the soldiers but tried to get Elise's attention. There was no way they could unleash that weapon.

The Shiansan soldiers gave way, taking intentional steps back as a unit. The crumbled walls of the tower would at least give them something to hold against so that they wouldn't get overwhelmed.

Thankfully, Siwen caught Elise's eyes and he gestured to her to lower the weapon. Her throat bobbed as she gulped, but she tucked the weapon into a bag and drew her sword to join them. The conditions were still too bleak for Siwen to feel reassured. Perhaps the weapon was a viable option at this point. The Gogobans had already seen it used once before. How bad could it possibly be to use it again? It could mean having even more of their neighbors to declare war. There would certainly be no recovery from such a scenario. He had to dismiss the idea. He couldn't be responsible for such a thing as that.

But could he be responsible for their army falling here and now even if he knew there was a way out? His answer came as he saw a pale yellow flag flapping in the air over the tower as their lookout signaled them. That was their sign. Siwen hurried to assist his soldiers as the battle progressed. They only needed moments, but this was critical. One of his soldiers fell away as his arm was crushed by a hammer. Siwen moved the injured man behind him and jumped in. Like his soldiers, he was fatigued, but a distant thundering sound signaled their salvation, reigniting his fervor enough to keep his blade swinging and feet moving to the rhythm of battle.

The source of the thundering came in the form of several hundred mounted soldiers charging around the hill on the flanks of the Gogoban army. They pierced through the forces at the back, drawing the advance of the Gogoban army to a complete halt. The enemy's hesitation gave Siwen enough of an opening to attack briefly, striking down two more opponents before their officers called for retreat.

Siwen shouted a cheer as their enemies fell back, his voice joined by those of his comrades. The king's soldiers had arrived just in time, even though they'd come without the monarch himself.

With the reprieve, Siwen had the soldiers form up just in case the Gogobans tried something, but after another pass from the cavalry, the enemy pulled back in quick order. Even though he wasn't the highest ranking official among the nobility present, the soldiers and nobles alike knew to follow the combat instructions of a Huan.

A few of the Shiansan soldiers under Fennu's command fired a volley of arrows into the backs of the retreating army. It wasn't the best etiquette on a battlefield, but this was an instance where Siwen supported the idea. They needed to devastate this invasion force and send them back to their own lands as hastily as possible.

An officer from the cavalry along with three other riders approached. Siwen stepped out from among the soldiers so the officer knew who to approach. They pulled up in front of Siwen, horses snorting and stamping. They must have been riding hard to get here on time. The officer removed his helmet, revealing the face of a man with a thick brown beard and bald head. A knotted rope on each of his shoulders marked him as a captain of the Shi-enn, an elite group of soldiers who served directly under the royal family. If there were soldiers more talented than Siwen, it was them.

"I'm glad you could make it," Siwen said, his aches and pains rising with sensation as the thrill of battle subsided. That wound where the spear had jabbed his side was especially sensitive.

"I'm only sorry we did not make it here sooner, lord," the Shi-enn said, tone grave, though seeming to hope that Siwen would provide his name.

"Huan," Siwen said.

"Lord Huan," the Shi-enn said with a nod of his head. "Are you in charge? Who is the commanding officer on site?"

"Technically, that would be my father," Siwen said, realizing he hadn't seen his father since before the battle. He didn't want to assume the worst. "I can lead you back to the command tent. We need to discuss the situation. Are there other officers that will need to attend?"

"Lead on, Lord Huan. I am captain over the Shi-enn," the officer said, "and by extension, I command the cavalry force that has just arrived. My presence should be sufficient."

"Very good," Siwen said, wanting to wipe the grime from his face, but his gloves were so equally covered in filth that it would do him no good. He turned and led the way back toward the command tent after issuing a relief order to the soldiers.

"I assume you are aware of the news regarding King Nikato?" the officer asked.

"We all are, yes, but we are prepared to forge on," Siwen said, answering the question while looking about, still hoping for a glimpse of his father.

Hesh was barking orders at some people who were tending to the wounded, her own armor finally mottled with blood. Both of Fennu's children emerged from the crowd and trailed behind Siwen as they aimed for the command tent.

Siwen was relieved to see them alive. For a while there, he'd been worried they'd be more of an impediment than a help, but they bore the signs of battle. Fennu stood outside the tent, arms folded, armor still completely spotless.

"Well done," Fennu said, his voice far louder than necessary. "For a moment there, I thought we were going to lose the battle."

"Lady Halimah's rally brought us back together long enough," Siwen said, nodding to the woman as she joined them."

Hesh laughed. "For a moment there, I thought myself as powerful as the cavalry only to realize that we made very little impact at all with me and my two riders."

"Still," Siwen pressed, "the rally brought the forces together long enough for us to hold. It was paramount to our success."

"You call that success?" Fennu said, lips turned in disgust.

"Seeing that we aren't all dead, yes," Siwen said, then changed the subject. "Has anyone seen my father?"

"Perhaps he was less successful," Fennu said, turning his eyes to his children.

Siwen experienced a rare moment of temptation, having half a mind to punch Lord Fennu Kye right in the nose. He would never succumb to a base action like that of course, but a lord such as he should have known that words like that were not appropriate. Instead, he glared at Fennu for a moment before turning his attention back to the Shi-enn officer, who dismounted to stand with them.

The officer wasted no time to speak, starting by introducing himself formally. "I am Davis, captain of the Shi-enn regiment. As you know, His Majesty King Nikato is gone, most likely dead. It did delay our progress here, unfortunately, but I saw fit to bring the cavalry force ahead. The rest of the troops should arrive shortly, but it will be our recommendation that, with a show of force, we can meet with the Gogoban leaders and propose a truce. You are undoubtedly aware of the declaration of war from Kombida, but we've also received one from Tiamjin *and* Colandia."

This information was met with even more cursing. Siwen could only close his eyes and grip the bridge of his nose to contain his own roiling frustration. He couldn't even begin to fathom what the next few years look like.

Davis cleared his throat before continuing. "They are not mobilized yet from what our sources say, so it is likely similar to the situation with Kombida, which is why we need to end this threat with Gogoba immediately. This will allow us time to prepare for invasion on the other fronts. Luedan has officially agreed to uphold their defensive alliance with us though, so they will be reinforcing us against both Kombida and Colandia, which means we'll need to focus the bulk of our forces against Tiamjin."

"So you would abandon me here?" Fennu said, his cheeks tinged with red.

"It's hardly an abandonment, Lord Kye," Siwen said. "You will still have your forces. We will not try to call them elsewhere unless things are secure on this front."

"Which is also why we propose making some kind of arrangement with the Gogobans," Davis said.

"Arrangement? What in the blighted blister does that mean?" Fennu demanded.

"It may very well mean ceding a bit of land, Lord Kye," Davis said flatly.

For a military man, Davis did seem suited for conversation with nobility.

Fennu's face turned an even darker shade of red. "This is *my* land we're talking about."

"If I understand correctly, you are a servant of the royal family of Shiansan. This is their land," Davis said. "You are a steward. If losing some of this land allows you to retain the rest of your stewardship rather than losing it all, we believe that would be a better result."

"Pah!" Fennu spat.

"Fennu, there is wisdom in this," Hesh said, her voice sharp but lowered in a sympathetic tone. "This is the duty we all have."

Fennu folded his arms and bit his lip, a rare sight. "Neither of you are losing your lands," Fennu muttered.

"We understand, Lord Kye, but such is the way of war," Davis said.

"So do we send word for negotiation?" Hesh asked.

"Not yet, Lady Halimah," Davis said. "It's best we wait for the rest of the forces to arrive. Negotiations will likely go more favorably under those circumstances."

"That is wise," Hesh said.

"It should also be noted," Davis added, "that we passed another group of soldiers on our way here. I would expect them to arrive any moment, but they said they were under your command, Lady Halimah."

"Yes," Hesh said. "And we are expecting another small force from Lord Kye's provinces as well."

Davis stroked his beard and said, "Very good, though I don't want to wait too long before meeting with the Gogobans. If they receive word about the other nations, then that puts our chances for peace at risk."

Siwen grunted.

"Do you have something to add, Lord Huan?" Davis asked appraisingly.

Siwen folded his arms and let out a sigh before deciding how to word his concerns. "None of what is happening here is coincidence.

It is orchestrated. There will not be a simple solution. We need to prepare for the very real possibility that the only way Gogoba is backing down is through force."

"You really think they'd sacrifice themselves here for the sake of their allies?" Hesh asked, hands on hips.

"I would not be surprised," Fennu said, "given the way they treated me the last time I attempted negotiations. You'd think they were bent on extermination."

"What do we do in that case?" Hesh asked.

"Give them what they want," Davis said. "We will lose lives that I would rather spare, but if we eradicate them here, then we at least eliminate a looming threat. The rest of this war with the other nations will not be so simple as this."

Siwen nodded. City fortresses like Xhi and Nansha were built to withstand sieges. The war with Kombida would need to be fought in places like this on the grasslands and hills. Such open battle would be an incredibly unfair advantage against their superior numbers, and Kombida was known for being extremely methodical. He would anticipate them to have a much more drawn-out offensive than Gogoba.

Worse still, he couldn't help but feel like this entire thing was just wrong. Every person he'd killed or injured over the last few days didn't need to die. All of his own soldiers who'd fallen should have been at home with their families, not out here, their blood decorating this hill. He'd lost sight of what they were fighting for. What were they defending?

Their families.

His fists clenched. If he wasn't here fighting, other people would be dying. And if he had the power to prevent some of their deaths and did nothing, then it would be the blood of the innocents on his hands instead of the blood of his enemies.

It was a cruel trade, but a necessary one.

"Send an emissary," Siwen said. "Ask if we can arrange a meeting with them tomorrow morning. Let's have every soldier dressed and prepared to launch a counterassault. As soon as they say no, I want us hammering down on them. Once they our out of the way, we can allocate our resources elsewhere."

"I'll have it done, Lord Huan," Davis said. He saluted to them as a whole before mounting back up and whistling to his men before they rode off.

Siwen nodded to the others, dismissing himself as he hurried back out to help those who were assisting the wounded into camp. Ignoring his own injuries, he bent down to assist a man with a stab wound on his knee who was not able to rise.

"Have you seen Lord Yubo Huan?" Siwen asked as he helped the man limp back to camp.

"Not since the beginning, lord," the man said through clenched teeth.

Once he'd safely deposited the man at the medical tent, he went back again.

"Over here, Lord Huan," a soldier called out to him. Siwen approached to find three soldiers bent over a single body. A spear haft still protruded from the man's leg, but his armor was dented and torn from several wounds. Despite the large gash across his face, they all recognized him.

Siwen bit his lower lip and bent down, closing the eyes of his dead father. "Help the wounded back to camp," he said in a voice that was more solid than he felt. "We can worry about the dead later." He knew that saying the words made him seem callous, but there were so many wounded that they needed all the help they could get.

It was strange to look at his father and see no movement at all. He'd been alive just moments ago, stoic and brave in the face of battle. His first instinct had been to close the eyes because the emptiness there was more grisly than all the wounds on his body. There was more finality with them closed.

He wondered if it would help the Gogobans to know that the man responsible for the dragonblood harvesting was now dead. They'd had their justice. He knew it wouldn't be enough though. They wanted more than justice.

Taking his own advice, he rose and went to help the others. They'd still have time to gather and burn the dead, but tomorrow, others would be joining them.

Chapter Twenty-Nine

In Pursuit of Justice

Mia

Mia took the last two steps to reach the top of the hill. The height provided an excellent view of the city of Xhi. A wall surrounded the entire city, but it also boasted a large castle ringed by another, even larger wall, all constructed of the same gray stone. The buildings were taller than she would have thought, and greater in quantity. It was the most populated city she'd seen by a large margin.

She was not far from one of the city gates, which were wide open as people came and went, mostly in large groups with only the occasional individual. Despite the bustle, it seemed a calm place, not far from the beauty of nature.

This was a flatter region than most of the places she'd visited so far. Only the faintest hint of a mountain peak rose on the horizon. The rest of the landscape was riddled with fields and thickets. The hill she stood on was covered in various plants, though she did not have the liberty to look down at them for closer observation.

Her will was not her own.

Rowan strode up beside her and folded her arms.

"I had siblings," Rowan said, her voice softer than Mia had ever heard. "Dragon clutches usually come in three to five eggs. I was one of four." Rowan was silent for a moment. Contemplative. "I remember that I had three siblings, though I can only remember the face of one of them, just before he was brutalized. We were very young. I think we'd only been hatched for a couple weeks at most. It was probably about the time where we would have gone off on our own." She looked at Mia. "Dragons have a very different society than humans. We aren't so dependent."

Rowan returned her attention to the city as she grabbed her lower lip between two fingers. "They took me then, but I remember hearing that they'd killed all the other dragons." She shook her head. "It was so long ago. I'd forgotten what outside even looked like. I lived in that prison cell where you saw me ever since then. They'd found a way to prompt me into my human form and once I was chained up, that was the end of it. You know a little of that."

There was a silence around them, and Mia realized that the buzz of insects had ceased. Perhaps they were instinctive enough to recognize what Rowan was.

"Dayelle told me all about your friend, Dami," Rowan said. "He was impulsive. Reckless. He was blinded by his own conceit. He considered himself invincible, free to choose whatever he wanted without consequence, and then completely convinced that whatever choice he made was the right one. Justice and vengeance do not look the same."

Rowan paused to sigh as she folded her arms and regarded the city. "There is more to it than that. I believe there's a proper order to things—a hierarchy if you will. It needs to be restored. Dayelle has operated under secrecy for a long time, but there are other strategies to achieve the same goal. The action I am about to take serves multiple services, and justice is only one of them. A message must be sent and understood without misunderstanding."

She regarded Mia for a moment before nodding to herself. "You will observe and behold."

Normally, Mia would have said something snappy or simply yawned to express boredom, but all she did was stare. Her frustration at her inability only lasted a moment. There was something strangely lethargic about having no control over herself.

Rowan stepped a good distance away from Mia, rolling her neck and shaking out her arms. Her body changed quickly as her arms, legs, and head expanded, wings spawning from her back, long tail erupting out behind her. It took less than a couple seconds, but Rowan had assumed her complete dragon form, a sight even more shocking than Mia had ever expected.

Rowan was enormous, her long body covered in red and black scales that glittered under the sunlight. The wings that spread out to either side could have covered Zein's entire facility twice over in their embrace. She flexed, shaking out her limbs as a guttural sigh vibrated from her throat. Four powerful legs pounded the ground, tearing up earth. Her tail whipped over Mia's head with a whoosh.

After stretching her back, Rowan's voice came out as an earth-trembling growl. A few people walking on the street in the distance had taken notice, pointing and screaming. Rowan answered with a bellowing roar that drowned out everything else. The roar almost sounded like two different voices, a deep sound that registered like an earthquake, and a higher pitched note that warbled.

With a single bound and pump of her wings, Rowan burst into the air, showering Mia in clods of dirt as the ground exploded beneath the monstrous feet. Mia didn't even flinch. She would be forced to watch this scene, and she was all too aware of what was about to unfold.

Gusts of air buffeted against Mia as Rowan launched into the distance. The people on the road scattered in all directions, leaving everything behind as they ran for their lives.

Rowan passed over them, liquid flame pouring from between her jaws like a geyser. Even from that distance, heat washed over Mia. Nothing would survive that, not even her. She would have melted beneath it.

Every surface the fire touched immediately became a blackened ruination that simmered like an ember. The screaming from the road ended immediately, but the flames trailed all the way to the gate which exploded with more fervor than she would have thought possible. She didn't know stone could burn like it did.

The jet of flame ceased as Rowan flew higher over the city. This was a spectacle for her. Everyone would see their impending doom, and nobody would be able to stop it. From what she understood, the vast majority of Xhi's soldiers had just been sent out to fight a different battle. Nobody would have been expecting something like this.

Mia tried to retreat from the scene—if only her consciousness could vanish—but she would get no such opportunity. She was the witness, after all. But why? What did Rowan gain by having Mia watch such horror? Anger burned in her.

Rowan swooped around, aiming low on her way back toward the city. The creature was magnificent, and Mia might have thought she was beautiful if not for the absolute terror that it truly was. More flames poured into the city streets. Tall, splendid buildings fell to the inferno. Rowan kept at it, burning more and more with every pass.

Picked up by Mia's enhanced hearing, the screams spoke of the absolute nightmare within the walls. And for her, it was like being back on that first mission when they'd been sent to acquire the bottles of dragonsbane from that production plant. She'd had to watch as Dami and Ambrose tore through the people there, but that was nothing compared to this.

Pain boiled in her chest.

There were thousands of people within Xhi. Tens of thousands. All of them were burning because this was where King Hinam Nikato's living family resided. But why did the whole city have to burn? Couldn't Rowan have sent Mia in to kill them more discreetly? Then all these innocents wouldn't have to die as well.

Mia staggered to a knee as realization struck her.

That was why she was forced to watch. Rowan wanted her to believe that there were only two ways to go. In one way, the dragons could handle things on their own, burning down the entire world, but in the other, Mia could be their tool, taking precise strokes to root out their enemies. It only confirmed her suspicions more. Rowan wanted her complicit.

Then she wondered about Ven and Zein. They'd had the same transfusion, but they weren't here, forced by Rowan to watch the massacre. Did that mean Rowan couldn't control them?

A tremor shook across Mia's body, but her eyes remained fixated on the burning city, drying at the intense heat that radiated over her.

A few people stumbled out of the city, somehow escaping the flames. They moved at a ragged pace. She could only imagine how they'd managed to get through, but she watched as burned garments fell away as they discarded their smoldering remains. The people trudged on.

Then Mia realized she was watching them and couldn't look away. That meant *Rowan* was watching. She didn't want any survivors, and Mia was operating as her agent.

Mia's muscles tensed. She couldn't stand to do this. Why wasn't she strong enough to resist? She'd done it before, she *had* to be able to do it again. This was *her* body, even if it had Rowan's blood flowing through it. Her muscles twitched and trembled. It shouldn't have felt so hard to move her own body, but she realized with utter fear that if she'd been able to resist all along, she never would have hurt Ven. She never would have killed those other people. If she could stop now, then wouldn't it mean she could have stopped then as well? That would mean she was responsible for the consequences of those actions.

I was being controlled. The muscles of her arm twitched. It was true. She *was* being controlled.

Her hands tightened into fists, but still her eyes remained open.

A sharp breath filled her lungs, and the vivid memory of Ven's words from a year ago came flooding in. *You are important. You are beautiful. You are good, and smart, and caring. You have value. You have the ability to do great things.*

Perhaps this was one of those great things. Regaining her own will. Her own sense of self. The dragons would ruin the world, but that didn't mean she had to help them. She *was* important. Ven believed so. Rowan clearly believed so.

Her voice growled within her as the pain ebbed. Her eyes finally tore away from the fleeing citizens to regard the dragon burning the other side of the city. The whole place was up in flames.

Body shaking, Mia struggled to her feet. The pull from Rowan did not release. She was too close. She took trembling steps backwards, retreating from the carnage. Every step was like wading through mud, but each one worked to settle her resolve. Gradually, her senses became her own.

I have the ability to do great things. She repeated the words over and over in her mind until she moved more steadily. With a scream she turned and jumped forward, trying to run but feeling like she'd almost forgotten how.

Behind her, Rowan roared, perhaps recognizing that Mia was breaking away. Maybe she would come for her and burn her with the others, but wasn't that a better fate than serving the dragon's purpose? She gritted her teeth and tried again, her feet finding ground as she struggled to pump them forward. Finally, she burst into a sprint, gaining speed, exhilarated by the air she gasped into her lungs. The ground zipped away beneath her as her legs pumped faster. Tears blurred her vision, and she didn't look back to see if Rowan pursued. She only ran faster and faster, creating as much distance from the dragon as possible.

She would be free.

Chapter Thirty

Teamon

Ven Yashke

"Sitena Rosars," Ven said, his voice a growl. He could scarcely understand her betrayal. Why would someone of her status ever need to swear allegiance to the dragons? She'd made a grave error. Ven, Morgan, and Valerie were still armed. Perhaps she was confident that they were not skilled enough to resist. "You will lose everything for this betrayal."

Sitena remained seated, shaking her head. The soldiers were about to come around the couches, but Morgan and Valerie also shot to their feet, sharing a look.

Ven did not know if they would comply with this ridiculous arrest, but he had come too far to let his too-trusting self fall into someone else's hands once again. Sitena certainly had no reason to believe that Ven was the type of person who would fight unless he was hiding behind Mia, but he held no such reservations now that he knew her true colors.

His mace was in his hand in a flash. Without warning, he bashed the man behind him directly on the skull. Valerie and Morgan dispatched the respective soldiers on either side of them almost as quickly. Valerie moved to close the door while Ven stepped right over to Sitena and clapped a hand over her face, clasping the back of her head with his other hand after dropping his mace on the floor.

Sitena tried to yell for help, but Ven kept his hands firmly in place, surprised at his own strength.

"What do we do with her?" Ven asked, tone harsh.

"She's a dragonsworn, Ven," Morgan said. "We kill her. There is not an alternative."

"Could we escape with her as a hostage?" Valerie asked.

"No," Ven said darkly. "She has many trained soldiers here. They'd stick us through the back with a crossbow bolt before we made it out of the courtyard."

"Then with all due haste, stab her so we can leave," Morgan said.

Ven gritted his teeth. "Hold on." He blinked down at Sitena who was still wriggling beneath his grip, struggling to break free. She was in her fifties but still a very strong woman. If not for his impervious trait and lots of recent training, he wasn't sure he'd have been able to hold her like this.

"Why, Sitena?" Ven asked. Morgan and Valerie both scoffed at him. It may very well have been a useless question, but Ven had to understand how someone could willingly serve the dragons, especially someone with Sitena with so much at stake. "You will lose everything over this. What could the dragons possibly have offered you?"

Sitena's eyes settled on Ven's, her eyes filled with barely concealed rage. Ven pulled his hand down for a moment, allowing Sitena to speak. "You will not make it out of here alive."

"Answer my question or we end you now," Ven said.

"Ven, hurry this up. The sooner we move on the better," Morgan said, bloodied sword in hand.

Sitena's glare could have shot bullets through steel. "You don't understand, Ven. Everything I have is *because* of the dragon."

Ven narrowed his eyes. That could make sense. He had no idea how wealthy she was in Earth terms, but she was probably the equivalent of a billionaire. "How long have you been involved with them?"

"Since I was thirteen," Sitena said. She stared back at him. It wasn't a quick response, but he had to realize that she was going to try anything to delay the time. The longer it took to answer Ven's questions, the better it was for her. "She has been good to me, as you can see."

Very young. Ven's mouth gaped open just a bit. He was about to ask more, but Sitena pressed on.

"I had just lost my parents, inheriting an estate on the brink of ruin. She came to me with a proposition that she would be able to save the estate. She was successful, naturally. Living for hundreds of years clearly endowed the dragon with knowing what kind of investments to make." Sitena would have kept going, but Morgan groaned in frustration.

"Alright, Ven, I think that will suffice. She was in distress, dragons offered help, she became greedy, and here we are. Let's be done with her."

Ven still hesitated. His situation was not much different from hers. Perhaps this was one of Dayelle's signature techniques. Approaching and beguiling children when they were most vulnerable did seem rather effective.

Sitena made a move for it, trying to spring up from her chair. She screamed before Ven could clap a hand back over her face, but Morgan was quick to the stroke, plunging her sword through Sitena's gut.

Ven was too shocked to react to the sudden end, but Morgan finished Sitena off without fanfare before rushing to the closed door where Valerie waited.

"Hurry," Morgan said to Ven.

Blinking once more at Sitena's body, Ven shook his head, retrieved his mace, and came up beside them. "Weapons away," Ven said, doing so with his mace. "We should proceed through the castle briskly. It's not uncommon to see people dashing about here as I'm sure you noted. We should take a similar approach to our own pace."

Morgan and Valerie cleaned their swords off on the clothing of the soldiers they'd killed then came up behind Ven as he braced the door handle. One final glance at the room had him considering how much he'd changed. Killing was coming easier to him. When the conditions demanded it, he would deliver.

"Close the door behind us," Ven said before swinging the door open and leading them out. There was already another soldier approaching from the opposite end of the hallway, but their best hope was that he was not heading for Sitena. Ven avoided looking at the man as they passed in the hall. The three of them quickened their pace and started descending the first flight of stairs.

"Do they have anybody with Zebadons?" Morgan hissed at Ven.

"I wouldn't be surprised," Ven said.

"They will hunt us," Morgan said.

Ven didn't respond. He had no idea what they would actually do. Didn't Sitena lack an heir? He imagined there would be utter chaos trying to resolve what would happen with her estate, but he didn't want to be around in case anybody wanted retribution. Tons of these people were now out of a job. Ven also didn't know if all these people were dragonsworn. In fact, he was almost certain that many of the people who were working for the Drekis Alliance didn't even know that it was being run by dragons, especially if even someone like Siwen had worked for them.

They reached the bottom floor and strode across the large entryway. Several others milled about their business, and if there were a time to come across an issue, it would be here. Ven kept his eyes ahead, focusing on the exit as they walked briskly to the other side. Once they got outside, they could start to jog without too much attention.

The woman who'd escorted them up to Sitena was there, a deep frown across her face as she regarded them. Ven averted his gaze and shifted his expression to appear slightly upset, hoping it would indicate that he was displeased with the way things had gone upstairs.

The woman made no move to stop them, but a pair of footsteps echoed loudly from the stairway behind them.

"Run," Morgan said just loud enough for them to hear.

Ven broke into a sprint just as he heard the voice behind them. "She's dead!" The words echoed through the large room. "Murdered!"

As others gasped, the woman who'd escorted them jumped out to grab Ven, but he shoved her aside. They were almost out the door when a guard popped in front of them to block their escape. Ven plowed on even as the guard called for them to stop, his spear aimed for Ven's chest.

Ven pushed at the spear, taking the point in his arm. The pain was sharp. Pain was something he could manage, imprisonment was not. His shoulder slammed into the guard, sending the man to the side. They were outside, but they still needed to cross the courtyard as well as the whole lower section of the castle grounds, which was essentially a small village. There were two more gates to get through before they'd reach their horses. Even then, if there were Zebadon riders among their ranks, the massive horses would easily catch up to them.

Morgan outpaced Ven, taking the lead now that they were in an open sprint. It seemed Ven had a lot more of his own limits to test if he wanted to take full advantage of his adaptive trait. He was a long way from becoming like Mia.

Ven finally had the thought to touch the device still stuck to the inside of his ear. He pushed the button and spoke as he ran. "Zein,

Sitena was a dragonsworn. You were right not to come to her. She's dead, but I'm probably in trouble."

Besides a quick look from Morgan, neither of them had anything to say about what Ven had just done. There was simply no time to ask. Ven didn't know how much trouble they were really in right here, but he had to hope that Zein would be able to provide some insight if needed.

Before they reached the other side of the courtyard, a few other people burst out of the keep behind them and shouts filled the air. Maybe coming here was a bad idea after all, Ven conceded.

"What's going on?" demanded one of the two guards who stood at the base of the first gatehouse.

"Some kind of attack," Ven said, voice shaking in the most dramatic, terrified voice he could muster.

Thankfully, there were so many voices shouting that their words were unclear, though Ven did pick out the word "halt" being used at least once.

Morgan didn't pause her stride. She ran right by the two soldiers. Ven made it by as well, but one of them grabbed Valerie by the arm. She gasped, making Ven skid to a stop so he could turn to help, but before he was able to do anything, Valerie headbutted the man in the nose and twisted out of his grip. She was off at a sprint right beside him. Morgan was a few paces ahead.

The one guard whose nose was *not* gushing with blood shouted out to some other soldiers and the sound of metal clanging rang out across the stone walls.

By the time Morgan reached the lower gate, four guards barred the path ahead. She paused there and started yelling at them. "Lady Rosars is dead!" she declared.

"We'll get that sorted," said one of the guards, "but we shouldn't be letting anyone in or out until we know what's—"

"Dragonsworn!" Ven said, panting as he drew to a halt beside Morgan. "They say dragons have returned." He had to hope the shocking news would convince the men to let them through. He glanced behind them. Other soldiers were charging down. They didn't have time for this. "Please, we must go to warn others."

"All in good time, sir," the soldier affirmed. It was the same man as earlier with the large mustache.

A couple other people also came, waiting to exit. The gate was still open, but some more guards were standing on the other side, keeping people from entering. They could maybe force themselves through both sides, but he knew his quick healing was making him take greater risks than normal. Morgan and Valerie could not afford such inconveniences. Perhaps he would have been better off without them after all.

"At least let these two through," Ven said, gesturing to Morgan and Valerie. "That is Lady Morgan Lauron, and she needs to return to her family at once."

The soldiers behind were getting closer.

"Sorry, Lady Lauron, but this is protocol," the guard said.

"Don't let them through," a voice shouted.

Ven bit his lip as his muscles tensed. They needed to get out. He sprang forward, shoving the nearest soldier and kicking away the one next to him. They both fell back. With the guards' attention on him, Valerie and Morgan slipped around to either side him.

A fist collided with Ven's jaw, snapping his head to the side. His vision exploded with stars and he stumbled back. Something sharp pressed against his chest and hands gripped him on each arm. Ven was strong, even without the imperviousness, but he hadn't had enough time to stretch that adaptation very far. He assumed it required years to reach the level at which Mia performed. Thus, he was unable to free himself.

When his vision cleared, he found himself restrained by two soldiers while another held a spear to his chest.

Valerie and Morgan had been caught as well, and more soldiers dragged them over.

Zein's voice buzzed in Ven's right ear.

"Ven, you forgot to turn the device off. What has happened?"

"We are being arrested?" Ven said, half to the guards and half so that Zein would hear and understand what was happening.

"They were the last ones to meet with Sitena," said another man through panting breaths.

"I can confirm," said a woman, panting even harder as she came up behind them. It was the woman who'd escorted them.

"She's actually dead, then?" said one of the other guards.

"She is, I saw it myself. And three other guards," reported one of the soldiers.

All eyes turned to Ven, particularly to his tunic. He followed their gaze down to his stomach where red flecks of blood went in a line across the surface. He'd be hard-pressed to get out of this one.

"She was a dragonsworn," Morgan said. "We had no other option but to kill her. Any honorable among you would have done the same."

"That's an extremely bold claim, especially regarding someone like Lady Rosars," the woman said.

Many of the people had begun conversing amongst themselves, clearly startled by the revelation, but the hold on Ven's arms did not slacken. Someone else took off running back toward the keep. There was shouting echoing from one of the smaller buildings, and more guards were animatedly discussing things from atop the walls. The chaos he'd expected was slowly unraveling.

"Who's in charge?" Ven asked.

"Shut it," said the guard holding Ven's right arm.

"Sitena was in possession of several dragonsbane weapons," Ven pressed, ignoring the pain as the man beside him tried to wrench it back. A warmth was spreading across his body as the wound on his side started to recover. "There are dragons. We will need to be prepared."

"Those villages that practically vanished are because of the dragons," Morgan added.

"I heard of those," one man muttered.

"This is not the place to discuss this," the woman said sternly.

"Frankly, I don't care what you think," said another soldier. "We all suspected Lady Rosars was involved in illegal activity."

Zein's voice came to Ven's ear again. "This is a lot worse than I could have imagined. It also means the dragons have no aversion to using the technology made from their blood. They could likely already be alerted to your presence there. You'll need to get as far away as possible."

"I'm arrested, remember?" Ven muttered back.

"We haven't forgotten," said one of the guards holding him.

"Regardless of what's about to happen," said the mustached guard, "we should put these three in a cell while we sort things out."

"You do understand that I'm a lady, correct?" Morgan asked.

"That does not make you exempt," the woman said. She made a gesture and the guards hauled the three of them toward the guard-house. Everyone else started running to and fro, with several people dashing up to the keep and a few people still gathering around the exit to try to leave. Even the soldiers escorting them bickered among themselves, one of them suggesting that they should leave.

Despite any further complaint, they ended up standing behind bars within the darkened building.

Ven heaved a sigh and leaned his head against the bars, ignoring the glares from both the women. Their confiscated weapons were set on the stone floor across the room.

One soldier drew the short straw and was forced to remain in the building with them as the other guards ran back over to the gate as the crowd grew. The guard stood in the doorway, arms folded as he watched the people, their panic rising. Voices crescendoed as more people filled the area.

"Did you really kill her, then?" the guard asked. He had a crooked nose and a raspy voice.

They didn't respond. Admission would only bring condemnation, and Ven was not prepared for anything like that.

Zein's voice buzzed in his ear with more than just a hint of panic. "Xhi burns! One of the dragons is destroying the entire city! You need to get out and locate that army immediately." The voice was loud enough that it gave Ven a shock of pain. He flinched and pressed a hand to his ear before sharing a wide-eyed look with Morgan and Valerie, his heartbeat racing.

"What is it?" Morgan said, eyes not only worried but narrowing in suspicion.

Ven gulped and shook his head. "Xhi is being destroyed by one of the dragons."

The clamor outside rose even more. Ven could only imagine that if Zein had received word via dragonblood technology communication, then perhaps some of Sitena's people were hearing the news as well.

"How do you know that?" the guard asked, his face bouncing between looking at Ven and out the door at the rising panic.

"The same way they do, apparently," Ven said, gesturing at the door.

"How do you know Sitena was a dragonsworn?"

It didn't go without notice that the guard did not refer to Sitena as a lady. Ven tried not to smirk. "We gave her information regarding the dragons, and she immediately ordered our arrest. It wasn't a difficult conclusion to make."

"So you know what's happening?" The guard placed a hand over the hilt of his sword, rubbing his fingers across the pommel with obvious nervousness.

"From what we can tell, the dragons are planning to regain their dominance over humanity, which they may have already done in many political aspects." Ven cleared his throat. As he'd suspected, there didn't seem to be a clear leader over the castle, giving him a glimmer of hope that he'd be able to negotiate his way out of it. "It's imperative that we get out of here. We're supposed to be gathering intelligence on the location of the dragonsworn army. That is why we'd stopped here. Sitena was bent on preventing that."

The guard chewed his lip while his hand continued stroking the hilt of his sword.

"Please," Morgan said, her features softening. "We do not have any time to waste, and who knows how long it will take all those other people to sort things out."

The guard shook his head to himself and gave Morgan a hard look. "Are you really a lady?"

"Of course," Morgan said, holding out her arms as if she was stating the most obvious thing. It was, certainly, very obvious, despite Morgan's meager attempt to appear more common. Her hair was too clean. Her clothes were too perfectly fitted.

"I suppose you do look the part," the guard muttered to himself, though still loud enough that Ven could hear. He let out a long breath. "I could get in some real trouble."

"With who?" Ven said.

"With Captain Teamon."

"Well did he order you to put us in here?" Ven asked. That name sounded vaguely familiar, and his first instinct was that they should avoid that man at all costs.

"No... But, well, I suppose we'll find out what he has to say now."

"You don't need to get him," Ven said.

"He's coming anyway." The guard took a step back so that he was no longer blocking the entryway.

Not a moment later, a man stepped through, body protected by thick leather armor. He had a sheathed sword at his waist with the familiar etchings and shape of dragon heads on the crossguard.

He was certainly familiar, but the memory was vague. Ven knew he'd seen the man somewhere. His wavy brown hair and scruffy beard had him looking like he should be the main character of a movie. The dragonsbane sword was a good indication that he'd probably been involved in the move against Dami.

"Let them out," Teamon said. He crossed his arms and regarded Ven. "Is it true about Sitena?"

"Yes," Ven said as the guard moved to release them.

"What made you believe it?"

"I shared a considerable amount of information regarding the dragons, and she immediately said I was too clever and ordered our arrest. She then said she had been working with a dragon since she was thirteen."

The barred gate swung open and the guard stepped aside while Teamon remained in his spot, arms folded.

"Well, I hope you're wrong," Teamon said. "Someone like her with the level of operation she's had... Well, it would mean that our greatest enemy has a lot of information. I've known something was off with her for quite a while. Quite frankly, you've relieved me of an obligation toward her." He gestured his head toward the door as the three of them emerged from the cell. "You'll find that many of the people she employed were not simply staying for financial reasons."

"What will happen here with the castle?" Ven asked, retrieving his mace since they made no move to stop him.

Teamon's eyes lingered on Morgan's dragonsbane dagger before she tucked it away.

"I will secure the keep. Sitena did not take adequate measures to establish inheritance of her property from what I know, so things could get violent. A few of her upper staff and I should be able to keep the business moving, and if what you say is true, then I will try to make the best use of the dragonsbane that was at her disposal."

Ven inclined his head. "If we locate the dragons and their army, could you be a reliable source for aid?"

Teamon withdrew his dragonsbane weapon, and Ven stepped back instinctively. He knew what that could do to him, and he'd brought some metal gauntlets along specifically for the potential need to wield one himself.

"There is something binding about wielding one of these," Teamon said. "An obligation. I may not have been much help against Dami's attack, but I will dedicate myself and any resources at my disposal to eradicating dragons."

"Even if it means no new development of dragonblood technology?" Ven pressed.

Teamon's expression darkened. "That was Sitena's endeavor, and I was... obligated to her."

Ven nodded. "I understand." He didn't have much room to question anybody given that he'd been directly employed by Dayelle. If that had been any judge of Ven's character, then he deserved the same fate as Sitena. "Will the guards let us out?"

"I'll let those people out," Teamon said, inclining his head towards those being restricted from leaving, then raised his eyebrows. "I think we've resolved the question of who killed Sitena, but there are also two dead soldiers and one who is severely wounded up there. Those soldiers weren't under my specific command, but the injured one could probably use a doctor before you leave."

"It's possible that he's also a dragonsworn," Ven said, considering the soldiers who'd tried to capture them initially. He'd thought they were dead and hadn't even considered the idea that one could have survived from his injuries, which was an embarrassing realization now that he considered the wounds they'd received.

Teamon shrugged. "That's a difficult thing to prove, but the man is somebody I've fought beside. It would be a shame to see him fall as another casualty of Sitena's deceit."

Ven regarded Valerie, who shook her head, and Morgan, who nodded hers. He sighed. "Alright, I'll see the man, but then we need to go as soon as possible."

"Understood. I will take you to him."

Chapter Thirty-One

Politician

Siwen Huan

Siwen panted as he stood over Zula Rakachi, the ruler of Gogoba. The other man's face was bleeding from a wound on his cheek, and one of his eyes was swollen shut. The battlefield was somber, with the last of the Gogobans either dead or captured. They'd refused any offer of peace, declaring that they would only accept a complete surrender of all of Shiansan. Even when offered all the land south of this battleground, they'd rejected it, Zula spitting on Siwen's feet. The absolute vehemence left them with little choice. The Gogoban force had to be eradicated. It was the only way to secure the border.

Save for a band of dissenters who'd left the night before, now the entire Gogoban army was gone. And to Siwen's distaste, it had not come without great cost. They'd lost hundreds of soldiers in the battle.

"Why couldn't you come to terms?" Siwen said, the words grating from his throat.

Zula spit at Siwen again, though this time it was mostly sticky blood, some of it clinging to his lips. "There are no terms for dragonsworn."

"We are not dragonsworn," Siwen said. "Your claim is bold. How do you dare use that as justification for what has happened? Look at this." Siwen gestured at the carnage that surrounded them, the metallic stench of gory death hanging like a fog that weighed upon his shoulders. The enormity of it made bile simmer in his throat.

Zula scowled, body swaying as he struggled to stay on one knee. "I saw all the records, Huan. House Nikato seemed to think it was important to record the imprisonment of the dragon and the assignment of the extraction labor to your family. I even saw black market records for the trade of dragon blood. I corresponded directly with your father and the handwriting on some of the records was completely identical. There's no denying it."

"I don't deny it," Siwen said, "and I don't defend it. Yubo is dead. King Nikato is dead. You had your justice yesterday. These lives were spent needlessly."

"The dragon needs to die. The taint of their blood needs to be purged."

"Then this is something you could have helped us resolve rather than invading our lands. Your actions were brash. Foolish." Siwen's tone was harsh. "Was it really worth the expense of your people's lives?"

Zula snarled. "Anything is worth the cost of eradicating the dragons. Not all of us were as fortunate as Shiansan, young Huan. Do you know why Gogoba is so desolate in the valley? Dragons burned the entire thing. All of it! A million people were slaughtered in a single week. Hundreds of years have not been able to restore that. This is what we all vowed to prevent. Harboring a dragon is not only extremely foolish, but it violates the most significant pact made by all of humanity."

"I understand exactly what it means," Siwen said, barely restraining his own growl. "Do you somehow believe that I and the rest of these people supported the decision to keep that monster in a cage?"

"It's more than that, Huan. Your nation has been using dragonblood instruments for too long. The only way to separate them from that is to purge it completely, and clearly the leaders of Shiansan are not reliable."

Siwen took a deep breath. He did not believe that using dragonblood technology would be so inherently evil that it would corrupt anybody who used it. Zula Rakachi, and by extension, the entire Gogoban nation, was a little more fanatical about it. Siwen had personally enforced confiscation efforts, turning items over to his father. That had probably only worked to drive up costs and put more money in the Huan family coffers. Somehow, it seemed, even King Nikato was profiting from it, which was revelation to him. It made sense though. No wonder the Nikato family always kept a force of superior warriors and a stash of dragonsbane weapons. They knew that the threat of imprisoning a dragon was a real one.

"You are wrong on that account," Siwen said, "but our concerns are greater than this squabble. The dragon is no longer imprisoned. It was freed by another one of its kind."

"Then I was too late," Zula said, lips curling back.

"No," Siwen said. "I suspect you were right on time. How did you come across that information regarding the dragon anyway?"

Zula only glared up at him for a long moment.

Siwen grunted in irritation. They should execute the man. He'd acted rashly, and it had cost the lives of thousands. The chances of changing his mind about this war also seemed slim, but the people of Gogoba would remember whatever action they took. If Shiansan actually managed to survive this war, then Siwen had to be able to make decisions that would be good for the long term survival of their people. "Have it your way," Siwen said. He bent down and hauled Zula to his feet. They would have to keep him prisoner until all of this could be resolved. In the best scenario, he'd wear down with time.

A couple of Siwen's soldiers came to assist him, and he ordered them to secure the Gogoban king as a prisoner.

With the Gogoban forces taken care of, they now needed to figure out how they would disseminate the rest of their forces to maximum effect. All of Fennu's forces would remain here, of course, and Hesh would move her entire force over to the west. Siwen was now completely in charge of the soldiers from Peskan, and they were the easiest to reallocate since their territory was the most secure.

Siwen was almost back to the camp when someone came sprinting towards him. The woman was young, and she was dressed in light, simple clothes, armed only with a long dagger. She worked as one of their scouts, and he'd taken reports from her plenty of times before.

More bad news most likely. He braced himself as she pulled up short and saluted.

"Anne, is it?" he asked, vaguely remembering her name.

She nodded and dropped her hand.

"Report."

Instead of speaking, she looked to either side then back at him.

"Understood," Siwen said, forcing back a groan. He led the way as he strode toward the side of the camp. They needed to speak somewhere where no prying ears could overhear. A couple other officers tried to get his attention, but he had to wave them off. It was clear that whatever Anne had to report, it was something that shouldn't wait. He walked briskly until they were a good distance away.

Anne kept her voice low as she said, "Xhi has been destroyed."

Siwen could barely contain his reaction as his heart sank. He glanced back toward the camp and folded his arms to keep them from shaking. "How do you know this?"

Anne held two fingers up to her left ear. "I have a... communication device. It is connected with a network of reports."

Siwen ground his teeth. This was only further confirmation regarding his suspicions. The use of dragonblood technology was so embedded into Shiansan society that his job of uprooting it had been an enormously vain effort. "Is this reliable?" he asked.

"Very," Anne said, but her eyes darted around and she looked like she was holding back a flood of words.

"Share everything," he said impatiently.

"Xhi was burned down by a dragon. It ruined the entire city. It even chased after survivors. Only one of our informants there managed to get away."

"Of how many?" Siwen asked, trying to wrap his head around the idea of a dragon destroying an entire city. That could have been Peskan. In a matter of days, it could be the entire world.

Anne shrugged. "Seven. Doesn't hurt to admit it now."

Siwen forced his arms to remain folded. "Who do you work for?"

Anne blinked at him, her eyes glossy with restrained tears. "Zein Huan."

"Of course you do." Siwen turned away from her and let out a long sigh. Despite his pretended disinterest, he had to wonder how deeply his cousin had entrenched himself in politics.

"There's something else, lord," Anne said.

Siwen composed himself and faced her, knowing that others would be watching their interaction even if they were out of earshot. "Go on."

"Your wife is no longer in Peskan. She was taken prisoner at Castia Mont. Lady Sitena Rosars has been discovered as a dragonsworn by Ven Yashke."

Siwen's hand clasped over his chest. That was not at all what he'd intended when he asked her to keep an eye on Ven. Perhaps he shouldn't have left her at all. They hadn't had enough time together. They would *never* have enough time. "Was anyone else with her?" he said, forcing the words.

"Yes, there was someone else named Valerie with them," Anne said, then paused and cupped a hand over her left ear. "Hold on."

"Are they speaking to you now?" Siwen asked, but Anne held up a hand to indicate that she was listening.

After a painfully long moment, she nodded to him. "It appears your wife was only held temporarily. They've killed Sitena Rosars and have been released, and they have a lead on the location for the dragon's army."

"Gah," Siwen sputtered. Receiving this information in such quick succession was causing his mind to spin. He'd been on the verge of abandoning his army to go storm a castle. The loss of the entire city of Xhi was a massive blow. Their entire hope for holding a defensive front had just collapsed. That left Peskan exposed and Nansha completely flanked. They could hold out for a while, certainly, but Shiansan was effectively doomed. The dragons were particularly bent on bringing it down, even risking their own exposure to see it through. The nations of men had once overthrown hundreds of dragons, but now they would struggle to defeat two?

But that had been a long time ago when there were no nations to divide them. It had simply been humanity fighting in defense of their very species. Unless they found a way to come together again, it was all too possible for them to lose everything their ancestors had fought to gain.

With all this fighting going on here, Siwen had almost lost sight of the true enemy. "Are you in direct communication with my wife?" Siwen asked.

"I am not," Anne said. "There is a central hub through which things are then relayed to the appropriate individuals. Also, Ven

Yashke is the one operating a communication device. We've received information regarding your wife through him."

Siwen nodded. The dragons needed to be dealt with, but he also needed to ensure that Shiansan did not get completely obliterated in the meantime. And, most importantly, he needed a way for this to happen *without* his wife getting killed.

"Where is the dragon now?" he asked.

"It could not be tracked. The surviving witness said it simply disappeared."

They weren't ready for this, even with what little preparations Siwen had been able to make. He'd been banking on the idea that the dragons would consider it too bold to strike personally. What would stop them from hitting Peskan next? Now he'd be scrambling.

This news changed everything. He nodded to Anne. There was work to do.

Chapter Thirty-Two

Assault

Mia

Mia moved briskly through the streets of Peskan. It took all her effort not to run. There was still this sense of something crawling down the back of her neck as though Rowan would drop from the sky behind her at any moment. The nightmarish scene she'd left behind her was never *truly* left behind. The fire and screams were behind every other blink of her eyes. She would *not* be a tool for that, which meant the next she and Rowan saw each other, one of them was going to die. And if that moment was right now, Mia would undoubtedly not be the one walking away.

She turned down a familiar street, ignoring the glances she got. After running straight here, she'd had no opportunity to acquire a cloak, so her features were fully visible. Though in reality, the eyes she lured were probably less for her attractiveness and more for her disheveled appearance. Running that quickly did not do wonders for her hair, and she imagined it would take at least an hour of brushing to undo the tangles. That was an hour she didn't have.

Before she even got to the building she was aiming for, she became aware of someone watching her, walking at an angle toward her. Her senses were so attuned that she could pick out the casual cadence of his steps on the ground, the breath filling his lungs, and the powerful heart that beat within his chest. All these and more combined into what she could only think of as a unique aura, one that was familiar.

She paused to face him. "Tem," she said, eyeing the doctor's assistant with his familiar dark brown hair and warm smile.

"You could knock, but no one will answer today," Tem said. The man had always been this casual. It was the opposite of disarming. Mia had been disenchanted by the idea of a man who could function the way Tem did even while assisting doctors who tortured their subjects. Zein at least fit the role of a heartless machine a little better.

"Where is he?" Mia said.

Tem shrugged. "He didn't share. He'll be gone for a few days from what I gather, but, I have something for you."

"That's alright, I need to find Ven."

"I can help you with that," Tem said. "Also, I can assure you that what I have for you will be just what you need." He headed toward the building Mia had just about knocked at. "Come on."

Mia worked her jaw for a moment as she considered him. "Were you expecting me?" she asked. This was certainly not the kind of interaction she'd expected. Her first priority was really to get on to Ven. If there was anything else he could do to help her resist Rowan's command, she needed it. And for all she knew, Peskan could be the next city to burn. She was actually surprised Rowan hadn't flown here right after. This had been the place that had imprisoned her all those years. Mia shuddered. What Rowan had shared about her life was horrifying, and it was decidedly best if she didn't think about it.

"Eventually," Tem said, opening the door and stepping inside. His pulse was calm and there was nothing unusual about his speech pattern or the heat radiating from his body. If there was any malice in his intent, she could not detect it.

Box it all, Mia really *did* get a lot better with her senses. It was amazing what she could do when she continued pushing her limits. She followed in after him.

Tem stood just inside, facing away from her to a single table. Sunlight came in from outside, lighting the place in a natural glow. A single, long box rested on the table in front of Tem. It was simple, like it had been crafted in haste. His attention remained rapt on the object before him.

"It has come to our attention that Dayelle and Rowan are intent on having dragons reassume control over Orund." Tem's voice took on a somber tone. "This... is something that should not be. I am not one who idealizes violence, thus my excitement when I heard of Doctor Huan's research. If the blood of dragons could heal people, that would be amazing. I could scarcely fathom the kind of harmonious coexistence that would have been possible between dragons and humans, but such was not our fate."

A somber moment hung with those words, but Mia only found herself confused by the sudden shift in Tem's mood. It made her all the more curious about what he could have inside that box. In fact, it made her a little wary.

"Life has required a lot from you, Mia," Tem said.

Mia said nothing. She'd felt the pressure ever since Dami escaped from the facility. She'd tried to run from it by escaping to Mavenda, and that had only brought destruction. Everywhere she went, problems followed.

"I don't know what will happen in the next few days," Tem continued, "but it will require more from you still. I hope I can at least help in my small way." He lifted the long box, revealing a plain, slender blade held within. The only thing that was particularly unique to it was the crossguard, displaying a single head of a dragon, not snarling or raging like the other swords she'd seen, but it was calm, mouth closed. It looked almost regal. "You will take this with you when you go to Ven."

Mia shook her head. She had not seen this particular weapon before. "Where did you get this?"

"That is a question for another day," Tem said. He closed the box without removing the weapon and tightened two leather straps that held it closed. "I have prepared a bag for you that also has a pair of gloves which should allow you to wield the weapon. I believe Ven has something similar. He has gained information regarding the general location of the dragon army, but I'm afraid the dragons might know his location. I think they incorrectly fear him more than you."

"The dragons fear Ven?" Mia almost smiled.

Tem shrugged. "Fear is a strong word, but there's something about him being an offworlder, I'm sure. That factor makes him almost a different breed. He doesn't have the same innate cultural and inherited traumas or experiences of the people of Orund. That can make somebody less predictable, which is apparently Dayelle's preference."

Mia regarded Tem open mouthed. "I didn't know you were so well-informed," she said after a moment.

"I've been catching up on things quite a bit the last few weeks," Tem said with a small smile. "What with the fate of the world soon to be determined, I can't be solely focused on research." He held out the boxed weapon to Mia. "Plus, with this in my possession, I'd be a fool to sit idly."

"You dodged my question regarding its origin," Mia pressed, taking the box from his hands. It had a strap that she could use to sling it over her shoulder. She didn't like having things brushed aside. It made her feel like he was withholding information.

"Which I did intentionally," Tem said, his expression stern. "I prefer not to lie. The simplest truth I can supply is that it has been with my family for many years." He gestured to a bag on the floor behind her. "You'll want to take that with you as well."

Mia didn't bother trying to hide her displeasure. If Tem didn't trust her, that was reasonable. At the same time, however, he was also handing her what was probably the most valuable possession Tem owned. She didn't imagine that his profession had earned him a large income. So he could trust her with valuable items and not valuable information. Perhaps he had something to be ashamed of, not that Mia would even know anything about that.

Tem was aware of her limited education, so the origin of the sword had to be something that she would personally take issue with. She'd have to address that later. Finding Ven was still the present objective.

"So where's Ven?" she asked, scooping up the other bag and sorting through its contents.

"He should have just left Castia Mont. He'll be heading east toward the village of Willow. It was recently destroyed in a similar fashion to Mavenda. I would strongly believe that the dragons know his location as well and will be making their own preparations."

Castia Mont. Mia shook her head. "Then I suppose there's no time to waste."

"Indeed." Tem gestured to the door. "Give Ven my regards. Help him stay alive. He's a little more reckless than you."

Mia knew that all too well. "Will do." Without saying goodbye, she slung the bag over her other shoulder and headed out. Simply carrying the dragonsbane weapon made her nervous, but she didn't feel anything strange as the container pressed tightly against her back after she tightened the strap across her chest.

Now that Mia was aware some people in Peskan knew what happened to Xhi, she was more conscious of the way different people were acting. It was clear who was informed and who wasn't. Most people milled about their normal business, but she noted more than a few different groups of people who seemed to be packing up their entire homes. Perhaps there was something else going on that she didn't know about. She didn't even know how many days had passed while she was being controlled by Rowan.

She kept her head down as she passed the part of the city that went near the castle. Despite the risk, she wandered up to the base of the castle where a couple guards stood. She asked after Ven, and they confirmed that he'd left days ago. Thankfully, they didn't seem to recognize her. She could imagine that her disheveled appearance certainly did wonders to disguise her, especially when compared to the last time she'd come through with her face exposed.

Mia also learned that most of the military force had left the city as well, under the direction of Yubo and Siwen. This gave her no other option but to pursue the information Tem had given her, though she was still suspicious. She knew he was Zein's man, but she didn't know him well enough to trust him. That being said, it was her only lead.

She wished she had a moment to eat something, but she had neither money nor the desire to steal. Her body could persist just fine without for quite a while, but not optimally. If she was well fed, her performance was almost double the capability versus when she was starved, and she hadn't properly eaten for three or four days now. Tracking time while she'd been controlled had seemed nearly impossible. At times, it was like she was half asleep, experiencing everything like a dream, especially when she was running, which was what she'd spent most of the time doing. The moments of greatest clarity were when Rowan wanted Mia to experience everything, like watching Xhi burn to the ground.

All that considered, she rummaged through the bag Tem had given her more thoroughly, relieved to find both bread and cheese. She'd eaten all of it by the time she got to the eastern gate. It still wasn't nearly enough, and she found herself eyeing a food stall set up at one of the last buildings inside the city gate. Traffic was considerably dense, and voices rose and fell in atmospheric fashion, but with her hearing, she still caught a few snippets of everyone's conversations. It was almost disorienting.

A sharp, quiet whisper stuck out from the other voices. It was a strange sound amid the cacophony, and she would have brushed it off if not for one very distinct word.

"That's Mia," the voice whispered. "I'm sure of it."

Mia spun off to the side, ducking behind the wall of the nearest building as she tried to hone in on the location of the voice. She stilled her breath and scanned the crowd, searching in the general direction of the voice.

"I lost her," the voice said.

She wasn't sure who the person was talking to, but this time she was able to locate them. They stood upon a second story balcony that overlooked the street. The balcony was concealed in afternoon shadow. There were gaps in the balustrade and several potted plants growing on the edges. It would be the perfect vantage point for someone who wanted to watch the comings and goings of those in the city. Mia blinked, her eyes adjusting immediately to see through the veil of shadow. There were two figures on the balcony. Now that she knew their exact location, honing in her senses was much easier.

"Send it in regardless. Dayelle will want to know," said a second voice.

Mia clenched her fists. They wouldn't be sending anything "in" about her. She hurried across the street, ducking beneath the general crowd now that she knew who to hide herself from. She didn't want to catch a lot of attention, but she knew how quickly communications could be sent. In a quick motion, she jumped, pressing her foot against the side of a passing wagon to leap high enough to grab the edge of the balcony. She pulled herself up, grabbed the top of the balustrade, and swung herself over, trying to keep her movements visibly feasible enough for an extremely competent human and nothing *beyond* that. Someone below did gasp, but Mia's movements were quick enough that probably very few people would have actually seen it happen.

The two people atop the balcony, a man and a woman, staggered back in surprise. Then the man fell out of his seat completely, a shriek escaping his mouth when he realized who Mia was. The woman held a device in her hand, poised as though ready to use it. Quick as lightning, Mia snatched the device from the woman's hand, prepared to crush it in her grip.

She needed to choose her words carefully. Even though her initial impulse was to grab them by their throats.

"Were you really about to blow my cover?" Mia said, cocking her head at them. "You weren't informed that these were compromised yet?" She said it as a question, and tightened her grip so the device shattered. Her tactic felt ridiculous, trying to convince them that she was still under Rowan's control.

"Wait," the woman said, "so you're still—"

"Yes," Mia said, not knowing what the woman was about to say, but trying to assert herself how Rowan would.

The man's eyes remained downcast as he spoke to her. "So how do we maintain contact?"

Mia narrowed her eyes at him, exuding confidence. Pretending was another of Ven's strengths, but Mia *was* confident. If not in her ruse, then her ability to violently enforce her will otherwise. "You have your protocol, don't you?"

"Yes, of course, but we can't go there," the man said. "Isn't the city... well... not safe?"

"What do you mean?" Mia said, stretching herself. Her instinct was that these were agents operating under the dragons, but she had to acknowledge that it was entirely possible that they worked as informants for a potential myriad of other options. Working for someone like Sitena Rosars was not out of the question. "I told you, communications are compromised."

"The assault," the man said, but the woman's eyes were narrowed at Mia. She suspected her.

The man had already said enough. They feared the city wouldn't be safe due to an incoming assault. Her idea that Peskan was only temporarily safe had just been verified. She needed more information, but asking any questions was likely to give her away since Rowan would already know the answer to any of them. Giving them any brief moment to act against her was not in her best interest. There was no other way to deal with them.

The two people shared a look.

Resolved, Mia slung the long wooden box off her shoulder and smashed it down at the woman. She'd already been reaching for something, but she was nowhere near fast enough to react as the wood connected with her skull. The man gasped and scrambled to his feet, turning to run. Mia clamped a hand over the man's mouth from behind and braced his back with her other hand. With a quick jerk, she twisted his head, neck snapping out of place. The heartbeats of both the man and woman were stilled. Dead. Her efficiency with killing was no longer bizarre, but she took no pleasure from it. Satisfaction, perhaps, but not pleasure.

Now she had to wonder what else these people had known. From what she gathered, there was at least some kind of fallback location for the dragons' agents within the city, but there was probably no simple way to find it. That was all she'd been able to glean.

She wished she knew what kind of assault was incoming. If it was another attack from Rowan, she didn't imagine they'd have any means of defending themselves. How humanity had overthrown dragons was beyond her comprehension at this point. An outright battle seemed nigh on impossible. A dragonsbane sword wouldn't do anything to keep her from completely burning up in the dragon-fire. Even with her resistance to flame, she doubted she could survive anything like that. She'd never felt more inclined to start building her adaptiveness for something in her entire life.

A peek back over the edge of the balcony let her know that nobody else was looking for her. She honed in on surrounding sounds, and nobody else appeared to be speaking about her. Satisfied, she turned her attention back to the building. It was not a small structure, and there was the possibility that she could learn more by scouring the place. She opened the door to the interior and proceeded method-ically, remaining as silent and thorough as possible to check each room. There were three rooms on the top floor. Two of them had beds and the other was empty. There were some weapons stashed, but little else.

The bottom floor was similar, aside from some cookware and general living supplies. No papers or other people. No other devices. She'd destroyed the communication device which had probably been a bad idea. She could have potentially used it to listen in. She'd acted too quickly, but it was better to be safe than to risk her location getting out.

Once certain she'd cleared the whole place, she headed outside, unconcerned with the bodies left behind. If she had to guess, it wouldn't matter in a short while anyway. She needed to get to Ven, but this information needed to get to their network. The only person she could speak with was Tem. With a groan, she ran back to go find him, hoping this assault would be something they could handle, but knowing that had absolutely no chance.

Chapter Thirty-Three

Refugees

Ven Yashke

By the time Ven, Morgan, and Valerie were outside of Castia Mont, Ven was eager to create as much distance from the place as possible. They steered to the east, making good time since their horses were equally excited to be moving. When checking the map Siwen had given him, he'd been able to locate the village of Willow almost directly east of Castia Mont, near the border of Okwan.

"At least our visit wasn't a complete waste of time," Morgan commented.

"Oh, come on," Ven said. "Minus the obvious risks, we got some good things out of that."

"We almost got killed," Valerie said.

"And then we *were* imprisoned," Morgan added.

"Yes, but we came out fine," Ven said. "In fact, we even killed a significant dragonsworn. I think that will cause some positive ripples in our favor."

"That still pales in comparison to us losing an entire city to drag-onfire," Morgan said, eyes distant.

"Yes," Ven said, their conversation dropping into somber silence. He couldn't even imagine the horror the people of Xhi might have experienced. Part of him felt inclined to rush out there and see how he could assist them. If there were any survivors, recovering from burns like that would be devastating and extremely difficult without the proper care and equipment. Despite the knowledge that going there to provide assistance was completely unreasonable, it did not alleviate the burden of wishing he could.

They were only four hours into their ride when they noticed a wave of people coming up the road toward them.

"Is that the army we're looking for?" Valerie said, placing her hand around her sword.

Ven shielded his eyes from the sun to get a better look as they stopped their horses. This did not seem like a normal occurrence. "They don't look like soldiers," Ven announced. In fact, they looked rather worse for wear, as some were clothed in little more than tatters.

"Then who are they?" Valerie asked, clearly wary about leaving one trouble behind just to find another.

As the people slowly got closer, they came into better detail. Many of them were haggard, emaciated. Ven sighed. He'd seen this kind of thing before. "Where I come from, we call them refugees."

Morgan and Valerie looked at each other.

"I think refugees are the same thing everywhere, Ven," Morgan said.

"It was kind of a joke," Ven said, though it was more of a mutter to himself.

"Are we all suspecting the same cause of their displacement?" Valerie said.

"I'm sure we can make a safe guess," Ven said. He heeled Butch forward. "I'll see if I can talk to some of them. If the dragons attacked Xhi, then perhaps their moment for subtlety is over, which means we're all in pretty big danger anyway."

Morgan and Valerie followed but stayed farther behind. He didn't blame them. With the way things had been on Orund, he wouldn't be surprised if there were agents hiding among all these people. In fact, he expected it and knew he'd need to proceed with extreme caution.

The number of refugees wasn't the largest Ven had seen before, but he estimated there were somewhere around two hundred. Possibly more.

"Hey there," Ven said, pulling up beside the first two people at the front of the group, a man and a woman who looked to be in their early twenties. "I take it you aren't traveling for leisure."

"What?" the man asked.

"Sorry," Ven said. "I was trying to lighten the atmosphere a bit. What happened?"

The woman scoffed. "Invasion, of course. Everyone's been slaughtered or taken."

"From where?" Ven asked, noting the woman's slight accent.

"From where?" the man repeated, giving the woman a worried look. "You haven't heard?"

"Are we the first ones you've seen come through?" the woman asked.

"I'm afraid we're in the dark," Ven said. "There were others?"

The man placed both hands to his head as tears welled in his eyes, face twisting as he held back a sob.

The woman's eyes took on a glazed appearance. "There should have been hundreds coming through here not more than a few days ago. They fled well ahead of us."

"I'm sorry, we haven't seen them, but we're just passing by ourselves to investigate," Ven said. "You never said where you're coming from, though."

The woman shook her head as other refugees now passed them on either side. "Hitar," she said.

Morgan shot Valerie a wide-eyed glance before recovering. "What happened there? What can you tell us?" Morgan demanded

"There's not much to say," the woman said. "There's a war. Something to do with kings and queens and their stupidity. It has nothing to do with the likes of us, yet we are the ones who suffer the consequences."

"Best get yourselves behind a castle!" shouted one of the other refugees. "That silver army is coming."

"What's the silver army?" Ven asked, keeping his voice loud so that any other person could answer.

"You see them, you die, that's all you need to know," the same refugee said.

The faces of the people who passed were still blank with shock. These weren't just the faces of people who'd lost their possessions. They'd seen death, and lots of it. That changed a person.

"Could that be them?" Valerie asked, her tone more hushed.

"The dragon army?" Ven said for confirmation. "Possibly. Mia did say they were all pretty well-equipped with metal armor. I could see the silver army being used as a descriptor."

Screams jarred them out of their conversation. As one, they all drew their weapons and looked about to locate the cause of the disturbance. It wasn't hard to find as a wall of soldiers appeared from the side of the road, emerging out of the cover of thick trees. They matched Mia's description exactly.

"Time to go," Ven said, but the mass of bodies around their horses caused just enough hesitation that one of the soldiers reached Ven on the left side. He swung down with his mace, batting the soldier's helmet.

Despite the blow, the soldier grabbed Ven's leg and tried to yank him from the saddle. Morgan and Valerie had successfully navigated out of the main traffic, but the refugees made a run for the woods on the opposite side. The attackers poured over the refugees. They didn't even have weapons drawn, opting instead to simply tackle people to the ground. Ven worried he was about to witness the exact horror Mia had described.

Ven smashed his mace into the arm that had grabbed him, bone crunching beneath the blow. The man didn't even react as his grip went limp, arm dangling with a terrible fracture. Ven decided now was not the best time to make an elongated observation and heeled

Butch forward. The horse jerked into a run, quickly outpacing the refugees on foot, reminding Ven of that old joke about how the best method for getting away from a bear was to run faster than your friend.

Watching the people around him get snatched up by the dragonsworn made his stomach clench with disgust. He hated the idea of simply running away so these people could be taken. There was a very specific reason the people weren't being killed. He knew what fate awaited them, and from what he understood, it was probably worse than death.

Now was not the time to fight. There were at least as many soldiers as there were refugees, and with the way the soldiers didn't seem to care at all about the damage their bodies received, the three of them wouldn't provide any real resistance. The best thing they could do was run away and report. Only an army would be able to face up against a force like this.

Ven tapped his communication device as he fought to catch up with Morgan and Valerie, but they were now veering the other direction. More soldiers were coming to ambush from the other side. "We found the army," Ven said as his communication connected. "They've been picking off refugees from Hitar. There are hundreds. We've been spotted. We're fleeing." It was hard to focus on what words to say as they wound through the trees.

Morgan was in the lead, and they managed to get back onto the road ahead of the army ambushing from either side. Such would not be their luck, however, for a line of soldiers ran out to block their retreat. Morgan and Valerie didn't slow as they steered right for the center of the dragonsworn soldiers. Their weapons were drawn.

Butch wasn't trained for this sort of thing. If those enemies hurt his horse as they stampeded through here, Ven worried about the very stupid decision that would force him to make. He was certainly no Mia, but he was still a subject.

The soldiers crouched at the ready, but Morgan and Valerie increased their pace , Ven falling a few more steps behind as Butch struggled to maintain speed. The women rode side by side as they crashed into the soldiers. Their weapons flashed, gouging into flesh and tearing armor. One soldier was trampled beneath the horses while another was battered away, two more getting struck by their weapons. Morgan and Valerie broke through, reaching the road beyond.

Ven aimed for the same place. The soldiers tried to fill the gap, but he slipped right through, jumping over the trampled body. Ven batted a sword away, protecting Butch's flank. They'd made it to the other side and Ven allowed himself to let go of his breath as Butch pounded down the road toward the others.

The dragonsworn did not give chase, so they slowed to a trot after a while.

"Well, I think we found them," Ven said to the women.

"That was terrifying," Valerie said. "Did either of you two notice how those soldiers didn't make any sound at all, not even when I nearly cut one of their arms off."

"That was an unnecessary detail," Ven said, "but yes. Mia described them as being lifeless." It was even worse than he'd imagined.

It was like they had no souls. That blank expression in their eyes was equally as haunting as looking at the eyes of someone who had died. Holy crap. Maybe they *were* dead. Did the dragonblood make them zombies?

"And we can safely assume they are capturing the refugees so that they can make their army even larger, correct?" Morgan said.

"That's the general idea," Ven confirmed.

"We need to evacuate everyone out of here," Morgan said.

"To where?" Ven asked.

"I might have recommended Castia Mont since it's the closest stronghold, but we don't know how reliable that will be. From here, they'd probably need to get to Peskan or all the way north to Colminan, but those are far enough away that they might not be able to reach them in any reasonable amount of time." Morgan heaved a long breath.

"So Castia Mont is probably still the best place," Ven said, realizing the issue.

"Even if we usher everyone there, we could be leading them to the same predicament," Valerie said.

Ven shrugged. "Maybe not. If Teamon was able to secure leadership of the castle, then it might at least be better than leaving villagers out here to fend for themselves. He did let us out at least, and we are very clear enemies of the dragons at this point. They tried to have me killed. I think if the dragons had influence over Teamon, we would not have left there alive."

"I am inclined to suggest people still go to those other cities," Morgan said.

"Better yet, straight up into Colminan," Valerie said. "With Xhi gone, Peskan might not be as secure either, leaving Colminan the safest stronghold they could get to."

"But it's still too far," Morgan said. "At least with Peskan, we're in charge. We have a greater guarantee of security even if we have to defend on more fronts. The city is well stocked, and my family has already sent a contingent of warriors from Wood Haven."

"Wood Haven?" Ven asked.

"Yes, it's the name of the county over which my family rules," Morgan said.

"And this contingent will be arriving in Peskan?"

"Yes. Part of our marriage included a continuation of a defensive agreement. I have no doubt it was upheld immediately upon the war declaration from Gogoba."

"Wait, you don't have confirmation that there's actually a contingent on the way?" Ven asked.

"We don't employ the use of the communication devices," Morgan said. "My family is the sort that would be trusted to uphold their agreements."

"Alright," Ven said, feeling decided. "Let's focus on getting people evacuated then. It seems like the dragonsworn are a lot closer to Castia Mont than I would have thought, but we could let the soldiers there know, and they might be able to help with the efforts." That was, unfortunately, the best they could hope for. Ven still wanted to know if there was some kind of headquarters for the dragons and their zombies, but the pressure to get people out of here was more significant. Every person that got caught was another soldier to fill the ranks.

He pressed the button on his communication device and reported everything back to Zein, who still hadn't responded from the earlier message. Hopefully that wasn't an issue.

Chapter Thirty-Four

Lost

Siwen Huan

Siwen gaped in utter shock as he watched the city of Sal burn. It was not the consequence of dragonfire, but of pure human brutality. An army from Kombida was currently inside, occupying the city and burning many of the buildings. In their haste to defeat the Gogoban forces, the Shiansan forces had neglected to consider that Kombida already had a ready striking force. Fennu Kye had failed to leave enough soldiers within the city to defend against potential attack. The Kombidan war declaration could very well have been delivered on the same day as the invasion itself.

Beside him, Lord Fennu Kye wept openly. His son and daughter also cried, though with less wailing.

Siwen was still trying to process the magnitude of all this, but there was little time to consider. A stream of fleeing survivors was rounding the edge of the mountain, heading towards the next nearest fortification, which would be Peskan. The Kombidan army was not pursuing, but there was still that risk.

"What do we do, lord?" said Commander Elise Sherwood from behind him.

Siwen didn't know the best course of action from here. It appeared that Peskan was perhaps already ruined as well, though he suspected Anne, Zein's little spy, would have reported to him if that had happened. It seemed possible that even Nansha was in ruins.

Lady Halimah was on her way back to her city to make preparations for the anticipated invasion there. A single platoon of riders from the Shi-enn force had accompanied her, while the bulk of them were riding to Xhi, hoping to confirm that the information Siwen had shared was incorrect. The very idea that Xhi had been burned to the ground by a dragon felt impossible, but Siwen still believed it. Once they confirmed the destruction of Xhi, they would reallocate troops to Nansha and Peskan. Those were the only two major defensible locations that remained.

Siwen and the remaining troops under him were supposed to stop in Sal on the way back to Peskan so that they had a general assessment. This was not at all what they'd expected to find.

"Sir?" Elise said.

"We should get to those people who've escaped," Siwen said, making a quick decision. "We need to defend their retreat and get them back to Peskan."

"What of Sal?" Fennu bellowed. "What of those swine who have taken it? We should slaughter them."

It was not an unexpected reaction from the man. Siwen chose to be direct with him. "We still need our allies from Luedan, Lord Kye. The best we can do is care for those who are yet living."

"What of Mother?" Du Kye asked.

"She may very well be among those fleeing," Siwen said. "Come. We can learn more from them."

Siwen heeled onward without waiting for a response. He knew others would follow, which meant they all would. Fennu did not possess the right charisma to go against anything Siwen had to say, especially not where war was concerned. Commerce was a different matter, but this was not the time for that.

Their timing was good, because a few soldiers were trailing after Siwen's fleeing countrymen. They seemed intent on picking off those who straggled at the back of the crowd. Pounding horses behind him let Siwen know that he was still in good company without looking back. He drew his sword, charging ahead of the others. His Zebadon was the perfect warhorse, never faltering.

It still took several minutes of galloping before Siwen reached the first opponent. The Kombidan soldier wielded a spear, so Siwen quickly pulled up his scavenged shield in time to block a glancing blow. It crashed hard into his shield but then deflected off, and Siwen leaned to the same side, sword jabbing, scoring a hit right in the man's neck. He toppled, and Siwen was already cutting down the next rider.

The other Kombidan soldiers halted their scattered pursuit and started falling back to the city. Wise. He'd actually hoped to cut a few more of them down to at least increase the losses on their side. Any death suffered by their enemies would reduce the chances of them invading Peskan, though he already knew that was probably inevitable. The best-case scenario was that Kombida had suffered heavy losses in taking Sal.

He felt terrible for thinking about it. More lives lost. Perhaps this was exactly what the dragons wanted. People killing people. It would certainly aid their chances at regaining dominance. Zein's informant, Anne, was giving Siwen regular updates now from the communication device. There were reasonable arguments against allowing dragonblood research, but he'd be a fool to not admit the convenience of the technology. He wasn't sure how reliable all of it was, but apparently his wife and Ven had learned of some kind of war in Hitar that had resulted in hundreds of refugees seeking shelter. Some of them would maybe make it all the way to Peskan.

Peskan had no news at all, which was a good thing. Siwen would have been lying if he said he wasn't worried that the city had been destroyed as well. After all, that was where one of the dragon's had been held prisoner for years. How it had been spared so far was beyond him, but if his suspicion was correct, then the dragons wanted more people to kill each other. They'd been rather successful with that so far.

Once certain the Kombidan forces were no longer in pursuit, he directed his troops to join the survivors of the invasion. He got a report from some of the civilians about the sudden appearance of the Kombidan army that was painfully reminiscent of what happened to Fort Sal. This was so well executed that he had to imagine some mastermind pulling all the strings, perfectly informed about the location of all their forces. He'd bet money that there were spies among their ranks.

Hearing the tale of Sal's defeat only made his own worries grow. He didn't know how they'd get out of this. Their odds were bleak even before both Xhi and Sal had fallen, but now? Would surrender be an option? Anything was better than another takeover by dragons, but if he surrendered, he was certain they'd execute him. He muttered an apology to Morgan, wishing that she were here with him. He'd been a fool not to have her join him.

They may have only met eight months ago, but even with everything going on, she was his first thought every morning and his final comforting thought every night. When he'd first seen her brown eyes, glittering in the evening sun, he'd known she was the one he would marry.

Every passing, enchanting moment since then had solidified his resolve that she was the one who would make him whole.

Even thinking of Morgan made him stronger. His chest swelled with determination, the hopelessness of their predicament diminishing. They'd find a solution.

Anne rode up toward Siwen, and he found himself bracing against whatever new misfortune he'd have to navigate. Seeing his expression, Anne's lips twitched before she spoke, pulling up directly beside him to lower her voice just enough for him to hear. "Scouts between Peskan and Xhi have reported sightings of an army en route to the city. It seems Peskan is next on the list. Estimates have them at three days out."

Siwen nodded acknowledgement, aware of the frown that deepened his expression. This was a battle they'd be ready for. "Thank you," was all he said, and Anne rode off, leaving him alone for at least a moment.

If there was any sensible way for them to end this war without total annihilation, he would take it, but he also wouldn't hesitate to defend his lands and eradicate any who sought to destroy the lives and freedoms of his people.

A quick glance revealed that Elise Sherwood rode close behind, and it had him pondering to what extent he would go to live up to that commitment. Would he be willing to use the weapon she carried? He'd been tolerating the use of the communication devices. Would using the power of a dragon's breath be much different?

Yes, it certainly would. He'd reached the point where he didn't think things could get worse than they already were. Using the weapon, however, would potentially eliminate the option to end this war any other way that through violence. He had to believe that there was another solution, and using the weapon felt like it would be giving up on that hope.

Chapter Thirty-Five

Calling

Mia

Mia stood atop a third-floor balcony in the middle of Peskan. It had been two whole days since she'd killed the agents. Tem had confirmed that they weren't Zein's, much to her relief, but they still wouldn't ever be able to identify if the pair had been working for the dragons.

She listened as Tem provided instructions on the use of the communication device. It was simple, requiring only the touch of a button. After she was confident enough in her ability to use it, Tem nodded to her.

"I'll leave you to it, then," he said, heading back inside.

She waited until she heard his retreating footsteps going down the stairs before she leaned over the balcony and stared out at the evening sun. The city was on high alert. Everyone knew what was going on at this point, and a large militia force was being mustered in addition to everyone making hasty preparations for their homes and stores. War was coming.

A shiver went up Mia's back as she thought of the impending terror, and she hugged the strap holding the dragonsbane sword to her back just a little tighter. She absently tried on one of the gauntlets Tem had provided her before pressing the button on the communication device. She flexed her hand and spoke quietly. "Hey Ven. It's Mia. I'm... back for now. I broke away again, and I'm here in Peskan. I almost came to find you, but it sounds like the city is about to be attacked. As much as I hate to admit it, I think I need to stay here and help. I don't think Rowan will interfere here as long as the other nations are attacking." She paused, trying to collect her thoughts before saying more.

To her surprise, Ven's voice came through, the sound penetrating as if through a rainstorm at first, but then it cleared up. "Mia!" The excitement in his voice brought a smile to her lips. "Oh my heavens, I'm so glad you're back. I'm so sorry for what has happened. Are you okay?"

There was a pause, and Mia found herself somewhat nervous about which words to use. She'd done some terrible things while being controlled, and she knew Ven would have something to say about how it wasn't her fault. She decided to skip that conversation altogether. Perhaps another time. "I'm alright for now. I've been giving a lot of thought about the dragon's control. I take it you didn't get pulled off anywhere by Rowan?"

"I did not, no," Ven said, "but I did feel a strong inclination that same day you disappeared, like something was trying to drag me away. It didn't work though. Zein had a similar experience to me. Are you concerned about the different reaction you experienced?"

"Yes," Mia said. "I don't like that she's able to control me, especially if you and Zein are both more resistant to her somehow. It's like something's wrong with me."

"There could be a lot of factors for that, Mia. Rowan might not even know that I exist."

"Yes, but she knows about Zein."

There was silence for a moment, and she could practically see him rubbing his lower lip in thought. She smiled despite the serious topic.

"What do you think it is, Mia?" he asked finally.

Mia took in a deep breath, practicing the very skill that Ven had taught her as she steadied her senses and cleared her mind. "I've been thinking about it a lot and... I think it's me. I think it's because I'd rather run from my problems than face them."

Ven remained silent, but she could imagine his clear blue eyes observing her with his steady, caring gaze. She'd abandoned him, she realized. Hiding in Mavenda was just her way of leaving behind all responsibility. She'd been afraid. Afraid of caring about something. Afraid of caring about some*one*. After losing all her friends, it seemed like too much of a burden on her mind. All she'd wanted was reprieve, not realizing that pushing Ven away had brought the opposite.

She couldn't put those thoughts into words. What she really wanted was to hold Ven's hand and feel the strength of his presence, but talking to him like this offered her some comfort as well. Tears welled in her eyes. "I think I'm trying so hard not to care what happens so I don't have to feel the pain. That is why it's easier to just let Rowan control me. Then I can distance myself from everything. I can just watch instead of experiencing it firsthand." Her cheeks flushed as she considered what Ven must be thinking of her. She was horrible for letting all this happen. He would hate her for hiding from all of this when she, of all people, was probably the most likely person to turn the tides completely.

"I see," Ven said. "You've really had a lot to carry. I can only imagine the burden you've been feeling." There was no judgement in his tone. Only sympathy. His voice wrapped around her like the warmth of a hug. "I've felt the same way too, but if there's one thing I've learned recently, it's that sometimes, the burdens placed on our backs don't ever go away. They might weigh on us forever, and it's on us to grow and build ourselves up so that we have the strength necessary to carry them."

A sob broke from Mia's chest as the words struck her to the core. "And what if I can't do it, Ven?"

"What do you think I came back here for?" Ven said, his voice quieter and earnest. "You see, we're not meant to carry these things alone. Just by talking to me right now, you've grown a little stronger. And that's saying something, because you're already the strongest person in the whole world."

Mia breathed a laugh, breaking up the next sob that threatened to break loose. Ven was right. Something about this conversation had already lifted her. She hadn't even known she was so weighed down, but he'd worked more of his doctorly magic on her. "Thank you, Ven." She'd underappreciated him, even after all he'd done. There was not one single person who had ever cared about her the way Ven did, even when she'd mistreated him. There was still a lingering fear that if she allowed herself to care about him too much that it would somehow come back to hurt her, but instead of forcing it down, she embraced it, letting herself care about him. A warmth spread down her back, and she smiled.

Oh, how she wished she could hold Ven's hand again. Her memory flashed back to that moment they'd stood on the balcony at Castia Mont before facing Dami. It was not long after Ven had said he loved her. She'd manipulated him to some degree, and he'd almost kissed her before they were interrupted. She would have let him do it. She'd *wanted* him to kiss her. And now, she found herself wishing they'd have another chance.

"Any time," Ven said. "And don't you go thinking I'm just out here doing charity work, because you strengthen me a lot too, Mia. I've done way more than would have ever been possible if not for you. You have a lot to offer."

"Oh, I certainly do," Mia said, standing a little taller. She laughed, but the moment was cut off by a sensation that tugged at her gut.

Catching the strained sound Mia made, Ven spoke to her. "What is it?" There was a sense of panic to his words.

Mia clenched the balcony with both hands, eyes scanning the sky as the tugging feeling intensified. Her gauntleted hand nearly crushed the wooden beam as her muscles completely tensed. She groaned and grunted with the strain of the all-too-familiar sensation.

"Mia!" Ven also spoke to other people who must have been with him, urging them to hurry.

Mia's heart pounded and her muscles bulged. The sweetness of oblivion awaited her if she just let go. There would be no more internal struggle. Perhaps this was just what she really needed. If she gave in one last time, she could free herself. Decided, she let the urge pull her along, and she mounted the top of the balcony before jumping down.

Rowan was calling, and Mia would answer.

Chapter Thirty-Six

Saving a Life

Ven Yashke

Butch couldn't run fast enough as Ven urged the horse onward. His heart thundered within his chest as he fought off the anxious pain that tore at his insides.

"Ven!" Valerie shouted from behind as she and Morgan fought to keep up.

"This isn't sustainable," Morgan said. "We're still about a day away from Peskan."

Ven ignored them as Butch pounded along the road, passing dozens of other refugees heading towards the city. They'd made several stops along the way, warning anyone they could find about the army marching across the country. All signs pointed to Peskan as the final target.

Sitena Rosars had been helping cover up some of the raids. Teamon had uncovered more information regarding her operations. It appeared that she'd initially been pulled into the Drekis Alliance over thirty years prior to oversee transactions for the trade of dragonblood technology. Somehow, that had resulted in her knowingly swearing allegiance to Dayelle. Much of the details were hazy, but they'd been able to connect the dots.

Ven couldn't care less. She was dead now, and the best they could do was move forward and save those who remained. Teamon agreed to harbor those he could, but he'd also been warned that he was in grave danger given Castia Mont's proximity to the last known sightings of the dragonsworn army.

"Mia," Ven said again, knowing it was likely in vain. The final sounds that had come through Ven's communication with Mia haunted him. He knew exactly what it meant. It also indicated that Rowan was close to Peskan again. Their time was short. He'd come back to Orund to save Mia, not watch her get controlled by a monster.

He thought they'd made amazing progress. Surely, she should have been able to resist the dragon's pull, but he knew her traumas ran deep. Healing something like that would take a lot more than a couple sessions, and he was no professional. It stung. Never had he wanted more for someone to feel safe. Never had he wanted more to simply carry her burdens for her, but he knew that it wasn't possible. All he could do was offer his measure of support. From there, it was as he'd said. She needed the strength to bear the weight.

But if she didn't have it, all of Orund would burn.

He knew he wasn't being very pragmatic. Butch was already growing tired, and Morgan and Valerie didn't stop shouting at him to slow down. With a huff of repressed frustration, he urged Butch to halt and then dismounted, opting to hold Butch's reins as he walked beside the horse.

Morgan and Valerie didn't mask their own annoyance as they came up beside him. "What was that about?" Morgan asked sharply, though her expression was better masked than Valerie's open frown.

"Mia was possessed by the dragon again," he said in monotone, trying to distance his emotions to remain sane. Sometimes, it was absolutely reasonable to let emotion control his actions, but now it was not practical. They were right. Peskan was too far. He'd get there and Mia would be long gone, probably off assassinating people again to suit the whims of a maniacal dragon. He could scarcely believe his circumstances.

"What, and you think you'd get there in time to make any difference?" Valerie asked.

"I am aware of the implausibility," Ven said, resisting the urge to lash back. He could understand her annoyance.

From the corner of his eye, Ven didn't miss catching Morgan pat Valerie's leg as if to calm her down. Ven paused as they reached a stream so the horses could drink, and he scratched Butch's side, whispering to the horse that he'd done a good job.

There were a couple abandoned campsites beside the stream where the grasses were matted down and campfires had diminished to small circles of black ash. Ven splashed his face with some water while the women stretched. They'd been riding for a few hours already, and though his body still ached, Ven seemed to be dealing with the conditions rather well. Every once in a while, he would feel the warm sensation indicating that his adaptive trait was triggered, though most of the time, he didn't even know what it was adapting to. It could have been pain, heat, intestinal issues, bacteria, eye damage, or any other number of random things. Without some kind of immediate wound or visible issue to observe, he wasn't sure he'd ever be able to confirm what was changing.

A little ways off to the side of the road was a tower just tall enough for Ven to see it over the top of the trees. "What's that?" Ven asked, pointing to the building with his chin. He was hoping that some other kind of conversation would lighten the darkened mood. He'd seen the tower a few times before, and there was a wide trail that veered off to it from the road.

"It's a manned watchtower," Morgan said after taking a drink from her waterskin. "I've been up there before. It provides a good final view of the valley before going through the pass toward Peskan. They can see the whole road from up top as well as another road that crosses through, coming up from Kombida. It would be a great location for the Huans to station a castle, but there hadn't ever been a need before now."

Ven nodded. "So they'd see if an army was coming through this way?"

"Yes," Morgan said. "And they have a system of two other stopping points between here and Peskan to swap horses for reporting any security issues. It's a good system. We have one like it in Luedan, though it has been used more for communication between cities."

Ven smiled as he patted Butch. He could have sworn that was similar to a story he'd heard about Butch Cassidy setting up a route of horses in order to outrun the law. Or was that the Pony Express? History hadn't been his primary topic of study.

He mounted onto Butch's back. "I apologize for my overreaction earlier," Ven said.

"All is well, Ven," Morgan said as she cast a glance at Valerie. "We understand the pressure you're experiencing. You care for her. I would have difficulty keeping my own composure if I'd heard Siwen was in trouble. Love can be a powerful motivator."

"Oh, I don't..." Ven stopped his words short, biting his tongue. He couldn't lie. Not about that.

"You have a healer's instinct," Morgan said. "Like at Castia Mont. You couldn't help but go assist that soldier we'd injured even though he would have killed us."

"I suppose," Ven said with a shrug. "It's hard to say no when you have the means."

"Not for most people," Valerie said.

Ven only nodded, still squirming inside knowing that Mia was out there struggling. He didn't want to admit it, but a sense of loneliness loomed over him, filling his chest with something dark. With the deaths of all those people at Mavenda, there was nobody left in this world that Ven had much of a connection with. Siwen was perhaps his only friend, other than Mia. Zein was... well, just a doctor, really. Somebody who'd known his parents? He could count the number of people he knew well with one hand.

Valerie and Morgan had overheard everything Ven said to Mia. Ven meant all of it. When he'd been talking about the strength of a good support system, he hadn't just been talking about her needing to lean on others, he'd been talking about himself.

Ven cleared his throat. "It's just how I've always lived." He remembered years of traveling with his parents. They'd gone all over the world, often taking critical medical supplies to various places that had never seen a good doctor before. He shared a bit of the details with Morgan and Valerie, and they remained quiet as he related their visit to a village in Thailand. His parents had performed four straight surgeries all day, saving the lives of all four patients. "They couldn't afford to travel to the hospital and certainly couldn't pay for the operations. One of the patients," Ven said, remembering the man's face perfectly as tears had streamed down his face, "kept asking why. Why were we helping? Why had we come all this way? He kept saying they had no money and wouldn't be able to pay for our services. My dad stopped the man to tell him that not everything in life is transactional. A true physician is someone who is willing to help somebody else without the expectation of reciprocal treatment. I'm not entirely certain I've adopted that ideology as well as my parents." Ven shrugged.

"Is that why you want to help Mia, then?" Morgan asked. "It just comes from the kindness of your heart?"

Ven shrugged. Truthfully, he'd done a lot of things in life due to expectations. He had medical training, so of course, he would help when somebody was in need. Did that mean he wanted to? He didn't have to come back to Orund. Sure, Dayelle *hoped* Ven would come merely so she could track him, but that hadn't been his responsibility. No, that feeling of something hooking his gut had been there for months, only diminishing slightly after arriving in Orund, and then considerably more after being reunited with Mia. He'd come because of a deeper feeling, one that he simply couldn't voice.

They fell back into silence as Ven filled his lungs with air, trying to enjoy this moment in nature. There were probably somewhere around one hundred other people within sight, most heading toward Peskan, though a handful were going the other way, despite warnings. The vast majority of people were on foot, some of them traveling with their animals.

They'd just passed the trail that led to the watchtower when the thudding of hooves pounded behind them. A soldier wearing light leather armor thundered by. "Run!" was all the soldier said.

The others on the road started to trail after the soldier. After hearing what Morgan had just described regarding the messaging system the watchtower guards used, Ven was quite certain they were in for some bad news. The other watchtower soldiers, six of them, came running around on foot. There were at least thirty people on the road behind them and the only sign Ven could see of any issue was a small billowing of dust from the road.

Valerie sighed. "Is there ever a moment where we'll catch a break?"

"My guess is that we won't get one of those until the dragons are dead," Morgan said.

Ven rubbed his lower lip, but he kept them at the same pace, waiting for the fleeing soldiers to catch up. "What seems to be the issue?" Ven said to the soldiers, making sure to show his own weapon so that they knew he wasn't just some refugee.

With a glance at the three of them, a soldier quickly said, "Riders are coming. Probably fifty of them."

"And why are you fleeing? Are they hostile?" Morgan asked.

"Judging by the way we saw them destroy a cart and kill a few people, yes," said another soldier. They passed by and increased their pace.

Ven regarded his companions. "This could very well be a slaughter." He gestured at the hundred or so people now scrambling away.

"The refugees won't get away. Not while facing mounted troops," Valerie said, her grip tightening over her weapon.

Ven pinched his beard. "What would be the best tactical decision here, Morgan?"

Morgan grunted and shook her head. "We would be well advised to ride straight to Peskan. Those on foot would be better off abandoning the road and making for the hills. The gap ahead has no space to either side. Anybody caught there would have nowhere to flee. They'd have to get through to the other side, otherwise the riders would overtake them."

"What if we could fight them at that same gap?" Ven said. "Would that allow more people to make it to the other side? How long would we have to hold them for that to work?"

"I can see what you're getting at, Ven, but we'd need to hold them a lot longer than we'd be able to."

Ven narrowed his eyes as the first of the enemy riders came into view. "But we might save a few of them still, right?"

Morgan sighed and patted her horse's neck.

"Alright," Valerie said. "Well, if you both are committed to this suicidal objective, then I suggest we get into position."

"No," Ven said. "The two of you should go. Urge everyone along. Leave me here to fight them."

"Against fifty riders?" Morgan said, her eyebrows as high as they could go.

"Yeah, that does sound pretty crazy, but I mean... at least I will heal if they stab me, right?"

"And if they cut off your head?" Valerie said, staring at him like he was a complete idiot.

"I'm tall. They won't even reach it."

Morgan pinched the bridge of her nose. "Ven, just come with us. You will only stall them for a few seconds at best. Maybe a minute. You won't be saving any lives by sacrificing yourself here. If this is because you're afraid of admitting you love that woman you just fawned over—and we all heard that conversation you had with her, Ven—then I request that you apply your fullest mental capacity to make the best decision here."

"Great, I'll stay and defend. You two get back to Peskan."

"Ven!" Morgan's nostrils flared. "I told Siwen I would keep an eye on you."

"We both know he didn't mean standing beside me when I make stupid decisions." Ven maneuvered Butch up the road. The two of them didn't hesitate to move as well. "Get anyone else you can through the gap."

Despite the angry expressions both of them wore, Valerie and Morgan herded the people toward the gap while Ven situated himself at the front of it. He pulled out his mace and tried to settle with the idea that he was very much an idiot.

People looked up at him as they passed by, many of them with mouths hanging open. They could see what was coming. They knew he was a fool for even bothering to make a stand. A father and mother ran by, a young girl clutched in the father's arms, crying as they dropped some things aside so they could go faster. "It'll be alright," Ven said, knowing it would be ridiculous to take comfort in the words.

They said nothing.

He refused to analyze himself, knowing that he would identify logical fallacies. Willful ignorance. Despite these efforts, he recognized that his disappointment about not being able to save Mia was crushing him more than he wanted to admit. He'd been working to become a doctor all his life. The whole reason he was in Orund was to save Mia, but he simply couldn't. It was not within his power.

And if he couldn't save her, then he at least wanted to save someone. Perhaps that family, clinging to their daughter. His stand here would be for them. Mind made, he sat up straight as the riders approached. There was probably a minute left before they'd reach him.

Valerie and Morgan paused beside Ven. Morgan shook her head, and Valerie didn't even look at him. "Survive, alright?" Morgan said. "My husband likes you, and he doesn't have many friends."

"You're also a fairly adequate human," Valerie added. "It would be a shame to lose one of those."

Ven smiled. "I'll do my best."

"At least take my shield," Valerie said, handing it over to him. "I know you can take a hit, but not too many."

Ven accepted it, putting it around his arm before nodding back.

They said nothing else as the two women took off down the road, leaving Ven alone to face an impossible number of foes. Even if there were ten, he doubted he'd be able to defeat them. If these were some of those possessed soldiers, then their inability to be affected by pain meant they would be a lot harder to take down than an ordinary person, even with the evening sun shining right in their eyes.

Ven hopped down from Butch's saddle. "I don't need you to get hurt because of me, too," he said, then slapped Butch and urged him to run. The horse did so, and Ven hoped he would get all the way back to Peskan. Taking deep breaths, he bent his knees and took a stance, just the way Siwen had shown him. As the riders got closer, he allowed his thoughts to go unchecked. This was a terrible idea. They'd charge right by him. He wouldn't even buy a single second. Many of the riders were armed with spears. He'd get run through before his mace would be able to harm any of them.

But there was no turning back now. He'd just sent Butch running off, which meant his chances for getting away were approximately zero. "I made a mistake," he muttered to himself. "I'm not even going to get a chance to properly regret this."

And then they were on him.

Chapter Thirty-Seven

Infiltration

Siwen Huan

Siwen marched to the top of the walls of Peskan. He had just arrived earlier in the day, but now he wanted to meet with his officers to determine the best course of action. He'd gathered a lot more information during the ride back. Two armies consisting of Tiamjin and Colandia had marched on Peskan and were now setting up camp around the city, a safe distance from anti-siege equipment. Kombida was also hot on their trail, with estimates indicating they would arrive tomorrow. After a day of setting up camp, he assumed the invasion would begin.

There was no word back from Lady Hesh Halimah yet, but Anne had shared that they still had a couple agents inside Nansha and that the city hadn't been taken yet either. This meant Shiansan still had one other stronghold, though their enemies all seemed to have bypassed that in order to attack Peskan directly. He had to assume that this was in part due to the dragon's vendetta against Siwen's family.

The complete destruction of Xhi had also been confirmed. There was little more than a handful of people who had survived, but they all attested to the same thing. Death and fire had rained from above carried by a flying beast of black and red. He shuddered to even think how his ancestors had destroyed the creatures. Here he was, about to defend his city from other people, when really they should have been coming together to attack the dragons. Wherever they were.

He folded his arms as he looked out at the gathering armies, wondering how Ven and his wife were getting along. They'd gone to find the dragons' location so they would have somewhere to direct their attention, but from what he'd gathered, it sounded like an entire army stood between them. So while humans were here distracting each other, the real enemy grew stronger.

Also gathered on the walls were several officers, including Fennu Kye. The lord had taken a more somber demeanor since losing his land, and he was eerily quiet. Additionally, Commander Elise Sherwood was there, though she had lost all of her troops. She wore a leather bag on her back which no doubt contained the devastating weapon. He'd yet to see its power demonstrated and hoped it wouldn't come to that.

"Let's go in order," Siwen said. "Offer reports if you have them." He pointed at an officer at the end.

The man cleared his throat and said, "A group of two hundred and twenty soldiers just arrived from Luedan. It's a small force, but well-equipped. They could reinforce the walls or be on reserve for special assignment."

Siwen nodded and the next officer spoke up. "We've been receiving refugees from all over. Most are ill equipped given the speed of their flight, but we should be able to find places for them all."

Then the next. "We have gone through the city for militia volunteers and have pledges from over twenty-three hundred people so far. Some have limited equipment, but we should be able to supplement all of them with at least a spear."

Siwen nodded again, fully aware that his family's castle had an entire building dedicated to the storage and maintenance of weapons. It was a practice they'd had in place ever since the establishment of the city. "Dispense those immediately. Trying to coordinate that in the moment of need will be a disaster."

He continued discussing things with them for several more minutes before a disturbance within the city drew their attention away. Identifying the issue didn't take long. From their vantage on the wall, a fight had started among the streets.

Siwen drew one of his swords and headed for the stairs.

Somehow, the enemy had infiltrated the city.

Chapter Thirty-Eight

Friend

Ven Yashke

A spear leveled at Ven's chest as the soldiers charged towards him. They weren't wearing the distinctive armor of the dragon zombies. Ven thought it was better than calling them dragonsworn. Rather, they wore some other kind of uniform, indicating that they were probably not under any kind of dragon control spell, but were probably from one of the nations now at war with Shiansan. This would work slightly in his favor.

Once the speartip was but a heartbeat away from striking home, Ven sidestepped and pushed the spear away with Valerie's shield. His mace smashed into the rider's knee. None of the other soldiers had expected Ven to survive, so they weren't prepared as he jumped and grabbed another rider's belt with the same hand that was also holding his mace. The force yanked at Ven's arm as the horse charged on, but he kicked off the ground and pulled hard, managing to force the rider off while Ven barely hooked the other side of the horse with his left leg. He righted himself just in time to deflect a sword from the soldier to his left. With his knees, he urged the horse forward and bashed the soldier to his right on the shoulder with a blow hard enough to knock the man down.

A spear was thrust at Ven from behind, jabbing him on his belt hard enough to poke through and dig an inch into his flesh. It was the first of what he knew would be many injuries. In fact, he'd already lasted longer than he thought he would. The riderless horse beside him continued to run, but other soldiers tried to cut him off. His horse slowed, and he had to keep his sword and mace moving in a wild blur to deflect all the attacks aimed at him. He struck another rider on the head and then another with the edge of his shield.

One soldier was bold enough to jump from his saddle and grab at Ven. He latched onto Ven's shoulder and they both fell from the saddle, crashing to the ground. Horses pounded over them, dodging for the most part. One hoof landed square on Ven's stomach. His imperviousness certainly hadn't had a chance to adapt to getting stampeded over.

Grunting against the pain, he pushed away from the other soldier, who immediately got kicked in the head by a horse. Ven shot to his feet just before another horse crashed into him. He managed to keep his feet and ducked under a hacking axe. The smell of dust and horse was heavy as Ven filled his lungs and swung his mace, crushing another rider's leg. He struck three more before the soldiers stopped charging altogether.

"He's still alive!" One of them shouted, trying to jab his spear at Ven. He took in a sharp breath as warmth spread through his body. Something was adapting, but the pain in his stomach remained. Ven dropped his mace, grabbed the spear shaft, and yanked hard. The man tried to maintain his grip, but Ven nearly pulled him off his horse, so he let go. Ven swung the spear around and stabbed it into another soldier's back.

At the warning, the other soldiers all turned their horses to face him again.

Another spear bounced across Ven's shin, causing more than a simple scratch. He screamed back the pain and started jabbing the spear over and over, using his shield to deflect whatever he could. Other soldiers fell, and with the density of horses, several now without their riders, the soldiers had a harder time reaching him. That wasn't enough to keep him protected. An axe tore past Ven's head, cutting across his ear and scratching a little across the back of his head. Somebody who was unable to reach him threw their spear, which effectively sliced across Ven's thigh accompanied by searing pain and a splash of his own blood. He staggered back with a cry, stumbling into the side of a mountless horse. The beast whinnied and tried to get away, cutting off another soldier and buying Ven just enough time to reassess.

There were only five riders behind him. All the others had charged right by initially, but they'd apparently stopped, turning their full attention on him. This was exactly what he'd hoped for, and now he needed to buy whatever time he could. That would only work if he stayed alive.

Though when another spear caught him in the back and glanced off his shoulder blade, he couldn't help but feel his optimism start to fade as it was overwhelmed with pain and dread. His actions became frantic as he jabbed wildly. He knew he had somewhat enhanced strength and quick reflexes, but that meant little against the five soldiers who'd managed to surround him. A sword bounced off the top of his shield and the blade's tip slapped the top of his head, breaking the skin and cracking against his skull.

His vision blurred. He roared and stabbed at the man, spear sinking into the flesh of his thigh. The warm feeling of adaptation worked constantly, but his wounds were not recovering. Pain he could deal with, but he'd received enough wounds and lost enough blood that his body would no longer function optimally. His right leg trembled and threatened to collapse whenever he tried to put weight on it. His left shoulder started to sag, and he was barely blocking any more blows. Another spear took him in the chest, almost cracking his ribs.

He was going to die. Hopefully the family had gotten through to the other side. If they could reach the woods then they'd have a chance to escape. Something battered Ven's face, and after recovering from the initial shock, he couldn't see out of his right eye.

Ven fell to his knees. *I'm so sorry Mia*, he thought. *I'm sorry I couldn't save you.* He'd failed her once before, but his death would seal that with more finality. A soldier lifted their spear up, preparing to jab down at him. The killing blow never came.

When Ven blinked up with his one good eye, he watched in utter surprise as a body soared through the air, crashing into the man who was about to stab him. A second later, Zein Huan himself spun up next to Ven, a spear twirling in the doctor's hands. He batted away weapon after weapon, his own movements a blur as he punched, stabbed, and threw people around as though they were no more than small children.

Zein was clearly no soldier. His tactics were painfully clumsy, and he was struck multiple times, though none of the attacks broke the man's skin. He'd had years to develop his imperviousness, and apparently that time had not been wasted. He was nothing like Mia. Ven imagined she would have torn through each of the soldiers like they were nothing more than paper, and they wouldn't have even grazed her with their weapons. Zein had none of that grace, but he was still effective.

One of the riders cursed and turned his horse around, about to flee back the way they had come. Ven shifted the grip on his spear and raised it over his shoulder before hurtling it at the soldier's back. It drove right between his shoulders and the man fell to the ground as his horse left him behind.

They had the full attention of the soldiers. Ven hoped they'd all stopped here to take him on, though he recognized it was quite possible that some might have charged ahead. He was in no shape to do much. Not unless his leg healed up at the very least. He'd lost a lot of blood, and even if all his wounds healed with adaptation, he'd still feel exhausted.

Zein was a relentless force. His lack of skill as a warrior didn't even matter since the enemy's weapons could not harm him. Ven felt a pang of jealousy at the fact that his own impervious trait was so selective with its adaptations. He doubted it would ever reach a level where he'd be as impenetrable as Zein or Mia.

Another shiver of warmth tingled across Ven's skin and suddenly he could breathe better. A gasping breath filled his lungs, and he grasped along the ground to retrieve his mace, disgusted by all the fluid that wetted the dirt road in spatters of dark red. The world shifted back and forth as though his vision was going, and he was almost certain he was about to black out, but the darkness never came.

He wasn't sure how much time had passed, but Zein was there in front of him, holding a canteen out.

Ven nodded and opened his mouth, not even saying a word before Zein helped Ven take a drink. "How did you find me?" he said after he'd taken several gulps.

Zein grunted as he tried and failed to get blood off the edge of his jacket. His clothes were riddled with tears, holes, and blood. "The communication device allows me to track your location as well."

"Figures," Ven said.

"This did not seem like a wise engagement, Mr. Yashke. Your adaptations are not like Mia's."

"I am aware," Ven said, trying not to sound too annoyed. Some of his other aches started to fade as more warm waves triggered.

"Mia has been lured away by Rowan again," Zein said, reaching down a hand to help Ven stand.

"I know," Ven said through gritted teeth as he rose to his feet. Several horses stamped around, unsure what to do now that their riders were all dead on the ground. "I failed her yet again."

"I need you to heal quickly."

"It's too late. We won't catch her," Ven said.

Zein cocked his head and pulled a device from his pocket with a plain black screen. "There is a tracking device on Mia. I know exactly where she is. And from what this indicates, she's somewhere on the side of the mountain east of Peskan. If we hurry, we might be able to follow her straight to a dragon."

Ven shot to his feet, ignoring the pain in his thigh as he did. "She's a lot faster than us."

"Then we'd better hurry."

Chapter Thirty-Nine

Control

Mia

Mia's body slowed to a jog as she reached the edge of the trees. She'd traveled southeast of Peskan, which made it hard to avoid the road. Rowan had kept Mia traveling at a careful pace so as not to alert people of her unnatural abilities. The road had been thick with traffic bound for Peskan, which wasn't something she would have expected for a city that was about to be invaded. She would have thought they'd be going in the opposite direction. Perhaps nowhere else was safe.

The familiar pull to let her mind sink into oblivion tugged at her, willing her to let Rowan handle everything. This time, Mia didn't give in. She forced herself to be completely present. Mia still had a communication device linked to her ear, not that she could speak. Ven had stopped calling out to her. That pain in his voice when she'd been taken this time was haunting. He'd tried so desperately to keep her from falling into the dragon's control, but he was powerless to aid her.

All she could do was follow the impulse. This was the best course of action. She'd known it would come to this eventually.

As her feet crunched carelessly on the underbrush, Mia had to hope that Rowan would still find her useful. If not, then the dragonsbane sword strapped to the box on her back might very likely be the tool to end her. But if the dragon remained in control, she wouldn't see a need to have Mia killed, would she?

Mia proceeded up an incline through the woods until she reached a flatter space spotted with boulders and clear of trees. It provided a distant overlook of Peskan off to the northwest.

Rowan stood atop one of the boulders, hands clasped behind her back as she stared off at the city. She looked over her shoulder as Mia went to stand beside her.

"We meant to make you a queen, Mia," Rowan said. "When the humans have been culled, we'll need a face they can look to for leadership. I thought it would be you." She paused to let the words sink in.

Mia's eyes would have widened if she had control of them. Instead, only her mind could reel as she considered the implications. This was similar to what Dami had wanted. He would have tried dominating all of humanity, installing him and his "queen" as dual rulers. But the dragons differed. They desired a puppet. She would have shaken her head in disbelief. It seemed common sense to her that not everybody shared the same vain ambitions. Mia did not want to be a queen. She wanted peace in her own way, not to enforce it on others.

"You are too weak, Mia," Rowan said. "You cannot bear to witness the cost of justice. Too much mercy enables people to repeat the same mistakes." She faced Mia directly. "You saw what we have the ability to do. We can force our will on humanity, but they lose their souls in the process. This is not how we want to rule. Our victory is inevitable, and we would prefer willful submission. In order to achieve that optimally, we need the face of a human to represent us."

You mean you need someone to be your decoy? Mia didn't know if Rowan could read her thoughts while controlling her body, but if she could, then Mia's fate was already sealed. It made more sense now why Rowan bothered talking with her. She planned to use Mia's body for very long term goals.

"You will be a god among your people," Rowan said, her eyes glinting with red, "but I will need more commitment out of you, which is why I'm going to watch you kill your friend this time. And if you don't do it, then I will torture him until you do."

A shiver crawled down Mia's spine as the pressure from Rowan intensified. Fear coiled in her chest, threatening to overwhelm her. It would be so easy to sink back into the comfort of oblivion. She almost believed that what Rowan described was what she wanted, but she knew it was wrong. Mia had already decided how this night would end, and it would not be with her killing Ven. Nor would Rowan do such a thing.

Mia would not run. Retreating into mindless oblivion was *not* going to be her legacy.

Ven's words came back to her as her body trembled under Rowan's command. *You are important.* Mia took in a sharp breath.

You are beautiful. She flexed her hands. *You are good, and smart, and caring.* Rowan's eyes widened in shock, a sneer slowly forming on her lips. *You have value.* Mia smiled back at Rowan, knowing the dragon had recognized her ruse. *You have the ability to do great things.* In one quick motion, Mia swung the wooden box off her shoulder, tearing it open with her powerful grip as Rowan's face changed drastically into more than just a frown. It was bestial.

Mia grabbed the hilt of the dragonsbane sword in her gauntleted hand. She would do great things. Tonight, she would slay a dragon.

Chapter Forty

Dragonblood

Ven Yashke

"**S**hould be just ahead," Zein said as he and Ven sprinted up the mountain slope.

Ven's lungs and legs burned with the push, but he could feel the adaptations working on him. He was getting stronger with each passing second. Every time he convinced himself that he could do a little bit more, he found that he *could*, in fact, do more. All of his wounds from the battle earlier were healed, and he'd downed three waterskins and a considerable amount of food, plundered from the dead riders. They'd ridden a couple of the riders' horses as fast as they could manage in order to make it this far. Zein was entirely convinced they could reach Mia before Rowan sent her off on some other mission. He was certain the dragon's eyes were set on Peskan.

They'd actually passed Morgan and Valerie on the way. The two had offered to join them, but Ven urged them on to the city. Without the impervious trait, they would only have slowed them down. Besides, if Zein was correct, then they were about to face down a dragon, possibly two. Even with their imperviousness, the odds of Zein and Ven making it out of such an interaction alive were extremely slim.

A thunderous roar so loud it rumbled the earth rattled Ven's bones. He stumbled and fell, failing to catch himself before his shoulder crashed into a rock. He hurried back up as Zein spared a glance back at him.

That sound was all the confirmation they needed. Zein checked his device one more time to determine they were on the right course, but a brilliant light like a bolt of pink lightning flashed just ahead of them. More growls and the screeching of metal on stone suggested they were walking into a battle.

Zein carried the dragonsbane dagger from the Huans' castle. He'd stolen it before coming to find Ven and held it in a gauntleted hand. Even this proximity to the weapon made Ven's skin tingle as though he were close to a fire. He had no idea how any other subject had been able to wield the items.

When they reached a clearing, Ven had the distinct impression that he'd just stumbled onto the scene of a nightmare. Rowan was there in dragon form, scales glittering in shades of red and black. She stood on four legs with a whip for a tail, her massive wings mostly held back, occasionally jabbing in to try to stab Mia with the jagged spikes on the ends.

Mia was a blur before the monster, moving with incredible speed to dodge the oppressive onslaught from the humongous beast. Even when Rowan's clawed talons raked across Mia's body, the woman merely spun out of the blow and slashed with her sword, scoring a cut along the dragon's leg.

"She has resisted," Zein remarked, stopping at the edge of the clearing.

"And we must help her," Ven said, running ahead.

"Wait!" Zein shouted, but Ven ignored him. He was not sure if even a dragon would be able to get through Mia's imperviousness, but he knew what a dragonsbane sword looked like when he saw it, and Mia was clearly using one. If Rowan was able to get that away from her, then Mia was truly at risk.

With a flick of her tail, the dragon whipped Mia across the stomach, knocking her back with such impact that she crashed into the side of a boulder hard enough to crack the stone. Rowan snapped her jaws at Mia, but she spun to the side, blade sliding across Rowan's snout.

Ven could barely process the details as their battle proceeded. Mia moved so impossibly fast that Rowan struggled to place a blow. Whenever she did, Mia rebounded quickly, usually scoring a hit as she did so. As Ven neared the dragon, his body shivered violently, and he stumbled to a knee as Rowan's tail flicked over his head. He tried lifting his mace to swing at it, but his muscles were stiff.

His eyes widened with recognition. Perhaps he wasn't as in control as he thought he was. He looked across the dragon's body. That, or he was so abjectly terrified that his body refused to fight with such impossible odds. Though he wasn't completely immobile, it was extremely difficult to move, almost like he was underwater.

Ven gritted his teeth. This was why he'd come back to Orund. He was going to save Mia. It didn't matter if Mia felt the same way about him that he did about her, there was still something that always drew him to her. Their souls were connected somehow. Fighting for her wasn't conditional on her reciprocal feelings, it was only dependent on *his* devotion for her.

"Get out of here, Ven!" Mia shouted to him. "She will kill you!"

Ven rose to his feet and nodded over to Zein, who still stood off to the side. He'd only taken a few steps into the clearing, exercising caution in the face of two powerful beings. Instead of drawing closer, Zein tossed the dragonsbane dagger to Ven. Ven already wore the two gauntlets he'd brought for this exact purpose. Feeling deft, he dropped his mace, caught the dagger out of the air, and ducked under Rowan's tail for the second time.

Mia and Rowan still fought in a relentless barrage of attacks and counterstrokes. Before he could make it another step, flames erupted from Rowan's mouth. The fire burned as though the sun had just arrived to immolate them. Even though it wasn't directed at him, the heat of the fire singed the hairs on Ven's exposed forearms. He watched in horror as the flames burst by Mia like a laser beam of molten air. Mia was a blur as she dashed away, but he could see that she was not unmarked. Part of her hair had been burned away, and the side of her face showed a terrible burn.

The dragon could kill her. It could absolutely kill her.

Resolved now more than ever, Ven ran up to the beast while holding the dagger in an underhanded grip. He reached Rowan's flank and jabbed the dagger into the nearest bit of flesh, stabbing her near the base of her tail.

Rowan twitched, pushing toward him in immediate response. Her body crashed against him so quickly that he didn't even have time to withdraw the dagger before its pommel struck him in the head. He fell back, still keeping a grip on the dagger even as it tore free and he tumbled away, forehead burning where the pommel had touched his skin.

He wheezed and lifted his head. He'd been knocked back nearly twenty feet, and he could have sworn he'd hit every rock on the way over. Ignoring the aches and pains, he hurried back up, surprised to find that he'd dropped the dagger in the tumble.

Mia was still alive, but she was scrambling to stay out of Rowan's reach. The burn extended from the side of her face down to her shoulder, and clearly the damage had shocked her. She was fighting much more cautiously. After another jet of flame that Mia thankfully dodged, a nearby tree exploded in fire.

Before Ven could take another step back toward the dagger, Zein was already ahead of him, scooping the dagger off the ground and running at Rowan. A spark of anger flared in Ven. *He* wanted to strike at Rowan. *He* wanted to kill this beast for what it had done to Mia. But a single stab didn't seem to make much of a difference. How many thorns would it take to bring down something as enormous as a dragon?

The pressure of what they were facing squeezed down on Ven with crushing force. He'd at least overcome whatever disabling influence Rowan had placed on him, but the reality of their task made him feel as though they were attempting the impossible.

Ven was no warrior. He'd trained for a few weeks—that would mean nothing when facing such an opponent. He may as well have been an ant.

Mia was batted away again, followed by another stream of fire. She barely rolled away and tried to close the distance. Her eyes flicked to him for the briefest of moments, and he could see the sorrow that enveloped her, but there was also determination. She was fighting. He couldn't begin to fathom how difficult it was for her to be doing this, but she had not given in. Whether or not they defeated Rowan today, Ven was proud of her. *She* was a warrior. *She* was a fighter. If anyone could take down Rowan, it was her.

Ven filled his aching lungs and could only watch as Mia rolled under a swipe from Rowan and her sword glanced off the dragon's leg. While distracted, Rowan didn't see Zein duck under her chest and attempt a jab somewhere between her two front legs.

Rowan roared at the wound and grabbed Zein in one of her talons before slamming him into the ground. Zein's body went limp. Mia lunged forward, slashing across Rowan's head, but the dragon turned her head so the sword slid across some of her horns, one of them severing completely. With a flick of her leg, Rowan flung Zein into the forest, his body crashing into a tree before falling to the ground.

Without any time to consider if Zein was still alive, Ven moved in closer while Mia jumped high, avoiding a gnash of Rowan's teeth.

He wasn't sure what he'd be able to do, but Zein had been knocked away, and Ven *had* to help somehow.

Mia dodged around another blast of fire as Ven saw a glittering light reflecting off the dagger on the ground beside Rowan's leg. The dragon shifted to pounce at Mia as she ran, skirting the edge of the forest.

"You can't do this," Mia's voice suddenly said in Ven's ear. She must have remembered the communication device. "This is my battle."

Ven growled before responding. "Remember what I said earlier? You don't have to do this alone."

She didn't respond, but another jet of fire streamed from Rowan's throat, igniting even more trees. Mia had jumped so high that Ven caught sight of her outlined against the evening light with the sun setting on the horizon. She landed near the back of Rowan's head, sword jabbing down. Her stab broke through Rowan's scales, but only went a few inches deep. When Rowan reached up to scrape Mia off, she jumped down, sword flashing as it broke through one of Rowan's claws.

Ven ran in at that moment, reaching for the dagger. All these cuts and stabs from the dragonsbane weapons had to be doing something to the dragon. It was poison after all, but Rowan's strength and speed never diminished. They'd severely underestimated the creature. He could have sworn Zein or Siwen had instructed him on how to kill a dragon, and one of them had said something about going for her neck or heart. He hadn't realized how difficult that would actually be now that he was facing one and seeing how enormous she was. If he ran and jumped, he wouldn't be able to reach her neck, and he didn't know where her heart was, but he had to assume that's what Zein had been attempting to hit.

Dagger in hand, he rushed toward Rowan, hoping to succeed where Zein had failed. "Neck and heart," Ven said to Mia, though as he approached, a single glance from Rowan let him know that he'd already failed. He saw the attack coming and already knew he wouldn't be able to dodge. He tried skipping to the side, but a massive wing snapped down at him, the sharp spike at the tip skewering him straight through the gut.

In vain, he stabbed at the wing with the dagger, managing three jabs as he was lifted off the ground and then slammed down a few paces away from Mia. He gasped and sputtered through the pain as the spike withdrew from his body, leaving a gaping hole. He could guarantee that his intestines had been critically damaged and likely his liver. His legs could barely move either, suggesting damage to his spine. If he didn't die, then at least he would develop some imperviousness to getting stabbed through the gut by a dragon's wing.

The angry scream that bellowed from Mia's throat shook him out of his pain. He looked up at her as she stood above him, dread washing over him. He was dying, and Mia was going to join him. By now, he'd learned to recognize the sign that Rowan was about to breathe her devastating fire. Her chest would swell just a bit and her head would coil back before extending in a form that was reminiscent of a cat vomiting. A sound like the great rushing of wind came as the dragon inhaled.

Perhaps Mia had grown to recognize the signs as well, but instead of waiting to dodge, she ran forward. Rocks sprayed out behind her with each of her powerful steps. Rowan stomped at her with her claws, but Mia merely dodged to the side before crouching and leaping up straight at Rowan's face. She braced her sword in both hands, though only one was gauntleted.

"No, Mia." Ven could barely mutter the words. His functions were failing.

Rowan didn't have time to breathe her fire as Mia's sword arced toward her head. Instead, the dragon snapped at Mia. The sword crashed into Rowan's snout and shattered a tooth, but Rowan chomped down directly on Mia, catching her in her mouth with such force that the sound thundered off the rocks.

Ven tried to sit up, which only caused him to shudder in pain. Rowan snapped her jaws again, tilting her head back to toss Mia to the back of her mouth. The jagged teeth pressed against Mia's flesh, and he was shocked to see that one of the teeth had actually broken through Mia's leg.

Ven's breath left him completely. His pain became meaningless. He used his arms to heave himself into a sitting position, eyes fixed on Mia. The back of Rowan's throat glowed as though she were about to launch a bout of flame, incinerating Mia in her jaws. Mia screamed and bellowed from within Rowan's jaws as the dragon snapped again.

A scream issued from Ven's own throat as he struggled to raise his arm. He couldn't stand. There was nothing he could do. He'd come all this way just to watch Mia get burned and eaten alive.

He attempted to throw the dragonsbane dagger still clutched in his hand. His throw was terrible, and the weapon merely clattered over to Rowan's leg, falling among the dragon's talons.

Rowan tilted her head all the way back, opening wide. Mia's mangled form fell deeper, but her own voice pierced through a roar released by Rowan. The light from within the dragon's throat flared.

"No!" Ven yelled. His heart sank as tears flooded his vision.

Fire exploded from Rowan's throat, engulfing Mia.

Chapter Forty-One

Siege

Siwen Huan

Siwen arrived at the scene of the disturbance to find a crowd of people pushing and shoving each other. Others were running away, but the shouts sounded more angry than afraid. That was at least a decent indication that things were not going to be too dangerous. Recognizing who he was and seeing him with his sword drawn, people backed off and the scuffle ended quickly.

This was not what he'd expected. Given the warning he'd received, he would have expected there to be dead bodies in the street. After asking for an explanation, he was told there were neighborly squabbles over resources, but while the people answered him, Siwen noticed a hooded figure watching him from the nearby alley. Once they made eye contact, the figure turned and disappeared.

Siwen cut off the conversation and ran over to the alley, but by the time he arrived, the person had vanished.

This whole situation was bizarre, and the hair on the back of his neck prickled as though he should be expecting an ambush at any moment. It seemed too convenient that this had happened so close to the wall where he was meeting with the other officers. It could have been his paranoia, but he was convinced this had to be a distraction. They'd drawn him and the others away from their position for a reason.

When Siwen looked over his shoulder, he saw Elise Sherwood standing there, scanning the scene as though prepared for an attack as well. She'd been sticking close to him ever since he discovered her secret weapon. Two other officers stood beside her, ready for orders.

"Be on alert," Siwen said. "Something isn't right here. We need boots on the street and a couple crossbows in—"

A whoosh over his head cut him off, and the building beside him exploded in a shower of stone and wood as a massive boulder crashed into it. He dove to the side and debris pelted him and the others, dust billowing out into the sky. He got back to his feet, relieved to find that he and the others were uninjured.

"We're under attack," said one of the officers as another whoosh sounded before a boulder smashed into a building across the street.

The siege had begun.

Chapter Forty-Two

Oblivion

Mia

As the flames tore across Mia's body, her flesh sizzled away. Her face was flat against the rough, dry surface of Rowan's tongue, but in the gaping space provided for the fire to erupt from Rowan's throat, Mia was able to move her arm which still tightly gripped the dragonsbane sword. She thrust the weapon up, pushing with all of her might despite the torrential flames that roared across her body.

She felt the sword tear through more flesh and crash through bones. A cacophonous sound rattled her entire body like a hundred reverberations of thunder. A second later she was slapped against something cold and hard. The burning sensation across her body didn't stop. In all the torture she had endured through the years, nothing had ever been so painful. She felt dry as a husk. She couldn't breathe. She couldn't even move. The only sensation was the burning pain that seemed to scorch every fiber of her being.

If she could, she would have cried or screamed. Her hand was empty, she realized. She wasn't sure where the sword had gone. Despite the heat that smothered her senses, her body shivered. Perhaps Rowan had swallowed her and this was what it was like in the stomach of a dragon.

All that she'd done had still meant nothing. The image of Ven's ruined body tormented her mind. The researchers had done things like that to each of the subjects when they were still young, but this was already years after they'd had their operation, and they didn't have the strange limitations that Ven experienced. Tests that attempted to examine recovery of deeper organ-puncturing wounds were among the kind that actually killed a few subjects, and those were people who'd had a lot longer to adapt than Ven had.

Whatever she was lying upon continued to rumble, and Mia mustered her strength to roll to her side. She dared to take in a sharp breath, but it hurt like daggers through her throat. When she opened her eyes, she could only see out of one of them. Rowan thrashed about in front of her, which meant she at least hadn't been eaten.

The tip of the dragonsbane sword was stuck out of the top of Rowan's head. Mia must have stabbed her all the way through from inside Rowan's mouth.

But the dragon was still alive.

Gritting her teeth, Mia pushed to her feet, trying to ignore the fact that the metal gauntlet on her right hand had melted onto her flesh. She absolutely would not think about how her skin was practically gone. Whether she moved or held still, she was in utter agony either way, but making herself do something was at least more bearable than lying in a heap as she died. Her boots were gone, and her bare feet padded against the stones. With her one good eye, she saw the dagger near Rowan's foot as the dragon stomped about.

Rowan was likely suffering a similar surge of pain. Mia could only imagine what it would feel like to have the dragonsbane weapon with its burning poison searing into her flesh. She took no satisfaction in seeing the creature suffer. Rowan had endured so much torture—much more than Mia ever had—but Rowan chose to act on her suffering in a way that only resulted in more pain. It was a mercy to end her.

Mia picked up the dagger, holding it carefully, though some of it touched the back of her thumb. She screamed through the pain as she jumped towards Rowan's writhing head. Rowan appeared lost in her suffering, oblivious to Mia as she slammed into her neck, driving the dagger into the scales with as powerful a thrust as she could manage. Bracing her legs against Rowan's body, Mia heaved, dragging the dagger across the neck until it ripped free and Mia fell back to the ground.

Rowan roared again, though the dragon's voice was garbled. Her head lowered and she looked as though she would vomit, but blood merely spurted out of the wound, some of it splashing across Mia's body.

Dragonblood. So much of it.

This was the resource that had made Mia what she was.

In her mind, she would have thought of it as being the color of gold or something special, but it was just like any other person's or creature's.

Rowan struggled to keep her head up, but Mia didn't want to take any chances. When Rowan tried roaring again, Mia lurched inside the dragon's mouth and grabbed the hilt of the sword, tearing it free in a quick stroke. Rowan barely even snapped at her before Mia pulled away. Every portion of Mia's body screamed at her to simply fall to the ground and let oblivion take her, but just as before when Rowan's will pressed against her own, Mia would not back down.

This was her life, and with her last remaining seconds, she would spend them how she willed.

A moan escaped Rowan's mouth as another wave of blood seeped from the neck wound. Mia went to it and, with all her might, brought the sword down in a powerful stroke. The blade tore through muscles and tendons. Mia screamed and sliced again, breaking through the spine, severing the head of her former master.

Only then did Mia fall to her knees, dragonsbane sword clattering from her hands. Her body shook, and tears streaked down her face. Oblivion awaited her.

Chapter Forty-Three

Free

Ven Yashke

Ven held a hand over his wound, trying not to think about how it might be the only thing keeping his insides where they should be, as he used his other arm to help him crawl across the ground. The limited mobility in his legs made every movement a struggle. Every breath he took came in sharply, held for a moment as his body surged with pain, then released in a gasp as though each one was desperate not to be his last.

His jaw shook. "Mia." The word croaked from his throat. Mia was just three feet away from him now. After killing Rowan, she'd dropped to her knees, body shivering. Now she was slumped forward on hands and knees.

Mia fell to her side before he reached her. Half her body was completely burned. Much of her hair was gone. It was a miracle she'd even survived the initial blast. How she'd managed to stab Rowan while inside the fire and then have enough strength to come out and cut off the dragon's head was beyond him. She was so strong.

"Ven." Mia's voice was no more than a whisper. She only had one good eye, but it searched for him.

Ven shoved himself forward with one extra grunt so that he was just beside her.

Mia's lip trembled as her eye settled on him. A tear welled and dripped down the side of her face. "I thought you were dying, Ven."

Ven took off his cloak and shoved it under Mia's head before helping her to her back. "I'm..." They were both dying. He'd seen it a hundred times as the life fled a person's body. Perhaps she'd be able to recover. She was impervious, after all. He couldn't bring himself to tell her that he was probably minutes or even seconds from bleeding out. "I should recover," he said.

Mia closed her eye as another tear streamed out. The burns on her skin were terrible, like she'd just been pulled from a furnace. After seeing some of her exposed muscle on her shoulder, he couldn't bring himself to look at it. Instead, he focused on her eye as he struggled to keep his own tears from forming. A pain grew in his stomach, more bitter and sharp than anything else Rowan could have stabbed him with. This was far worse.

"Mia—"

"I'm so sorry, Ven," Mia cut in. She reached her hand up to him, the one that was less burned. She touched his shoulder. "I was too afraid to admit how I felt—everyone else always betrayed me but you..."

"It's alright." Ven risked pulling his hand away from his stomach so he could stroke Mia's face. "I understand."

Mia cast her eye toward the dead dragon. "I'm free, Ven." More tears streamed down her face, and Ven could no longer restrain himself as he blinked his own tears out, one of them splashing onto Mia's shoulder.

"Yeah, you're free, Mia," Ven said. "You did it." He stroked the side of her face as softly as he could despite the tremble in his arm. "You are so brave. So strong."

Mia nodded and sniffed, her movements slight. Her face twitched as she winced at some unseen pain. "It hurts so much, Ven." Her eye clamped shut, squeezing out another tear. Ven bit down on his quivering lip, knowing there was nothing he could do until one of them simply died. Her body shook with a tremor as she took a sharp breath and blinked up at him, eye glistening. "I wish we'd gotten that kiss." Her lip twitched in a movement that was half smile, half wince.

Ven spared his own smile, though it was still more of a frown. A kiss was something he could give her. He bent towards her face, forcing through the pained tension in his stomach as he did so. His tears pattered on Mia's cheeks as he placed his lips to hers. She did not kiss him back. When he withdrew and regarded her eye, it was half-lidded, staring blankly. She did not breathe.

Tears poured shamelessly down his face as Ven shimmied to lie beside Mia. He took her hand and cradled it to his chest as silent sobs wracked his shoulders, doing nothing to ease his pain.

In the end, he had not failed Mia. He'd helped her face her fear. She'd stood up for herself. She'd earned her own freedom.

But if he'd known this would have been the result... well... He closed his eyes and squeezed Mia's arm against his chest until his body grew too weak. His own breath became shallow and uneven. He wanted the pain to end—not just the stab wound and the broken bones—but the ache that squeezed at his heart to see Mia's last moment. He'd seen death before, but nothing ever hurt so much.

And there was only one outcome that would give him that relief.

He let out a breath, willing it to be his last.

***

Zein watched from the edge of the forest until his body finally underwent the adaptation. Both his legs had been broken, but he'd managed to wedge himself into a slightly upright position, giving him just enough of an angle to watch as Ven and Mia battled the dragon. Now, as he approached the carnage, his heart pulsed with anxiety.

He had put everything into his research, and if both Ven and Mia had died, then all he'd worked towards had been for naught. He would be the lone survivor. Worse still, he would have failed to save the boy's life. Giving him the procedure was supposed to keep him safe, not force him into taking greater risks, but it seemed that, for Ven, greater capacity and greater risk went hand-in-hand. Perhaps that was a characteristic of all the Yashkes.

"We're near the site," a voice said in Zein's ear. That would be Taye Mansen. He'd sent her out of the facility after the first mission run by Dami, Mia, Ambrose, and Baze when it had become immediately clear that things would only escalate. He knew he'd need somebody on the outside, and she had the incredible organizational skills necessary to coordinate all his efforts between his different contacts and to maintain the resource management he'd needed to keep his operations afloat. "Is it safe to approach?"

Zein took in the scene with a sweep of his eyes. Ven and Mia lay beside each other, and he could not sense life from either of them. The dragon, Rowan, was also dead, a treasure trove of blood and tissue that could be further examined and used for almost limitless research. It was the kind of hoard he would have never expected to chance upon.

"You're clear to approach," Zein said. He stepped over to Ven and Mia, almost confused at the tightness in his chest. Part of him knew that he should have felt something more seeing them dead. Maybe he didn't entirely believe it. As a doctor and researcher, he needed empirical evidence as confirmation. He bent over Mia first, knowing she had the ability to mask her own pulse and breathing, but Zein had spent much of his own focus of adaptation on honing in his ability to hear and feel beyond normal senses. Pressing his fingers against her neck, he found there was no pulse—not even in the slightest.

He let out a deep sigh as the last of his hope escaped him. Perhaps he should have tested them against fire even more to build up her resilience. They'd only tested against it four or five times. Not enough. Swallowing back his failure, he moved over to Ven. The stomach wound was severe enough to have killed anybody, and—his eyes widened. Ven was still bleeding.

Zein dropped to a knee beside Ven. He knew Ven's adaptations took longer to take effect, but he would have thought the boy would be dead by now. Perhaps there was something applying the right amount of pressure inside to prevent him from bleeding out. That was the biggest concern. Zein could see better in the dark than a normal person, but even with that and the distant, burning trees, he couldn't identify anything he could actually do to help.

It appeared that Ven did not require any assistance. Right before Zein's eyes, Ven's flesh started coming together all on its own.

"Come on," Zein muttered, willing it to go faster. Of all the people Zein wanted to survive the coming days, Ven was at the top of the list. He'd meant what he said about failing Ven's parents, and he wanted to do his best to make sure that Ven didn't face a similar fate.

"You were serious," Taye said as she emerged from the forest with a crew of fourteen other trusted agents and employees.

"Take care of the dragon, but leave the head alone for the moment," Zein said, keeping his eyes trained on Ven's wound. If the adaptation was taking place, then he had to assume that Ven's chances for survival were now quite high. He wished he could say the same for Mia.

Taye directed the others to start working on the dragon's body. There was more blood in there than they'd be able to extract, but they'd want to get everything they possibly could for now. There was also the chance to experiment with other tissue, so they would focus on extracting various organs.

"Avoid using dragonsbane wherever possible," Zein instructed. "We don't want to corrupt any of the tissue." He wasn't sure how much more harm it could possibly cause, especially when this dragon had already undergone several years of torture using dragonsbane weapons, but he didn't want to take chances where it wasn't necessary.

His one fear now was that, with Rowan's death, Dayelle would be coming for them. And if Rowan was scary, he imagined Dayelle was far more formidable. She had to have been free for hundreds or thousands of years with all that she'd been able to establish. After scouring records, that mansion he'd escaped from had been owned by the same family for nearly six hundred years without ever changing hands. Previously, Sitena Rosars was the wealthiest person he'd ever known, but after learning that the majority of her funding actually came from the Drekis Alliance under Dayelle's direction, he could scarcely begin to fathom what kind of influence Dayelle had behind the scenes. The combined war against Shiansan was no surprise at all.

Ven's eyes snapped open as he took in a sharp breath. He immediately loosed that breath in a cry of pain, baring his teeth and looking down at himself where he still clutched Mia's arm to his chest. He dropped his head back and groaned, "Why? Why am I still alive?"

Zein reached out and squeezed Ven's shoulder, as it seemed like a reassuring kind of sentiment. "You still have work to do." More than the boy realized.

Ven looked over at Mia again before pinching the bridge of his nose and holding back more tears as that final resolution settled in.

Zein stood and averted his eyes. He did not know any words that could help. This situation complicated things, and it was not something Zein would have hoped for. Despite all the destruction the world had seen in the last few days, he had the inclination to consider Mia's death the most grievous blow of them all.

"There will be time yet to mourn, Mr. Yashke," Zein said. "Peskan will fall tomorrow without our aid."

Ven sniffed and swallowed. "Tomorrow?"

"Yes. And with its fall, the freedom Mia fought to obtain will be gone for all of us." He regarded Ven carefully, knowing how much actually rested on his shoulders. "Walk with me when you are able. There is something you should know about the true history regarding the overthrowing of the dragons."

Chapter Forty-Four

Hostages

Siwen Huan

It was later in the night when Siwen finally headed back to his room. The invading forces intermittently launched stones at the city. Admittedly, their efforts did not impact the defenses of the city very much, but he knew it was more of a scare tactic than anything. Citizens and soldiers would be up all night, wondering if their home would be struck or if the enemy forces would somehow come charging through the city.

What he still couldn't pin down was why there'd been that distraction on the wall. Perhaps he was only imagining that something else strange had happened at that moment, but he also didn't want to doubt his instincts.

A good night's sleep would hopefully help him figure out what was going on. When he passed under the gate of the castle, a wave of relief washed over him as two figures approached under torchlight. One of which was the most beautiful woman to walk the planet.

"Morgan!" he said, running over until he reached his wife's embrace. Valerie stood dutifully to the side, torch in hand.

"I heard about your father," Morgan said as she sank into him, her head pressing down beneath his chin. "I'm so sorry."

Siwen merely rubbed a hand along Morgan's back and held her more tightly. "He went with honor," he said, though he preferred not to speak on that topic. "I'm glad to see you returned safely, though perhaps Peskan is no longer a safe place to be."

Morgan breathed a laugh. "I'm not sure there's anywhere safe currently. We had more combative engagements than you might like to know."

"I'm sure," Siwen said before kissing Morgan on the forehead. "We can talk about this more in the morning." He nodded to Valerie. "Thank you for staying with her."

Valerie bowed her head. "My pleasure."

With that, Siwen took Morgan's hand and they went into the castle. She clung to his side, her sword pressing up against his hip as he held her close. "I should have had you come with me," Siwen said.

"You missed me terribly, didn't you?"

"Absolutely, I did." She poked his rib and smiled at him. My, how he loved that smile.

"Well, I missed you too," she said. "It's peculiar how we can go all our lives without each other, and now just a moment apart is difficult to bear."

"Here in Shiansan, we call that love."

Morgan squeezed his hand. "Ah, of course, and where I come from, there's a lot more to it than that."

In the dimness of the castle halls, nothing shined so bright as Morgan's eyes. It may as well have been broad daylight with the amount of light and warmth that filled him. Then everything went black. The last sensation he had was that of something terribly hard and painful cracking into the side of his jaw.

***

Ven jogged beside Zein, the two of them rushing to Peskan. In his hand, Ven held one of Rowan's teeth, part of the flesh still stuck to the root end. The dragonsbane sword was back inside a wooden box and slung over his shoulder. Zein held both an eye and one of the talons. The gates to the city were unsurprisingly closed, but when Zein identified himself, they had no issue opening a side door that went through the adjacent guardhouse. When asked about the body parts clutched in their hands, Zein shook his head at Ven, but Ven figured that the more who knew, the better.

"Parts of a dragon head, of course," Ven said as they got back out into the city.

Zein gave him a disapproving glance but hurried off at a run again. Ven sighed and struggled to keep up as a guard shouted his disbelief that dissolved into an argument with the others. Ven might have smiled at everyone's reactions before, but he was feeling distant. It was hard to connect with anything, and the more he forced himself away, the better. The grief was still there on the fringes of his mind, threatening to seize him if he stopped moving.

A loud crash sounded in the distance, and when he asked Zein about it, he was informed that the city was under siege to the west. Tomorrow was bound to be interesting.

They skidded to a halt outside the castle as Zein pressed a finger to his ear.

"What is it?" Ven asked. Despite his weariness, his body screamed for him to keep moving, fearing what would happen if he stopped. The constant warm floods as his body continued adapting were a comfort. Something told him that the more he adapted, the better equipped he would be to fight. He wanted to fight—he needed it.

"We're too late," Zein said. "Siwen has been taken."

"Now what do we do?" Ven asked, unable to bear the idea that they would lose him as well.

Zein sighed, expression hardening. "We save him, of course. Otherwise the city is lost."

***

Siwen jerked back into consciousness, dimly aware that he was heavily restrained and his feet were dragging on the floor. It was still night, but a line of torches carried by those who'd taken him lit the way as they proceeded to some bonfire that waited ahead. He was gagged, but other than dragging him, his captors made no attempt to restrict him from looking around even though it was evident he was awake. The fact that they didn't care about him identifying their location made him assume that they didn't believe he'd be getting away. His chances of surviving the night were slim.

The bonfire was lit outside of a large farmhouse. Judging by their elevation and the lights of the city behind them, Siwen determined they were west of Peskan, probably very close to where the enemy armies had been assembling. The farmhouse must have been requisitioned for their own use.

They reached the fire as a man stepped up to look Siwen in the face. The man wore a thick cloak over elegant armor. His hair was a bright blond, not too dissimilar from Ven's. Siwen almost immediately identified the man as Max Lidius, king of Colandia. "It's him. Well done," Max said.

Siwen cursed himself. He'd underestimated their operations. They had managed to sneak people not just into Peskan, but into his castle, to capture him and get him outside of the city without being caught.

"Get him inside. Send everyone else away," Max said.

"Everyone?" asked another man who stood beside the door to the farmhouse. With another quick lookover, Siwen realized he was in the presence of Lord Monarch Jihu Nin of Tiamjin as well.

"Yes," Max said, gesturing to the soldiers restraining Siwen.

The soldiers moved him into the farmhouse and set him on a chair. His hands were tied behind his back. There was the chance that he could headbutt the soldier to his left and steal the sword from the soldier to his right, even with his hands bound. He'd have to roll back to get his hands in front and cut the restraints, and then he'd be in a position to break his way free, but there were still several other soldiers in the area. He wouldn't make it far.

Instead, he sat as Max and Jihu stood opposite him in the main living area of the farmhouse. The door was closed as the soldiers left.

Max folded his arms and said, "Queen Sophie. It's just us." He kept his voice low so that it could barely be heard above the crackling of the fire in the hearth.

Queen Sophie of Kombida emerged from the shadows of a room, arms folded in the sleeves of a dark robe that also covered most of her face. He took it that the soldiers outside weren't supposed to know she was here.

Only then did it dawn on Siwen that, with the deaths of his father and King Nikato's entire family, he was next in line as the ruler of all Shiansan. Whatever was left of it, anyway. This was some impromptu council of kings and queens. Only, he was a prisoner, so he had to assume that it was merely to decide his fate and that of the rest of Shiansan. It made him wonder if Lady Halimah had fallen as well.

Sophie gestured to Siwen. "Can we get that out of his mouth, then?"

"I suppose," Max said, stepping up to remove Siwen's gag. Once removed, Max stepped back and the three leaders stood side-by-side as they regarded him.

"Would you accept a surrender?" Siwen asked, working his jaw.

"But we just got started," Jihu said. He was younger even than Siwen, not a day older than twenty.

"I have more important things to attend to," Siwen said flatly, trying to sit up straight in the chair.

"More important than the collapse of your nation and loss of your land?" Sophie asked.

"Yes," Siwen said flatly. If they'd brought him here merely to convince him to surrender, then he just needed to find a way to do so that didn't result in Peskan being sacked.

"And you'd willingly be executed and have your property dispensed among us?" Max said.

"I would prefer not to be executed," Siwen said. "I am familiar with the law. I have not been involved in the trading or creation of dragonblood technology nor the harboring of a dragon. Those responsible for that are already dead."

"You really expect us to believe that you were not involved in your family business?" Sophie asked.

"I tell the truth and expect nothing."

"Nobody would believe such a claim," Max said. "I'm sure you understand that."

"I believe you are capable of making up your own minds," Siwen said. "Is this what you brought me here for, though? To execute me? You could have had your people slit my throat."

"We are not brigands, Lord Huan," Max said.

"It's war, King Lidius," Siwen said back to Max. "Assassinations are not beyond the morals of combat. So why am I here?"

"Where is the dragon?" Jihu demanded, stepping closer.

Siwen adjusted his wrists to try and alleviate the tightness, but that proved ineffective. "I don't know," Siwen said. "You saw the condition of Xhi, I assume."

"You are trying to blame that fire on a dragon?" Max said, lips curling in amusement. "We had several agents within the city who set fire there."

"You didn't see it with your own eyes, then?" Siwen asked. He hadn't seen it, but the description was horrifying. Everything had burned. Every last surface, scorched until it was black. "No fire started by your agents could have burned down the entire city in a single moment like that."

"You underestimate the ability of our agents," Jihu said with a sly smile.

Siwen glared back. "Better than underestimating your intelligence."

"Lord Huan," Max said, tilting his head. "Let's remain focused. We were discussing the terms of your surrender."

"What do you propose?" Siwen asked.

"Your lands and property are forfeited," Max said. "We would need the gates opened to our troops so we can occupy the castle and legitimize our claim to the lands. You as well as any close relative would need to be executed, of course, to eliminate risk of anybody trying to claim otherwise."

Jihu stepped up. "Or we just kill him, catapult his body back into the city, and then bombard the place until they give up or we crack a big enough hole in the wall. They can't be able to resist us for more than a week under those conditions."

Sophie raised her eyebrows. "That seems fitting. Match barbarism for barbarism." She narrowed her eyes at Siwen. "Did you know Zatla was my dear cousin?"

Siwen frowned at that. He knew the name, of course. Zatla was the noblewoman who ruled over Red Bridge. "Of course. I am well educated on royal families. Why is this relevant?"

"You also want me to believe that you don't know about her assassination?" Sophie's gaze was cold as steel.

Siwen straightened himself in the seat to look her in the eyes. "Why do you believe that I would know anything about that?"

"The woman who killed her was wearing one of your uniforms," Sophie said.

Siwen grunted. "That sounds suspiciously convenient. Did each of you receive a similar provocation? That wouldn't be very politically wise of Shiansan to do, now would it?"

Max frowned. "No, the rest of us heard of your nation's development and continued use of dragonblood technology, and we were called to enforce international law."

Siwen held back a growl. "Yes, and Kombida was incited against Shiansan via assassination because they also have considerable use of dragonblood technology while Hitar was practically overthrown internally as a nation that thrives on dragonblood research. All of this happened around the same time, and you mean to tell me that you are not concerned with how all of this was orchestrated simultaneously?"

"That's a bold accusation!" Sophie said.

"Hardly," Siwen said, fixing her with a firm gaze. "I worked firsthand on eliminating dragonblood research operations and personally imprisoned and fined more people from Kombida than Shiansan natives, but that's not what we're here to discuss. The point I was making is that we are all here because somebody wanted us here."

"And I take it you know who that person is?" Jihu said with a shake of his head, practically scoffing.

"I do."

"Let's just execute him and take the city," Sophie said, interrupting their conversation. "This conversation is unnecessary. We can disseminate the assets afterwards."

"Who?" Max said after holding a hand up at Sophie to silence her.

"The dragons, of course," Siwen said. "They want us to kill each other so they can regain control." He didn't have much hope that sharing what he knew would be effective, but he had to hope that the others were not complete fools. There was also the likelihood that they would regard this war as an opportunity to simply seize property, and Sophie's comment made that possibility seem all the more likely.

The other three leaders shared a look, each frowning in their own way. Jihu gave the slightest nod before Max drew his sword and stepped toward Siwen.

Chapter Forty-Five

Royal Council

Ven Yashke

Ven ducked under the window ahead of Zein. They'd slipped past the guards with ease as Zein was able to direct Ven through the darkness. Zein handed him the dragon parts before climbing in behind him. It was dark inside, but a light glimmered at the bottom of a door as voices spoke animatedly on the other side.

The constant movement was good for Ven. It harnessed his emotions and kept him fixated on a goal, filling him with energy. They were saving Siwen. He'd been in this situation enough times already after tragedies and disasters. Sometimes, a patient was lost, but that shouldn't prevent him from trying to help the next patient.

It *shouldn't*.

But Ven still felt the occasional squeeze against his heart or tightness in his chest. The activity was all that kept him from falling back into despair. He was all too familiar with the sensation. It had been similar after losing his parents.

He was also distracted by their conversation on the way here. Zein explained that a large majority of the dragons had been killed through surprise attacks or by sneaking dragonsbane into their food. Outright combat had only happened on a handful of occasions, which, if it ever reached that point, was absolutely devastating. Entire populations had been massacred. The fact that the battle with Rowan had only resulted in the loss of a single life... Ven couldn't finish the thought.

But if Dayelle was as ancient as Zein suspected, then she could possibly destroy every soldier in Shiansan by herself in an outright battle. And if she was backed by an army of Dragonsworn? The chances weren't good.

Zein moved to the door, listened for only a second before pushing it open and hurrying into the bright room beyond. Ven came after him as he heard metal thunk against a hard, dull surface. Perhaps they'd been too late.

But when Ven saw what was beyond, he nearly dropped the dragon parts from his arms.

Siwen stood in a room with three others, all of them dressed in much finer clothing than his friend. One of them was helping Siwen remove the bindings on his wrists after apparently having just cut the rope. The man helping Siwen stopped and leveled his sword at Zein once their presence was known.

"Ven? Zein?" Siwen said, eyes settling on the dragon parts clutched loosely in Ven's hands. His jaw dropped. "You did it?"

Ven had a sudden lump in his throat as he answered. "Mia did. It was just one of them, though."

"Is that what I think it is?" said one of the others, a woman whose widened eyes were fixated on the dragon parts.

"Yes," Zein answered. "We came to provide proof that the dragons are at large. We just killed the one that was previously imprisoned inside of Peskan, but there is still one remaining."

"You... killed it? How?" asked the thick man who still had his sword drawn. He had an imperious look about him, like he was accustomed to being worshiped.

"Well, King Lidius, we had access to a couple dragonsbane weapons and a very formidable warrior who..." Zein paused to glance at Ven, "did not survive the encounter."

Siwen's expression dropped as he gasped audibly. "Please don't say it was who I'm thinking."

Tears stung Ven's eyes, but he blinked them away to answer. Zein remained silent, leaving the burden of the announcement on Ven's shoulders. He was the person who'd been closest to her. "It was Mia," he said to Siwen.

Siwen ran a hand across his face before striding over to Ven and clasping him in a tight hug. Ven squeezed back, surprised by the warrior's sudden show of emotion, reminding him of the stark contrast between Siwen and his cousin. Sorrow wriggled up Ven's chest, releasing some of the tightness he'd held there.

"I'm so sorry, Ven," Siwen said, pulling back but keeping a firm grip on Ven's arm. "We'll end this for all of us."

Ven nodded. "It's alright. She made her own choice in the end."

"And where is this other dragon?" the woman asked.

"We're not sure exactly," Zein said, "but she has been amassing its own forces to the southeast."

"Amassing forces?" King Lidius said.

Zein gave one of his signature sighs. "We... have much to discuss, if you are willing to listen."

Siwen gestured to the other three nobles. "I suggest we sit. This will be a long night."

***

Ven watched the sunrise, arms folded against the morning chill as he sat on the bench outside the farmhouse and leaned against its wall. He remembered the look in Mia's eyes when she'd watched her first sunrise. That was only a year ago. He didn't know how he was supposed to react to all that had happened and was still happening. The one sense of direction he clung to was that he wanted to make a difference.

He understood that he wasn't the most capable individual, and without Mia, he felt a little like the wind had gone out of his sails, but if there was something he could do to rid this place of Dayelle's influence, he'd do it.

As the rising sun glistened across the city and reflected off the morning dew clinging to the grasses near his feet, he acknowledged that this was a place worth fighting for. It was strange to be here in a different world, caught up in the wildest politics he could imagine, watching as people fought and bled for their causes. These battles seemed so petty. What was worth the price of a life? To think that people killed over things like money or pride made his stomach churn with disgust. War was terrible and meaningless.

But a dragon seeking to regain control by butchering thousands and causing thousands of others to kill each other? It angered him. There *had* to be a way to coexist without the need to seek dominance, but these people hated dragons with a passion, even after generations of freedom, and there was no way Dayelle would listen to reason.

Political science was not one of Ven's strengths, but it suddenly felt like he should have paid closer attention to that textbook he'd had to read through a couple years ago.

The door to the farmhouse opened and closed, and a short time later, Ven was joined by Siwen, who sat on the other end of the bench, staring out over Peskan.

"My father died," Siwen said.

Ven kept his eyes ahead, squinting at the grass. "I'm sorry."

"The fool had it coming," Siwen said. "For years, I thought he was the epitome of honor." Siwen paused to shake his head. "But he was a fraud all along."

"That's... disappointing, Siwen." Losing a parent was not something Ven really wanted to relate to somebody with, but he knew at least a little of what Siwen was experiencing. "At least there were plenty of good things about him as well, right?"

"There were." Siwen glanced at Ven. "I'm sorry about Mia. She was one of a kind. These past few days have been a tragedy for many."

Ven nodded. He could only imagine what it had been like at Xhi. An entire city had been turned to rubble. They needed to end this.

"You know, something doesn't quite add up to me, actually," he said, giving Siwen his full attention.

"What is it?"

Ven cocked his head. "I know Dayelle. I've possibly spoken with her more than anybody else here. She's... smart. Like, really, really intelligent. She manipulates everybody like some kind of mastermind. Surely she would have realized that we'd catch on to what she was doing here—wanting us all to kill each other. She had to know we'd find out and that we wouldn't actually fight, right?"

Siwen pursed his lips and shrugged. "Perhaps." His eyes narrowed, a visual cue that he was coming to his own conclusions. "You think there's some other point to all this?"

"Yes," Ven said with a nod. "Rowan had been able to level an entire city by herself. Dayelle is supposed to be even older than Rowan, and she hasn't lived in a dungeon her whole life. She's probably healthier, more talented, and more cunning than Rowan was. What if—"

The ground trembled. There was a sound so deep and visceral that he felt it more than heard it as it dulled all other sensations, like his ears were suddenly filled with vibrating water. It was gone a second later, and the sun blotted as two enormous wings stretched out to either side of it.

Assuming it was Dayelle, she was massive, like a flying skyscraper. Her scales were gold and violet, her horns jagged, and her wings large enough to envelop half the city. She would sweep over them in a wave of destruction. Why she had ever felt the need to hide was beyond his imagination. How could anybody hope to fight against something like that?

"She gathered us here for an extermination," Siwen said as he drew his sword and rose to his feet.

"Yes," Ven said, his voice a whisper.

Dayelle flew high and released another roar, the ground rumbling once again.

"But that won't stop us from fighting," Ven said, getting to his feet. It was time to put on his gauntlets and pull out that dragonsbane sword from the wooden box.

Chapter Forty-Six

Everything

Ven Yashke

A dull, warm sensation tingled on the skin of Ven's right hand as he held the dragonsbane sword. The gauntlet muted the poison from causing direct harm, but it didn't completely stop the discomfort.

"She could probably reach us within five minutes," Zein said, standing beside Ven and Siwen.

The armies of Colandai and Tiamjin camped nearby were a bustle of activity. A few people completely disbanded, fleeing to the west, ignoring the orders for them to form ranks. It would make little difference whether they stayed or left. What difference would a few more ants make against something like Dayelle?

"Dayelle is larger than Rowan, I assume?" Siwen asked.

"Like, ten times as big," Ven said. "How did your ancestors ever beat these things?"

"Mostly through assassinations," Zein said. "Not in outright battle, excepting Gogoba, which is partially why that country remains mostly desolate."

Ven tensed as Dayelle flew over Peskan, but she did not release a bout of fire as expected.

Zein placed a finger to his ear as Ven asked the obvious question. "Why isn't she burning the city?"

"The city is under attack by human forces," Zein said. "They came in from the southeast. It's likely the dragonsworn."

"So she doesn't want to kill us all," Ven said.

"She wants to enslave us, then," Siwen said.

The panic from the armies heightened as Dayelle drew closer. More people broke away and fled on foot. People screamed and fought, their survival instincts flaring.

Tem ran up the hill to meet them, panting when he stopped before Zein. "I have another update," Tem said to Zein. "There's another contingent of soldiers that arrived in the city just before the invasion began. They came in from Castia Mont and are equipped with a few dragonsbane weapons, including some vials and crossbows."

King Max Lidius and Lord Monarch Jihu Nin rode over to join them, each with their own retinue.

"You were serious about the dragons," Max said. "I was hoping it was just a bluff to save your hide."

"I wish it was," Siwen said. "Do you have dragonsbane weapons?"

"Not here," Max said. "We came to fight people, not demons."

"This is exactly what she wanted," Ven said, not sure if he was supposed to address anyone a particular way. They never seemed to mind that he didn't use the proper formalities. That, or their situation was dire enough that nobody cared.

Dayelle was less than a minute away.

"Get your people out of here," Siwen said to the other monarchs. "This whole thing is a trap."

Dayelle was heading straight at them.

Max and Jihu turned their horses and charged back towards their armies, barking orders.

Pressure dulled Ven's hearing as Dayelle tilted her head, her jaws snapping as a single beam of light shot from her mouth. The projectile smashed into the combined armies of Tiamjin and Colandia with an explosion that rivaled that of bombs from Earth. Screams erupted and the entire army started to flee.

Ven hefted the sword as Dayelle was nearly upon them. Another burst of fire blazed around them before Dayelle's entire body ignited in flames as she shrunk rapidly to the size of a person and crashed to the ground in front of Ven, Siwen, Zein, and Tem. A ring of fire encircled them, preventing them from running away, not that any of them intended to do so.

Dayelle's body remained aglow with fire.

"I'm rather disappointed, Ven," Dayelle said. "This isn't what I brought you here for. Mia wasn't supposed to die, and now I have to do things a little differently. I was really hoping to avoid all this." She gestured at the army as screams and clashing metal filled the air. Her thralls had arrived here as well, and they were murdering the fleeing soldiers. "And unfortunately, I don't believe you would be a suitable replacement for Mia. Your disposition is too... free-thinking."

Siwen didn't wait for Dayelle to say more. He rushed her, sword swinging. Dayelle dodged two strokes before striking Siwen in the chest with her leg, his ribs snapping audibly as he tumbled across the ground.

The sound of clashing metal crescendoed. When Ven spared a quick glance away from Dayelle, he saw that her heavily armored army of dragonsworn were wreaking havoc on the armies as they tried to flee. She meant to change all of them. There were also flames erupting out and engulfing the dragonsworn, something he would never have imagined. It was almost like one of the soldiers was equipped with a massively powerful flamethrower. Whoever it was, they were probably saving countless lives if they were able to hold off the dragonsworn long enough.

"Funding your research proved effective for me in the end, Doctor Huan," Dayelle said as her own eyes flicked in the direction of the battle. "Not in the way I hoped, but effective nonetheless. I should have the rest of Orund subdued in no more than three months." She shrugged, which looked strange as her shrunken wings still protruded out behind her. "Your work is finished, and you will be the first that I consume. Ven will be second." She smirked just a little before she looked at Tem, eyes narrowing slightly before snapping wide. Her body began to change immediately.

Dayelle erupted into dragon form, her jaws becoming the size of two massive trucks in the blink of an eye as she moved to chomp at

Tem. There must have been something she'd seen in him to change her mind so quickly

Ven jumped away, but something bronze crashed into Dayelle's neck, knocking her head upward. Another dragon had clamped its jaws onto Dayelle, claws scratching at her underside. The other dragon was much smaller, though still about twice as big as Rowan had been.

Ven barely rolled out of the way to avoid a tail smashing him into pulp. He had no idea where physics came into play with the dragons changing form, but he did notice a sudden decrease in air pressure after they'd transformed.

Dayelle's massive claws dug into the side of the smaller dragon as she pulled it away, ripping her neck free of its teeth. Was that... Tem?

Ven scrambled to his feet. Beside him, Zein also got up. He had jumped in the opposite direction, which was less fortunate, and Zein's left arm hung limply at his side. "Tem is a dragon?"

"I suppose," Zein said, seemingly unconcerned about his broken arm. It would heal—and a lot quicker than Ven's would have if it had been him.

The dragons tumbled down the hill, tearing the side of it away and ripping out every tree in their path.

A sudden rage burned inside of Ven as he fixated on Dayelle. According to Zein, *she* had killed his parents. She was the one who'd released Rowan. She was the one who'd butchered the people of Mavenda and countless others.

If there was one thing Ven had learned since coming to Orund it was that, yes, he could help people heal, but box it all, he could kill. And kill he would. Even if it would kill him. Hefting the sword, he charged down the hill toward the dragons. Clearly, his odds were atrocious, and even the smaller bronze dragon was getting absolutely ravaged. A scrape of claws sent bronze scales showering towards him. The ground itself threatened to tear asunder. This was not the kind of battle one could hope to escape alive, but he would give his all. For Mia. For his parents. For Siwen, Morgan, and the whole of Orund.

Zein ran beside Ven until they were cut off by a group of dragonsworn. Ven sneered, impatient with the obstacle that prevented him from reaching his quarry. Ven had little training with actual swordplay, but he at least had momentum as he charged down the hill. He ducked under a stabbing spear, swinging the dragonsbane sword. It hammered across the waist of the soldier, breaking through the armor and hacking into flesh beneath. He spun, barely dodging another sword that stabbed through his shirt. He could survive wounds, but he did not have the time to wait through a recovery. The best chance he had at getting to Dayelle was while she was distracted by the bronze dragon. Was that really Tem? A dragon had been working for Zein for how long now? Perhaps Zein hadn't even known.

Ven stabbed his sword, the tip slipping just under the noseguard of the soldier's helmet. Zein had killed three other ones in the same time, but when the older doctor suddenly gasped in pain, it caught Ven by total surprise.

The soldier who stabbed Zein was holding Siwen's dragonsbane sword. An emotionless face regarded Ven as the soldier kicked Zein aside, sending him tumbling down the hill and off a torn apart rockface, body vanishing from view.

There was no way Zein would survive such a wound. That stab had been right through the shoulder. And Ven wouldn't survive either if he didn't get his crap together and focus. He stepped back to avoid a swing and jab from the soldier. It was the only one left after they'd killed the five others, but the energy from his fearless charge was dwindling as he was once again faced with mortality.

He forced himself to keep his eyes focused on the soldier's movements, even as a glaring flash of light exploded to his left from the battle between the dragons. Gritting his teeth, Ven held his ground instead of backing away. Indecision would not prevent him from getting to Dayelle. A thick breath filled his lungs as he looked the soldier in his lifeless eyes and said, "I'm a killer."

Their weapons clashed several times as Ven's heart thundered in his chest, fixated on getting the advantage. When his blade slid across the soldier's thigh, he didn't even react. He continued striking at Ven, though with lessened mobility. Even though Ven was not a particularly skilled swordsman, neither was the thrall. He relied on his armor and inability to feel.

Ven risked a feint and stepped close to the thrall as his sword jabbed dangerously close to Ven's stomach. He smashed his elbow into the soldier's nose then kicked up with his knee while bringing his other arm down on the enemy's sword arm. This resulted in snapping the soldier's arm back at the elbow, rendering the arm useless. The sword dropped from his hand, but he grappled at Ven's throat with his other hand. Ven reversed the grip on his sword and stabbed him through the gut. This did little to stop the dragonsworn from trying to strangle him, but Ven used the leverage to jerk the soldier over his shoulder and slam him into the ground.

One more quick stroke to the thrall's neck brought the battle to a close.

Bending down, Ven retrieved Siwen's sword with his other hand before settling his eyes back on Dayelle. She had Tem pinned on the ground, one of her massive arms pressed against his neck. Tem's claws scratched and tore at Dayelle, effectively ripping away a few of her iridescent scales, but it wouldn't be enough to save himself. Ven recognized the early stage of Dayelle preparing to breathe fire directly down into Tem's face.

Ven took off at a sprint, keenly aware that if he tripped and stabbed himself with either of the dragonsbane swords in his hands that he was as good as dead. When the flash of light from Dayelle's fire erupted, it was like a second sun blazing to life. He wasn't sure how resilient dragons were to their own fire, but he had to imagine that Dayelle knew what she was doing.

People had killed dragons before. Normal people. He had to keep reminding himself that as he got closer to a creature that would put all the dinosaurs to shame. He was no Olympic athlete, but he had to believe that the adaptiveness had helped him have at least above average abilities, so that would make him a slightly more annoying ant, increasing his odds from all but impossible to infinitesimally possible.

He ignored the math and ran, letting his simmering anger drown out thought. Rowan had been killed by getting stabbed in the brain and then having her neck chopped off. Ven had basically no chance of achieving that simply due to the extreme height. The other option was to try stabbing Dayelle in the heart, and he was not particularly familiar with dragon anatomy.

Now that the blazing light of Dayelle's fire diminished, he got a closer look at the results. Tem wasn't dead, but Dayelle clamped her hind legs onto his body to stop him from clawing at her. Then she reared back as if to pound into him with both her front legs. Tem's own fire erupted, dull when compared to Dayelle's, but he targeted her chest.

It was only then that Ven saw a few scratches across Dayelle's chest where several scales had broken away, revealing some of the pale pink flesh beneath. That revelation gave him enough hope to be able to penetrate the dragon's hide with one of the swords. If only he could reach it. Tem was equally riddled with such marks, and he bled profusely from more than a couple spots. When Dayelle's weight dropped down onto Tem, it struck with the sound of a car crashing into a boulder.

Ven was nearly upon them, and he held the swords out to either side.

Dayelle reached down and snapped her jaws around Tem's neck, cutting the flames short.

Ven jumped over a fallen tree and dodged around the sprawling limbs of another. He was right beside Dayelle's front left leg when she yanked her head up, jerking Tem in the air. She chomped once, teeth sinking into Tem's flesh.

Ven leapt as high as he could before slamming into Dayelle's leg. He jabbed both swords into her flesh with underhand grips. The blade in his right hand sank almost to the hilt, but the one in his left had barely broken through a scale. He heaved himself up as Dayelle whipped her head, flinging Tem into the side of the hill with an explosion of earth.

Ven heaved himself up and stabbed again with the looser of the two swords. His efforts did not go unnoticed. He doubted that stabbing a dragon with a poisonous sword would keep him off her radar for long, and he was right, because her left hind leg twitched up to scratch him away. He kicked up and tore out the deeper sword, barely dodging the initial swipe, but Dayelle looped her neck around to peer directly at him.

Just then, something crashed into Dayelle's side, not far from where Ven hung, clinging to his swords that were both stabbed into her flesh. It had been a boulder, probably fired from one of the siege engines from the camp. Though it had probably done close to nothing to the dragon, it was at least an indication that people were still fighting.

Dayelle was unfazed, and she jerked her arm down, which would result in him getting smashed into the ground. It appeared like climbing up her body was not going to work. He tugged out the swords and tried to jump clear of the path. When he slammed into the ground, Dayelle didn't follow through to crush him. Instead, she turned her full attention to him, massive head lowering down as a single claw from her right foot pressed down against his chest, pinning him.

A voice filled his consciousness, virtually banishing all thought and sensation as it left no room for any other sense. The voice was clear, reverberating through him as though shaking every molecule. "I was going to eat Zein first and save you for second, but I can make an exception." She shifted her grip and pinched him between two pointed claws, lifting him into the air.

The idea that he'd even tried to kill her spoke volumes of Ven's insanity, but if there was any chance to kill her, he'd take it. She hadn't even bothered to dislodge the dragonsbane swords from his grip. In fact, looking at them in relation to her size, they truly seemed inconsequential. It would take a one-in-a-million jab to be worthwhile. Perhaps he could get lucky. If she threw him in her mouth, he could potentially stab her from inside like Mia had done. He had to hope for the best, even as his body started to tremble.

After rising to her full height on two legs, Dayelle tossed Ven into the air, and he flipped before falling back down, straight toward Dayelle's gaping mouth. She would swallow him whole. There was no way out of this.

Ven clenched his jaw and gripped the swords tightly, prepared to throw in the only strike he would get. Before he fell into the dragon's mouth, however, Tem had returned, shoving into Dayelle's side just enough for Ven to fall right past the snapping jaws. His sword glanced off the edge of Dayelle's mouth, and he screamed as he plummeted toward the ground below, his body falling parallel to Dayelle's long neck.

He tried the next best thing he could think of, switching to an underhand grip as he tried stabbing into Dayelle's flesh. If he could somehow wedge a blade in enough, he might be able to stop from falling all the way to the ground. In only a couple seconds, he stabbed at it three times, but was unable to pierce through the tough scales.

Then he saw the portion of flesh that Tem had exposed by Dayelle's chest. That was his one chance. He would get less than half a second to prepare a stab. With both hands reared back, he thrust them forward right as he passed Dayelle's chest. Both swords punctured through. He tried holding onto them, but that nearly tore his arms from his shoulders. His body flipped from the sudden tug, and he went off to the side before smacking hard against the Dayelle's knee. His vision exploded with stars, and the air left his lungs before he slid off and plummeted once again, crashing legs first onto the ground below, his last sensation being that of immense pain as he heard his own body crack.

He was spent. He'd given his everything. All that remained was to embrace the cold oblivion that had been gaping at him ever since he'd clutched Mia's dead hand to his chest.

Chapter Forty-Seven

The Broken

Siwen Huan

Siwen clawed his way back to his feet, wheezing for air. Dayelle had kicked him hard enough to crack two or three of his ribs, and the initial pain had been enough to make him lose consciousness. He had no idea how much time had passed, but his sword was gone and the sounds of battle were all around him.

Dayelle had resumed her dragon form, but she thrashed about, clawing at her chest like she was attempting to rip out her own flesh. Dark blood issued from a wound there, showering the wooded area below. The idea of what he was witnessing was insane. It was like watching liquid gold fall from the sky. People had paid unbelievable amounts of money for even a vial of dragonblood.

Little did they know it would come to this, costing them their own blood in turn.

A group of seven dragonsworn had spotted him, though they were still several paces away. Unarmed and broken as he was, Siwen was as good as dead. Or worse.

Siwen stumbled away, knowing he'd be no use in battle in this condition. The best he could hope for was to survive. Another earth-shattering roar bellowed from Dayelle, and a burst of light sparked across the sky like lightning.

The footsteps of the approaching dragonsworn grew louder as they neared him. He tried increasing his pace, but the bouncing made breathing almost impossible as his muscles seized with the sharp pain from his ribs. He worried there was even worse damage than just broken ribs, and he was possibly even bleeding in his lungs.

Many of the soldiers from the armies had all fled. Nobody dared challenge Dayelle without their dragonsbane weapons, and then the armed dragonsworn flooding in had completely shattered morale.

Siwen would have no assistance.

He neared the farmhouse, but the dragonsworn were now sprinting. They'd intercept him before he reached the door. It was over, and Siwen would not die a coward's death. He stopped in his tracks and turned to face them, prepared to go down swinging, but thundering hooves caught both him and the dragonsworn by surprise as twenty mounted soldiers pounded up the hill and swept through dragonsworn with precise strokes. At the head of the troops, much to Siwen's surprise, was Morgan.

"My queen," Siwen said, staring up at her in awe, daring to flash a smile.

"You need to pick your fights better," Morgan said. "You promised me at least one child, so I'll need you to deliver on that. Understood?" She raised a dark eyebrow at him.

Siwen barked a painful laugh. "I will survive."

"Good," Morgan said, looking over her shoulder at a soldier who was familiar. Siwen recognized him from their visit to Castia Mont as Teamon, one of the dragonsbane wielding soldiers under the employ of Lady Sitena Rosars. Several of the other soldiers were equipped with crossbows, and he could see they were laden with bolts affixed with glass vials, no doubt filled with more dragonsbane. One of the riders was Valerie. "We need to deal with that." She jerked her head toward Dayelle who was still bleeding and thrashing, sometimes slashing out at the bronze dragon that occasionally attempted to bite at her. "Promise you'll stay safe?"

Siwen only nodded, but the soldiers were already turning their horses, eager to go take care of the dragon while it was seemingly distracted.

Morgan nodded back, and the twenty soldiers charged down the hill.

Against his better judgement, Siwen followed after. Besides, if he was dying, he would die. He didn't see how walking would make the condition of his chest even worse. The pain had changed slightly, becoming at least a little more tolerable.

The riders spread wide so as not to be an easy target, and they drew out their crossbows, but their approach did not go unnoticed.

Dayelle turned to face them, and fear gripped Siwen by the throat as he imagined his wife getting snapped by the dragon's teeth. Knowing he was unarmed did not stop Siwen from pushing forward. A couple of the riders released their bolts a little early, poison spattering across the dragon's scales.

Siwen had the thought that perhaps Dayelle was already dying. That wound in her chest was terrible and had not stopped seeping. It was possibly only a matter of time, but nothing short of complete certainty would be acceptable.

Dayelle roared and snapped her jaws. Most of the horses stopped their charge and several riders were thrown from their saddles, Morgan included. Siwen kept his eyes locked on his wife as he struggled forward.

The first bite was aimed directly at Valerie, who had retained her mount. She was unable to avoid the quick snap, and both she and the horse were completely enveloped in the dragon's mouth. A couple bolts shattered across Dayelle's face, and the poison steamed where it touched her. She paid it no mind and kept snapping at the various riders, biting once, then throwing back her head to swallow. The horror of it made his mind scream at him to turn and run, but he was familiar with the sensation of facing a terror. In it, there was a thrill, though not if it involved watching his wife get devoured.

When Dayelle snapped at Morgan, Siwen's heart lurched, but Morgan leapt from her horse's saddle and actually stabbed Dayelle's snout with that dragonsbane dagger of hers. She was still knocked aside as her body impacted with Dayelle's nose, and she hit the ground with no minor velocity. The horse had been ripped in half from the bite.

"No," Siwen tried to shout as he drew closer. Dayelle was about to bite at Morgan again when the bronze dragon crawled up her side.

With a snarl of rage, Dayelle whipped around, slamming her claw into the other dragon before biting its neck and crushing it into the ground. Blood sprayed from the bronze dragon's neck as Dayelle tugged. When she let go, the bronze dragon lay limp.

That had given Siwen enough time to reach Morgan. Her teeth were bared in pain as she lay prone. She gestured. "The crossbow."

Siwen followed her direction and held his breath as he bent down to retrieve the fallen crossbow. A bolt was already in place with the poison affixed.

After killing the other dragon, Dayelle swiveled back to face them, though her movements were sluggish compared to how quickly she'd been moving before, and her legs seemed to tremble, causing the earth to shake beneath her.

Dayelle growled and Siwen raised the crossbow, gritting his teeth against the pain in his ribs. Leveling the crossbow, he knew not to bother aiming for the head, but instead pointed it at the existing wound on the dragon's chest. Before she could move to protect it, Siwen released the bolt. It shattered against the dragon's chest, splashing into the open hole.

Dayelle fell with a shiver, her face crashing down directly in front of Siwen, one eye glaring at him. With a final tremor, the dragon stilled, and a puff of steam coiled out from Dayelle's mouth.

The crossbow dropped from Siwen's grip as he went to kneel beside his wife. She had a terrible gash on her left leg but was otherwise in good condition. Relief washed over him.

Morgan grunted before smiling. "You did it. You killed her!"

Siwen smiled back, but he felt that the credit was certainly not his alone. He had no idea where the other dragon had come from, and he had not seen Zein or Ven at all. Perhaps they'd been eaten.

He would search for them, of course, but he had to take a moment to drop beside his wife and place his forehead to hers.

They'd won.

***

After Dayelle had fallen, the thralls had stopped fighting. They simply collapsed, each of them dying. That result had been worse than Siwen hoped for. At the very least, he'd been wishing they would return to normal, but whatever process their bodies had undergone with the takeover, it had indeed killed them.

It had taken several hours to scour through the absolute massacre, but there was no sign of Zein at all, leaving Siwen with the only conclusion being that his cousin had been eaten by the dragon. Actually confirming that detail would be... gruesome, and nobody was about to try digging through Dayelle to find out.

Much of the city had actually held out against the dragonsworn, though they had breached the wall in one portion, overwhelming the guard and sweeping through a few buildings. That was a tragedy all on its own.

Siwen felt like he'd been too fortunate. He'd been the first person to attack Dayelle, and he'd only received a single kick.

The one surprise he hadn't expected was to find Ven. His body was mangled, to say the least. They'd brought him back to the castle at Siwen's order. He was alive, but in critical condition and stuck in a coma.

Siwen knew however, that if the boy was able to survive long enough, he would possibly make a full recovery. It had been a few days, but Siwen was still recovering from his own injuries as he leaned out over a balcony that overlooked the city of Peskan. Morgan came behind him and rubbed a hand along his back before joining him.

"The delegations have all officially left. You made a wise move there," Morgan said.

Siwen grunted, finding it ironic that he was the one who'd presented the idea of legalizing the use of dragonblood technology by assuring the other leaders that they could then monitor the trade, development, and regulation. Not all other nations were on board initially, but, knowing that they were all probably using dragonblood technology to some degree anyway, it didn't take too much effort to persuade them otherwise. This was all the more relevant now that they had two dead dragons to harvest. Were there more dragons out there? Possibly, but if so, they hadn't taken part in this conflict, which he felt was a better sign than not.

A knock came at the door, and Siwen received a hurried notice from Carina. "He's awake."

Siwen nodded to Morgan then hurried through the castle, stepping carefully to be mindful of his healing wounds.

Carina was one of the only servants Siwen had trusted with knowing about Ven's unique trait, so she'd been watching over him. She held the door open for Siwen as he entered the small room, and Ven blinked back up at him as he sat at the edge of the bed, which was a miracle of its own.

Ven's eyes were heavy, but he managed a sad smile. "Siwen."

"Ven, it's good to see you well. I... We have a bit to catch up on."

Chapter Forty-Eight

Pyre

Ven Yashke

Ven took in a deep breath as he stood before the burning pyre. Within the flames, Mia's body disintegrated to ash along with part of Ven's soul. He stood so close to the fire that it burned him. Behind him stood Siwen and Morgan, the only other people he would have allowed to be here now that Zein was dead.

They made no move to pull him back. The heat of the fire seemed like the only thing keeping Ven alive. The fire lasted three hours, and Siwen and Morgan remained with him the entire time.

Tears ran down Ven's cheeks in a steady, silent stream. He wanted to give up for a moment. He was so angry that he'd survived. Stabbing the swords into Dayelle's chest had started the process of the dragon's death, and Siwen had sealed it with that final crossbow bolt. They'd done something tremendous—something practically impossible—and yet it was still no victory.

Here he stood, defeated.

Words from both his parents tried clawing their way from the back of his mind, but he'd been struggling to ignore them for so long. They'd both said that he would do great things. He'd never understood that there would be such heavy costs as well.

In the end, Mia had finished strong. She'd fought for what she believed in rather than succumbing to her own weaknesses. Ven nodded to himself. Instead of being bitter about his own survival, he knew it would be wise to be grateful. It meant that he wasn't finished. He'd already done some great things, but there must be more for him to do. It was like Zein had said. He wasn't done yet.

He'd spoken with Siwen for a couple hours last night. Zein had gone missing after getting stabbed by the dragonsbane weapon and his body was never found. Ven hadn't voiced his thoughts, but he wanted to assume that Zein had survived somehow and was back to operating underground with that wealth of dragonblood they'd harvested from Rowan's body.

Tem was still a mystery. He'd been killed by Dayelle, but Ven couldn't get past the idea that dragons had been working against each other. It made him think that perhaps others were out there, still hiding in plain sight. Siwen knew that he would still need to locate wherever Dayelle had been keeping a den. She would have a hoard of supplies there, including one of the portal keys that she used to travel between worlds, which, Ven realized, was a treasure beyond value. Siwen wasn't entirely optimistic he'd be able to locate it in time since there were several people who had been serving Dayelle willingly under the Drekis Alliance, but he'd promised to root it out now that he knew what he was looking for. The other nations had all agreed to something similar, but Ven's interest in the political structure had waned.

For his part, Ven knew he needed to find his own purpose. He'd had more than his share of killing. It was time to go back to what he'd always trained for.

"Goodbye, Mia," he whispered just loud enough that only he could barely hear it.

Ven gripped the marble—no—the key in his palm tightly. He had more to give. He was not done yet.

Afterword

I hope you enjoyed exploring the world of Orund! If you love fast-paced fantasy, then you can expect a lot more.

This whole story really came about because I wanted some world-altering science to be a part of a fantasy world. It really just spiraled from there. If you enjoyed it, please leave a review somewhere. Word-of-mouth is a big deal in the indie author world.

Is this the end of Orund? Maybe. Probably. Is it the end of Ven Yashke's story? I guess we'll see.

Get a free eBook novella of *MALAHEM* by joining my newsletter: FREE BOOK

Acknowledgements

Massive thank you goes out to all the wonderful readers of Dragonsbane. I had somehow convinced myself that this story was only subpar, but with all the amazing comments and reviews, I knew I had to come back and finish this series.

Another big thank you goes to my wife for being so accommodating. Authoring is basically a second job for me, so that means I have to carve out special time once in a while to make deadlines, and she is an amazing support.

Thank you to Alexandra Leonhardt for her editing services and fitting all of that into my crazy deadlines.

Also a big thanks has to go out to my wonderful beta readers, Tori, Christopher, and Zachary. You guys are rockstars!

Also by

Be sure to check out my other works, particularly the Grimnir Chronicles, starting here with Depths of Vanalf. I consider this my best work so far, and it should be another fun world to dive into.

About the Author

Brady was born in a stronghold at the base of the Rocky Mountains. He currently resides there with his wife, their three daughters, and a few domesticated house lions of a rare breed. He set out with the goal to write fantasy that anybody could read with characters who face real life struggles. Everyone deserves to feel like there is hope.